A BOND SO FIERCE AND FRAGILE

COMPELLING FATES SAGA
BOOK THREE

SOPHIA ST. GERMAIN

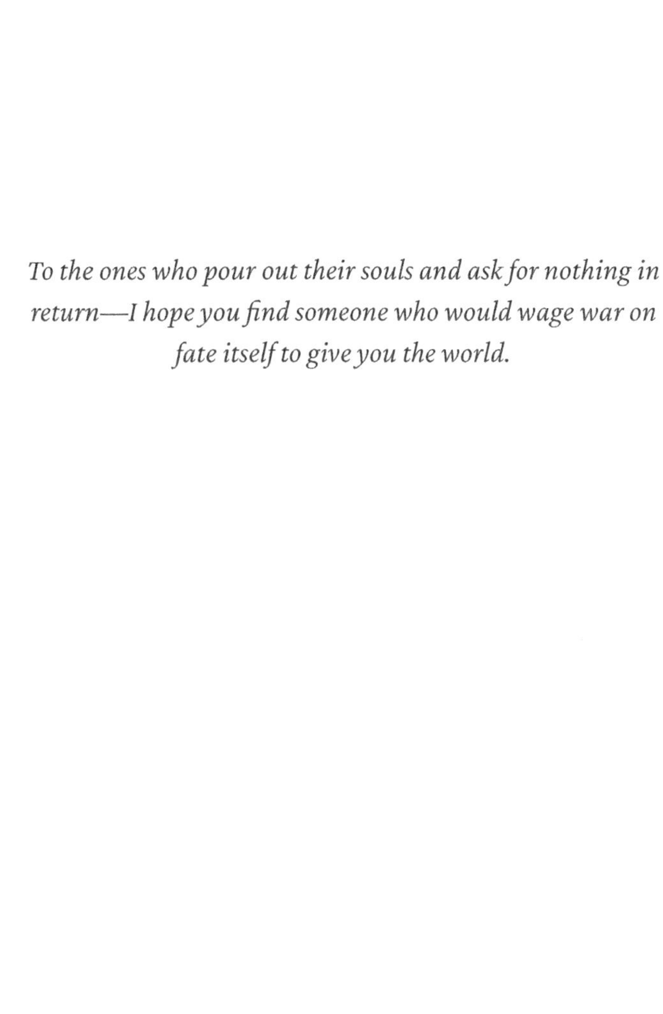

To the ones who pour out their souls and ask for nothing in return—I hope you find someone who would wage war on fate itself to give you the world.

HAVLANDS
N
S

Ellow
Asker

Korina
Eiatis
Sea

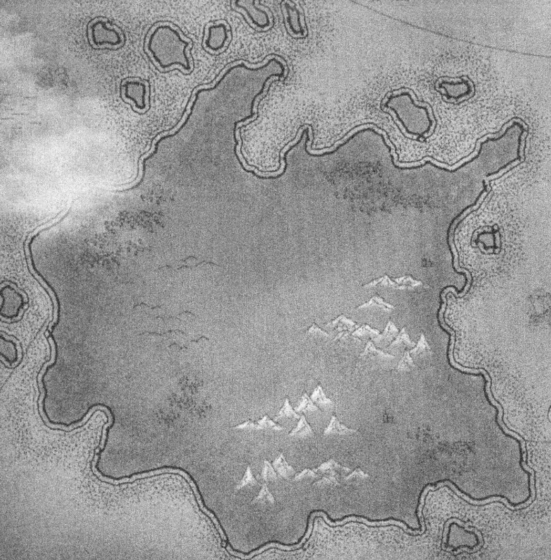
Vastala

CHAPTER 1
LESSIA

Merrick grinned at her as he opened his arms, and Lessia couldn't help but break into a run to reach him where he stood upon one of the cliffs beneath her childhood home, his silver hair dancing around his face in the warm summer breeze.

The sun blasted her skin as she pushed herself to move faster, and she had to fight to keep her eyes from closing against the bright light as her feet dug into the sand to close the distance between them.

But as Merrick's arms wrapped around her waist, she gave up and let her lids fall shut, allowing her other senses to take in the male she loved.

Merrick.

Her mate.

His wild scent whirled around her, and she couldn't get enough of how it filled her nostrils—nor how it filled her with that sense of freedom, of casting off shackles, of being utterly and entirely herself.

"I missed you," he murmured into her hair, and his

heart began pumping faster, the drums tapping against her own chest and filling the air like a soft melody.

Pulling back, she finally opened her eyes to his, and the ones that usually held the darkness of the night sky were now nearly pure silver, the flecks appearing to whirl as they flickered over her.

"I missed you too," she whispered before she crashed her lips against his.

The groan ripping from him nearly sent Lessia to her knees, and only because his strong arms held her did she not tumble down onto the white stone beneath them.

Gods, she had missed him so much.

Lessia wasn't sure how long it'd been, but any time away from him was too long.

She'd gotten too used to him always being there.

I'm here.

I'm always here.

Lessia smiled against his mouth, interrupting the kiss, and when Merrick pulled back to search her eyes, she let her lips pull even wider until he also broke into a grin.

"I'll never get used to that." Merrick shook his head so wildly his hair flew around it, sparkling against the blue sky behind him. "I'll never get used to you being mine."

Lifting her hand to caress his cheek, her palm rasping against the silver stubble growing there, she responded, "I'm always yours. Always."

Merrick brushed his lips against hers again. "As I'm always yours."

"Are you coming or what? We've waited forever!" A voice broke through the clear air, and Lessia hadn't thought her smile could go any wider, but her cheeks began hurting when her sister impatiently waved at them from behind Merrick's tall frame before she sprinted up the trail toward their home.

After a final look at Merrick, who nodded and released her, she grabbed his hand and began dragging him the familiar path up to the stone house where she'd grown up—where she'd spent her first twelve years of life.

Large green bushes flanked the road, and the bird-song she remembered loving as a child filled her ears as copses of trees popped up on either side.

The sound of small animals rushing across the forest bed joined the chirping and the wind rustling the leaves, and Merrick pulled at her hand when a rabbit crossed their path, to stop her from stepping on it.

Lessia drank in every sound, every smell, every familiar curve of the road.

She'd missed this island so much.

Thirteen years...

That's how long it'd been since she'd last been here.

Her favorite place.

Her home.

She felt Merrick's eyes on her and quickly tried to shake the melancholy that had begun filling her upon remembering the night she'd left, upon remembering the mother who'd made this place a haven.

The mother who was no longer.

The hand wrapped around her own tightened its grip, and when it pulled her to a stop once more, gently tugging at her to turn around, she let it.

"It wasn't your fault, Elessia." Merrick tried for a smile, but the darkness that now filled his eyes betrayed him.

And when a second voice—another familiar one, but this one filled with anger and resentment and disgust—broke the gentle melody floating around them, his grin collapsed completely.

Lessia spun around even before her father could finish his sentence, her heart shattering at the twisted grimace on his face.

"Of course it was her fault." Alarin took a step toward them, and Lessia's blood ran cold when she realized his white tunic and breeches were splattered with something dark...

Something red?

Despite the warning blaring within her, Lessia sniffed the air.

Iron overtook all the summer scents that had twined around them before.

Blood. It was blood that painted her father's clothing—blood that ran down his hands, dripping onto the light stone lining the path as he continued to walk toward them, his amber eyes crazed as they flitted between her and Merrick.

"She killed her sister. And then she killed her mother." Alarin stopped a few feet away, but drops of spit still landed on her face as he forced the words out. "She's a monster."

"No." Lessia stumbled toward him, but Merrick's grip on her hand held her back. "No, Father. Frelina is alive! I just saw her."

Her father's face crumpled with pain, before his arm shot out behind him. "If she's alive, how do you explain the graves?"

Lessia didn't want to look, but she couldn't stop herself from following her father's shaking hand, and when it revealed two white stones—one with *Frelina Rantzier* carved into it and the other *Miryn Rantzier*, both with dark stains marring the shiny fronts—a scream burst from her lips.

"You should feel pain," her father spat. "You killed my mate. My daughter. You should suffer like I have."

No.

No, this was all wrong.

Lessia shook her head, barely able to see through the tears that welled up in her eyes.

Still, when her father unsheathed a sword hanging by his waist, she didn't shrink back.

Instead, her eyes fixed on the graves of her sister and mother.

Two of the people she'd loved the most.

She did deserve this, didn't she?

If they were dead...

If they'd truly left this realm to move on to the afterlife?

It must be her fault.

Out of the corner of her eye, she noted the sword flying through the air, the whistling sound brushing her ears, but it wasn't until Merrick's hand ripped from hers that she snapped her head up.

Tears spilled down her father's cheeks as his arm fell to his side. "Now you'll know."

Know what? It was as if her thoughts refused to collaborate.

But then a gurgling sound—a horrible, wet, blood-curdling gurgling sound—reached her, just before a loud thump accompanied it.

Turning her cotton-filled head, she found Merrick's body crumpling to the ground, the sword he ripped from his gut clinking as it fell to the stone. His arms and legs splayed out in strange positions across the grass-peppered path, almost as if he'd taken a great fall.

Lessia wasn't certain if the sound that split the air came from her own mouth.

It was animalistic, a primal roar of pain that should break worlds apart, that should carry all the way to the Old World... perhaps even to the gods.

And when that thread she'd just begun to notice, the flicker of awareness between them, went dark, something broke inside her.

Hands flying to her chest, she fell to her knees beside her mate.

"Merrick!" Lessia's voice sounded as if from far away, as if it wasn't her own anymore, as if the pain was too great to let anything else in. "Merrick!"

She dropped her hands to his face and forced it her way, but the eyes that met hers...

There was no light behind them.

No dancing silver flecks.

No deep darkness.

And his face?

There were no hard lines that she loved to watch soften.

There was no twist of his mouth to hide a smile.

"Merrick!" She snapped her head down to his chest, but no heart thumped against it, and no air drove it up and down.

Another eerie, spine-rattling sound exploded through the air.

"Now you know," her father echoed. "Now you know how it feels. What you did to me."

She couldn't look at him.

Not when anger began working its way through the pain.

Not when that anger turned to rage, and her magic flitted to life behind her eyes, burning under her skin.

He'd killed him.

Her father had killed Merrick.

A hiss flew through her clenched teeth.

Squeezing her eyes shut, she gripped Merrick's bare arm to keep herself from storming toward her father and from allowing the voice in her mind to urge her to avenge her mate.

To kill like he'd been killed.

As Lessia dug her nails into Merrick's smooth skin, something touched the edge of her consciousness.

Don't lose focus.

Her forehead scrunched.

How many times do I need to tell you not to lose focus?

Merrick's deep voice bounced within her mind, and her eyes flew open.

He still lay there beneath her, chest unmoving and face serene, the bloodied sword beside him and the wound it had caused still oozing blood, pumping it from his gut, and Lessia fought another cry weaving its way up her throat.

Focus, Merrick's voice snapped.

I'm trying, she wanted to scream back, but the words caught in her throat when she dug her fingers further into his arm.

Her eyes trailed the golden skin.

The *smooth* golden skin.

As she released her grip, her eyes followed the marks her nails had left.

But...

There was no dark traitor mark.

She glanced at the other arm, but it was as smooth as the one she'd held—no raised scars, no black letters contrasting against his skin.

Lessia moved to look at her own arms, realizing with a start that the skin on them, too, was smooth and unbroken.

No traitor mark.

No outline of the blood oath she'd once sworn.

It... it wasn't real.

This wasn't real.

She pushed at her mind, forcing it to focus.

What was the last thing she remembered?

There had been water.

A ship.

The king.

Loche and Merrick standing before her.

Suffocation.

Something warm being pressed into her hand when cold lips collided with hers.

Pain shooting up that same arm when heavy wetness surrounded her.

She took a shallow breath.

The king had figured out she was the one the curse spoke of.

And this?

This wasn't real.

She could see it now.

The muddled edges of her consciousness, the mistakes that whichever of Rioner's guards was doing this to her had made, the impossibility of being back in her childhood home.

Lifting her head and making her stiff legs straighten,

she captured her father's eyes again.

Only now, those eyes were a few shades darker, the golden-brown hair more auburn in the flickering light of the sun.

"Rioner." Lessia clenched her fists when the king met her glare head-on. "So you dare meet my eyes now?"

The cool laugh he let out should have made goose bumps rise across her skin.

But she was done being afraid of him.

Absolutely fucking done.

Merrick had trained her for this.

She'd decided to walk this path.

To save their realm, whatever the cost might be.

And the king was terrified of her.

She could see it in the slight creases around his eyes—the twitch of the palms hanging by his sides.

He was terrified of the curse and her magic.

A corner of her mouth lifted.

He should be the one to cower now.

Wiping the straggling tears, she let the magic sizzling under her skin burst out of her eyes as she stepped toward him.

The Fae king didn't move as she locked eyes with him and purred, "Don't look away."

"I won't." Rioner's mouth twisted into a cold smile. "But you realize this cellar is filled with guards, don't you? They'll kill you before you have time to take a breath if you so much as threaten to stain my robe."

She made herself smile back at him, trying to get the smell of iron that still filled her nostrils to fade.

It wasn't real. Nothing of what had just happened had been real.

"See, I don't think they will. They know of the curse, I

assume?" Lessia cocked her head. "I've understood you can't kill me yourself. Perhaps not even order it."

Rioner's brows popped up for the smallest of seconds before he caught himself. "I thought your mind was clear. The guards told me you hadn't broken yet." He began turning away, his eyes still meeting hers over his shoulder. "They must have been mistaken. I'll need to find another to help with this mission."

"Don't turn your fucking back on me!" Lessia nearly tripped over an uneven stone as she followed him. "Where are you going?"

Rioner halted. "You're demanding to know where your king is going?"

Something like unease coiled deep within Lessia's gut. "Stop playing coy. We're past that point, aren't we, *uncle?*"

A shocked laugh escaped Rioner. "Uncle? That's a new one." He waved to someone she couldn't see. "Her mind has gone. Please take care of her."

The salty breeze shifted into a worryingly familiar one, and Lessia's magic faded away with every whiff of iron-tinged stale air.

Sounds she never wanted to hear again drowned all others.

And then... the darkness.

Darkness that engulfed everything—that nearly swallowed the king as he walked toward a thick stone door.

Her eyes widened.

Not to get used to the shadows that danced all around her but because she recognized that door.

Lessia met the eyes of a dark-haired Fae standing guard beside her.

A Fae she also recognized.

The memory of agony had her muscles flex, but she pushed it away, forcing herself to speak up again. "I know this isn't real! I left this cellar years ago! This isn't real!"

Spinning around so his robes flew all around him, Rioner drawled, "You've been in these cellars for years, Lessia Gyldenberg. I thought I had use for you—something only a halfling could do—but alas… I'll have to find another."

"No!" Her greasy hair slapped against her skin as she shook her head. "No!"

This wasn't happening.

It wasn't real.

It couldn't be real.

Focus.

She tried to get Merrick's voice to give her strength.

"Merrick," she whispered. "Merrick, please help."

She needed him to growl at her.

To make her snap out of this nightmare.

"Yes?"

Her eyes flew to the king again.

Then to the dark ones of the male who opened the creaking door.

A choked sound traveled from her chest when Merrick's passive eyes trailed across her face, then moved back to the king.

"Do you know the halfling?" Rioner asked as Merrick pulled the door wider for him.

"Never seen her before." Merrick's eyes didn't seek hers out again. "Is she important?"

"No. Perhaps you can do me the honor of killing her? I need more space—"

Her heartbeat slamming in her ears muffled the rest of the king's words, and before anyone could react, Lessia sprinted forward, grasping at the king's robe and pushing him up against the wall.

"Merrick would never look at me like that," she snarled as she gripped his head and forced his eyes to her own. "You can't fool me into believing this is real."

"Lessia, no!"

She ignored the vaguely familiar voice fighting to break through the haze of rage.

"You can't breathe," Lessia purred softly as her magic sizzled to the surface once more. "The air in this room is gone."

She couldn't help the smile that pulled at her features when the king tried to draw a wheezing breath, and when his eyes bulged after only seconds, the grin turned into a humorless laugh. "Doesn't feel too good, does it? I hear you like to drown your enemies."

"Stop! It's not what you think."

That voice again.

Who was that?

Lessia nearly turned her head, but when the king's face turned blue, she couldn't deny herself the pleasure of watching him suffer.

"I think water replaced the air in your lungs. Can you feel it?" she cooed, savoring the fear in the amber eyes as the male shook his head.

"Please!" someone begged, and this time the voice tugged at her heart. "Lessia!"

Tugged so hard her heart skipped a beat.

Frelina. That was Frelina's voice.

Focus.

She whipped her head around, but the cellar was empty.

Where had the guards gone?

As she brought her eyes back to the king, her question got stuck in her throat.

Soft, bright amber eyes met her own.

Not muddled, hard ones.

Her father's eyes flooded with tears as he grasped at his throat, the gurgling sound no longer pleasing her but driving a cold sweat across her skin.

"Lessia! Please!" her sister called out again.

Was this another mind trick to stop her from getting to the king?

Focus.

Rubbing her arms, she tried to get her mind to close, tried to force the magic within it away, tried to understand what was real.

As she trailed her fingers across the scars, the letters marking her arm, she reminded herself that the king had had her sister and father.

The letters were real.

They couldn't create those by capturing her mind.

It's the same one.

That's what Merrick had told her.

You and me.

They were real.

Elessia and Merrick.

They were real.

That meant...

Fuck!

Lessia quickly pulled on the magic that had drifted away.

"Breathe. You can breathe!" she urged her father, and

when a rattling sound rumbled in his chest, she released a breath, catching him when his knees buckled.

As she pulled one of her father's arms over her shoulders, her magic burned behind her eyes and she snapped it inward, the way she'd done when training with Raine, Kerym, and Frelina, and upon finding blazing green eyes —the eyes she'd cursed for so many years—she screamed at them to get out, to leave her alone.

And as soon as they flickered, her walls flew up.

The cell vanished.

Only the sound of water remained in the small wood-encased space, and as Lessia looked around, she realized the room they stood in was a ship's cabin, with the heaving water sloshing against the sides of the vessel.

Her father still hung limp by her side, and as she glanced to her right, she found Frelina, Kerym, and a male who must be Thissian chained to a wall.

Whipping her head around to the other side, her heart stopped.

Rioner actually stood tall there, a lazy smile on his bent face.

And beside him...

Three of the vilest guards she'd gotten to know during her stay in his cellars.

The green-eyed one, the one she believed was named Torkher, flashed his teeth, but when she couldn't help but show her own back, Rioner slammed a hand into the Fae's chest as he made to approach Lessia.

"That was quite the entertainment." Rioner fixed the gilded crown atop his head. "I thought you might kill my dear brother."

Lessia's nostrils flared, but she kept her mouth shut,

her gaze following the guards who began filing into the rounded room from either side of her, their eyes trained on her and the other prisoners.

"See, you were right. I can't kill *you.*" Rioner's frosty smile lifted further. "But I can kill everyone around you. Make you watch them suffer until their last breath. Force you to hear their screams every minute of every day until you're begging to be able to kill yourself. I think it shall be quite entertaining as well."

"Fuck you," Lessia snarled, tightening her grip on her father and inching toward her sister and friends.

"Such a mouth on you." Rioner chuckled as he began walking toward a rounded metal door. "I'll see you tomorrow, little halfling. And… I think perhaps we start with the other Faeling."

Red colored her entire field of vision when Rioner jerked his head toward her sister.

But she didn't have time to respond before the first door slammed shut behind him, closely followed by the other two, the metal clangs telling her they were bolted shut, leaving them all in the little light that shone through the gaps in the planks of the side of the ship.

CHAPTER 2
MERRICK

One day.

One fucking day without her and he was losing his mind.

Merrick paced back and forth on the deck of Loche's ship, the one Raine had dragged him onto when he'd refused to stop trying to beat the regent into carrion in the cabin beneath.

Glaring at the wild sea crashing around the ship that Elessia's friends had sailed in on to pick them all up from the water, he tried not to imagine what the king was doing to his mate right this moment.

But it proved futile when images of the first time he'd seen her forced themselves into his thoughts.

Her pale and too-thin body lying on that dirty stone floor beneath the king.

The shaking voice begging for it all to end.

Her unseeing eyes when she swore the blood oath to Rioner.

Fuck!

He'd thought the pain he felt when he realized what she was would be the worst he'd experience.

It had nearly killed him to follow the king's orders.

But now?

Now that he knew her?

When he truly knew who she was—that she was his?

His to save.

His to protect.

His to love.

Merrick cursed again, stepping up to the railing and digging his fingers into it so hard that chunks of wood crumbled under his palms.

He would rip the flesh from the king's bones like he did this wood for what he'd done to her.

"No more. Please no more," Elessia had begged that first day he'd seen her, and Merrick wouldn't stop until the king did the same.

Until he fucking kissed his feet, begging for mercy.

And then...

He'd unleash the souls that always pressed all around him.

He would let them rip into the king—bring him over to their side of the veil or whatever it was he could open and close between their worlds—and continue the torture there forever.

Merrick hadn't missed the thirst for revenge in some of them, the hunger when they beheld the king, whispering what they'd like to do to him.

An exceptionally tall wave hit the side of the vessel, splashing small drops of salty water onto his face, and he was about to curse again—curse the fucking seas for daring to still exist when Elessia must be hurting—when something flickered within him.

Holding his breath, he froze, trying to sense it once more.

There. The fragile thread that used to shimmer in gold like Elessia's eyes when her magic surfaced now sputtered like an almost burned-out candle.

But it was there.

She was alive.

And she was fighting.

Merrick didn't know how, but he could feel it.

His little fighter.

The woman who'd been through so much—too much—in her young life, but who refused to give up. Who believed in him even after everything he'd done. Who believed in the good in all the world even after everything it had done to her.

The good Merrick had thought to be long gone until he watched her fight for a better life.

Until he'd watched her save those Faelings, watched her find friends, watched her build a life, and watched her... fall in love.

He knew Elessia believed he'd been hurting for years because of the mate bond...

But he hadn't.

He hadn't been happy—it'd been long since he'd felt happiness, until the past few weeks—but he'd been content seeing her find purpose, find comfort, even find love.

Still, knowing now what it felt like to give in.

To claim her.

To call her his...

He understood why Raine never regretted meeting Solana, even if he now had to live without her.

Merrick would have stiffened at the slow footsteps

sounding behind him if he hadn't smelled the stench of alcohol that constantly whirled around Raine.

"The drinking helps." Raine waved a flask his way as he leaned against the railing beside him. "You'll see."

"No," Merrick mumbled. "I need a clear head to find her."

Raine nodded, his eyes shifted out across the dark sea. "The human—Amalise—is making some food. It didn't smell too good, but it'll be hot."

Food...

As if he could eat anything when Elessia...

"You need strength, too, Merrick. I've heard those whispers all day—you'll be drained soon." Raine moved so he faced him. "Remember what happens..."

Fighting not to roll his eyes or give in to the urge to slam his fist into Raine's face to relieve some of the tension coiling his muscles, Merrick thought about the last time his energy ran out.

It'd been after he was forced to torture her.

The worst fucking day of his life.

Hearing her ribs break...

He ripped another chunk from the railing and threw it into the sea.

He'd nearly died that night.

Would have happily gone if it hadn't been for Elessia and what he knew she'd still have to face.

Not just with the king but the rebels... and the fucking Oakgards' Fae.

He'd been drained before, of course.

But it had been centuries before that night.

He'd learned quickly that if his magic drained him, it wasn't like it was for other Fae, where they just couldn't access their gifts.

Of course it fucking wasn't.

Merrick's gift—those damned souls whispering to him —tried to claim him and take control over *him* whenever he wasn't strong enough to resist them. Tried to pull him over to their side and tried to rip that thread that separated their worlds apart, so they could come and go as they liked.

He wasn't certain what would actually happen if he died.

Perhaps they'd go with him.

Or they'd run free.

Not that he'd care, if Elessia...

Merrick shook his head.

She was alive, and he'd ensure she stayed that way.

"Fine." Merrick glared at Raine, responding to his earlier suggestion. "I'll eat. Then we need to find her."

"Do you feel... Is she..." Raine winced.

"She's alive," Merrick snapped.

She was. That he was certain of.

"Good." Raine gave him a weak smile. "We'll find her. And that little sister of hers."

Merrick didn't miss the shadow of guilt that crept across Raine's face at the mention of Frelina.

Not that it had been his fault.

None of them could have known what Meyah was planning.

Still, although he probably should have, Merrick didn't offer him any encouraging words.

It was good that he felt guilty—then he'd also have some urgency to find them.

Raine's narrowed eyes told him he knew precisely what Merrick was thinking, but he didn't say anything as they walked into the dimly lit cabin.

The low murmurs quieted as Merrick's foot landed on the wooden floor, the squeaking of the planks seemingly echoing across the cramped room.

To his left, a few foul-smelling cots stood, and atop them sat the sisters who'd saved them back in the cabin in that damn forest on Asker.

Venko was perched on his own bed beside them, and the merchant briefly met his eyes as Merrick walked farther into the room.

Those blues of his still held some fear—even after all the weeks they'd spent together—and when Merrick curled his lip back, Venko quickly averted his eyes to the clasped hands in his lap.

Merrick would have snickered if there was any humor left in the world.

He could smell the loathing from Loche even before those steel eyes met his own, and his lip lifted farther, letting his teeth rasp against his bottom lip. The regent openly glared at him from where he sat watching Ardow and Amalise cooking something whose musty smell permeated the entire square room.

"Watch it, human," Merrick purred when Loche grumbled something under his breath. "I wanted to kill you before all of this happened. Now... it might just be a necessity."

"Merrick," Raine warned. "She won't like it."

He's right.

Merrick jerked when her voice rang in his mind, as clear as if she'd been right there, and the raspy sound of it was the most beautiful thing he'd ever heard.

She *wouldn't* like it if he killed Loche.

He couldn't read her mind, but he knew she still

cared for the dumb human, and he wouldn't hurt her. Never again.

She'd told him she would never deny him anything.

And neither would he her.

"Fine," he finally muttered. "I won't kill you."

When Loche smirked at him, one of those smiles the regent deserved to get his teeth knocked out from, Merrick added "yet" under his breath.

Perhaps Elessia would tire of his smug smiles and searching eyes.

If so, Merrick would be ready.

"No one is killing anyone." The guard who had trailed Loche during the election—Zaddock, Merrick seemed to remember—stepped out from the small bathing chamber, where he must have dunked his hair in the only bucket, judging from the drops of water running down his leather tunic. "At least no one in this room."

"Z, you're ever so grumpy now." Loche leaned back in his chair, his hands resting behind his head. "You seem a little frustrated... What happened those weeks in the cave?"

A plate clattered to the ground, and when Amalise bent to pick it up, it was impossible to miss her reddened cheeks and the sour look she cast at the regent.

Ardow appeared to have caught his friend's discomfort as well, as he quickly broke in, "Let's just eat, and then we can argue."

No one seemed to disagree because when Ardow and Amalise set out the plates on the table for Raine, Loche, Zaddock, and Merrick, it remained entirely quiet.

Ardow brought four bowls with him to the cots, and when he sat down next to Venko, the sisters began a hushed conversation, but as Merrick—very unfortunately—was coming to know, a never-ending torrent of words spilled from their mouths, reverberating softly through the entire room.

Blocking them out, he focused on the blonde woman who'd slipped onto the chair by his side, much to Zaddock's dismay, from the open glares he shot across the table.

"So you're with Lessia now?"

Merrick nearly choked on the piece of bread he'd popped into his mouth at the openly hostile tone, the fierce blue eyes, and the lifted chin of the human beside him.

She didn't seem frightened of him.

At all.

"Well?" Amalise tapped her spoon against the bowl.

"I am." Merrick stared right back at her. "She is mine, and I am hers."

"So you're going to get her back?" Amalise raised her chin another inch.

"Of course I'm going to fucking get her back." Merrick couldn't help but let anger seep into his tone. "It's the only damned thing I am going to do."

"Good. You can't be too sure with the Fae. I've heard some horrendous stories from Lessia. You seem to be pretty ruthless, so I wondered if perhaps you'd leave her behind."

He couldn't help it.

His whispers boomed through the room as a snarl dropped from his mouth.

"If anyone else doubts my intention to find Elessia and kill the king and every single fucking male or female who has hurt her..." Merrick emphasized each word. "Feel free to let me know now."

Every person in the room turned a shade lighter at the thick air, and the souls, he knew, were whispering their innermost fears back to them.

Even Raine, the male who'd fought beside him for centuries, shrank into his chair.

When the whispers continued, Loche's hands twitched toward his ears, but Merrick had to give it to the regent: he fought bravely, especially since Merrick allowed the souls to creep all the way up to him.

Zaddock flew from his chair when a small sound escaped Amalise, but the blonde pushed him away when he tried to wrap his arms around her to shield her.

"Good," she huffed again. "You seem like you can protect her. Even if you're fucking terrifying."

A startled laugh burst from Merrick's throat when he met her hard eyes—the ones that were not glossy from fear—and the whispers softened until only a low humming bounced between the dark wooden walls.

She was fucking testing him.

Merrick heard Venko mumble "I hate it so much. So damned much" to Ardow before Amalise spoke again, and that was enough for him to rein in his magic completely.

"Now that that's settled... How are you going to find her?" Amalise demanded.

"Yes... tell us, Death Whisperer, how will you find her when she could be anywhere in the Eiatis Sea?" Loche's voice sounded stronger than it should have, as his coloring still hadn't returned to his usual shade, and Merrick wanted nothing more than to rip the regent's smug face off.

But then...

Something flashed in those gray eyes.

Something he realized the regent was fighting hard to keep under wraps.

Fear.

Sorrow.

Heartbreak.

That's what rotted within him.

That's what that smirk tried to hide.

That's what those tightly clenched fists, as he made himself meet Merrick's eyes, tried to control.

Merrick's rage melted faster than butter on a piece of newly baked bread, and it was replaced with something cold—something he didn't like.

A feeling he didn't care for one bit.

He knew what it was like, watching the one he loved fall for someone else.

So Merrick swallowed the snarky response he'd planned to retort with, and instead looked to Raine. "Where do you think he's gone?"

Raine had studied the king's movements and habits for centuries.

It was how he'd decided on that island in the middle of Midhrok.

Raine shook his head, his reddish hair falling into his eyes. "I-I honestly do not know. I doubt he's gone to Vastala. Not with his brother in captivity. You saw his guards back on that ship... They weren't too sure of that decision. He's probably somewhere remote... somewhere no one would think to look."

"What about Korina?" Merrick suggested. "Even rebels haven't returned there yet."

The dark waters around Korina had been nagging at his thoughts the entire day.

For some reason, they resonated with what the king was doing—betraying his own blood.

Exactly like the shifters had betrayed the Fae and humans.

"Perhaps..." Raine sighed. "It's a start."

Merrick ground his teeth, telling himself not to snarl at him.

It wasn't Raine's fault.

It was no one's fault.

Well, apart from the regent.

He couldn't help but send the raven-haired human another death stare.

If he hadn't stepped forward...

"I gave her the stone." Loche glared back at him as if he knew precisely what Merrick was thinking. "That's all I did."

"What stone?" Amalise asked, her brows drawn in.

Merrick didn't look away from the gray eyes as he responded, "It controls the sea wyverns. The stone can call them back here—can make them fight for us."

He refused to thank the human.

Loche should have fucking given them the stone before.

Now it might be too late.

"Wyverns..." Zaddock mumbled. "So she'll be able to protect herself?"

"If the stone allows her," Raine said softly.

The blood in Merrick's veins froze to ice.

"What. Do. You. Mean?" he got out, his voice lowering into that frosty one he'd noticed always gave Elessia goose bumps.

He'd never wielded any of the stones—his gift too

precious to the Rantziers to have him part of the fleet—so he wasn't too certain how they worked.

Raine's features twisted at whatever he saw in Merrick's face, and his voice lowered so much that Merrick knew the humans by the cots wouldn't be able to hear what he said next.

"After the Rantziers' misuse of them, the stones don't respond to just any Fae anymore. Only those who are worthy—of pure heart—may call them back."

Merrick's shoulders dropped two inches.

Elessia was the most kind-hearted, loyal, and pure soul he'd ever met.

Of course she'd be fucking worthy.

Raine's eyes dropped down to his bowl with gray mush. "Merrick... she's not just a Rantzier, she also compelled Ydren when she first met her."

His heart ached so much in his chest he was surprised it didn't break through his ribs, and as Merrick sucked in a breath, he felt all the eyes in the room fly to his face.

The silence was too much.

The stares too heavy.

Flying from his seat, Merrick ordered, "Tell your captain to steer toward Korina. We'll start there."

Then he took the stairs four steps at a time to get up into the rain-filled air again, keeping his eyes on the horizon and screaming into the bond, *I'm coming for you! Please, just keep fighting. You're strong enough. I'm coming!*

CHAPTER 3
LESSIA

You're strong enough.

Lessia jerked as she awoke, trying not to panic at the rattling chains and the damp blindfold Rioner's guards had tied around her head, which irritated her skin.

Merrick's voice still echoed in her mind from the dream, and she could almost hear him tell her *Only you and me,* could almost taste his soft lips against hers, could almost smell his familiar wild scent fold around her.

She couldn't stop the sob that left her lips.

"Lessia, are you in pain?" Her father's voice sounded somewhere to her right.

She hesitated for a moment, listening to the metallic rustles and Kerym's whispered words to his brother, who still hadn't responded in the hours they'd been here; to her sister's soft breathing; and to her father's repeated "Lessia?"

Was she in pain?

Not physically.

Although she still had a strange aching sensation traveling up her right arm...

Not even mentally.

She didn't know how, but... the tears that fell from her eyes as she thought of Merrick weren't of sorrow.

They were of resolve, of what she knew she must do.

She'd made a vow back on Raine's island: to fight back—to do whatever it took.

It was time now.

It was really time.

Before it all ran out. Before something happened on this ship that she couldn't control. Before her family or friends were harmed because of her.

Lessia had already suspected back on Ellow that Rioner would somehow figure out she was the one the curse was about.

The king wasn't dumb.

But she hadn't told anyone her suspicions because she knew she needed to be close to him if she was to fulfill the gods' prophecy—if she was to kill him. So she'd let them all believe she'd trusted their plan to confront the king, all the while knowing it was quite likely Rioner would take her away.

If her friends had suspected what she expected to happen, even Merrick might have locked her up in one of Loche's cellars to keep her away from King Rioner.

Especially if he'd known the entire prophecy...

But now... she was only a few feet beneath Rioner if, as she suspected, some of the thumping footsteps above them belonged to the Fae king.

Lessia had prayed that her father and Frelina might

be out of the king's claws when she had to do this—that they wouldn't be put in harm's way.

But that wasn't her reality now.

So she would need to act quickly.

Alone.

Ensure no one, not even the people in this room, knew her plan.

It wasn't the best one.

Perhaps it was only *a plan*, as Raine had once so rudely stated.

But she knew the king underestimated her.

He still believed she was the broken Faeling he'd dragged out of his cellars, and she'd make sure that was precisely what he continued to think.

That Elessia was only a broken, weak halfling that the king could drive to the brink of absolute despair—that he could break and shatter and snap.

Because if she didn't convince him of that, Rioner *would* ensure she truly broke. He'd kill or perhaps even trick her into killing one of the people in this room.

There was no more time to lose.

So when her father demanded "Lessia, please answer me," she forced the guilt out of her mind and began screaming.

Given everything, it wasn't too difficult to make her body shake, each scream that left her more heart wrenching than the next as she thought of her mother, as she made herself think of never seeing Merrick again, as she thought of the risk to the rest of her family.

"Lessia. You're all right! You're not there."

She ignored Kerym's urgent whisper, ignored her sister's small hand trying to lace with her own, ignored her father's panicked question, "What's happening?"

and she definitely ignored Kerym's answer: "She believes she's back in Rioner's cellars."

"Fuck!" Kerym swore as she heard what must be his chains clinking. "Didn't think I'd miss Merrick so quickly. Lessia! You'll make all the guards on this ship come down here."

That's exactly what she hoped for.

Lessia continued wailing, shaking off all loving touches, and even when a creaking door opened and heavy footsteps moved the planks they sat upon, she let her cries reverberate around the ship.

"Stop that!" someone ordered.

Lessia screamed louder.

"Enough, halfling!" Hands grasped her shoulders, shaking her.

She filled her lungs and put every pent-up emotion behind the next scream.

"What is this ruckus?"

Lessia fought a relieved grin and cried out again when the king's voice drifted toward her.

"Stop her right now!" the king demanded. "She's so fucking loud, any ships within a mile will hear her."

She almost nodded to herself as she let out another harsh shout.

She'd known the king wouldn't want to be found. Not with her father chained up beside her. Not with the Siphon Twins—the twins still considered heroes amongst the Fae—shackled beside him.

The sound of her scream died in her throat when her head flew to the side, and sharp pain exploded behind her eyes as whoever had slapped her used far more strength than her sister had done that one time.

Still, she forced out another shriek.

"Enough!"

The fist that connected with her nose was entirely unforgiving, and hot blood flooded her mouth when her bone crunched.

Head-splitting pain burst through her face as she tried to scream again, but it was muffled when whoever hit her stuffed something foul-smelling into her mouth, hindering her ability to breathe.

The moan that followed was a real one as Lessia had to draw a breath through the nose she expected was shattered, and when her body twitched to curl into itself as the air stilled, she let it.

The next strike still rang true.

Her head slammed so hard into the wall behind her that she must have lost consciousness for a second, because when she came to, her father was screaming at Rioner.

"—enough! She's a child, Rioner! My child! Your niece!"

Lessia shook her head, realizing the blindfold had slipped off somewhat from the beating, and by squinting, she could make out Torkher grinning coldly where he squatted before her, the king standing behind him with four guards on either side.

Even though the dirty piece of fabric still covered some of her vision, Lessia could tell the guards—apart from the damned sadist Torkher—were uneasy.

Their gazes flitted so fast between her father and his brother and then back to each other, she wouldn't have been able to make it out if she hadn't been half-Fae.

But this was good.

They were loyal enough to the king that they'd kill her—or at least find a way to break her entirely.

But she didn't believe they'd let her father die.

Hopefully not even her sister.

Her family was innocent.

She'd bet on that as soon as she'd seen how they stared at her father in that cage on the ship—how they'd hesitated at the king's orders, mumbled to each other when they followed his demands, and the disapproving jerks of their heads as they led Thissian onto the deck.

Only she would be the one to lose her life.

And Rioner, if she was able to bring him with her.

Blood trickled down her throat as she pulled in another wheezing, painful breath through her nose, but she ignored the agony when the king opened his mouth.

"It's enough when I say it's enough, brother." Rioner's face remained bored as his eyes flew across the chained group. "She is meant to dethrone me. I will sooner die than let a fucking halfling—one that's related to me, at that—"

"Don't say another word, brother."

Lessia flinched at her father's warning—his tone so eerily similar to the cold one of the king's as he glared up at him.

She twisted so she could see him better, and another jab of pain stabbed at her.

But not from her nose.

No, her father's raging face was almost identical to his brother's, standing above them.

Cold.

Calculated.

Furious.

A primal rage born only of Fae blood.

She'd never seen him like this, and she couldn't help but think she'd brought this on them. On him.

This is bigger than you, she tried to remind herself.

It was bigger than her family.

She was doing this for all Havlands.

Lessia tried to repeat the words to herself, but when her father continued and his voice broke—from pain or anger, she wasn't sure—that cold, sticky feeling of guilt crawled through her veins.

"She is my *daughter*, brother. My... my daughter! She's a Rantzier! Have you no mercy?"

Disgust pulled at the king's features, twisting his already cruel face into one of nightmares. "It makes me feel sick that you made these two, Alarin. Sick! I should have them killed right now just for tainting the Rantzier name."

Red painted her vision, and Lessia tried to hiss "Don't you dare" through the dirty rag stuffed into her mouth when the king glanced at her sister, who sat with a straight back, eyes ahead, not an ounce of fear dancing across her soft features as she shifted the chains lying across her lap.

But when Rioner's cold gaze moved, landing on Lessia's tightly bound hands, then moved to follow the blood she was certain trickled over her chest, a chill whispered down her spine.

"So you're not completely broken yet..." The king cocked his head. "Say, how does it feel being separated from Merrick? From Loche? Did it make you feel good, breaking their hearts?"

She didn't want to, but she couldn't help the slight grimace twisting her features upon remembering Loche's eyes turning aware again, and when Merrick's wide, angry gaze met hers as Loche slammed his lips against her own... she physically recoiled.

Shaking her head, she had to fight not to press farther back into the wooden wall behind her.

Why had Loche done what he did?

Something tickled her consciousness, but it was so hazy, the memory still filled with so much pain, she huffed a sharp breath to battle it.

Rioner chuckled. "I saw the regent kiss you. I doubt he's alive if the Death Whisperer has any backbone left. Merrick probably unleashed those souls of his as soon as he came up for air. It's what I would have done..."

"Enough! It's fucking enough," her father snarled. "Leave her alone. Or I swear..."

The king whipped around so quickly that another jab of pain struck her when she moved her head to follow.

"You do not give me orders, *brother.*" Spit flew from Rioner's mouth as he snarled at her father. "You are the reason there is a risk to our family's throne. You gave life to this... this disgusting, vile abomination."

Chaos erupted as Kerym flew forward as far as his shackles would allow, as Frelina screamed something at the king, as her father growled so loudly some of Rioner's guards blanched.

Lessia couldn't help but do the same, managing to spit out the fabric in her mouth.

Fighting for her life, she tried to get to the king, wanting to tell him to tell her that to her face, to look her right in the eye as he called her those names.

But it was useless.

Rioner only laughed at the group, and when he ordered "Make them more agreeable, will you?" before spinning on his heel to leave the room, Lessia cried out again.

A harsh, raspy, agony-filled cry as five guards lingered, each with their eyes on one of them.

She tried to get in front of Frelina—tried to press her sister behind her—but Torkher wouldn't have it.

With a sharp order to another guard, he slammed another fist into Lessia's face, and the pain pulsated through her so violently she wondered if she'd be sick before he pulled the blindfold down once more.

Sounds she knew she'd never forget began echoing through the ship's cabin.

Moans.

Cries.

Huffs.

Crunches of bones.

Harsh sounds of breaking skin.

Her sister's defiant scream.

Her father's desperate cry.

Kerym's swearing and threats.

Thissian's muffled groans.

But still, Lessia didn't miss the king's demand: "Torkher. Break her completely. Not just physically but mentally. Whatever it takes, I want her to jump off this ship willingly."

The laugh brushing her ear as the Fae guard leaned in was the same one that filled her nightmares.

"I missed you," he whispered, his wet lips dragging across her cheek and his hands roving across her body. "I've learned a thing or two since last time, and... I can't wait to play."

The scream that burst through her mouth wasn't forced this time.

CHAPTER 4
LESSIA

Lessia shook so much that the putrid water in the cup she held sloshed over its sides, and she barely managed to get a few drops into her parched mouth when she brought it to her lips.

Dropping the mug after trying to lick up the remaining water, Lessia leaned back against the wall, her head throbbing with such force she wasn't certain if it was her body or the ship they were on that trembled.

She didn't know how many days had passed, not with the blindfold they kept over her eyes day and night, but she guessed at least a few, based on the aching hole in her stomach and the dried blood that seemed to coat almost every inch of her skin by now.

The guards had beaten them every few hours since Rioner left the room, and no matter how much Lessia tried to persuade them that she was broken—that she'd willingly step off this ship—she hadn't been convincing enough, and Rioner hadn't bothered showing up a single time since he'd ordered the torture.

Even when they'd begun bringing the others outside the room, to somewhere Lessia could no longer hear their screams, and she'd truly panicked—had truly meant it when she cried that she'd slit her throat right there and then—they hadn't budged, believing she still harbored some strength inside.

And while she might... might have that burning love inside driving her not to give up, she wasn't sure how long the flame would flicker.

Lessia knew her time was running out.

She could feel it.

If she didn't convince Rioner's guards soon, they'd do something to someone in this group she wouldn't be able to reverse.

That she couldn't bear.

"F-F... Lina," she managed to stutter through chapped lips.

Her sister had become worryingly quieter with each day that passed, and Lessia wasn't even able to use her eyes to understand how injured she was.

If it was anything like herself...

Lessia had a few broken ribs and fingers, one of her cheekbones was crushed from the last beating, and she was pretty certain her left shoulder had been dislocated a few times, based on the searing ache shooting from it every time she moved that arm.

And her nose...

Well, it hadn't healed straight, and she still struggled to breathe through it.

"I'm here," Frelina rasped somewhere to her left, and Lessia couldn't help the tears that sprang into her eyes at her small voice.

"She's by me," Kerym added softly. "She's strong, Lessia. Like you."

Kerym's arm nudged her when she sniffed, and Lessia made herself nod.

"This would be a great time for your mate to come to the rescue, I think," Kerym continued, and Lessia could tell he was fighting to keep the cheer in his voice. "I am excited to watch Merrick rip these fucking guards' heads off."

"Sh-she is his mate?"

Kerym stiffened beside her as a deep, unfamiliar voice broke in, and although she hadn't heard it previously, she knew it must be Thissian's, since he was the only one in here she didn't know.

"She is." Kerym's tone held so much love that Lessia would have had to look away had she not been blindfolded. "He finally found her."

"Only to lose her."

The choked sound that followed Thissian's words shattered Lessia's heart.

It was so much worse than Raine's agony and Kerym's sorrow.

It was resignation.

As if Thissian had merely yielded to the cruel twist of fate they all lived.

"He'll come for her," her sister hissed. "I saw how he looked at her. He'll rip this world apart if that's what it takes."

Despite everything, Lessia smiled.

He *would* come for her.

She knew it in her bones.

She wasn't sure how, but she could feel him.

Every time she hurt, she heard his voice telling her she was strong enough.

Every time the darkness moved in on her, she felt his lips press against hers.

Every time she thought she might finally break, the love she felt from him wrapped around her and healed those broken, jagged pieces she was made up of.

While Lessia knew she shouldn't have hope—because there was only one way this could end, after all—she wished for a little more time.

A few more days with him.

Staring into those night-sky eyes.

Making him smile.

Having his hands travel across her skin as if she were so precious he needed to touch every inch of her.

But even if it was too late for her...

She had to believe that Merrick would save the others.

That he'd care for her sister. For her father. For her friends. For Havlands.

Because, despite what the Death Whisperer thought of himself, he was good.

A cough ripped her from her thoughts, and Lessia leaned to her right, trying to get closer to her father, whose breathing appeared as labored as Lessia's.

"Father," she whispered, wanting to say something more, wanting to tell them all that it would be all right, that she would get them out of here, that Merrick would come for them.

But the thickness in her throat choked her words.

Lessia tried to tell herself it wasn't her fault, but when another clipped breath rushed past her father's lips and a low, pained moan escaped someone else as they shifted on the floor, guilt knifed its way through her chest.

It felt like it *was* her fault they were being hurt.

The guards were doing it to break Lessia, and she hadn't convinced them they'd succeeded yet.

"It's *not* your fault," her father rasped as he moved closer at the involuntary sound leaving her, his arm aligning with her own.

And even though none of them could move much due to the restrictive chains, his mere presence was soothing, and the burning sensation behind her eyes that had started when she heard Frelina's voice grew hotter.

A silent sob shook her body.

Then another one.

And another.

Another.

They kept coming until her entire frame trembled so hard the chains rattled in sync with the violent shakes.

Both her father and Kerym tensed beside her, and she tried to control her limbs when Kerym urged, "Do not let them win, Lessia. Do not break. He's coming for you, so hold on for him."

"W-will he know?" she managed to ask, and while the question was vague, the others knew what she meant—knew that she needed to know if Merrick would feel her die, should it come to that.

"Yes." The haunted word came from Thissian when the others remained silent.

She wanted to scream.

Either way, someone would hurt.

Merrick if she succeeded. The people in this room if she did not.

"It's not your fault," her father said again, his voice

stronger now. "Nothing that's happening is your fault. If it's anyone's, it's mine."

"Father, no," Frelina whispered, while Lessia managed to shake her head.

"Lina," her father pleaded softly. "I kept you both so sheltered because I wanted to protect you, but it seems... it seems all I did was set you up for failure. Lessia would never have left if I had found a way to integrate you into our society—to teach you what being Fae truly meant. And I... I should have listened to you, Frelina. I knew! I knew something was wrong, but I... I was too weak when your mother died. I..."

Her father's voice broke, and Frelina's louder sobs joined Lessia's silent ones.

"I'm so sorry. My beautiful girls. I am so sorry for all the pain my brother, my blood, is causing." Alarin drew a trembling breath. "I failed to protect you, and for that, I'll never forgive myself. But I *promise* you, I will find a way to get you out of here."

"Such pretty words, brother."

Lessia jerked when the king's voice floated through the room, and she wasn't feigning the way her body curled into itself, how it tried to become as small as possible when a low laugh that she knew belonged to Torkher followed.

"I wonder how you expect to keep that promise," Rioner continued, and in the silence following his words, Lessia could hear at least four pairs of feet making their way toward the group.

Kerym shuffled away from Lessia when a distressed sound left her sister, and from the way Frelina quieted and the chains clinked, Lessia understood Kerym was trying to hide her behind him.

But the wave of gratefulness that roiled inside her turned to glacial dread when her father spoke.

"Brother. Let them go. I'll have them get as far away from Havlands as possible. You can take out your revenge on me instead. Kill me if you like. But let them go."

"No!" she tried to scream, but the sound was barely more than a whisper.

Frelina also let out a muffled sound, although it was quickly clipped, almost as if Kerym had managed to stop her from speaking.

"Kill you... Perhaps," Rioner mused. "But letting them go?"

The clanging of an expensive metal, not like the chains they were all bound in but like the gold that made up the king's crown, had Lessia suspect he shook his head so violently the dangling gemstones adorning it clinked against each other.

"I don't think so," Rioner declared.

"Rioner," her father snarled, his begging tone rising into a fury-touched one. "You're starting a war you'll lose control over. You will not survive this. With their bond, he'll tear through this world to find her, and you know he's strong enough to kill you."

Lessia's pounding heart stopped in the heavy silence that followed, and she could tell from the sharp gasp of air flying into her father's lungs that so did his.

"He'll find her," Rioner repeated. "I must assume you're referring to the dear Death Whisperer?"

The next silence seemed to stretch on for what felt like an eternity, the soft breaths from the people in the room the only sound, and Lessia's heart remained quiet, as if its beats were too fragile to echo in the tension-filled room.

"So they've mated after all," the king said, almost as if to himself.

The laugh that followed was like a bucket of cold water thrown over her head.

"The Death Whisperer mated to a mere halfling? Oh, how the gods must have laughed at that one. The embarrassment it must bring him..." The king cackled again, and Torkher's blood-chilling laugh accompanied him, bouncing against the damp walls in the room.

"Tell me, halfling, how long did it take you to forgive him for all he's done to you?" Rioner asked, a hint of humor playing in his tone.

While Lessia could tell her father stiffened again, the air filling with the taste of confusion, she refused to respond.

Refused to give in to this one thing.

She would break for the king.

Gladly. It was what she had been trying to do every hour of the past days.

But not for this. Because if Merrick heard this was the moment she broke...

She bit her lip so hard it muted the pain within her.

She couldn't go there.

A hand laced around her arm, and she winced when the nails broke through her already sore skin.

"Your king asked you a question," Torkher spat. "Answer."

Lessia didn't even bother giving him a shake; she only kept her chin up.

Then her head slammed to the side, the ringing in it joined by Kerym's and her father's outraged screams.

"Answer!" Torkher screamed into her face, his vile breath fanning over her.

She remained quiet.

Another blinding strike had the back of her head slam into the wall so hard the crack echoed in the room. Or perhaps it was all in her head. Lessia didn't really know.

"Answer!"

She kept her lips firmly shut.

"Stop this!" her father screamed at the same time as Frelina whimpered.

But when Kerym's soft words reached Lessia's ears, she realized her sister wasn't making noises of pain for herself.

"She'll be all right, little Lina. Your sister is strong."

Kerym was right, Lessia thought as another fist crashed into her already broken ribs.

She was strong.

Because of Merrick.

Huffing a breath, she tried not to let her body coil farther in, but the pain wouldn't allow her to straighten her back.

"May I?"

She vaguely heard Torkher utter the question, but when her body was roughly shifted to the side and her shackles clinked, she realized he must have asked whether he could free her to get better access.

That's what he liked to do when they were alone too.

Having her strapped to something didn't allow him to hurt her *everywhere*.

"Fuck!" Kerym exclaimed when she was dragged away from his side.

"Lessia!" Frelina cried, the sound making Lessia's knees buckle.

But the Fae guard only tightened his grip, his arms sliding in under hers to drag her across the hard floor.

Pain pulsated in the darkness of her blindfold, and when Torkher released her, she tumbled to the wet wooden planks beneath her.

"Keep her conscious," the king warned. "I do not wish to have to come back. Especially if Merrick is on the way... we need to move quickly."

A low sound rumbled in the Fae's chest, and Lessia couldn't help but whimper when he ripped her tunic off, the scent of iron telling her the force opened some of the wounds from yesterday that the fabric had clung to.

"I want him to come," Torkher hissed into her ear as something cold and sharp played across her exposed back. "See, I want him to find your broken body and know exactly who did this to you."

The blade dug into her skin, and Lessia couldn't stop another scream when Torkher broke down the mental shield she'd managed to keep up for the past few days.

She was standing over her own naked and broken body, and the pain slicing through her was like nothing she'd ever felt before.

It was like a thousand daggers striking at once.

Like a fire blistering across every inch of her skin.

Like a darkness that swallowed the world, never to allow the sun to shine its soft light on it again.

With her hands on her knees, she tried to breathe.

But it wasn't possible.

Neither was the scream she tried to force from her lips.

Instead, her eyes widened when they snagged on large, golden-tan hands, and she quickly straightened.

Behind the pale and bruised body was a lake, and as she stared at her reflection, she realized she wasn't Lessia at all.

It was the Death Whisperer that stared back at her.

Her mouth fell open, her eyes returning to her own body.

Merrick *was carved into every bit of skin visible from this position, and she started shaking her head.*

No.

No.

He couldn't see her like this.

No.

"Enough, Rioner!" Her father's growl cracked the image before her eyes, and for the first time in her life, she was grateful when darkness once again surrounded her.

But her face crumbled when she realized that even though the image wasn't real, the sharp kisses of pain dancing across her back were, and so was the metallic scent of blood that whirled all around her.

"I'll do whatever you want," Alarin begged. "Please, just stop this. *Please.*"

She wanted to tell him no—to be quiet.

But she couldn't.

Not when fighting to keep the magic invading her mind out.

Not when fighting to stay awake, to not let the other, thicker darkness lurking at the edges of her eyes win.

She didn't even have the energy to wince when more letters were carved into her skin, the movements fast and determined, almost as if Torkher had done this before.

"Please!" Her father was crying now, and it was all she could do just to stay alive when a low cry left Kerym as well, a deeper one following it.

Rioner laughed again, and she briefly wondered whether one practiced the evil sound that penetrated what was usually something merry.

"You can't handle this, brother?" the king taunted. "She was with me *for years*. Years when she believed no one was coming for her. You left her. This serves you right."

Lessia braced herself when the familiar sound of water rushed into the room.

Droplets stung the wounds on her skin, and she bit down another whimper, knowing exactly what was coming, when Torkher stepped back.

The rushing inched closer, the sound roaring in her ears.

"Rioner, *please*. I beg you! I'll do anything! Anything!" Alarin's desperate voice barely carried over the sloshing sounds, and Lessia swallowed, quickly pulling in whatever air she could through her broken nose and dry mouth.

You're strong enough.

Merrick's voice drowned the sounds around her.

Do you want me to tell you no one—mate or not—has loved anyone the way I love you? That I would laugh as the world fell apart as long as you stood by my side? That even if I could only have one fucking night—one night pretending you're mine—I'd take it?

"I love you," she whispered back, trying to be grateful for the two nights they'd had.

It was at least more than one, she argued with the Merrick she'd conjured in her mind when he frowned at her.

Then the water swallowed her.

But not like it had when she dove from that boat to escape Ydren.

No, this water was invasive, forcing itself through her nose, through her mouth, filling her lungs in what felt like mere seconds.

Even her eyes brimmed with water, washing the image of the beautiful Merrick away.

She couldn't stop her body from trying to pull air into the now water-heavy lungs, nor when it convulsed from being unable to do so.

Shards of wood pierced her skin as she rolled on the floor, desperately trying to escape the king's magic, and she thought she should have appreciated it when Ydren was the only thing she needed to fear from the sea.

Lessia tried to focus on Merrick's lips and his words when she panicked in that cell in Ellow, but her mind snapped to another mouth, one that had pressed against hers right before the sea swallowed her last time.

A vague memory fought its way through her frantic mind from her last seconds on the ship in Ellow, and it wasn't the water that made her jerk when something warm traveled up her arm.

Loche...

He'd... he'd given her the stone.

But where was it?

The warmth spread from her arm across her shoulders, to her other arm, quickly making its way through her body, and then... then something other than crashing waves filled her ears.

Voices.

Low mumbling voices speaking to each other with words that Lessia couldn't make out.

Voices of which she wasn't certain who—or what—they belonged to.

But she didn't care when the darkness pressed on her mind.

Instead, she screamed in their direction, begging that

her gut feeling was true: "Please help me. Help us! Help Havlands."

CHAPTER 5
MERRICK

Please help me!

Merrick jolted upright in the cramped cot he'd tried to get a few hours' sleep in when Lessia's voice exploded within his mind.

I'm here!

I'm coming for you!

Fuck, hold on!

He tried to scream back at her with all his might, but he had no idea whether she could hear him, and he almost lost it when the only thing that joined the anger within him was fear—pure, vein-chilling dread—that couldn't come from anything other than his mate.

She was terrified.

Fuck! Merrick threw the blankets to the floor as he flew from the small bed, ignoring Raine's moan as he accidentally bumped into his cot on his way up to the deck.

He needed to get out of here.

He needed...

Merrick slammed a hand into the damp wall as he climbed the rickety stairs.

He just needed to be with her.

Preferably after killing every fucking bastard who ever hurt her.

We'll help.

Gladly.

We'll kill them all.

The souls pressed all around him, and since the deck was empty save for Zaddock—who should be at the helm steering, as it was his turn to guide them through the night—Merrick didn't bother leashing them.

Their roaring whispers joined the waves crashing against the port side, and Merrick understood why Lessia had screamed at the top of her lungs that night on the ship.

His entire body buzzed with wild, untamed energy—the feeling so foreign he clasped the railing and leaned over, as if the depths of the sea might have an answer to what the fuck he was supposed to do.

Merrick cursed when the water drops spraying his face did little more than rile him further, pushing those souls to spread out from the ship, their whispers reaching farther and farther, perhaps even deep into the sea to scare whatever swam beneath them.

He swore loudly again as a wave of sticky helplessness rippled across his skin.

Before he'd met this wildly loyal, pure, kind, intelligent, and beautiful woman, little had been able to provoke him.

He hadn't cared enough after everything that happened to Raine and the others, believing the punishment of being blood-sworn to the Fae king was sufficient to compensate for the pain his friends lived with day and night.

But now?

Gods, he couldn't fucking stand it.

He had no idea how Raine did it.

How Kerym was alive.

How Thissian still set one foot in front of the other.

Lessia wasn't even dead, and it still was as if she'd ripped out everything that made sense within him, as if she'd taken every other reason to live.

He was hers.

Fully and entirely.

And if she didn't exist...

The whispers turned to bellows.

Neither would this world.

We'll wipe all Havlands out.

Kill every soul and bring them over to us.

Create a new world in the shadows.

We'll rule there together—make your mate our queen.

Merrick finally reined them in slightly.

He fucking hoped not.

If he had to continue dealing with these assholes when he was dead...

That thought alone was enough to quell the final whispers, driving up the veil, or whatever it was, that kept them away from the living side.

Footsteps thudded in the silence that followed, but Merrick didn't turn around as the scent he'd come to hate—the one he could barely stand after it had enveloped Lessia during the election—drifted across the deck.

"Careful, regent. I'm plotting how I'm going to kill everyone who's ever hurt her, and you're high on the list." Merrick kept his gaze on the light starting to break over the horizon as Loche sidled up beside him.

Although the dark-haired human kept a few feet of distance.

Perhaps he was smarter than Merrick had given him credit for.

"You know I did it because I loved her."

Then again... perhaps he wasn't.

The urge to slam a fist into his face and then throw the regent overboard crushed Merrick's chest, and even though he quashed it, as he knew it wasn't what Lessia would want for the man she'd once loved, the warning rumble in his chest hopefully encouraged the regent to tread carefully.

"I know, I know."

Merrick threw a glare to the side when Loche shifted to face him, one of his arms leaning against the railing and the gray eyes that he worked to keep sharp, but where pain shone through like the sun now peeking over the sea ahead, locked on his own.

A shudder traveled up Merrick's neck, pricking his scalp.

Was this how Merrick had looked to everyone else during the election?

"She chose you." Loche bowed his head for a second before he continued. "I know that. I respect that. But I..."

Loche didn't have to finish for Merrick to know what he meant.

He still loved her.

It was as clear as the anger and despair tangling within Merrick.

Could he really blame him? Merrick had barely

spoken to her, apart from growling Rioner's orders, when he fell for her and knew he'd never get back up.

And a small voice within Merrick told him that it was a good thing Loche still cared for his mate.

Though he was a bastard, he wanted the same thing as Merrick.

Unfortunately, he wanted *many* of the same things as Merrick.

He had to look away from the regent's imploring eyes when the night Lessia kissed Loche in that library invaded his mind.

He'd nearly broken down the fucking bedroom when she came in, smiling and covered in another man's scent. Only the sight of her happy grin had stopped him.

Seeing those beautiful lips lifted in a genuine smile, not the fake ones she reserved for most people, broke through the rage—the possessiveness—and he managed to tell her to continue seeing him.

But then the regent had hurt her.

Not just hurt her... but done it in the worst way possible.

Loche knew—he fucking knew!—she'd always felt like she didn't fit in, that Fae and humans alike shunned her... and still he'd forced her away from the one place she'd found an ounce of happiness.

Merrick would do a lot to save her life—anything, really—including sacrificing every soul in this realm, and any others he might stumble upon.

But hurt her like that?

He could never.

"I can see you disagree with how I chose to protect her."

Merrick snapped his eyes back to the regent's gray ones.

"I had to think on my feet, Death Whisperer." Loche threw out his arms. "The king was there. You were in the cellars. I was fucking terrified he was going to figure it out. It was the only way for the king not to get suspicious."

Merrick forced a nod.

"But you still hurt her," he said quietly.

Loche's eyes flicked to the dark deck. "I know. I'll never forgive myself for that."

"Is that why you're here? Because of guilt?" Merrick refused to let Loche's eyes escape as he awaited his response.

He'd suggested Loche and his men leave to go back to Ellow several times already.

It's not like a few humans could stand against Rioner and the lethal guards Merrick was certain he had brought to accompany him on this mission...

They might even be in the way should Merrick and Raine have to work to keep them safe.

But Amalise had refused as soon as he brought it up, and the guard that followed her like a puppy had obviously stayed.

Same with Ardow.

Guilt appeared to be permanently etched into Lessia's friend's features these days, and Ardow had not even looked at Venko—who, to his credit, also agreed to stay—before he violently shook his head, declaring he owed Lessia this much.

A huff flew through Merrick's lips.

Ardow truly did.

It was almost like he'd been fucking compelled by that rebel leader, the way he sang her praises.

And while Merrick wasn't happy about how that meeting on the ship had gone, at least Ardow had seen the shifter for what she was.

Fickle.

Power hungry.

A liar like the rest of the leaders in this realm.

Merrick bore his eyes deeper into the regent's ones.

But Loche...

He had a whole rebellion to quell.

Why was he still here?

"I can't... I just... My men will prepare for the rebellion, but given what we know, I don't think it'll be enough. I think we need..." Loche hesitated when Merrick's eyes narrowed.

"We need?" Merrick demanded.

"We need her to kill him. Ellow needs her to kill him." Loche's mouth twisted to the side as he shook his head. "I wish it wasn't her. But... it's all we have now. I fucked up so bad. And while I owe it to her to save her, I also owe Ellow to do everything I can to save it. I already let her get away, and... I gave her the damned stone. We have nothing left now."

Merrick was about to snarl at him that Lessia would do whatever she damned pleased, when something between a cough and a sob lodged in the regent's throat, and a feeling he didn't like at all chilled Merrick's chest.

He clenched his fists by his side.

Surely he wasn't about to feel empathy for this man?

But damned if that feeling didn't fucking grow as Loche's shoulders hunched as he stared out over the brightening sea.

Like Lessia, he was so young.

Too young to fucking lead a nation, and a divided one at that.

Too young to take on a war that would be devastating, especially if those rebels got their claws in his people first.

Merrick didn't know Loche's whole story, but he'd seen enough during the election to know his upbringing couldn't have been close to the ones of those snotty human nobles.

Perhaps not even close to the comfortable life he expected Venko had led before getting tangled in this mess.

Loche let out another strangled breath.

Flicking his eyes to the sky where the sun fought with dark clouds wanting to cover it, Merrick sighed.

As he moved his gaze back down, he couldn't help but take a step toward the human.

"She will." Merrick sighed again as he put a hand on Loche's shoulder. "She will kill him. I'll make sure of it."

Loche nodded, and for a few beats, silence layered around them as they watched the sun slowly rise.

The wind was warmer again, the scents filling it those of wet cliffs and burned grass—the smells Merrick knew still wafted from Korina.

If he squinted, he could make out the towering island ahead, the black cliffs skirting its entire border, the slippery, steep stone seemingly impossible to scale.

But Merrick knew better. There were several hidden paths—one with stairs, and a few with meandering, narrow trails, where one misstep would cause someone to fall to their death.

He'd taken one of those paths in the war, and he

scowled remembering how slick it had been from all the shifter blood running down it.

He could almost smell it.

The death.

The destruction of every town.

The fear that had permeated the air as the shifters realized no one—not even women or children—would be spared.

Merrick dropped his hand from the regent's shoulder.

For him, it felt like yesterday that the last fucking war had ended.

But humans and shifters forgot quickly... and even for the Fae, even for Rioner, the memories appeared to be hazy.

Merrick scoffed to himself.

He'd seen Rioner and Alarin in tears, bent over their father's cold body only a century ago.

And they'd be there again soon.

With people crying for loved ones.

People pissing themselves on the battlefield because the glory they'd been promised faded in the bloodshed and pain that fighting truly brought.

People screaming for a mercy that would never come.

"We'll find her."

He nearly lost his grip on his magic when Loche spoke again.

Whirling to face the regent, he couldn't help but let his nostrils flare. "I know we'll fucking find her. But it needs to be soon."

An image of himself kneeling next to Lessia's broken body, the horrid smell of death assaulting his nose, flashed in his mind, but he pushed it away, especially as that guard and Amalise ventured down from the ship's quarterdeck.

"How are we doing?" Merrick barked at Zaddock.

It was Amalise who responded. "We're probably two days out from Korina. The winds aren't in our favor, so we can't go faster."

The fucking winds.

As if he'd let some fucking weather dictate how fast he could get to her.

If she was even there.

Merrick's chest vibrated from the growl building in it, and he couldn't help but roll his eyes when Zaddock stepped in front of Amalise.

Moving her own eyes upward, Amalise pushed him aside. "Stop trying to babysit me."

Zaddock mumbled something about "Stop putting yourself in danger, then," but he backed off when Amalise sent him a glare so cold it could rival King Rioner's.

Merrick's eyes flitted between them for a moment.

It was clear that the guard had it bad for the blonde.

But she was holding back.

He wasn't certain exactly why, but in the few times he'd caught her eyes when she hadn't been prepared, especially when they were out on deck, the pain there mirrored what he'd seen in his brothers' eyes.

She'd lost someone. That he was sure of.

Amalise's gaze narrowed when he continued staring, and her voice dropped an octave when she spoke again. "How are we going to find them? Korina is massive, and I've heard you have to have a death wish to try to climb those cliffs."

Merrick finally tore his eyes from hers. "They won't

be on Korina. The king is a water wielder, so he will stay over water on his ship to be as strong as possible. He's worried, and when he's worried, he'll not take any risks. He'll have his most lethal guards with him, including one who is a stronger mind-bender than even Raine."

"That's never been proved." Raine walked up to the group, throwing Amalise a wink when she stared at him as he took a sip from his flask, which had Zaddock pull her behind him again. "He'll probably also have one of his beloved fire wielders, though—they can cause so much lovely destruction from afar."

"But so can we." Merrick couldn't help but curl his lip to show off his teeth. "They'll probably have Kerym and the others dosed with Vincere to keep them docile, but you and I can take on a little fire wielder and the mind-bender."

"Kerym will probably still want to fight, if I know him." Raine wiggled his brows. "I'm guessing the little Rantzier will as well. She seems quite feisty."

Merrick nodded back at him, but he didn't voice the thought that touched his mind.

They would want to fight *if they were alive.*

He knew how Rioner worked by now.

He was probably doing everything in his power to break Lessia.

And the easiest way?

To threaten those she loved.

His fingers curled until his knuckles blanched, but Loche interrupted the snarl wanting to break free.

"So let's say we find them there. What do we do then?"

Raine met Merrick's eyes as he responded, "I'll try to

take out as many as I can, the ones who forget to protect their mind, so that we can get close to them."

"Then I get on the ship first," Merrick continued, falling right back into their usual planning as if it hadn't been decades since the last time. "Whoever is the best fighter comes after me, and I will protect Raine so that he can continue controlling their little minds and search for Lessia and the rest. No one apart from our friends stays alive."

"I'll go after you, then," Loche said as he patted the sword by his side. "I may not have fought Fae, but I was one of the best in our navy."

"I'll join you." Ardow walked out from the shade of the upper deck. "Venko is no warrior, but he will manage the ship, keep it ready if we need to leave swiftly."

The merchant who hovered behind Ardow nodded, his eyes flickering across the group before meeting Merrick's and offering him a quick bow of his head.

"I will go as well." Amalise raised her chin as she pulled at the hand Zaddock still held on to. "I might not be a fighter, but I am quick and quiet, and I know how to sneak in and out undetected."

Zaddock's grip on Amalise's hand tightened until she hissed at him, but he refused to let go, his face turning as white as the woman's fingers he squeezed, and he appeared not to care who listened as he spoke. "The fuck you are. Amalise, I need you to listen to me. You're staying behind with Venko. It's too dangerous."

Amalise ripped her hand free, moving to stand between Merrick and Loche. "I am not going anywhere. Lessia is my best friend, and I would gladly sacrifice my life for her."

"She doesn't want you to die for her!" Zaddock was

nearly screaming now, the desperation so sharp it would have pierced Merrick's chest should he have space for more emotions within him. "You're staying behind."

"I am not." Amalise's eyes burned Zaddock's way, and Merrick shook his head when the guard glared right back.

"He might be right, blondie." Raine grinned at her, ignoring the vicious stare she shot him. "It's not like sneaking away from the men that I am sure chase you back home. These people won't stop because you're pretty. They'll rip your head off all the same."

Merrick gripped the blonde's arm when she lurched toward his friend, pulling her back even though Zaddock looked as if he'd take the sword and stab it right through his chest for touching his woman.

"Calm down," Merrick hissed into her ear. "This isn't about you. It's about Lessia."

Amalise panted as she stared up at him, but when Merrick continued to keep her gaze, she finally relaxed. "Fine. But I am still going."

These stubborn humans.

They all thought they were invincible.

It must have to do with their short lifespans, Merrick thought.

Being twenty-five or eighty was perhaps not that big of a difference.

"Z, just stay by her side on the ship," Loche offered. "Merrick is right. It's not about us, it's about Lessia, and who knows... maybe Amalise will be helpful when we find her."

Zaddock's jaw was so tight Merrick was sure he'd have a raging headache after this, but he finally gave a curt nod as he walked up and dragged the still seething

Amalise to his side, ignoring her "Stupid, possessive bastard" mumbles.

Merrick snapped his gaze to Raine, but he still didn't miss Zaddock snarling "If you die on that ship I will come to the afterlife and haunt you for fucking ever, and then we can talk about possessive."

Despite everything, his mouth twitched, and so did Raine's as he shook his head at the two humans.

He knew what Zaddock was feeling very well.

But while he was a possessive bastard himself, he'd never force Lessia to do anything.

She'd had enough of that in her life.

He'd be whatever she needed him to be—be whatever she wanted him to be.

Unfortunately, he doubted an overprotective Fae male was her dream.

Even if she did seem to like it in the bedroom.

He couldn't stop her grinning face from popping into his mind.

The sounds she made when he devoured her.

What she'd said to him that first night they had together.

I love you. And one night is not nearly enough. I told you. I want everything. *I want to be your fucking mate, and I don't know the right words, but I accept our bond—I welcome it—I'm proud of it.*

Merrick closed his eyes, and her scent immediately slammed into him.

She'd always smelled like warm grass on open fields to him. Like a summer day full of possibilities he'd never had. Like a calm sea begging to be swum in.

Freedom, he'd decided that day he finally got to meet her eyes.

That's what she smelled like.

That's what she was.

Absolute perfect freedom.

That fragile bond that seemed attached to his heart flickered in response to heat welling within him, and he wished there was a way to grasp it, tug at it until he found her.

It flickered again, and his brows creased.

Why was it swaying?

Merrick focused on the bond, and only the bond, Lessia's face fading into the background.

It flickered again.

Flickered like a candle about to go out.

Fuck!

His eyes flew open, immediately meeting Raine's, and Merrick didn't even realize his knees buckled until his friend's arm wrapped around his back.

"What is happening?" Raine urged. "Merrick!"

He could only get out two words. "Bond. Breaking."

CHAPTER 6
LESSIA

Help us! Help me!

She wasn't sure if she was dreaming when air finally traveled into her lungs, but she continued screaming at the voices that now drifted further and further away.

Help! Please!

As the fog in her mind lifted, the large shapes that had danced before her eyes, who had turned their heads in her direction when she screamed at them but who hadn't spoken back to her, faded until only darkness remained.

"I'll do anything, Rioner! Please stop this. Please! She's my daughter!"

Her father's raspy voice was the first thing she heard as she came to, but the coughing fit that followed swallowed all other sounds.

Lessia hacked with a raw throat, tears streaming down her face, until the choking sensation finally left her, although both her nose and throat still burned from the salt in the seawater Rioner had forced down them.

"You're a fucking coward, Rioner." Kerym's voice was stronger than her father's. "You've always been. She's a fucking Faeling!"

"Careful, Kerym," the king said in a low voice. "Your brother isn't doing too well. You wouldn't want him to take her place, would you?"

"Oh, fuck you." Thissian's deep voice didn't waver either. "You've already ruined our lives. Do you think you can hurt Kerym and me more? You can't. You've already taken everything. I'd gladly welcome whatever you can muster with that water and more if it just ended the misery that is this life."

"Is that so?" Rioner mused. "And you, Kerym? Did losing your mate also break you?"

Lessia focused on her shallow breathing as Kerym's silence told the king everything he needed to know.

"What about you, dear brother? You're still fighting? Is it because of them? The halflings?" Rioner must have started walking around because a chill breeze peppered Lessia's bare back with pebbles, and she pulled her legs up, trying to keep some of the warmth, to cover herself as much as possible.

"I-if you had... found your mate... you'd never do this. *Please*. Y-you saw... our parents. Y-you saw... what losing Mother did to our father." Alarin was begging now, sobs interrupting each word, and the sound was so horrible that Lessia closed her eyes even though she still couldn't see anything with the blindfold.

Chains rattled before her father continued, his desperate voice rising. "T-they're my children! Lessia is twenty-five years old! Frelina a year younger! They haven't *lived*! I-I know you... believe this prophecy... but what if it was just a way for the gods to get to us one last time? Y-you're the one breaking apart the Rantzier family right now, brother!"

Rioner only laughed. "Those two are no Rantziers. But you all have given me an idea, so thank you ever so much for that. Torkher, take off her blindfold but hold her in place so she doesn't get any ideas, will you?"

Before Lessia had time to react, the Fae guard she couldn't stand the smell of—as pure evil wafted directly from his skin—dragged her into a seated position, ripping the fabric from her head, and gripped her shoulders when she wrapped her arms around her front.

The first pair of eyes she found were her father's tear-filled ones.

Then Frelina's panicked ones.

Then Kerym's blue ones, darkened with pain.

Thissian's ocean-colored ones waited for her next, and she wasn't sure why his were the worst, but perhaps it was because she'd believed him to be almost numb from how he'd spoken before, but now...

Fear flickered within his eyes.

"It's all right," she tried to tell them, but her throat hurt too much for words to form, so instead she mouthed them, trying for a weak smile after.

Her father and Frelina both let out gut-wrenching sounds in response, but Kerym kept her gaze, mouthing "Hold on. He's coming" back to her.

Thissian didn't move, his eyes flitting to the king before moving back to her, and she didn't like the look contorting his features.

She didn't like it at all.

Lessia couldn't even nod as Kerym yet again

mouthed “Hold on” as Torkher violently shifted her so her back rested against his chest, and she shuddered when his lips tickled her ear. “You’re dying today. And he won’t get here in time.”

Lessia stared straight ahead, refusing to let Torkher’s words sink in.

“He’ll find your broken body floating amidst the waves beneath us. Unless any of the creatures in the sea eat you first, of course,” the Fae spat, but still Lessia didn’t react, forbade herself to even swat at the hands that roved over her bare skin.

The king spoke again as he waved forward the other two guards behind him. “Get my brother up here.”

Lessia watched silently as they unfastened her father’s shackles, an ember of gratefulness trying to warm her chest when Kerym stopped her sister from getting in their way.

Catching his eyes, she wrangled to offer him a smile, but it mustn’t have been too encouraging, as Kerym’s face fell as he stared back at her.

The two guards dragged her father’s body until he was only a few feet away from where Lessia half sat, half lay against Torkher.

Placing Alarin on his knees, they tied his hands behind his back again, then straightened, staring at Rioner standing somewhere behind her.

Despair filled her father’s eyes as he looked at her, and she willed her own not to mirror it, tried to give him hope, tried to send him the belief that she would find them a way out of this.

But her own fragile hope was fading quickly.

Especially when the image of Merrick finding her

body that Torkher had conjured earlier pressed to reveal itself in her mind again.

She'd clung to the glimmer—the chance that those shapes she'd seen when the water enveloped her were what she thought they were—but when nothing stirred within her again, those voices worryingly silent, Lessia realized it might have been a fool's dream.

"Give him the antidote," the king ordered, shattering the silence, and Lessia barely had time to understand what was happening before one of the guards pulled out a small vial and shoved its contents down her father's throat.

Her father's eyes bulged as he nearly choked on whatever they'd forced him to drink, but the Fae behind him wouldn't relent, pushing his head up until a loud swallow reverberated within the square cabin.

More tears spilled down her father's cheeks when his eyes found hers again, and she couldn't help the hiss escaping her lips at the pain that tugged at his expression, that curved his usually straight back, that had his hands ball into fists.

But when she tried to turn her head to glare at the king, demanding to know what he was doing to her father, Torkher wrapped his hand in her hair, pulling it so hard she yelped.

Kerym and her sister growled in outrage when Torkher only chuckled as he tugged even more, forcing her to nearly rest the back of her head on his shoulder.

"Don't get any ideas, halfling," he snarled into her ear, and when a heartbreaking sound pierced the silence that followed—one she wasn't certain who it came from—she forced herself to utter some sound of agreement.

As Torkher released her, her eyes flew across the

room, and her brows snapped together, intensifying the ache in her head when she realized it must have been Thissian who let out that awful, sorrow-filled cry.

His eyes touched hers for only a second before they fell, the sorrow in them spreading to his entire frame as he hunched over, folding into himself where he was chained next to her sister.

"Thissian, what is it? What's happening?" Kerym urged, but his brother wouldn't respond—he only pressed himself further into the wall, making himself as small as possible.

"I knew you were the cleverer brother." Rioner snickered as he approached her father, carefully keeping his back to Lessia. "I believe dear Thissian might have begun to grasp what I'm thinking."

Kerym's brother let out another soft cry, and the hair on Lessia's neck rose when Kerym stared from Thissian to the king, then slowly shifted his gaze back to Lessia, the crease between his dark brows deepening.

Even though her mind was muddled, she tried to rack her brain for what the king could be planning now—to prepare herself or to come to terms with it, she didn't know.

He'd given her father what he called an antidote...

She stopped herself from trying to move her hands to press against her pounding temples.

If Torkher struck her again, it would be even harder to think.

As her eyes snagged on the blindfold on the floor instead, she realized they'd kept her from using her magic with the blindfold, as she needed to meet people's eyes to use it.

For the others...

They must have been using Vincere.

So the antidote would be to allow her father to use his magic again.

But why?

While useful, his magic only undid other magic...

What had they been talking about that could have given the king ideas?

Lessia's eyes flew open, and it was impossible to stop the rush of air that forced its way into her lungs.

She started shaking her head.

Then she did it more violently when she met her father's eyes and saw the same realization dawn in them.

No.

Please no.

She couldn't help it.

A whimper followed the gasp.

Then a sob.

Frelina's eyes fought to meet hers, and as soon as her sister's amber ones bore into her own, Lessia knew it was true.

Huge drops of tears rolled down Frelina's round cheeks.

Thissian began rocking back and forth beside her.

Kerym's face whitened, and the smirk he'd fought for his life to keep whenever she'd glimpsed him drained from his face entirely.

A sound she didn't even know she could make escaped her as the king and Torkher began laughing.

"I should thank you, brother." Rioner began pacing back and forth, stealing a look at Lessia when that sound—the otherworldly sound she didn't even know how to describe—continued to pierce the air. "I would never have thought of it if you hadn't been going on and on about your mates."

Please.

No.

Help us!

Help me!

Help!

Please!

Lessia started begging.

To whom she didn't know.

Because there weren't any voices in her head anymore.

The gods no longer walked this realm.

And Merrick...

Merrick, I love you.

I love you.

Please hear me.

I love you.

She screamed it inside her head.

Screamed it down the brittle bond connecting them.

Even if she knew he wouldn't hear her.

"Alarin, look at me," Rioner demanded.

When her father didn't move fast enough, the two guards dragged him to his feet, his head hanging between his shoulders as he gave Lessia a final look.

"P-please," she whispered, tears nearly blinding her. "Please, don't."

Don't do this to him.

Please, no.

Not yet.

Torkher laughed so hard it shook her entire body, and she couldn't help it when her muscles slackened, the powerlessness driving all strength from them.

The Fae let out a disgusted sound as he pushed her limp body off him, but she didn't catch herself as she fell to the floor, one cheek resting against the wet wood, the rest of her body lying at a strange angle.

"Alarin, I'm sure you've figured it out by now... But please. Break their bond." She could hear the smile that must have twisted Rioner's features as he spoke.

Lessia couldn't stop herself.

She screamed when the words she'd feared slammed into her heart.

Break their bond.

Like everything that was gifted by the gods, the bonds were magic.

And her father...

She screamed again.

"Brother..." Alarin pleaded. "Do not make me do this."

"I need her broken," Rioner snarled. "And you've all just informed me this is the best way. And... I won't lie. The Death Whisperer believing she is already dead? He won't survive it. Not after everything they've been through. It'll give me some more time to figure out what to do with all of you."

No.

Lessia lifted her head from the floor.

Ignoring the panicked looks from the three others chained to the wall, she made herself face her father.

"Please," she begged him, her voice so small she wasn't certain if he heard her.

But he couldn't miss the agony she was sure warped her face.

"Please," she whimpered again.

She couldn't do this to Merrick.

Not yet.

She *would* die.

Probably soon.

But she'd promised him more than one night.

You had two.

She felt like screaming again at the voice reminding her of what she'd thought earlier.

It wasn't enough.

Two nights weren't enough.

"Do it," the king ordered. "Now!"

"No!" Frelina screamed from where she struggled against her shackles. "Father, no!"

Her father's eyes left hers to look at her sister, and his face crumpled as he stared back and forth between her and Frelina.

Lessia couldn't breathe.

Scrambling up to sitting, she didn't care about trying to shield her bare torso.

Instead, she started crawling toward her father.

Toward the king.

She... she needed to kill him now.

Because if she was actually broken...

If her father followed through...

She might not have the strength left.

She needed to fulfill the prophecy.

For her family.

For her friends.

For any half-Fae out there.

For Merrick.

But a heavy boot on her back stopped her advance, and even when she started fighting, Torkher wouldn't let up.

Pinning her to the planks, he again twisted her hair,

pressing her face down into the floor as he drove a knee deeper into her back.

"Do it now!" Rioner screamed. "Or I swear I will let Torkher kill her before your eyes, prophecy or not."

"I'm... I'm so sorry, my beautiful child."

Lessia lifted her head in time for the air to fill with the vibrations of magic.

"No!" she cried when those flickers wafted toward her. "Please! No!"

Merrick! No! It's not me!

I love you!

Please!

Something within her chest tugged, like a frail rope mooring a ship that was too heavy, fighting against the strong waves that inevitably would bring it out to sea again.

"No!" she screamed. "Don't do this!"

Lessia fought with everything in her, fixing her golden gaze inward, trying to compel her father's magic to leave her mind.

But it was no person. It had no soul.

It was like trying to compel the floor.

Ignoring the knee still pressing into her injured back, she started squirming violently, talking to herself as if she'd lost her mind.

Maybe she had.

"Merrick, there were so many things I never said. I love you so much. You brought me all the light. You brought me everything. Freedom. Hope. Trust. Love. Fight. I love you. Don't die because of me. Please don't die because of me. Live! Save this world. Please. Please. Please."

The tugging stopped.

"Please," she whispered again, feeling for the tether.

It was still there.

As frail and fragile as before.

But it was there.

Still barely able to breathe, Lessia raised her head again.

"I won't do it." Her father stared right into her eyes as he spoke. "Enough, Rioner. There is nothing you can say that would make me do it."

"Is that so?" Rioner's dark cape flew out behind him as he stormed up to her father, bridging the few feet in two or three long strides.

Alarin lifted his chin. "It is. It's time for your rule to come to an end. Your guards won't stand for this. Only the wretched ones in this room, perhaps. But I've heard the whispers. I've been approached by the council. I know what they're saying about you in Vastala. They believe your greed is driving you mad, Rioner. I didn't want to believe it, but the cruelty in this room... No. I won't do it."

"That's unfortunate." Something glimmered in the air as Rioner leaned in farther. "I guess it's a good thing I don't need you anymore."

The room filled with choking silence for a moment.

Then a scream—a blood-chilling, bone-shattering scream—followed.

Chaos erupted.

Lessia fought to see as more screams followed and chains shrieked so loudly she wondered if Kerym and his brother had gotten free.

But it wasn't those sounds that terrified her.

It was the gurgling, choking sound, and the thud that followed.

And when the guards who had held her father in place backed away, their faces so ashen she wouldn't have been surprised if they fainted, terror wasn't enough to describe what she was feeling.

Blood pooled on the floor where her father lay motionless, a dark gash stretched from one side of his throat to the other.

And when Lessia tried to catch his eyes...

They were unseeing, amber circles staring into nothing.

Into the afterlife.

She screamed then.

At least that's what she thought she did.

Then her vision went crimson.

And with every last bit of strength in her, she somehow forced the knee off her back, jumping to her feet and sprinting to where the king was wiping his blade on his cape.

She was going to kill him.

Rip out his throat with her teeth.

But something struck the back of her head.

And it all went black.

CHAPTER 7
MERRICK

He couldn't hear what the others around him were screaming as outraged whispers exploded across the deck, so violent and furious that he wouldn't have been surprised if the world was to end soon.

Had he not felt that frail tether still connecting him with Lessia, he would have let go entirely, would have unleashed the storm of souls that now whirled all around him, would have fucking laughed as they took whatever was left of this wretched world.

But he did feel it.

She was alive.

She was somewhere in Havlands.

Still, she was too far away.

Merrick closed his eyes as the whispers roared louder, screaming out the frustration and rage and wrath he kept within him, crying for revenge, for death and destruction, and punishment.

Lessia might believe he was good, that he was *kind*, as she'd once said...

But Merrick knew better.

She was the only thing he cared about.

In this world and any other.

Everyone and everything else could burn or drown or be demolished, for all he cared.

Let's do it now.

Let's kill them all.

It would be easy to give in to the whispers filling his ears.

But as Merrick opened his eyes and stared at the people surrounding him—the cowering Ardow and Venko by the wall; the regent holding on to the railing, his face filled with torment; Raine staring at him with worry tightening the corners of his eyes; the dark-haired guard holding his sword in his hand and the other pushing Amalise behind him—Merrick tightened his grip on the veil keeping those souls from doing anything other than whisper whatever they wanted to the living.

He nearly scoffed when Zaddock continued to wave his blade in the air.

As if a sword could do anything against his magic...

Merrick's eyes snapped to a door opening as those copper-haired sisters ventured onto the deck, their faces strained but with no fear brightening their eyes as they stared out over the chaos.

He shook his head when they came closer.

Did they have a death wish?

The memory of them saving him and Lessia in that cellar flashed within his mind, and Merrick cursed silently when another surge of fury consumed him.

He'd been nearly as damned angry then as he was now.

When those fucking men had marked her...

The dead guards should count themselves lucky that he hadn't been able to use his magic when he killed them.

He would have honored his promise—would have let them be tortured through all eternity by the souls he now began pushing back to wherever they resided when they weren't trying to break into the living realm.

Lessia was alive, he reminded himself.

And he needed these people to find her.

At least some of them.

He doubted they'd be as eager to help if he killed off the useless ones. Fear unfortunately wasn't as much of a motivator as the king of Vastala believed...

With a sigh, Merrick tightened the leash further, using some of the anger to force the souls to move faster than they usually liked.

They shrieked at him as he drove them farther and farther away, but he didn't even bother snarling back.

They knew who their master was.

When the last one finally left the deck, Merrick slumped against the railing, the anger and frustration and despair draining him as much as the pressure of his magic.

"You are terrifying," one of the sisters—Soria, Merrick seemed to remember—said as she walked up beside him. "No wonder they call you the Death Whisperer. That's exactly what that felt like."

He shot her a warning glare before growling, "We need to sail faster. We're running out of time."

"You're not even going to apologize?" Zaddock hissed as he finally sheathed his sword.

Raising a brow, Merrick moved his eyes to his, and thankfully, the human closed his mouth before Merrick shut it another way.

"I. Said. We need to sail faster," Merrick repeated when no one moved to the upper deck. "Something has changed... I don't know what, but we need to find her today! There is no more time."

"We can't." Zaddock apparently didn't fear for his life as much as Merrick expected, and he stepped toward the guard when Amalise broke in.

"There is a storm coming. Look over there. We won't be able to search while also keeping the ship from sinking."

Merrick's eyes drifted to the darkening horizon.

Of course a fucking storm was coming.

But weather—fucking weather—wouldn't stop him from finding her.

"Then I'll go myself." Merrick shifted his scabbard so that his sword lay across his back instead of resting against his hip. "If we don't find her today, it'll be too late. I'll fucking swim."

"No, you won't." Raine gripped his arm, flashing his own teeth when Merrick bared his sharp ones in warning. "You'll die too. And for what? You know what she wants."

What she wants...

She was fucking twenty-five years old!

She shouldn't have to save the world.

She should still live at home, safe in a room where her parents could still teach her what being Fae meant, perhaps prepare her for moving out and trying her wings soon.

And Merrick?

Merrick should have stumbled upon her when she walked into whatever village was closest and realized what she was without having the damned king breathing down his neck.

He should have approached her, maybe bought her some flowers or something else, like he'd seen his friends do for their mates, and then the first thing he should have done would be to offer her his arm to walk her home.

Then he would have courted her.

And after that...

He would have asked her father for her hand.

Paid for and organized the most expensive mating ceremony there was.

Married her after because he wanted to tie himself to her in every way he could.

This...

This fucking life?

It wasn't what she deserved.

"I don't care what she wants." Merrick shoved Raine's arm off. "I don't want to live in a world where she doesn't exist."

Raine lifted his hands and groaned. "I can't believe I'm saying this, but we have a duty to this world, Merrick. We once swore to protect Havlands from whatever harm may come to it..."

"Like you give a shit," Merrick spat as he ensured his boots were securely laced. "You made it very clear you were only here to die a hero's death."

"I know," Raine mumbled. "But she... that passion you saw in her, Merrick. We see it too. We feel it too."

"We do," Loche echoed, his voice gravelly. "We all love her." Loche raised his hands when a rumble shook Merrick's chest. "Not like you. But she has inspired all of us, and we all want to find her."

"You're not fucking listening to me!" Merrick gripped the railing, shifting his legs over it so he faced the wild sea below. "I know she inspires every person she comes across. She is the fucking light of this world! The purest soul. The kindest. The strongest. A leader, a friend, a lover, a woman, a Fae, a human. But it's almost too late. I can *feel* it!"

Something flickered in the corner of his eyes, and Merrick couldn't help but raise his brows when Ardow swung a leg over the wet railing as well, straddling it as he spoke. "Listen to him. If he's saying it's almost too late, it is. I am coming too."

"Ardow," Venko said, his voice soft but not in the pleading way Merrick would have expected.

Instead, the merchant walked up to them, the lines in his face deep with worry but his eyes steady. He put his hands to Ardow's cheeks as the latter turned around to face him.

"Bring her back," he whispered before he pressed his lips against Ardow's, the kiss so gentle everyone on the ship quieted, and it wasn't necessary to have Fae ears to hear the relieved sob leaving Ardow as he kissed him back.

Merrick tore his eyes away, locking instead with Amalise's blue ones, which now glistened as she looked away from the two men, and he noticed she didn't pull back when Zaddock laced his fingers with hers.

Raine cleared his throat, and Merrick knew the flask in his hands shook not because of the storm now beginning to rock the vessel but because he remembered those stolen moments with Solana.

They'd also had too little time...

Borrowed, cut short, wrong time.

This wretched world...

"If you're going to be so damned stubborn, I guess I'm coming too." Raine stuffed the flask into his tunic, pulling his sword across his back and securing Solana's dagger at his waist.

With another low groan, Raine hoisted himself up so he sat next to Merrick. "Of all the dumb things we've done..."

Yes, this was probably the worst one. Getting into the Eiatis Sea without any real idea of where to swim... It was probably a death sentence.

But Merrick couldn't just sit on his ass on that ship anymore.

He knew Lessia's time was running out.

He'd rather die fucking trying to find her.

"You always fought until the end." Raine gently elbowed him as rain began splattering the people and the ship. "Remember when that Fae nearly decapitated you and you fucking held on to your head while you chased after him?" He shook his head. "That's when I knew you were insane."

Merrick rolled his eyes, trying to keep that particular memory out of his mind. That wound had hurt more than any other he could remember. "If I hadn't gotten to him, Thissian would have won the bet that he was a better fighter than I. Couldn't have that."

A low scoff interrupted their exchange.

"I guess we should be lucky if you'll fight next to us in the coming war." Loche approached them, halting a foot or so away from the railing as he bore his eyes into Merrick's. "We will try to follow you as best we can. I would suggest going east. That's where the most secluded waters around Korina are."

Merrick shot him a sharp nod, but just as he was about to turn back, Loche grabbed his shoulder.

"Please. Bring her back," he said, almost in a whisper, and if Merrick hadn't known better, he might have thought the regent was about to get choked up. "And... get her revenge."

Merrick nodded again.

He would get her her revenge.

Serve it up on a silver platter for her if he could.

Lay the king's neck against the smooth railing of his own ship and let Lessia use her daggers to carve into his fair skin—carve until that stupid crown tumbled into the sea that Rioner loved so much and disappeared for all eternity.

Amalise approached him when Loche stepped back, and since that guard wouldn't let her more than a foot away from him, Zaddock followed, his hand still clasped around the woman's.

"We'll be there when you find her. She... she is strong, Merrick. But she is also sensitive. Y-you didn't see her those first months." A shudder went through Amalise's small frame. "We... we weren't sure if she'd make it."

Merrick could tell Ardow stiffened beside him even while holding on tight to Venko.

"I know," he said, trying to get his voice to sound gentle. "I'll protect her."

He would. If there was anything he could promise, it

was that once Lessia was back, he wouldn't be a step away from her.

His eyes lingered on Zaddock for a moment, and when he met the human's dark blue eyes, a moment of understanding passed between them, and Merrick couldn't help but think that... perhaps... the overprotective Zaddock had a point.

"I saw that." Amalise twisted her lip as she glared between them and wagged her finger in Merrick's face. "Do not justify him. He's an overbearing bastard."

"But you're here. You're alive." Merrick's words appeared to strike a chord because Amalise only opened and closed her mouth a few times before a pink tint crept up her cheeks, and she bowed her head, stepping back with the overbearing bastard following closely behind.

The two sisters were the last to approach.

The one with long hair—Pellie—placed a small hand on Merrick's shoulder. "Save the others too. Especially... especially the dark-haired one."

"She took a fancy to him in that awful cabin," Soria whispered theatrically, ignoring her sister swatting at her. "But please do. Lessia only just got her family back, from what I heard, and she, out of anyone, deserves to have those she loves around her."

"She's right." Pellie squeezed his shoulder before releasing him. "On both accounts. I wouldn't mind jumping that Kerym's—"

A mix between a chuckle and a huff left Merrick as Soria slapped a hand over her sister's mouth, pulling her back again and urgently berating her for being so blatant.

Those two were something else...

But he could imagine Kerym taking a liking to either of them.

With a final glance out over the deck, ignoring the heavy raindrops that now fell from the sky, Merrick told himself again this was the only way.

He would find her.

He would.

Somehow, he could feel her even from this distance, and something within him told him this was what he must do.

He might have cursed the gods many times... more than he could count, honestly.

But they'd made him her mate for a reason, and damned if he was going to let her down.

Merrick didn't look back as he pushed himself off the railing, nor did he look to the side to see if Ardow and Raine followed.

The water slammed into him, the height making it feel more like jumping into hard-packed mud instead of water, but he angled himself right, and without breaking anything, Merrick slipped under the cool surface.

He lingered there for a while, savoring the silence—a rarity, something those souls seldom offered him.

He could feel Lessia better down here.

She must be sleeping, or perhaps resting, because the emotions that touched his soul were not those of fear or even anger.

It was love that filled his mate right now.

Deep, devastating love.

The love he'd seen in her even before he got to experience it himself.

The love she had for a world and for the two people who had done nothing but hurt her.

He'd thought it was maybe an act at first, but Lessia truly didn't blame the world and the humans or Fae for her fate—she directed her ire to the gods instead.

And...

Maybe... just maybe, she was right in that.

Something touched Merrick's arm, and he reluctantly opened his eyes, muting the connection with Lessia, expecting to meet either Ardow's brown eyes or Raine's hazel ones.

But they were wide violet ones that met his, and he had to stop himself from reaching for his sword when sharp teeth came into view next as the beast opened its maw.

Ydren. It was Ydren, he told himself as every nerve within him ignited, his muscles coiling and his senses screaming at him to defend himself.

Instead of drawing his sword, Merrick pointed upward, and when the wyvern inclined her head, he kicked hard to breach the surface.

A scream—filled with raw panic—met him, and he realized the group still on the ship hung over the railing, shouting at him, Ardow, and Raine to "get out now."

Ydren let out something akin to a scoff as she twisted her body, allowing first Raine, second Merrick, and then a very hesitant Ardow to climb onto her back.

The wet scales were slippery, and when Ydren straightened her neck, towering over the sea to bring herself higher, Merrick had to admit he was forced to squeeze his legs with everything in him not to slide off.

Behind him, a yelp left Ardow, and Merrick sighed when the man began slipping backward.

Quickly snatching hold of his tunic, Merrick ensured

the human stayed on, albeit at an awkward angle, ignoring his grumblings.

They didn't have time for vanity.

"She's my friend," Raine called out to the faces, now level with them, still frozen in fear.

Even Venko, who should have been used to her after the days on Midhrok, seemed apprehensive.

And Loche...

The mighty regent couldn't hide the twitch of his hand toward his sword as his gray eyes swept across the beast, and Merrick knew it wasn't becoming, but he smirked at him, eliciting a narrow-eyed glare in return.

"She knows where Lessia and the rest are," Raine continued, and Merrick snapped his eyes to his friend instead. "She'll take us there. You need to follow. She'll guide you so that you can escape the storm, or at least the worst of it."

When Zaddock, of all people, nodded first, Merrick called, "Go now! We have no time to lose."

He didn't bother to ask how Ydren knew where Lessia was.

This was their best chance.

The wyvern whipped her head back to stare at him, and the same determination that blazed within Merrick could be found in her glossy eyes.

But it was the small ember of hope that also glittered in the dark that Merrick clung to.

The beast seemed to tell him to hold on.

At least that's what he imagined when she, with a cry that made him want to cover his ears, dove into the water and launched herself across the vast sea with a speed no ship could ever match.

CHAPTER 8
LESSIA

"Lessia!"

"Lessia! Come on!"

"Come back to us!"

Something shook her, and she groaned against the pressure building across her temples, squeezing her eyes shut harder when it exploded into what she could only describe as lightning hitting her mind from within her skull.

"Please..."

Lessia halted the move she'd made to fold into herself when the small voice followed the male ones.

"Please, Lia."

Frelina.

That's who that agony-filled voice belonged to.

Fighting against everything wanting to shut down within her, Lessia pried her eyes open.

She was surprised she could take in the scene before her—that there wasn't a blindfold in place—but the feeling didn't last long when Frelina's distraught face came into view, the tracks down her cheeks betraying the tears that had broken through the layer of dust clinging to them all.

Sitting against the wall between Kerym and Thissian, who looked almost equally distressed as they stared back at Lessia, Frelina let out a small hiccup, her tear-stricken face seeming so young, so lost, as she met Lessia's eyes.

"I'm glad you're alive." Kerym tried for a lopsided smile, but it didn't reach anywhere near his eyes. "That cut on your head didn't look too good."

Frowning, Lessia tried to reach up to touch her hair, but although she was no longer tethered to the wall, her hands were bound behind her back, and she could do little more than bend her elbows.

She didn't need her hands when she pushed up to sit from the floor. Her head pulsated, and the warm trickle down her still-bare back confirmed that she must be bleeding.

But why was she bleeding?

She found Frelina's eyes once more as she racked her jumbled mind.

She remembered Torkher carving something into her skin, and with a quick glance, she could confirm Merrick's name was etched all over the parts of her body her eyes could reach, dirt and what must be coal dust already settling within the healing wounds.

She remembered the king.

Water.

Her father...

Lessia whipped her head around, icy terror seeping through her veins.

As soon as her gaze snagged on the limp body on the

floor, on the dark stain spread out beneath it, she slammed her eyes shut.

It had to be a dream.

A nightmare.

Not real.

Her shoulders lowered.

Of course. It was Torkher using his magic again. He'd done this to her before.

Every person she'd loved had lain on the floor of this ship at some point.

Even Merrick, who wasn't anywhere near this cabin, had taken her father's place.

Opening her eyes again, Lessia shook her head.

She was too weak to use her magic, her body completely drained, so Torkher must have physically tortured her to get her mental walls down.

That wasn't new, either, and it would explain the deep wound in the back of her head.

A humorless laugh bubbled up her throat, and she threw her stare around the room, knowing already she wouldn't find the Fae guard.

He never showed his face in these visions...

"You can stop now, Torkher! I already figured it out. You can't hurt me with this anymore! I know you're making me see it!"

She was getting better at realizing when he used his magic, even when it seemed as real as this vision did.

"Lessia," Kerym called softly. "It's not Torkher."

She laughed again as she met his blue eyes. "You have to say that, you know. You always say these things."

Frelina burst into tears again.

"And you always cry like this. Apart from when it's you lying there." Lessia cocked her head as she stared at the fake sister, at how she lost her breath from sobbing so hard.

Torkher was truly going all out with this one.

"Listen to me." Thissian shifted so his chains squeaked. "And look at me."

This was new. Thissian had never spoken to her before. Her visions of Kerym's brother were usually of him crawling up in a corner of whatever room Torkher conjured.

As Lessia turned her head his way, she wondered whether the intense pounding within it would remain or perhaps even intensify once Torkher released her mind.

Thissian's blue eyes bore into hers, and she couldn't help but stare at how similar he looked to his brother, even with the sorrowful expression darkening his beautiful features.

But the longer she met his eyes, the more she realized they weren't a mirror of Kerym's at all.

Where Kerym's eyes were blue like the sea around Midhrok or the cerulean crystals sometimes found in the caves back in Vastala, Thissian's eyes were dark, like the evening sky right before the stars began shining or like the deepest parts of the lakes in Ellow.

She wondered for a brief second how that happened, until Thissian interrupted her thoughts. "It's not a vision, Elessia."

When she began rolling her eyes, Thissian snarled softly, and she barely had time to react before he threw something at her. Something that hurt as it bounced off her bare skin.

"Use it," Thissian hissed.

Shifting forward as much as she could, she twisted

her torso so her hands could grip the sharp stone that had fallen to the floor.

Staring at it—or as much as she could, with her hands barely able to pass her hips—she asked slowly, "What do you want me to use it for?"

This was also new.

They didn't usually interact this much.

The thing in her hand was a part of the stone wall from behind Thissian, the edge looking as sharp as either of the daggers she'd brought, but still, it wouldn't be enough to break through the cuffs around her wrists.

"What do you think? Hurt yourself!" Thissian urged.

She lifted her eyes, and a smile spread across her face as she met each pair of eyes of the three visions before her.

Of course.

Torkher wanted her broken.

Rioner wanted her broken.

And if she killed herself in this vision...

Lessia shifted the stone into her left hand, twisting the right one painfully to line up her wrist with the sharp edge.

"Wait! What are you doing?" Kerym exclaimed. "Just prick yourself to see that this is real!"

Lessia ignored him as she pressed her wrist down, moving it from side to side.

Fuck, that hurt.

Had visions always hurt this much?

Blood started welling around the stone, and the smell of it made Lessia dizzy.

But she continued.

Back and forth.

Back and forth.

"Fuck! What the fuck, Thissian! Stop her!" Kerym was screaming now, but she still disregarded him.

Better give Torkher and Rioner what they wanted so they'd let her real friends and family go.

If she had to kill herself in a dream to accomplish it... then so be it.

"Stop!" Frelina cried. "It's not a vision! You're hurting yourself!"

Lessia's wrist pounded in rhythm with her head now, but she continued the movement until the stone's sharp edge hit something hard.

She couldn't help the nausea slamming into her when she realized it was bone, and her own gagging joined Kerym's and her sister's cries.

"It's not real." Lessia hummed the words to herself as she pressed harder, her neck bent and eyes transfixed on the dark blood pumping from her arm.

She didn't have time to escape the boot that slammed into her, knocking her over and forcing the stone from her hand.

"What the fuck?" Lessia lifted her head, closing her eyes for a beat as darkness pressed at the corners.

When she opened them again, Kerym was lying across the floor, his bound arms over his head as he stretched to reach her.

Frelina's face was red and blotchy, her breathing shallow as she tried to do the same as the male beside her, and Thissian stared at her from Frelina's left with wide, sunken-in eyes.

"Lessia, listen to me. Listen to me closely." Kerym scrambled backward as he tried to right himself. "I know it hurts. But you need to let the pain in. Your father... Alarin... he is dead."

Something tugged at her heart, like a jolt shooting through it.

But she shook her head. "I know this isn't real."

"It's real," her sister cried. "It's... that's him. He wouldn't do it, Lessia. He wouldn't break your bond."

Lessia tried to push her hands into the floor, but she quickly abandoned the idea when her wrist screamed at her and a gasp flew from her lips.

That really hurt.

Instead of sitting up, she twisted her body to look back at her father again.

Then she moved her head to stare at Frelina.

Then back to her father.

Break their bond.

The king's face flashed before her eyes.

I won't do it.

Then something else glimmered, something the king had held in his hand. Something with an amber tint to it amidst the sparkling silver.

A dagger.

A thud followed the dagger's reflection.

No. No, this couldn't be real.

Because if it was...

I won't do it.

A whimper worked its way up her throat.

Father.

She curled onto her side so she could face the body.

The next sound stuck in her throat as she began crawling toward him, using only her legs and ignoring the splinters that lodged in her bare breasts and stomach, her torso pressed against the floor as she inched forward.

"Father," she whispered when she reached the body. "Please."

But the amber eyes staring back at her were filled with nothing.

And the hand she managed to touch with her own when she squirmed on the floor...

It was cold.

Hard.

As if...

He'd been dead for a while.

She heard her heart break then. A crack that must have spanned realms, that must have shattered every silence in Havlands and every realm beyond, echoed within her mind.

He was dead.

She didn't have to look back at the group to realize this wasn't a vision.

It had been a fool's hope—her mind trying to protect her.

Perhaps even her mind breaking a little... perhaps even breaking a lot.

Like the king wanted.

He wanted her broken and dead.

Lessia moved her gaze from her father down to herself.

Her exposed chest was scratched, blood—dried and fresh—mingling with the dirt lying like a sheen of sweat over her skin, and she again glimpsed the carvings Torkher had entertained himself with.

Twisting, she found the hand she'd damaged looking white—pale—as if she'd managed to drain all blood from it, and although the wound had already started closing, the part of her that was Fae trying to save her, it would leave a nasty scar.

The blood, though, made her wrist and hand slippery, and she could barely believe it when she tugged at the iron cuff around it and her hand began to fall out.

The pain was so intense that Lessia bit her cheek until it also bled.

But she didn't stop.

Not until the hand, which appeared to barely hang on, even if she could somehow still clench and unclench her fingers, was free from the chains.

Falling over onto her back, she panted, thinking she heard one of the others speaking, but it was as if their voices couldn't reach her, her ears filled with too much pain.

Lessia looked at her other hand and tugged at the shackles around it, then realized it was useless.

The chain the cuffs were bound to was fastened to the middle of the room, and although it gave her a much wider berth than she'd had before, she wouldn't be able to leave the space.

She stared at the hand again.

It was the only thing holding her back now.

She was already broken, wasn't she?

And according to the curse, she'd be dead soon anyway.

A flame of anger flickered to life within her, starting from her broken heart and burning hotter as it reached her lungs, then her ribs... then ignited all across her skin.

Her blurry vision cleared, the pain fading into the background as only one face remained before her eyes.

A face she'd hated for years.

A face that should have been comforting, familiar even...

A harsh hiss rushed through her teeth as the king's smirk mocked her.

She might be broken...

She might even be half dead.

But she wouldn't fucking go without a fight.

I won't do it.

Her father had refused to yield in his last moment.

Neither would she.

The voices around her buzzed louder now, and she could make out a soft "What are you doing?" and "Lessia, please come sit down," but she couldn't. She couldn't even look their way.

Instead, she searched the room for a larger stone, for something she could use...

There. A loose iron clamp, rusty and with a thick screw still in it, lay in one of the dark corners beside the door through which the king came in and out of.

She picked it up before she could second-guess herself.

Kneeling on the wet planks again, Lessia angled her hand, moving the cuff as far up her wrist as she could.

"Lessia!" Kerym screamed now. "Stop!"

"P-please, no," her sister begged.

Even Thissian urged, "Don't do this. Don't let him break you."

She didn't look up at them as she lifted the clamp with her injured hand.

The wound's jagged edges stared back at her, a reminder of the physical brokenness her accelerated healing permitted her to ignore, at least for now.

The funny thing was that the king had already broken her, hadn't he?

She'd still not recovered from the years in his cellars.

She'd changed during the years in Ellow.

Then, during the election.

Then again, with Merrick.

All things the king set into motion.

But just because she was broken... it didn't mean she was useless.

She just wasn't the same as she'd been growing up.

She was something new.

Something forged in pain.

Something born out of guilt.

Something bound by love.

Because every broken piece that remained now was just that...

Bound by love.

Unlike the king, what had kept her going all these years was love.

It was love that kept her together even when everything inside her seemed to shatter.

It was love that would make her do what she planned to do next.

It was also love—the love she held for her parents, the love she held for Frelina, the love she held for Amalise and Ardow, even the love she held now for Raine and Kerym, and it was especially the love she held for Merrick—that made her remain silent as she let the iron clamp fall onto her hand.

Again.

Again.

Again.

Again.

Until not just her broken heart's thumping reverberated against the wooden walls but also the crushing of the bones in her hand.

The others cried now.

She could hear more sobs joining her sister's—strangled, horrible sounds that shouldn't come from warriors like the ones in this room.

Still, she didn't look their way as she wrangled her broken hand out of the cuff.

Instead, she whispered, "I love you. I love you so much. Please, please don't let him die too," and with the bloodied hand—the hand that mirrored how she felt, battered but unbowed—she pressed open the creaking door and sneaked up the stairs, keeping her broken one tucked against her chest.

She could feel it now.

The tug of fate.

This...

Her end...

It had been inevitable.

Her father had bought her time, hiding her away.

Loche had bought her time, forgetting her.

Merrick had bought her time, training and protecting and loving her.

But now it was up to her.

She would die today, but so would the king.

Lessia didn't bother forcing the face of Merrick, Frelina, or any of the others she loved out of her mind.

This would hurt them, but the alternative was worse.

They'd understand like she understood why her father had done what he did.

Merrick... The others would keep him alive. She had

to believe they wouldn't let him fall in the darkness of despair.

I love you.

She whispered it every time she climbed another step, until she reached the top of the empty stairs.

A manic smile pulled up her lips when she saw a sword resting against the corridor wall leading out to the deck, where she could hear voices drifting toward her.

Despite her hand still bleeding, her fingers nearly numb, she gripped the hilt.

Perhaps fate wasn't so bad after all.

CHAPTER 9
MERRICK

They'd only been watching Rioner's ship for a few minutes, but Merrick couldn't shake the feeling that they needed to get on board—that they needed to get Lessia and the rest out. Now.

Fuck, it was as if he hadn't had centuries of training in war and fighting.

His entire being trembled as his eyes flew across the ship, one ear listening to Raine's recounting of the minds he could connect to—not that it was likely to be accurate, given the king trained his soldiers against mental Fae—and the other trying to pick up anything from the ship.

But the water roared too loudly, and Ydren didn't dare get out from behind the rock sticking up out of the water, offering them some protection from sharp eyes traveling their way.

That feeling roiled within him again, and he hissed "Quiet" when Raine asked what he wanted to do.

Something demanded his attention, and it was as if

the gods themselves turned his head toward the center of the ship, where a rusty door slowly opened.

Merrick could barely believe his eyes when a half-naked Lessia stumbled out of it, and he immediately froze, every nerve and muscle standing at attention when his eyes caught on the red hue tinting almost every inch of her bare skin as she pressed herself against the wall.

A growl built at the back of his throat, and soon it echoed within Raine, while the wyvern made soft noises of distress.

Merrick didn't need the scent of iron that tinged the wind to tell him how injured she was, but when it touched his nose, that growl within him tore from his lips so swiftly and viciously Ardow and Ydren jumped.

And when she limped, dragging behind her what looked like a sword that would be too heavy for her under normal circumstances, he couldn't stand it.

He couldn't read her, but it wasn't difficult to understand what was happening.

She was out of options.

Lessia was desperate—willing to do whatever she could attempt in her fragile state.

Another warning growl rumbled in his throat, his vision tinting with darkness, and those souls began their whispers when Raine's eyes found his.

"Don't say it," Merrick hissed. "We go now!"

He knew Raine wanted to plan.

Merrick would probably have suggested it himself if it hadn't been Lessia walking there.

If what she was doing could be called walking...

He could almost hear the pain she must be in, and it

wasn't just physical, judging from the streaks breaking up the blood and dirt on her face.

But it *was* Lessia who slowly made her way across the ship's deck. It was the female who'd stormed into his life and within a moment—a single second—had turned it upside down, had shifted it into something he could never have seen coming.

Not that he'd change a thing.

He loved her.

Utterly and completely.

With every dark corner of his mind and heart.

Even the souls loved her after watching her for so long together with him.

She was everything that mattered.

Another gust of wind brought her scent to him, and the urgency intensified, creeping up his neck.

"Go!" he roared when Ydren hesitated.

After the beast shared a look with Raine, she cried out, one of the battle cries that sometimes echoed within Merrick's nightmares from battles fought long ago, and with a jerk that had Ardow nearly fly off again, the wyvern set off toward the vessel.

It appeared that the ship's occupants didn't hear the cry, or at least Lessia didn't, as she continued her excruciatingly slow walk while the wyvern navigated the tough waves, diving and jumping and swimming atop them whenever needed.

Merrick still held on to the neck of Ardow's jacket when they neared, and he didn't even bother asking the male before he flung him off the wyvern onto the deck, where he tumbled into a heap of body parts.

Following as swiftly as he could, Merrick pushed off

Ydren's body, not giving a shit about her grumble of protest as he threw himself onto the ship.

His landing was better than Ardow's—the man was still struggling to get to his feet—and after one roll, Merrick stood straight on the ship, his perked ears picking up on the footsteps nearing the corner, his eyes glued to the frightened ones of his mate.

She stilled when she found his gaze, blinking a few times.

Then she blinked again, her pale face crinkling.

"Hi," he whispered when she only continued staring at him, tears filling her beautiful amber eyes, but he couldn't take it anymore when her bottom lip began trembling.

Sprinting the three or so steps he needed to reach her—three steps that still seemed too many—he tugged her against his chest, careful not to hurt her further, even though the only thing he wanted to do was tuck her into him, find a way to hide her away from this cruel world.

She shook in his loosely encircling arms, but when she pressed harder against him, he locked his arms tighter, resting his chin on her bloodied hair.

"I'm sorry," he whispered as he noted how Raine elegantly landed on the wooden planks before pulling Ardow into an upright position, each drawing his sword from his back as the rhythmic thumping of steps rang louder.

"I'm so sorry," Merrick echoed, the words seemingly the only ones he could utter as he tried to keep his voice from sharpening when his eyes rushed across her body and he noted the scratches, the burns, the carved marks on her back—his own fucking name, for gods' sake—the broken hand and the bloodied one, and the deep cut she still bled from on the back of her head.

Still... he could tell those weren't the worst wounds.

When Lessia tilted her head upward, he nearly crumbled right there and then.

The Death Whisperer thought he'd known horrible, agonizing pain.

He'd seen it in war after war, after all. In the souls that passed on but didn't find rest. In his brothers and friends.

But this...

What filled his mate's beautiful eyes...

There wasn't a word for it.

No human or Fae language could ever come near describing what she was feeling.

It was as if she wasn't there anymore.

Like this was Lessia... but it also wasn't.

It wasn't only Merrick who noticed.

Out of the corner of his eye, he caught Raine's crestfallen face even as he whipped his head back and forth, ensuring they weren't taken by surprise.

Ardow's face was worse. His mouth opened in a silent sob as he took a step toward them, but when Lessia's eyes drifted to meet his, he stilled, his arms flying to wind around himself.

The steps sounded louder now: they'd be here any second.

Merrick could feel a rage build within him. One he hadn't ever felt before—and he was no stranger to anger.

But this one...

It was wild.

Uncontrolled.

Primal.

So vicious he nearly stepped back from the woman he loved to protect her.

But then...

"Hi," she whispered in a voice so broken it sounded like someone else's.

Fuck, it hurt just to listen to it.

He loved her so damned much.

"Hi," he urged back. "Hi. I love you. I'm here now. You're safe."

He sounded like a rambling adolescent, but he didn't care when she dropped the sword and wrapped her arms around him.

And maybe he loved her too much, because the sound of steps faded from his ears.

There was only her.

"You're real?" she whispered, and damn, Merrick's eyes burned, and not from rage.

"I'm real." Merrick leaned down to kiss her softly, praying that her bloodstained lips could take it. "I'm real. It'll be all right. I'll make it all right. I promise, I promise, I promise."

Lessia's eyes remained closed as she got out, "He's dead."

He didn't need to ask who. Not when he knew there were only a few people that could have shattered her heart in this way.

"I'm sorry. I'm so sorry." Merrick pressed featherlight kisses against her full lips, managing to clear his mind enough to hear Raine call "Any second now," and shifting this beautiful creature into the corner of the wall they stood against.

"I'm sorry." He couldn't tear his lips from hers as he continued, so the next words were muffled. "I'm sorry,

Elessia. I just... I need you to hold on. Just for a little longer. Okay? Just a little longer. I need to take care of these men. But I'm here. You just... just call my name and I'll be right back by your side."

She didn't protest as he moved her so she stood fully covered in the shade, and while he knew it didn't matter —not with how warm the air was here—he tore his jacket off and wrapped it around her.

"I love you." Merrick bore his eyes into her dim ones. "You promised me more than one night, remember? We'll have that next one tonight."

When she nodded, the sight so reassuring the Death Whisperer thought he might cry for the first time since he was a child, he bowed his head in return before spinning around.

"Ardow!" Merrick couldn't help but bare his teeth when Ardow didn't move fast enough as he waved him over.

Taking hold of his collar again, he dragged the male the last step, positioning him in front of Lessia.

"You protect her with your life, you hear me? With your fucking life!" His whispers emphasized his order, but to his credit Ardow only gave him a sharp nod before planting his feet wide, his sword raised so quickly before him that Merrick had to spin out of the way.

Good.

Guilt drove Ardow's determination, but it didn't matter now.

Merrick had seen his goodbye with Venko.

He'd die for her, and that was all Merrick could ask for.

Something flashed to his right, and Merrick didn't have to think as his mind snapped into battle readiness.

Four guards flew around the corner, their swords raised and faces mirror to his own.

Merrick grinned—one of those smiles he'd noticed Lessia didn't like.

But he couldn't help it. Those guards might be armed to the teeth, but he'd always been better than them—magic or not.

Not even bothering to unsheath his sword or let his whispers free, he met the Fae guards straight on, ducking under the dagger that whistled by his head.

He sensed someone trying to pry into his mind, but before those claws—so similar to Raine's—got hold, he sprang forward and with a sharp jab of his arm disarmed the guard that he knew, from his days in Rioner's employ, was the one trying to control him.

The Fae faltered momentarily, and from the fear in his eyes, he surely realized who stood before him.

But it didn't matter.

Sprinting around him, Merrick gripped his head and snapped his neck so forcefully it separated from his body before he was even able to make a sound.

Blood sprayed, but Merrick jumped out of the way while throwing the still-twitching body toward another guard.

Rioner's guard's face scrunched as his friend's blood splattered onto it, and that was the expression he was allowed into the afterlife with as Merrick slammed a hand into his chest and ripped his heart out.

A scream sounded behind him, and he whirled, catching Raine's eyes where he leaned against the railing, apparently just enjoying the show, before a female charged him with her sword held high.

She screamed again as her eyes flitted from Merrick

to the male he'd just sent to live wherever they sent dead evildoers, as the souls already around him snatched up his essence and Merrick made his lips lift higher.

"Friend of yours?" he taunted as he circled the woman, keeping an eye on the male Fae who was trying either to sneak up on him from behind or to get away.

He was trying to get away, Merrick decided, when the souls and their whispers stirred louder, and even though he was disappointed, he bent down and picked up a wooden oar that lay by the railing. Without breaking eye contact with the female, he threw it.

His aim was still intact—or at least that's what Merrick inferred from the muted sound of flesh being ripped apart before the oar thudded against the hull.

The female's next outraged scream was also a clue.

Merrick kept his distance as he continued to stalk around her, hands behind his back, trying to rile her further.

He didn't particularly enjoy fighting females, but this one had hurt Lessia... or at least stood idly by as someone else did so.

He'd make it quick.

When the female rushed him, he sidestepped her to the right, having already noticed she favored her left side, and all it took was an angled kick for her to lose her sword to him.

Then another swift movement to bury it in her heart.

Silence stretched out around him, interrupted only by the whispers clinging to this soul as well, dragging it with them to the afterlife.

Merrick closed his eyes, locking down his magic when they were finished.

"You fought bravely, you served well, you honored

your people. Now rest," he mumbled into the iron-tinged air.

Even though Merrick hadn't even given these guards a chance to surrender—would not give any enemy on this ship the option—his commander had instilled respect for the fallen within him.

He'd told Merrick that perhaps it was even more important for him, as a guardian of death—or as they later called him, the Death Whisperer—to respect those who went before him.

"Sounds like there are more coming. Will you save one for the rest of us this time?"

Merrick nearly snapped his teeth at Raine's voice, but instead he opened his eyes and found his friend in the same position as before—casually resting against the railing.

"Seems you needed a break," Merrick responded as he jerked his head.

Thankfully, Raine was still in tune with how they used to fight, and with an eye roll, the latter started picking up the bodies and throwing them overboard.

Nothing could be done about the blood, though.

Shooting his eyes over to where Lessia and Ardow still stood, Merrick was relieved to find she wasn't watching him with fear in her eyes.

On the contrary, it seemed she had some more life in her, her cheeks a bit rosier under the dirt stains.

More steps sounded, and Merrick stiffened when the voice he'd never forget—that he might hate more than all other sounds—sliced through the air.

"The king is coming," he hissed at Raine, still keeping his eyes on Lessia.

Merrick cursed to himself when she also stiffened,

something flickering within her eyes that he'd never seen before.

At his words, she stepped around Ardow, that damned sword in her hands dragging against the wooden planks once more, the rasping sound rumbling through Merrick.

He quickly abandoned the spot he'd stood in, which would have ensured he was first to meet the approaching Fae, to get to her side, and he had to stop himself from lecturing her when she hissed at him as he gently nudged her behind him.

She was injured, he reminded himself—it was not the time for *brooding*, as she liked to call it.

Instead he leaned in and whispered, "*Please*. I nearly lost my mind the past few days, so *please* allow me to be an overprotective bastard. Just today."

Her eyes glimmered when he used Amalise's words, and warmth spread within his chest when something akin to a low laugh rasped through her throat.

Metallic sounds joined the approaching feet, and the air became heavy with the flickerings of magic, the scent of smoke joining it as the wind whirled around them.

Ardow eyed them as he stalked forward, taking up a spot slightly behind Raine, who came forward to stand almost shoulder to shoulder with Merrick.

Nudging Lessia a bit farther back, Merrick finally unsheathed his sword, keeping a loose grip on his magic as a group of guards rounded the corner, the king's gilded crown reflecting the sun where he walked in the middle.

CHAPTER 10
MERRICK

Merrick immediately found those green eyes he'd feared were on this ship.

Fucking Torkher Sordensen.

Raine stiffened beside him, probably noting the same thing Merrick had.

Merrick cursed to himself, the grip he held on Lessia tightening.

They'd grown up with Torkher.

They were all bastards—Merrick, Raine, the twins, and Torkher—and their parents had died in war, either fighting or as civilian casualties. They'd all lived together in one of the training camps, being raised by the soldiers and commanders there.

Also like Merrick and his friends, Torkher had become one of the best soldiers, not just because of his strong mind gift but because he was truly skilled in battle, and his prowess with the sword even rivaled Merrick's. But unlike himself and his friends, Torkher had not used his skills for good...

Or at least *tried* to.

That Fae wasn't just trouble.

He was fucking evil.

His soul was nothing more than a blackened, shriveled lump of coal that even the souls dancing around Merrick wouldn't touch—wouldn't want anywhere near their realm.

As Merrick allowed a warning to vibrate in his throat when Torkher held his eyes, he also thought of how, growing up, he'd sometimes found comfort in Torkher's evil.

It had helped to know true evil when Merrick feared he himself was turning rotten.

But now?

There was nothing comforting in the way Torkher tried to peek behind his back, continuing toward him and Lessia even when his king ordered the group to stop.

"Obey your master," Merrick purred, forcing the numbing dread of knowing Torkher had been alone with Lessia out of his voice. "Otherwise..."

He let his magic free—let those greedy souls surround Torkher—although it proved more challenging, since some of them recoiled from his mere presence.

Still, those whispers whirred in the air, telling the Fae whatever they could to unsettle him, mocking his horrid mind.

But although Torkher stopped in his tracks, what appeared like an involuntary shudder running through him, he still threw his head back and cackled.

A madman's cackle.

A male insane enough not to fear death.

Or a male broken enough...

Merrick had seen both before.

"I know death intimately, Death Whisperer," Torkher said after his laughter faded with the wind. "You do not scare me."

Pulling the reins on his magic, Merrick cocked his head. "Is that a challenge?"

"Perhaps." Torkher looked over his shoulder at his king and the frozen group of Fae. "Or perhaps it's an invitation. She begged for death, you know. Cried for us to kill her when we tortured her."

Lessia's breath hitched behind him, and Merrick's whispers exploded across the ship again, so loud that two of the king's highly trained guards covered their ears even as they gripped their swords.

"Yes," Torkher continued, his glacial grin widening. "I showed her again and again what will happen to you when she dies... She likes you quite a lot, you know. Truly *is* yours. I even took the liberty of putting your name on her. Remember? Like we did to our victims when we were young, to count them?"

Another sharp breath sounded behind him.

Merrick ground his teeth as he spun around, ready to explain, but his words stuck in his throat when Lessia only smiled at him, the sight still breathtaking, lighting up her bloodied face.

And when she said in a hoarse voice, "I claim that guard. I want to carve my name across his face," Merrick had to fight that burning sensation behind his eyes again.

He was just waiting for Lessia to become frightened of him—to realize just who he was.

But she seemed to be too damned stubborn, and wasn't he the luckiest fucking male in the realm for it.

Turning around again, Merrick realized his magic had snapped back without him needing to tug on it.

"You heard her," Merrick said quietly. "Hopefully she'll cut off your fucking dick and let you bleed to death first, though."

A cough got stuck in Raine's throat, and Merrick met his friend's eyes for a brief second, realizing Raine was trying not to fucking laugh.

He rolled his eyes as he faced the group again, readying himself when Torkher stepped toward them.

"Enough," the king snarled.

Torkher froze with one foot midair—almost as if the king's order had tugged on a blood bond.

But Merrick knew better. Torkher was loyal in the way the king always sought from him and his friends, wholly and utterly without reservation.

Only the roar of water sounded around them as Merrick, Raine, Ardow, and even Lessia, who had somehow managed to sneak up to his side, stared at the king and his men, all other noises muted in the charged air that seemed to wrap the ship.

A sense of foreboding settled over Merrick, the sight too similar to the one they'd had a week or so ago, and he couldn't help but step in front of Lessia again, his hand seeking her shoulder and holding on so tightly he was surprised she didn't try to pull away.

"You're not surviving this, Rioner." Merrick couldn't help an ember of smugness seeping into his sharp words.

Because the king wouldn't survive this. Not with the fury driving Merrick. Not with Raine in his element.

Merrick hadn't missed how two of the guards' mental shields must have slipped as their eyes now flew across the deck, bright from fear, but their bodies remained still, relaxed even, as Torkher and the other guard snarled at Merrick's words.

And the king wouldn't survive Lessia's determination, which Merrick could feel falling off her in waves.

She was angry too. Not in the raging, nearly uncontrollable way Merrick was, but in a guided, more focused way. As if there was only one thing she needed to achieve.

And from how her eyes remained locked on the king, even with Torkher trying to catch her gaze, Merrick knew precisely what it was.

You'll get your revenge.

He'd told her that once.

He'd broken too many promises already, but he'd make sure he kept that one.

As if she could read his mind, Lessia placed one of her broken hands over his own and squeezed his fingers, and he couldn't help but shoot her a quick smile and was immediately rewarded with one in return.

"Perhaps I won't survive..." the king mused. "But perhaps neither will you. My brother was stupid enough to believe himself untouchable, and would you know? He's dead. Not sure if your little mate there had the chance to tell you."

Merrick had to hold Lessia back when she charged toward the king.

"Not yet," he hissed as she struggled against him. "Soon. But not yet."

"He killed him! He fucking... slit his throat!" she screamed, her eyes shifting color, but not into the beautiful gold of her magic.

Instead, they deepened, the amber turning into dark honey... the shade eerily similar to that of the uncle who now laughed at her from where he stood, still surrounded by his guards.

"I'm so sorry," Merrick whispered urgently. "You will get your revenge. I promise. But you need to hold on a little longer."

Lessia continued shaking her head, but after finally letting herself meet Merrick's eyes, the movement slowed until she stopped struggling against his hold.

When her chin dipped, although barely perceptibly, Merrick allowed himself to look forward again.

His eyes narrowed on the guard closest to the king as he continued to let his arms loosely run up and down her sides, continued to try to get her calm enough to see what he and Raine had been trained on for so many centuries.

They needed a weak link.

While Raine and Merrick could probably take on other guards here themselves, Torkher would put up a real fight... and the king himself was not to be underestimated.

The one Merrick now focused on was a fire wielder.

Merrick didn't know him, didn't recognize his face, but the arms of his tunic were charred, and the scent of smoke that tinted the wind didn't leave any question as to what he was.

But there was something about the way he moved that was familiar...

Not as if Merrick knew him, but as if... as if he'd known someone like him.

There was a hesitancy in how he stared at the king, something... unwilling in his stance.

Merrick's elbow shot out to nudge Raine's arm, and

when Merrick glanced at his red-haired friend, Raine nodded, having noticed the same thing.

Leaning forward, closing any distance between himself and Lessia, Merrick pretended to kiss her cheek.

"That one is blood-sworn to him," Merrick breathed.

Lessia didn't respond, but the way her eyes shifted ever so slightly from the king when he straightened told him she'd understood.

If she released him from the oath, he'd probably switch sides.

Rioner feared the fire wielders almost as much as the mental Fae. Not that it was entirely surprising...

Being a water wielder, he could fight them, but Merrick had seen what some of the stronger ones could do during the wars he'd fought. Not even an entire sea could quell their destruction when they got started.

Something in the air shifted as Merrick flicked his eyes between the king, the fire wielder, the two guards Raine already was working on, and Torkher, and he was ready even before the king stated, "I guess we'll see who survives in the end."

Before whirling around, Merrick pressed his lips to Lessia's, wishing for nothing more than time to devour them again. But the kiss lasted no more than half a second as the roar of fire began building behind them and he heard the familiar sound of Fae battle cries.

"Get to the fire wielder!" Merrick ordered Raine before catching Lessia's eyes again. "And you two stay together!"

He didn't have to ask twice before Ardow stormed up to Lessia's side, the two of them looking far too young—and far too injured, in Lessia's case—for this battle.

Merrick would do everything he could to ensure they wouldn't have to fight—ideally lay both Torkher's and the king's heads at her feet—but he didn't have time to decide on the best way of doing it before Torkher was upon him, his sword slicing far too close to Merrick's gut for his liking.

Charging forward, using one of Raine's tactics to throw the Fae off, Merrick drove him farther away from where Lessia and Ardow still stood, while at the same time landing a strike squarely on the Fae's nose.

The crunch that followed was so satisfactory Merrick offered the Fae a half smile before kicking him back and lifting his sword between them.

A steady stream of blood ran down Torkher's chin, but the Fae didn't even appear to notice as he flung his sword out, meeting Merrick head-on.

"She begged for you, you know. Called out your name in her sleep. She didn't think you'd come. She thought you'd given up," Torkher taunted him as their swords clashed.

Again.

And again.

Pressing forward, Merrick used Torkher's words to fuel his anger and held back the souls begging to be released. He wanted to take this fucking bastard down himself.

"Sh-she won't survive... this." Torkher panted now as he lifted his sword once more, and Merrick lunged, refusing to give him a moment's rest. "Halflings don't belong in our world. You... you know this."

"She belongs wherever the fuck she wants," Merrick snarled as he cornered Torkher against the railing, his sword finally knocking Torkher's out of his hand.

As the blade clattered down the side of the ship,

Merrick's half smile lifted into a full one, and he angled his sword toward Torkher's neck.

But the Fae's eyes weren't on his as he said, "It appears the afterlife is where she wants to belong, then."

Merrick couldn't stop himself. He whirled around, and his heart nearly burst from fear.

While Raine had managed to get the two guards whose minds he'd captured to sit at the side of the ship, he was now fighting for his life against the fire wielder, with Rioner standing safe behind the flames, seemingly directing his guard.

But that wasn't what had Merrick let out a choked sound.

It was Lessia ripping her arm free from Ardow and sprinting around the flames to approach the fire wielder himself, or… the king.

The king, who'd already noticed her.

"N—" Merrick's scream was cut short as something lodged in his gut.

Pain struck him with such force that he couldn't hold back the jerk that racked his body.

Letting his eyes fall, he found a dagger—the damned dagger he'd gifted Lessia, the one with the rubies to complement his gemstone-decorated sword—sticking out of his side.

Let us go!

We will kill him!

The whispers screamed at him as he reached down and ripped the blade out, tucking it into one of his sheaths and refusing his body's wish to double over to protect itself from more harm.

No! he growled back.

He was doing this by himself.

Fucking quickly, so that he could get to Lessia.

Without a second's warning, Merrick spun around, and he had no idea what Torkher saw in his face, but it was the first time he'd ever seen the Fae shrink back.

Merrick didn't bother savoring the moment. Instead, he dropped his sword, and just like he'd planned, Torkher's eyes followed.

He had to resist shaking his head.

The dumb bastard.

Then he attacked.

Gripping the Fae's arms, he pressed them against the intricate wooden railing, and when Torkher began kicking for his gut or chest—exactly as Merrick knew he would—he ducked under them, forcing Torkher's legs up, so the Fae landed on Merrick's bowed back.

Shooting upward as fast as he could, before the idiot could realize this wasn't the best position for him to be in, Merrick flipped Torkher over the railing.

But Merrick still held on to his arms, and when they stopped the Fae's backflip...

he moved Torkher's flailing arms so he could hold them with one hand, and then he used the other to push harder, until a loud crack broke through the air and Torkher screamed.

Merrick didn't wait before he dragged the Fae back onto the deck. He wasn't letting him go until he was in fucking pieces—when Merrick knew he would never be able to recover.

Torkher moaned as his broken arms lay at awkward angles around his half-sitting body.

With a glance backward—his pulse thundering impossibly fast at the sight of Lessia still charging around the flames—he realized he still had a second. Maybe two.

And... Lessia *had* claimed this bastard.

Removing his belt and ignoring how that made the blood flow more freely from his gut, Merrick quickly tied the Fae's broken arms as tightly as he could, and when Torkher cursed him, he slammed a boot into his face so hard the Fae must have lost consciousness.

He didn't bother double-checking, though, as his hammering heart beat faster, his senses warning him of danger. As he spun around, a wave of heat immediately washed over him, forcing him to squint as he sprinted back toward the middle of the deck.

Smoke began twirling toward the sky, shrouding what was happening from view, and Merrick swore to himself as he stormed farther into the dark clouds.

He needed to find her. There wasn't another option.

"Lessia!" he screamed across the deck, not giving one shit if that betrayed his location.

The answering scream chilled him to his bones.

It wasn't his name.

It wasn't a word at all.

But it was hers, and it was filled with pain.

"No! Lessia!" He tried to run faster, but it was impossible as the smoke thickened.

Merrick had to slow his feet to walk, listening to try to see where everyone was.

"You're going to die! You..." Lessia's raspy voice sounded somewhere to his left, but that's where the wall of fire still burned bright, the crackling of the flames silencing the rest of her words.

"Lessia!"

Fuck, he was panicking now.

Merrick tried pulling on the bond tethering them, but it was still so damned weak. Probably because she was weak, a small voice in his mind dared pipe in.

Fuck that!

He needed to find her.

He needed to protect her.

Just fucking needed her.

"Lessia! Answer me!" Merrick screamed at the fire, but the flames roared louder.

And then... another scream. "Lessia, no!"

The cry was Raine's, and Merrick had no air left, only smoke filling his lungs, but he still tried to call for her, refusing to let the smoke consume her name.

"Lessia. P-please." His words were harsh whispers now, the smoke devouring his voice, and he stumbled within the shadowy world around them, begging to find her.

"No!" Ardow's voice sounded closer. "Lessia, don't!"

Something metallic clattered, and Merrick tried to see, pried his eyelids open as far as they'd go, but between the smoke and the tears they forced out, it was fucking impossible.

Lessia!

Please!

He screamed down the bond.

Tell me where you are!

I love you!

I fucking need you!

Don't do this!

The bond wavered for a second, but that second was enough. Merrick released every grip he had on his magic, letting it fly across the ship, the sea, everywhere in this damned world the souls wanted to go.

He knew they wouldn't be able to do anything—not against the elements; he'd learned that the hard way—and he couldn't control who they killed if he couldn't see.

But it didn't matter. He had to fucking trust they wouldn't kill her.

They'd kill Raine.

Ardow.

She'd hate him for it, but she'd be fucking alive.

Lessia!

"Stop!"

He froze in place at her voice.

"Merrick, please stop!"

He started pulling in his magic when something roared above him. Merrick flicked his gaze up, his eyes widening even within the painful smoke.

Ydren had risen from the water, using her large leathery wings—wings Merrick hadn't known she'd been able to control, since wyverns only used them in fighting—to keep herself half flying out of the water.

His eyes rounded further when Lessia climbed—fucking climbed with her broken hands and body—up her long spikes to reach the beast's head. Then his heart stopped.

Lessia screamed something lost in the wind for him, pointing down with her entire arm, and Ydren didn't wait a moment before she dove toward the deck.

Opening her massive maw, the wyvern unleashed a torrent of water on the ship before her entire body slammed into the wood, making the vessel quiver.

It was quiet for only a second.

Then the smoke cleared, and more screaming began.

But Merrick didn't call Lessia's name again. He could only watch as his mate slipped off Ydren's head and stormed forward, tackling the fire wielder as he gawked at the wyvern, and the golden glow that followed wasn't from flames.

No. Even though he could not hear what Lessia told the Fae, he knew she commanded him to be released from the blood oath. Because that's who she was.

She wouldn't kill him. Not when he hadn't chosen this himself.

That overwhelming feeling of love slammed into Merrick. He couldn't understand how it even fit within him. How his dark heart could survive it. But somehow... it did.

He loved her so damned much.

He could hardly take it when she pushed herself off the Fae and reached out a broken hand to help him to his feet.

The Fae didn't take her up on the offer.

Fucking thankfully. Otherwise, Merrick might have had to kill him.

His heart thrummed in his ears, and when Lessia's eyes searched the ship, finally landing on his own, he thought it might escape his chest.

She was so fucking beautiful.

Bloodied.

Sooty.

Her hair hanging like stringy curtains around her face.

Her skin barely visible under the dirt.

But those eyes... The amber glittered like gemstones in the sun that broke through the smoke.

She was alive. Alive and fighting, and he'd never loved her more.

He'd meant it when he said he'd fallen in love with

her more every day, watching her fight for her fucking life.

She was a force of nature, and when she beckoned for him...

The Death Whisperer's legs nearly gave out. But he forced himself to walk toward her—to close the distance he wished to erase forever.

She offered him a small smile as she slipped a bloodied hand into his, but then her nose wrinkled. "You're injured."

He was injured? Merrick nearly snapped at her that she was the one fucking injured when she rolled her eyes and sliced them forward instead.

His lips pulled at the sight, and they lifted farther when his gaze followed where hers had landed.

The king stood against the railing, Ydren and Raine closing in on him, and there was fear lacing his scent as his eyes darted toward Lessia and Merrick, who followed the Fae and wyvern closely. Ardow and the guard Lessia had released fell in step with them.

Seemed like it was the king's turn to die, and Merrick wished for nothing more than to taunt him, but he kept his mouth shut.

This was Lessia's moment.

They all halted when Lessia raised a hand, and she pulled Merrick with her when she took one more step to stand a bit ahead of the others.

"So here we are," the king spat.

"So here we are," Lessia echoed softly.

"I guess it was inevitable." The king rested his arms on the railing, and Merrick kept a close look to ensure he wouldn't try anything with the water that rushed below him. "You can't fight the gods' will."

Something tugged at Lessia's face, and a feeling—a very strange feeling—roiled within Merrick. His brows pulled as he stared at his mate—at the emotions fighting across her face.

"Oh, I think you can." Lessia cocked her head. "But you did it wrong. You did exactly what they wanted you to. Played right into their hands... So stupid for the mighty regent."

"Look at you, lecturing me like a child," Rioner spat. "You're exactly like your father."

"Do not speak of him," Lessia warned, her voice lowering. "You have no more right to do so."

Ydren reinforced Lessia's command with a growl that had her hot breath flying across the deck like the heat from the fire had before.

"As if a fucking halfling can tell me what rights I have." Rioner let out a cold laugh. "What do you think will happen now? Your sister takes the throne? No... They will not accept her."

Her sister? Merrick shared a look with Raine, and he didn't like what began to form on his friend's face.

"I don't know," Lessia admitted. "But it'll be something better than your rule."

Rioner seemed about to snap at her again when the guard she'd released from his oath called, "Just kill him! He'll continue to spew his poison otherwise."

Lessia didn't even look over her shoulder at the guard. Instead, her grip on his hand tightened, and for the first time, no warmth raced from her skin to his.

Merrick's eyes traveled across Lessia's determined face to the king and back again.

A harsh laugh forced them back to Rioner.

"She hasn't even told you." The smile on Rioner's face was genuine.

"Stop!" Lessia ordered, but the king ignored her.

"This is amazing!" He slapped his hands on his knees as more laughter bubbled out of him.

Merrick snarled softly, moving to place himself between the king and Lessia, not risking her for a second if this was the king's way to distract them.

But even as he did so, a small voice within him started speaking up, a warning blaring at the despair he could now sense from Lessia.

He didn't require another look at Raine to learn that he also had started to understand something was wrong. Truly wrong.

"What is going on?" that damned Ardow asked, his forehead creasing as he also took a step toward the king —as if that would help him understand better. "Lessia?"

His mate didn't speak, and for the first time in a long time, real, hair-raising fear gripped the Death Whisperer.

Not anger.

Or rage.

Or desperation.

But awful, skin-crawling, blood-chilling fear.

The whispers always brushing his ears went quiet, their silence, which he usually sought, so deafening he almost wished for the roar of the fire to return.

He could feel it. Could smell it in the air. Could hear it in the waves. Could sense it in how the world stilled.

He knew whatever followed now... it'd be the end.

The king laughed again. "The Death Whisperer doesn't even know his mate is destined to die with me."

Merrick's knees went out.

His vision began flickering, and something within him broke as the world around him exploded.

A torrent of water rose from the sea, and although everyone around him sprinted forward, including the vicious sea wyvern, it swallowed the king faster than they could blink.

The next moment, he was gone.

Merrick stayed on his knees.

This was what Lessia had kept from him.

He'd seen her on that other ship as she stared east, looking for her friends... The sorrow in her eyes had been there because she wasn't certain she'd see them again.

It's what he'd felt from her in her house... that deep need to be in control, the desperation as she'd clung to him.

Merrick's eyes drew to the sky, and he cursed the gods then.

He'd questioned them before, sure. But he'd thought there always was a purpose—that perhaps he'd been given his gift to protect Lessia, to keep her alive...

But this?

He couldn't even shake his head.

What was the purpose?

His gaze trailed across the deck as he fought with himself within his mind.

Raine tried to talk to him, but he didn't respond. The wyvern used her wings to return to the sea, but he didn't move. His eyes followed Lessia as she walked up to Torkher and slit his throat, silencing him so swiftly Merrick should have been proud.

But he couldn't...

For the first time in his long life, he fucking... couldn't.

He remained on his knees.

He heard Ardow ask Raine and the guard to join him in finding the others.

He remained on his knees.

But he met Lessia's eyes as she walked up to him, and when she also knelt, wrapping her arms around him, he didn't refuse her.

Instead, he folded her broken body against his broken heart and held her there.

They were both silent.

Because what was there to say?

CHAPTER 11

FRELINA

Her tears had finally dried.

Frelina's cheeks were stained from the salt that mingled with the dust and blood there, but she didn't move to wipe them. Instead, she kept her gaze on her father's crumpled body, letting her eyes wander from the dark stain on the wood to his dusty uniform to his unseeing eyes, which remained open, staring into the nothingness that was death.

The pain that had felt as if it would burst out of her, cracking her rib cage wide open, had also softened.

It hadn't disappeared, but it was as if the pain were shifting, finding room to fill every one of her cells, rebuilding her from within.

She'd thought the worst day in her life would always be the one when she said goodbye to her mother. Watching the woman who had raised her—the person Frelina loved the most in her small world—waste away, and not being able to stop herself from picking up her mother's visions of pain and suffering...

Frelina slammed her eyelids shut.

It had been awful.

But today? Today had been worse. Not just seeing her father—the only person she'd had for years—die.

But seeing—fucking feeling—how it broke Elessia...

Frelina couldn't help but whimper.

It had been so clear to Frelina, so clear to the brothers beside her, that when Elessia realized it hadn't just been one of the guard's visions, something irreparable shattered within her sister.

And when Elessia started hurting herself, not to numb the mental pain but because she believed there was no other choice? Bile still burned Frelina's throat after refusing to take her eyes off her sister's turmoil. As if by watching she could absorb some of it, take over the heavy burden Elessia appeared to carry alone.

I love you. I love you so much. Please, please don't let him die too, Elessia had whispered as she dragged her broken body out of the room.

Frelina's heart hadn't been able to take it.

Especially not when a vision followed—one Frelina was certain her sister hadn't shared with anyone: an image of a crumpled paper, of a sentence that had altered Elessia's course forever.

For only in their ultimate sacrifice can a new world be born—the world they have dreamed of, battled for, and wept over.

Another whimper forced its way out of her.

"It's all..." Kerym started, but then trailed off.

He finally decided on "We're here," apparently realizing as well as she did that nothing would ever be all right again.

Turning her head in his direction, she met his eyes when the ship lurched violently.

"What was that?" Thissian straightened from where he'd folded into himself, his arms wrapped so tightly around his legs that his ankles were white.

"I don't..." Kerym startled when the vessel tilted again, something loud thundering above them.

The entire ceiling seemed to vibrate, and for a second, Frelina was worried it might cave in. But then it stilled again, although the silence that followed was almost worse.

"Wh-what is going on?" Frelina asked shakily.

That couldn't have been Elessia, could it?

Her sister might have had determination blazing in her gaze when she left the cabin, but she didn't have any abilities that would shake a large ship like this one.

"I don't know," Kerym muttered. "Come here, little Rantzier."

The dark-haired Fae waved for her to move to the side so that he could cover her, like he'd done when Elessia had been tortured. "Your sister will surely come back to haunt me if I don't at least try to keep you alive."

Try to keep you alive.

While she hadn't spent much time with Kerym or the others before everything, she had noticed they weren't ones for false hope, and she very much doubted she'd be alive for much longer. Still, she shuffled into the spot where the wall curved slightly, allowing Kerym to shield her almost entirely.

If Elessia wasn't successful in killing the king... then Frelina would have to try.

She didn't expect to succeed, but like her father... like her sister... she'd go down fighting.

She was a Rantzier, after all.

Some of that wickedness their family was known for flowed within her veins, and she'd use every last drop of it should she need to.

They remained silent for a while, only their shallow breaths and wild heartbeats filling the musty air around them.

Then the ship heeled again.

Not as violently as the first time, more... focused, as if whatever was doing this wasn't in a rush anymore.

"Something left the ship," Thissian murmured.

"Yes, but what?" Kerym asked.

Neither Thissian nor Frelina responded, but a ripple went through the air once more, something like sorrow-filled acceptance thickening it, joining the stale and dead scent.

If Elessia had jumped...

If the king and his men had left...

They were stuck here.

Despite her best efforts, Frelina's bottom lip began trembling.

She didn't want to die in this stupid cabin. She hadn't even seen Ellow yet, the one thing she'd promised to do when her mother passed.

She hadn't gotten to know the sister she'd missed for more than half her life.

She hadn't even loved yet... had never been kissed, had not even been hugged by anyone outside her family, had never felt even close to what she knew Elessia felt for Merrick, and he for her.

She'd never even experienced heartbreak, not in the way Elessia had when that regent rejected her.

Perhaps that wasn't what anyone in their right mind

would seek, but after twenty-four years of life with parents who meant well but tried to shield her from ever feeling anything other than joy...

Frelina wanted that kind of pain—the kind she'd read about in books—that only love for another could bring.

Frelina wanted it all.

All the feelings.

All the joy.

All the sadness.

All the love.

All the hurt.

Even now... even seeing her father from behind Kerym's broad back, she couldn't regret those wishes.

She just... wanted to live.

"Someone's coming," Kerym hissed when low thudding made dust whirl from the ceiling, interrupting her thoughts. "Thissian!"

His brother shifted as well, trying to line up his shoulders with Kerym's to make sure they would face any attack first. But even so, Frelina could peek through the small sliver between their muscular torsos, and she held her breath as the door before them creaked, then flew open with a loud thud.

The brothers protecting her must have relaxed because the small space between them disappeared, but it didn't matter. Frelina recognized the voice shattering the silence immediately.

"You're alive!"

Raine. It was the grumpy drunkard who'd pushed his way into her mind so effortlessly that she'd spent every day after that finding ways into his, something she'd learned drove him crazy.

"Don't sound so surprised," Kerym responded, tiredness sneaking through the words she expected he meant to sound teasing. "Took you long enough to find us."

Frelina started to stir, moving to get out from the cramped spot, when Thissian stiffened again, pressing her into the wall.

"That one is one of Rioner's guards," he snarled. "Kill him!"

She could barely breathe as her back scraped against the damp wood, and only because Thissian appeared to move forward, pulling at his shackles, did she hear what Raine said next.

"He was blood-sworn... He's not any longer." There was a brief pause, and she wouldn't be shocked if it was because Raine drank from that stupid flask of his. "He is no threat to you."

Air was beginning to get scarce in the small space, especially with the large Fae refusing to give her an inch of breathing room, and she used the little she had to get out, "You're choking me."

"Is that the angry one?" Raine's voice was louder now. "You got her back there?"

Finally.

Finally, the brothers moved, allowing Frelina to peel herself off the wall, and she gulped down a few heavy breaths, grateful that the open door let in some of the fresh air from above.

Her eyes met bloodshot hazel as she lifted her head, and she quickly forced up the mental walls around her mind.

Raine's mouth twitched ever so slightly as he let his gaze trail across her face, and she glared at him until he moved his burning eyes away.

She didn't need to continue staring at him to understand where his gaze fell next, noting the shoulders flying up toward his ears, his back curving as if in pain.

"Can you get these off?" Frelina asked, letting her own eyes drop to her bound hands when it appeared as if everyone in the room had fallen silent, a wave of despair she knew could only come from Raine and Ardow realizing who lay in a heap those few feet away.

"Of course."

It was the guard who responded, and while she'd heard when Raine told them of his blood oath, she couldn't help but recoil as he bent down to unlock the clasps of her chains with a large, rusty key.

"I know." The guard spoke before she had a chance to apologize. "There, you're all set."

She was grateful he didn't offer her a hand, because unlike Thissian and Kerym, she didn't feel like getting right to her feet when her wrists were finally free.

If she got up...

If she started walking...

That would mean it was time to leave her father behind, and that she wasn't ready for yet.

More tears filled her eyes, even if she could hardly understand how she had any more of them within her. They soon started falling down her cheeks like a silent, soft stream weaving its way across an island, and Frelina bent her knees, hiding her face behind them.

"Let's give Lessia and Merrick some time alone before we go up. I think they need it."

Raine's voice was soft as he spoke, and even without the image he allowed her to see within his mind, showing her that she could take all the time she needed, she knew he didn't hold the others back just because of his friend and her sister.

Her body still shook when his large one slumped down beside her, and she didn't stop him when he pulled her to him, tucking her body under his arm.

Another image flickered before her eyes.

Her sister atop a wyvern, climbing up its head as a fire roared beneath them. Elessia hesitating before Rioner when the guard begged her to kill him. Rioner disappearing within the deep sea as Merrick fell to his knees.

Frelina lowered her mental walls for a second to let Raine hear a soft *Thank you.*

She hadn't understood how much she needed to see that there was still some fight left within Elessia, but that second of hesitation before the king had told Frelina all she needed to know.

Her sister might be broken... but she hadn't given up. Something within Elessia still wanted to live.

Lifting her head, Frelina blinked a few times.

Now there was some time...

Now that she knew, that Merrick knew, that the rest knew...

They could come up with a plan to keep Elessia alive.

She let her eyes find her father again, holding on to her legs as the pain struck her like a knife and allowing Raine to grip her shoulders more firmly—to keep her up or keep her together, she didn't know.

Moving so she looked up at him, she lowered the protection keeping him out of her mind.

He's dead.

She needed to say it somehow—to process it. But she couldn't do it out loud. Not yet.

I know. Raine's eyes didn't waver from hers as he responded.

It hurts.

I know. Another squeeze of her shoulders.

It's not fair.

I know. Raine's words wobbled a little bit, and she realized he did know.

Frelina watched the muscle in his jaw tense.

She'd heard about his mate being killed. She couldn't imagine his pain, not even having glimpsed it when she managed to catch him with his guard down once on the ship on their way to Ellow.

It couldn't even be comparable to her own.

A shudder racked her before she realized she hadn't raised her walls again.

I'm sorry! She tried to break away from his gaze as she quickly shut the door to her mind, but he wouldn't let her.

Don't be. Raine's eyes flitted between hers. *Solana always said no hurt was the same. We all hurt in different ways and for different things, but that doesn't take away anyone's right to pain.*

Frelina nodded as she watched his hazel eyes brighten to almost all green as he thought of Solana, of their love, of their hurt.

She felt it all.

It was beautiful and bright and utterly heartbreaking at the same time.

A sad smile pulled at Raine's features as he slipped his flask out of his tunic.

After taking a long sip, the emotions playing across his face muting, he offered it to her. But even though her pain was raw, fighting so hard within her that it felt as if it could burst through her skin from the pressure, she shook her head.

"I want to feel it," she whispered. "I need to feel it. I need to feel it all."

Because the way her life was shaping up, she doubted it would be the long one of the Fae, and if so, she needed to feel every damned emotion she'd longed for before the end.

Starting now.

CHAPTER 12
LESSIA

Merrick still hadn't said a word.

If she hadn't felt his heart thundering against her chest, she might have thought he had more serious injuries than the wound that had already begun clotting in his side.

Lessia tightened her arms around his neck.

It wasn't a physical wound that kept the Death Whisperer on his knees.

No. It was a mental one. One that cut through hearts and souls and tissue without drawing blood. But one that would scar all the same.

"I'm sorry," she whispered into his hair as he hugged her back, fighting the tears threatening to spill over.

Merrick only shook his head and held her closer, even though he was still careful not to press on any of her open wounds.

Gods, she loved him so much.

It felt as if it would choke her. It was as if it could

drown out all else, leaving just him and her together in this mess that was their reality.

Even now... even finding out what she'd kept from him, he didn't hold it against her.

The rage she could feel shifting within him wasn't directed her way.

Lessia couldn't help the sob that left her.

She didn't want to die. She didn't want to leave him. She didn't want to leave this world.

She just... didn't.

"I won't allow it." Merrick finally moved, altering his position so his back leaned against one of the wooden masts and gently tugging her with him so she straddled him, his arms remaining around her as if he couldn't stand having an inch of space between them.

"Merrick," she started, but the look in his eyes made her swallow the words she'd planned to say.

The sharp darkness in his eyes was eerily similar to what she saw there when she became lazy as they trained.

Gently removing her arms from where they'd rested around his neck, Merrick laid her hands atop her thighs, and he spoke quietly as he pulled straps of fabric off the tunic he wore, using them to bind her bloodied wrist, then moved her broken bones into place—letting her take small breaths when pain shot up her arm before continuing.

"I won't allow it, Elessia. I won't. There will be a way. There is always a way. And we'll find it. I promise you we'll find it together."

His eyes bore into hers.

"You've fought so bravely for so long. Please. Please just fight a little more."

She followed the silver swirls within his eyes, relishing the sense of falling—the sense of freedom and love and safety—they always ignited in her.

"Please," Merrick whispered when he finished, his hands moving to cup her cheeks. "Fight a little more for me?"

Lessia swallowed at the pain pulling at his sharp features—at the hope making the silver in the dark eyes before her glitter in the sun.

You and me.

She could see it so clearly.

How their life should be.

How their love should be.

The happiness.

The fun.

The excitement.

Everything they should have had.

It wasn't fair.

But the world wasn't fair, was it?

She'd learned that young. Had seen it in her own family. In the children on the streets of Vastala. Had heard it in the cries from the other prisoners in Rioner's cellars. Had seen it in Ardow. In Amalise. In Loche. In Merrick.

In everyone she loved.

Lessia's chin lowered of its own accord, and although it was only a small dip of agreement to his question, a rush of air left Merrick before he gripped her face more firmly and pressed his lips to hers.

"Thank you," he whispered when he came up for air. "Thank you."

She smiled against his lips. "People like you and me don't get happy endings, do we?"

She'd meant the words to come out playfully, trying to lighten the heavy wall of air pressing against them from all sides, but somehow they didn't. Something high-pitched worked its way into her tone, and the slight tremble was as clear as the sky above them.

Merrick stiffened in the way only full Fae could—like he was a statue, no blood flowing through his veins and no heart pumping life into his body.

Shifting so he could glare into her eyes, still with his fingers caressing every bit of the dirty skin on her face that he could reach, his nostrils flared.

"Perhaps we only get endings." Merrick's eyes searched hers, something in them flickering—an understanding, the way he always understood her, joining the night sky. "But let's make that ending one for the fucking books, shall we?"

A tear made its way down her cheek at the same time as low laughter sprang from her lips. Merrick's mouth twitched as well, and she couldn't help but grin wider at how he tried to hide his smile—exactly like he'd done on Ellow during the election.

A low growl interrupted her giggling, and she looked up to find Ydren's head bobbing above the railing behind her.

Lessia smiled at the beast as well.

She'd come.

She'd come for Lessia.

She'd come for all of them.

Lessia didn't even have to start getting up before Merrick lifted her and gently set her on her feet. But as he motioned to stay back, she gripped his hand in one of her bandaged ones and dragged him with her to the sea wyvern.

Reaching out with her other hand—the broken one—she placed it cautiously on Ydren's snout, forcing her features to remain soft when a sharp pain shot up her arm.

"Thank you." Lessia met Ydren's shiny eyes as the wyvern pressed into her hand. "Thank you for saving us."

She didn't know how, but it was as if Lessia could hear Ydren shake off the thank-you, as if... the wyvern shrugged her nonexistent shoulders.

"How did you know?" Lessia continued stroking the violet scales as she let her eyes wander across Ydren's large body and the wings she'd not seen before but which now seemed so obvious.

Of course the leathery, shiny wings belonged to this magnificent creature.

Ydren bent her head toward Lessia's left arm, and Lessia nearly jumped when the wyvern's snout dragged against it, and it lit up—Lessia's skin glowing like the sun above them.

"It's the stone." Merrick squeezed her hand when she continued staring at her skin with her mouth open. "It chose you."

The stone?

Loche's face, the rough kiss, flashed before her eyes.

He'd given it to her.

"It chose me?" Lessia echoed as she watched the warm glow fade when Ydren pulled back from touching her arm.

"It did. Of course it did." Merrick's eyes were pure silver now, and she fought the urge to look away when they swept over her with so much pride she almost couldn't stand it. "When you touched water with the stone in your hand, it chose to merge with you. It deemed you worthy."

"He's right." Raine's voice rumbled across the deck, and Lessia spun around so quickly that Merrick's hand was ripped from hers, and even Ydren let out a protesting noise.

Lessia threw Merrick a quick smile as he pulled her back, snaking his arm around her waist to keep her close as first Raine, then Ardow, then Kerym and his brother, and finally her sister and the guard exited the hatch.

Raine nodded toward Ydren. "The stones choose whether the Fae wielding them are worthy of their power. They haven't worked since the R... since your family abused them. I wouldn't be surprised if this is the first time since the war centuries ago. They're absorbed within you—live with you until you die—allowing you to call upon the wyverns when you're in need."

Lessia nodded slowly, glancing from Ydren back to the group.

She staggered when her gaze landed on her sister's tear-stained face, more tears wanting to gloss her eyes when Frelina tried for something Lessia suspected should be a smile but which seemed more of a broken grimace.

Lessia was about to step toward her sister when Raine froze, then whirled around and put a muscular arm around her sister's shoulders, pulling her small frame against his.

Sharing a quick look with Merrick, whose silver brows snapped together in the same way she expected her own did, she decided not to say anything.

If Raine wanted to protect her sister...

Who was she to interfere?

Instead, Lessia cleared her throat. "So... where are the rest of the wyverns, then?"

The voices she'd heard when Rioner was choking her must have been them. And there had been many.

Ydren made a soft sound, and something about it had the hair on Lessia's arms rise.

Slowly turning away from the group, she found the wyvern's eyes.

The seconds that passed seemed like they lasted an eternity, the cold that had begun running up and down Lessia's arms spreading across her body.

"They're not coming, are they?" she whispered when Ydren's eyes clouded.

The creature shook her head so fast that droplets of water flew around her, and Lessia's stomach sank.

She didn't need to ask why. Like before, she could somehow *feel* what Ydren was thinking. The wyverns didn't believe that Lessia was worthy. They thought the stone must have made a mistake.

One word echoed within her mind.

A warning.

Rantzier.

Rantzier.

Rantzier.

Closing her eyes, she drew a deep breath.

It would be all right. They'd survived Rioner today, after all.

But you needn't only survive Rioner but thousands of rebels and an entire nation of Oakgards' Fae.

She swore at the voice bouncing against the walls in her mind.

"Fuck. If the wyverns aren't coming, I think we have a problem." Kerym's curse had her eyes fly open again, and her gaze swept over the worried faces that must have started to realize the same thing she did.

Ardow's pinched one.

Her sister's devastated one.

Kerym's worried one.

Thissian's defeated one.

Raine's hardened one.

The Fae soldier's confused one.

But it was Merrick's face...

The fear twisting his features. The fear—not for himself, not for his friends, not for this world, but for her—that had her say what she did next.

"Then I must go to them."

Merrick seemed as if he was about to argue with her, a familiar vibration shaking his chest, but she captured his eyes and pierced them with her own.

"You made me promise to fight." She didn't care if the others heard their conversation. "This is me fighting."

"This will not save your life," Merrick growled. "Getting the beasts to help us might save this world, but those wyverns will not save you from the gods—from that prophecy. You promised me to fight for *your* life!"

"I also promised to save this world!" she screamed, her blood heating as his dark eyes refused to let hers go. "I promised the children... I promised it to myself when I left my home! I need to do this! We need them. I need them!"

"And I need you!" Merrick screamed back, color tinting the Death Whisperer's cheeks as he threw out an arm. "We need you, Elessia! Don't you see that?"

Tears blurred her vision as she followed his hand,

and she swayed at the looks she got from the group of Fae and part-Fae before her.

"He's right." Her sister stepped forward, her lip trembling but her voice still carrying over the wind whipping across the wooden ship. "You promised not to leave me, Elessia."

Raine nodded as he stepped with her sister, keeping Frelina steady. "This world needs you, Elessia. It will need someone with your heart and your loyalty and your passion to heal after the wounds it's about to suffer."

Kerym found her eyes as he also inched forward. "Trust us, Golden Eyes. The world will need as many of you as it can get."

Even Thissian gave a swift bow of his head. "If anything... don't do this to him."

It was as if Kerym's brother let all the pain from his own loss free, and Lessia actually stumbled back at the sight of it.

Was that what M—

No. She wouldn't go there.

Her eyes were desperate as they moved back to Merrick.

She didn't want to do this to him... to any of them. To herself.

But what choice did she have?

They needed the wyverns if they were to survive.

A deep, familiar voice broke the loaded silence. "Maybe she can do both. Save herself and this world."

They all shot straight up as wood slammed into wood and their ship creaked loudly, the sound rushing right through her, as another lined up with it.

Loche elegantly jumped onto their own, but it wasn't

his serious face that had her rip her hand from Merrick's and sprint toward the other ship.

A mess of blonde hair glittered behind him, and tears flooded her eyes when Amalise's blue ones met her own.

Lessia didn't care about anything within her body that hurt as she sprinted right into her friend's arms, slamming them both into the deck.

Wetness touched Amalise's cheeks as well as she hugged Lessia, and as she pulled back, the words Lessia knew Amalise meant to be playful instead carried a sorrowful note as they came out. "You look like shit."

Lessia forced a smile, easily picking up the jargon she and Amalise had perfected over the years to hide their pain. "Not all of us had the pleasure of hiding away in a cave with a hot man."

She cast her eyes to Zaddock, who jumped from the other vessel to their own, seemingly very bothered by Lessia's hurtling Amalise into the boards, judging by his dark, drawn-down brows.

Amalise's cheeks heated, and she mumbled something incoherent before apparently gaining control of her features and pushing Lessia off her.

After getting to her feet, her friend pulled her up, although not as gently as Merrick had done before, and Lessia winced as the movement made the bandage scrape against her still open wounds.

"Sorry, sorry!" Amalise rushed out.

When Lessia waved dismissively, Amalise grinned, something mischievous glittering in her eyes.

"Well... on the topic of men. I heard quite the opposite... I heard you got yourself a very hot man. Or maybe I should say male?"

Lessia couldn't stop her eyes from seeking out

Merrick's, and sure enough, his waited for her, love still filling them even after their argument.

"I did," she said softly.

Amalise's eyes widened for only a second before she pulled Lessia to her and slung an arm over her shoulder.

"Finally," Amalise whispered, almost as if to herself, as she started steering them toward the group.

"If you're done with all the man talk..." Raine threw them a forced smile, his eyes moving from Lessia to Merrick, worry still filling them. "What did you mean, regent?"

Cold crawled across her skin when she accidentally met Loche's eyes, and her smile faded at what she saw in them.

Pain.

Anger.

Hurt.

Confusion.

She didn't know which emotion in his storming grays was worse. But his turning away from her when she made to take a step toward him, moving to stand farther away, was like taking a slap to the face.

"I've heard from my spies in Vastala that the wyverns live near some place sacred to the Fae and your gods? The mirrors something? That you can call upon the gods there and get answers. Maybe you can ask how Lessia can do this without dying?"

Lessia swallowed at the fear that sneaked its way into Loche's voice, and she didn't dare look at Merrick, already sensing she'd find the same fear in his eyes.

"The Lakes of Mirrors," Kerym mused. "No one has been there in centuries."

"For good reason," Thissian broke in. "The gods can't

be trusted. They may not be able to lie, but they twist the truth until you don't know where in the world you are anymore. It's a dangerous place."

"But they allow us to speak to the gods?" Frelina asked, her voice not wavering, and Lessia shot her a grateful look.

"They do," Raine responded. "At least that's what the stories say. It's worth a try."

Lessia nodded, finally braving facing Merrick.

And when he reached out his arms, she wiggled out from Amalise's embrace, and forgetting about everyone else on the ship, she walked right into them, allowing him to shield her from the world.

She listened to his strong heartbeat, wanting nothing more than to stay there forever.

But she made herself whisper, "Is that enough fight for you?"

Merrick nodded, and she let him pull her closer, merging their bodies as much as they could as he whispered, "I love you, Elessia Rantzier."

CHAPTER 13
LOCHE

Loche leaned over the railing, letting the waves still crashing against the sides—even with the heavy anchors they'd lowered to keep the two ships from drifting too far apart—splash salty drops onto his face.

He wished the water could somehow scrub the memories of the last hours from his mind, but it did little more than sting his slightly sunburned skin.

Loche sighed as he straightened and dragged his hands down his rough face. He hadn't been certain if he'd ever see spring again—didn't even want to think about summer...

Not that he expected to see another in Ellow.

With the threat of the rebels and now the Oakgards' Fae...

No. Loche was quite sure he'd be joining Lessia's father within the next few weeks.

He clenched his hands by his side as Alarin's lifeless

body being carried across the ship flashed before his eyes.

The Fae warriors had given him a proper Fae goodbye, at least as worthy as they could out here in Korina's waters.

Loche had heard of them before, of course, but he'd never attended one himself.

It might even have been beautiful, how everyone on the two vessels—human and Fae alike—lined up on either side of Rioner's ship as Merrick and Raine carried the royal Fae across it, humming a mournful song in one of the Fae's old languages.

They'd each touched their heart and then laid a hand on Alarin's chest when he'd been carried past them—the way Fae expressed that he'd forever live within them, and that they'd carry his love with them always.

But Loche hadn't been able to stop staring at Lessia the entire time.

She'd been so strong. Standing straight-backed, she'd held on to her sister, who'd doubled over, screaming out her pain, letting the younger half-Fae lean on her as Merrick and Raine lowered a small boat with Alarin in it and let it drift away to be swallowed by the Eiatis Sea.

Lessia had been strong in the way she always was.

But Loche knew what she worked so desperately to hide behind the quiet tears falling down her face as she pressed her hand against her father's chest.

Guilt. Raw, all-consuming guilt.

That's what kept her going right now—what kept her standing.

It was the same guilt that lived in him—the one that had drawn him to her those first days of knowing her.

He'd seen the way Lessia moved—as if she didn't think she belonged anywhere, as if she asked the world for forgiveness for walking on its earth, as if she didn't believe she deserved the same treatment as the people around her.

But he'd also seen her kindness. The pure light that drove her to want to do good at whatever cost.

Loche had never felt so connected to anyone before, especially not so quickly.

Not his soldiers.

Not even Zaddock.

When Lessia spoke to him, it was as if she saw him. She saw Loche.

She saw him not as the regent everyone feared, wondering how he'd become so powerful, but as the boy who had been born into a cruel world, who'd made mistakes and paid for them, but tried to do what he could to make his nation a better place.

Loche shook his head as the memories of their final time together, before it all went to shit, replaced the ones of today.

He was pretty certain he preferred not to remember the good times with Lessia, and he balled his hands so snugly, it felt like all blood drained from them.

Loche didn't want to dream of her laugh—the one he'd heard too few times, but which appeared ingrained in his memory. He didn't want to see her twirl in the damned dress he'd purchased for her, when she stole his breath with how beautiful she looked.

He didn't want to remember the feel of her skin beneath his hands. The way her lips melted against his. The way she breathed when she was excited or scared.

She wasn't his, and... he knew now she never would be.

Not after what he did to her.

Lessia calling his name that day—the desperation, the pain, the fear in her voice—filled most of his nightmares, and he dreaded sleeping because of it.

Back then, he'd thought it was the only way...

But it had cost him everything.

As soon as he'd caught her eyes in that damned cabin after his men had captured her and the Fae warriors, he knew it was over.

The way she hovered by Merrick wasn't for protection. It was as if those two were drawn to each other wherever they went, like two forces that couldn't be apart.

Loche sighed.

He'd heard of the Fae's mates, but he didn't really understand it—didn't understand how Lessia, who resented anyone for taking away her choices, could stand it.

But...

At least Merrick loved her with everything in him.

Loche had seen the fear in his eyes today, and while he felt for the Fae, because that fear resounded in him as well, he was grateful for it. Merrick would die for Lessia—exactly like Loche would have if she'd chosen him.

"May... may I join you?"

He almost pinched himself to make sure that it wasn't another dream—that it truly was Lessia who walked over from the cabin inside, her matted hair and empty eyes illuminated only by the moon that hung high above them in the sky.

Forcing himself to nod, Loche stepped to the side, allowing her to take the spot by the railing beside him where he stood in the bow, and as she settled, he placed a hand atop the wooden sea wyvern that hung there.

"Can't sleep?" He couldn't meet her eyes again, not now, when her scent joined the salty wooden one of the ship, so he looked out over the restless sea, where the moon's reflection played in the waves.

"No."

Her voice was so small, so broken. So full of guilt, he could taste it.

Fuck. He had to turn to face her, and when he met those pain-filled amber eyes, saw the torment that seemed to hurt her more than any of the broken bones and wounds she carried, he opened his arms.

To his surprise, Lessia walked right into them, and he had to fight with everything in him not to burrow his face into her hair, pull that intoxicating scent of hers deep into his lungs.

"It's not your fault," Loche whispered when she continued trembling in his arms.

"Everyone keeps saying that." She sniffed. "But if not partly mine, whose is it?"

"Rioner's. It's only Rioner's fault." Loche pulled back to look at her, trying to keep his voice even as he faced the broken woman he still loved. "I know you think you're responsible, I know the guilt you think you must carry, but it's unwarranted, Lessia. You have done nothing wrong."

A mixture of a sob and a snort left her. "Nothing wrong? I spied on you! I told my king your secrets! I... I took your memories and feelings, and then I... I didn't know."

Her face crumbled. "I didn't know," she whispered again. "I didn't know, and I hurt you. Like I've hurt everyone."

Closing his eyes, he drew a deep breath.

He knew she'd feel guilty when she found out why he did what he did, especially because of what had happened between her and the Death Whisperer. But... it was still unwarranted.

Opening his eyes, he pulled her closer again—not into a tight embrace, but so she wouldn't miss any of his response.

"Listen to me." His hands rested atop her shoulders, gently squeezing them when she made to look away. "I love you. I probably always will in some way. But this was meant to happen."

He gave her a weak smile. "I won't be able to follow where you must go. I have a duty to my people, and I must see it through. He... Merrick has no loyalty to anyone but you. As it should be. As it was meant to be. As you deserve."

Lessia shook her head, her eyes darting between his.

"Yes, as you deserve. You deserve to be happy. For as long as you can." Loche's heart constricted when she continued to shake her head, and he moved his hands to her cheeks to stop the movement.

"People like you and me," he mumbled as he tried not to allow his heart to beat faster at the feeling of her skin, albeit dirty and bloodied, heating under his fingers. "We don't get these chances often. Please... for me, be happy when you can. It... it gives me hope I'll have it again before the end."

She stared at him for so long and so intensely that,

for the first time, Loche had the urge to look away from her imploring eyes.

But he kept her gaze until it softened, until the small creases around her eyes vanished and the frown that had marred her forehead faded.

Until she understood he meant what he said.

"Wh-where will you go?" She took a step back as she spoke, and Loche didn't have to turn his head to know Merrick was approaching them.

But as the Fae stalked up to Lessia's side, tucking her against him as if they were only one being, Merrick didn't threaten to kill him for touching her, or even throw him one of his death stares.

Instead, his dark eyes shone with gratitude, and when Lessia rested her cheek against the Fae's chest, he actually bowed his head.

Confused, Loche nodded back, remaining silent until Lessia softly cleared her throat.

Right. She'd asked him a question.

"I... I think I need to try to find the rebels." Loche tried not to stare at the hands running up and down Lessia's back, at how easily she molded herself against the Death Whisperer. "It's only weeks left until their attack, and while my soldiers are preparing what they can in Ellow, we won't survive two wars."

"Their leader is ruthless." Merrick sought his eyes as he spoke. "She harbors a lot of hatred in her heart. You might need to kill her."

Lessia gave a soft nod. "She reminded me of Rioner when we met. But... but her people are innocent. There were several of them that seemed worried when we told them of the threat of the Oakgards' Fae. They might follow you if you can honor their place in society."

Loche met Merrick's eyes, and a moment of understanding flowed between them.

Like himself, Merrick didn't seem convinced they'd be that easy to turn.

Still, Loche hummed in agreement. "We will try not to kill them if we can."

"Who will you bring?" Merrick had begun playing with Lessia's hair, and Loche had to tear his eyes away, throwing them back out across the sea.

"The people on this ship, I suppose," Loche responded. "I cannot spare more soldiers right now, nor do I have time to return to Ellow and then go out again."

It was quiet for a beat as Merrick moved his gaze to Lessia, then back to Loche.

"Kerym and Thissian will join you. I need Raine. I... I don't know what we'll face out there..." Merrick didn't need to finish for Loche to understand he feared whatever those Lakes of Mirrors could bring.

"Thank you," Loche offered when the Fae remained silent.

Merrick gave him the slightest dip of his chin. "Thank you as well," he said, so quietly Loche wasn't sure if he'd imagined it.

He made the mistake of glancing back at Lessia and Merrick, and his chest nearly caved in at the way they stared at each other. The look in their eyes held so much trust and love and fight, Loche couldn't breathe for a moment.

Without excusing himself, he started to back away.

Not that it mattered. Lessia and Merrick didn't look up as he made his way over to his own ship, and he could still see their silhouettes standing in the same position when he sank down against the upper cabin.

Pressing his hands to his aching chest, he thought perhaps he had lied to Lessia back there.

He didn't have any hope of finding what she had. And even if he did, he didn't want it.

Because that meant he would risk feeling like this again.

CHAPTER 14
MERRICK

Merrick had to physically restrain himself from whirling around and taking her somewhere he could protect her, distracting her forever, when he heard Lessia's soft sobs as she bid Amalise, Ardow, and the rest goodbye before her friends returned to Loche's ship.

While Lessia, her sister, Kerym, and Thissian were still injured, all of them needing rest, ideally for a long, long time... there wasn't any time left.

The threat of the rebels hung over the group like a heavy storm cloud, and he noticed several hunched shoulders amongst the group as they settled onto the respective ships: Venko's worried face even as he reunited with Ardow; the guard Zaddock's constant hovering around Amalise, and the hand he kept on his sword, ready for an attack at any moment; Loche's worried gaze flitting to the north ever so often—filled with unease for his nation, which lay there.

Even those talkative sisters were quiet, although he

did notice Pellie throw some suggestive comments Kerym's way and the Fae responding in kind, albeit in a more subdued way than his friend usually spoke.

Merrick nodded to the dark-haired Fae brothers as they walked over to the regent's ship, but when he caught Thissian's eyes, he quickly looked away. In his blues swam a mixture of sorrow, fear, and pity as they flicked between himself and his mate.

A shudder racked the Death Whisperer's shoulders.

Thissian had never been one to hide his feelings.

He'd openly wept on the battlefields when they were younger, disregarding how their commanders would sneer about it, because of how much he hated the waste that wartime death was.

He'd been seen as the weakest of the four of them for it, but Merrick wasn't convinced that was true.

To allow yourself to feel that utterly and completely...

Merrick shook his head.

Brave.

That's what it was.

Brave and strong.

He allowed himself a glance toward Lessia, eyeing her when she pulled Frelina close and quickly lowered her shoulders when her sister stared unseeing out across the others leaving—falling right into the older-sibling role she must have played growing up—and wondered for a moment if he'd be able to be as strong as Thissian.

Because right now...

Right now, he felt like begging Raine for one of his flasks and drowning himself in it as that burning sensation that had become worryingly familiar rose behind his eyes again.

He couldn't lose her.

He just... he fucking couldn't.

He'd promised to keep her safe. He'd promised to always be there—be whatever she needed him to be.

A protector.

A friend.

A trainer.

A lover.

Merrick pushed the urge for liquor and sweet oblivion away.

He'd need to be strong for her. Only for her. Continue fighting like Lessia had promised him she would.

For as long as she breathed, he'd take all the pain in the world. Fuck, he'd take hers as well if he could. But if she didn't breathe anymore... He ground his teeth when the souls around him roiled in fury.

"Death... Ah... Merrick, a-a word?" The Fae soldier sprang backward when Merrick spun around to face him, and his face whitened as he lifted his hands, fire sparking from his fingers—probably in response to Merrick's magic flickering in the air.

Merrick deliberately moved his gaze to the male's hands, wondering whether the decision to save him had been hasty, when the Fae spoke again, the sparks fading.

"I apologize." He jerked when Merrick's eyes landed back on his, but he didn't take another step backward. Instead the Fae straightened, trying to lift his chin.

He was young, Merrick realized as he observed him. Very young.

Barely older than a Faeling—perhaps thirty or maybe forty years old.

Still, Merrick didn't have it in him to be soft. Not right now.

Not when he needed to save whatever warmth there was in him for Lessia.

So he raised a brow when the Fae only opened and closed his mouth, and demanded, "Yes?"

The Fae's swallow echoed between them before he finally spoke again. "My name is Cedar Reinsdor, and I... I just wanted to say I am forever in your and your mate's debt."

Merrick froze, eyes flying across the Fae before him.

"You're not... Dedrick's son, are you?" Merrick took a step closer to the Fae, pretending not to notice how the younger one couldn't stop himself from shrinking back again even as he nodded.

"I-I am."

"How the fuck did you end up here?" Merrick frowned as he eyed the expensive clothing the Fae was clad in and the bejeweled sword and dagger hanging by his waist—so much more elaborate than his own... than the dagger he'd gifted Lessia.

He should have noticed it before—only the noble Fae could afford such extravagant weapons, and the clothing... It was something one was more likely to see in Rioner's castle's vast halls than on a warship in the middle of the Eiatis Sea.

And the Reinsdors... They were one of the oldest and most powerful noble families.

"I... My father owed the king a debt." Cedar's long blond hair fell into his eyes as he bowed his head. "Rioner... he wouldn't settle for anything else but my utmost loyalty to him."

Merrick flicked one of his teeth with his tongue, trying not to show the rage that burned so hot within him that he was surprised he didn't burst into flames.

Of course Rioner had wanted this male.

His flames were truly magnificent, and the king couldn't have someone like that on the loose...

Like with Merrick, Lessia, and most of the others blood-sworn to the king, his gift posed a threat to the king himself.

Merrick's whispers whipped the air—the oily vibrations from them sharpening with every moment he thought of the damned king.

Rioner needed to die.

A slow, painful fucking death where he was alive until the very last drop of his blood was drained from his body. Suffering. Suffering in the way he'd made Vastala and its people suffer.

Merrick had heard stories from other realms of bloodsucking monsters hidden within facades as beautiful as the Fae's bodies.

How he wished they had time to go in search of one of them.

The whispered legends told by far-traveling Fae spoke of these monsters being able to deliver the most gruesome deaths.

Not that that would be enough for the king. He deserved to die again and again and again—reliving the pain and fury of those he'd hurt for several lifetimes.

That's what the souls he now struggled to keep leashed whispered of.

Merrick's eyes focused when the Fae before him let out a straggling rush of air, but that rage within him still reigned, drowning all other emotions.

It wasn't until a small bandaged hand slipped into his that he could snap out of it.

Merrick's eyes drew to Lessia's when she sidled up

beside him, and he didn't know why he was surprised when she offered him only a small smile and a press of her injured fingers instead of wide, fearful eyes.

She's strong enough now.

The souls whispered the words to him as they huddled around Lessia, not in the threatening way they did around others, not anymore, but protective, as if they knew should anything happen to her, their own fate was uncertain.

She was meant for you. For us.

Lessia smiled wider, almost as if she heard them, before she moved her eyes to the cowering Fae.

"I'm Lessia," she offered softly. "And I heard you're Cedar. I believe our"—she swallowed before continuing—"fathers were friends."

Cedar offered her a shaky nod. "I... I've known Alarin since I was a child. I'm s-so sorry for your loss. And... I also wanted to say... thank you for what you did for me. I... I am in your debt."

A trembling breath made its way down Lessia's lungs before she appeared to catch herself—catch herself in a way Merrick wished she'd never had to learn, hiding the pain and the sorrow and the guilt somewhere deep within her broken body.

"Thank you." Lessia stepped closer to Merrick, and despite everything, warmth clawed into his chest when he realized it seemed to steady her.

"You are not in my debt." Lessia drew another breath before continuing. "Saving you is what any decent person would have done. But..."

Lessia cast Merrick a quick look before continuing, and his brows knitted when he tried to understand the feeling within her.

Guilt and sadness, yes. But also... purpose.

It was purpose, he decided, that drove what she said next.

"But still, I want to ask a favor." Lessia waited until Cedar nodded. "I need you to return to Vastala. I know it's probably the last thing you want to do, especially now, being free of Rioner. Trust us... We know."

Merrick clasped her closer when she shot him another glance.

Gods, he fucking loved her.

He didn't know how it was possible that he loved her even more every day.

But right now? It felt as if his chest would combust from pride.

She was... a leader.

He'd seen it in her before—it was one of the reasons he had trained her, after all, to ensure she could protect herself when she stepped into what he knew must be her destiny.

But now? It was so clear to him.

This beautiful, strong, kind, loyal, and gentle soul would be the one who saved their world. And he'd be right by her damned side while she did it.

"We need some of the Fae to see our side," Lessia continued after folding an arm around Merrick's waist, drumming up heat within him like she always did any time she touched him. "Loche and the others will take on the rebels and prepare Ellow the best they can. We will get the wyverns to fight. But we need you to convince your father to join us."

Cedar's mouth fell open as Lessia reached out a broken hand, sweeping it across the group that had gathered on the other ship, waiting only for Cedar to join them.

Raine and Frelina slowly approached, and Merrick only caught his friend's gaze out of the corner of his eye, but he still noticed the glimmer of admiration in it as it flicked to his mate.

"These humans, Fae and half-Fae, are the only thing standing between a Havlands ruled by cruel and twisted men and women, and a new world—a world where debts aren't paid in blood or children left to die in the streets. While I'll never force anyone to join us—not like the ones we stand against—I ask you to *please* do this. *Please* be a part of this. *Please* stand with us."

Merrick had to catch himself not to let his own mouth draw down like the Fae's before him, and he couldn't help but move to stand behind Lessia, folding his arms around her and whispering how fucking proud he was of her into her ear until those goose bumps he loved peppered her neck.

When he finally lifted his gaze, Cedar had managed to snap his gaping lips shut.

But his voice still wavered as he responded, "I will. I will do anything I can to help. I am certain that when I tell my father what you did for me, he'll want to stand with you, but I don't know what that will help?"

Merrick really tried to stop letting his lips drag across the soft skin of Lessia's neck when she spoke, but having her this close... breathing her in...

He couldn't fucking help himself.

And she didn't push him away—on the contrary, she leaned into his touch—so he hoped she didn't give a shit, either, that they were surrounded by so many people.

"Your father," Lessia started, but she had to clear her

throat as her voice became breathy, and Merrick knew it wasn't particularly mature, but more pride swelled within him when he sensed some of her pain dull, heat stroking its way within her like it did in himself.

"Your father," Lessia tried again. "He has power over the other noble families. I need him to convince as many of them as he can not to fight. Ideally, they would join us, but I realize it might prove too much of a challenge, so I ask only that they do not fight in Rioner's war. He lost today... and I have a feeling he will do anything in his power not to repeat what happened here. He will ask the Vastala Fae to join the Oakgards' Fae's fight to take down Ellow. So please... please help us convince them not to."

The silence stretching out across both ships as Lessia's words sank into frightened minds roared louder than the wind. While the thought had already crossed Merrick's mind, he had to clutch Lessia tighter as the reality of her words settled within him.

There would be war.

In only a few weeks, there would be bloodshed and death and pain, and Lessia would be right in the middle of it.

"I will do whatever I can." Cedar drew back his shoulders. "I will go straight there."

"Thank you." Lessia touched his hand with her broken one. "Loche has promised to take you as far as he can."

Cedar bowed to her before he backed away. Actually bowed in the way Fae bowed only to their monarchs, and another one of those waves of pride washed over Merrick.

Lessia was born for this.

She might not believe it, but she was born to be a

queen, and even though she might never take on the title —wear the crown her Rantzier blood entitled her—she would always be his queen.

He'd fall to his knees before her any day.

Worship her in the way she deserved.

Follow her every command.

When Cedar reached the other ship and they pulled up their brow, Lessia spun in Merrick's arms, and as she wrapped her own around him, lifting her face to his, he could see she needed to be alone.

Needed to not be the leader.

The sister.

The friend.

The...

He frowned as she continued to stare into his eyes, trying to read the many emotions tangled within her.

No, she didn't need to be alone. Not entirely. Despite everything, he smiled at her.

She needed *him*.

She wanted *him*.

And since she was everything he needed in the world —more than air, water, or food—he wasn't about to waste a single second as Loche's ship lifted its sails and began weaving its way through the waves.

Ignoring Raine and Frelina, Merrick swept Lessia up, cradling her to his chest, and took the few steps to the door leading down to the sleeper cabins on Rioner's ship as quickly as he could.

As he swung the door open, he turned his head and hissed, "Don't you fucking dare come down here," before stalking through it and letting it slam behind them.

CHAPTER 15
FRELINA

She stared at the closed door, and before she had time to think about what she was doing, Frelina took a step toward it.

"I wouldn't do that if I were you," Raine warned from behind her.

Halting, still with her hand outstretched to grip the handle, she asked, "Why?"

She'd seen Elessia in Merrick's arms. Devastation was too weak a word to describe what had blanched her features.

"She needs us," Frelina continued as her stomach clenched at the hollowness of the mask Lessia had worn while she'd huddled with Loche and the others to plan for the next few weeks.

She'd been able to observe her sister the entire time, since no one had invited Frelina to join.

Not that it was surprising...

What could she contribute if there was war?

But she could help her sister. She'd been too overwhelmed so far—had found comfort in Elessia being the strong one. But when she'd spoken to that blond Fae...

A chill raced down Frelina's spine.

It had sounded so ominous somehow—like she'd stepped into a role she didn't want to claim but that was hers all the same. As if Elessia had just... accepted it somehow.

If what she'd accepted was death... No, Frelina wouldn't have that.

She needed to be strong now for her sister. Protect her like she'd protected her parents back then.

Frelina let out a sharp breath as she took another step.

"I really advise against going in there." Raine wrapped his hand around her arm, pulling her back.

"I need to help her," Frelina snarled, trying to escape the Fae warrior's grip.

But Raine wouldn't budge, and she groaned when he only pulled her into the cloud of alcohol stench that always clung to him.

Let me go, you dumb drunk!

She opened her mind to him when her voice wouldn't cooperate, the thickness from all the crying choking her words.

Raine opened his mind back. *Merrick's got her. He'll distract her.*

I'm her sister! Frelina snarled into his head, trying to make it bounce against those thick walls Raine never allowed her through.

Exactly.

She hated the lopsided smile Raine threw her.

Then he sent her a memory, and her body became warm. Then cold. Then warm again.

Low sounds of pleasure, then gentle, loving words, touched a thick wooden door surrounded by white stone, and she could hear Raine sigh as he lifted a hand to knock on it—could feel how little he wanted to pull Merrick and Elessia out of that room.

That's what's going to happen in there, so unless you're someone who likes to listen—and trust me, I don't judge—I'd advise you to stay up here with the dumb drunk.

Frelina shook her head as Raine stepped back and released her arm.

Surely Elessia wouldn't...

Then memories from her growing up filled her thoughts.

How her father had done everything—everything in his power—to keep her mother distracted when they found out she was sick.

Their room had never been quiet. Their kitchen had never been without the newly baked bread her mother loved. Alarin barely ever let his hands leave her mother, even as they walked the forest, even as they bathed, even as they slept.

Even though Fae—including her parents—were open with their love, Frelina blushed, and the blush deepened until her cheeks burned when Raine chuckled and said, "You're as bad as Lessia. She could barely hear me say the word *fuck* before."

Frelina covered her face with her hands, shaking her head. "I'd just rather not imagine my sister doing it."

"So you'd like to imagine someone else doing it?"

Her nostrils flared when she peeked at Raine through her fingers. "No!"

"Are you sure?" Raine took a step toward her as he lowered his voice. "You don't want to imagine someone removing those dirty clothes of yours and using their hands to wash your body so excruciatingly slowly that you burn for them?"

Frelina's eyes widened, and she started backing up, still shaking her head.

But Raine continued approaching her, steadily and deliberately.

"You don't want someone to weave their hands into your hair and drag their lips across the heated skin of your neck, licking and biting every inch of it until you can't breathe anymore?"

Frelina's back reached the door.

Her skin was on fire now, and her face felt as if it were melting, not only because of Raine's words... but because of what they started within her.

Embers of warmth sparked within her core, and as she continued to meet Raine's eyes, meeting the challenge there head-on, she shook her head once more.

Still, Raine took another step.

She held his gaze, seeing something flicker in there, and she took a shallow breath, understanding beginning to form in her mind.

"You don't want someone to claim your lips until you're begging them to claim you entirely?" Raine rasped.

He took another step, and the embers within her became a kindling fire.

"You don't want someone to lift you up and press his co—"

Frelina stepped forward, a laugh bursting from her lips even if fire still touched her cheeks, the cool early morning breeze not helping one bit.

Raine froze.

"I know what you're doing," she purred, grateful when the playfulness hid the slight uncertainty within her that she was right.

"What am I doing?" Raine asked quietly.

Frelina lifted her hands and dragged them down Raine's chest.

He stepped back.

Cocking her head, she raised her brows.

A shadow of a grin brightened Raine's face, his white teeth glinting as light trickled off the horizon, his hair shining like rust in the sun.

"Clever little Rantzier," Raine purred back as he pulled out his flask. "Merrick isn't the only one who can distract people, you know."

Frelina shook her head again as she cast her eyes upward.

While she'd realized he was only doing it to get her to focus on something else—anything else—other than the pain, her own or her sister's, Raine's words had still ignited something in her.

She did want that.

She wanted all of it.

She wanted someone to kindle that fire in her, and she wanted a man's hands worshipping her body. She wanted to forget everything except the moment she was swept up in.

Ideally, she wanted it with someone she loved, but she'd settle for someone she liked too.

Maybe even someone she tolerated.

If war was to come upon them, Frelina probably couldn't be too picky—couldn't wait for a mate who might not even exist if she ever wanted to feel that way.

Raine's brows snapped together for a short second, but it was enough for pink to tint her cheeks again.

She'd forgotten to close her damned mind, but thankfully Raine didn't say anything else.

Not wishing to be left alone even though embarrassment still heated her blood, Frelina followed Raine as he pulled up the anchor—making dragging the thick metal hulk onto the deck seem much easier than it should have been—and when he ventured up to the top deck, taking the helm, she settled onto one of the wooden stools beside it.

He cast her a glance now and again as he began steering the ship west, heading to what she'd overheard being called a middle-realm, a realm that was never named, that never belonged to anyone or anything, and that most apparently thought should be left alone.

"Your sister is strong."

Her eyes flew to Raine's when he spoke.

"I thought she was broken when I met her... but she's not." Raine shook his head, an expression Frelina hadn't seen before crossing his face.

It was...

Hope.

It was hope, she thought, that made the Fae's hazel eyes burn as he stared back at her.

But hope for what?

"She's the strongest person I've ever met," Raine continued. "Even with all this. Even with what she's gone through—the people she's lost, the hurt she's been through and caused, she's fighting back. Not just for him..." Raine's gaze drifted toward the door for a second, although Frelina knew he was referencing Merrick.

"She's doing it because she truly believes in a world

where peace may reign and people of all kinds may live freely. For a world where we are stronger together—united instead of enemies." A scoff left Raine, but it wasn't one that made Frelina think he believed her sister delusional.

No. His eyes were wistful as they followed the sail shifting in the wind.

"She would have loved her." Raine continued staring up toward the sky as he continued. "She would have fought so hard by her side."

Frelina looked away when tears began rolling down the Fae warrior's face, and he quickly pulled out his flask and took deep swallows against the pain he wouldn't let her feel.

Because that's why Raine didn't fully open his mind to her.

She'd thought he was just showing her up. But now she could taste his pain on the wind.

It was brutal.

There was nothing beautiful about it.

It was a pain that should shatter bones. That should crush souls. That should end lives.

Frelina opened her mouth, but no words came out.

What could she say?

His mate—Solana, she'd heard from Merrick once—was dead.

There was no bringing her back—there was no soothing this pain.

So Frelina didn't say anything. Instead, she just sat there—let Raine decide if he wanted to speak again. Let him know she would listen.

They were quiet for so long that the sun moved across the sky, casting their side of the ship in shadows.

When the wind began whistling around them, a shiver worked its way through her body, and she was grateful when Raine sat down on the other chair and swept a blanket around them both.

Frelina stared into the wind, feeling some kind of relief when it wet her eyes again as she asked, "What happens now?"

Raine was quiet for so long that Frelina was about to ask again when he sighed.

"Now we face Ydren's relatives." He lifted a hand when the wyvern, as if called, jumped out of the water and nearly splashed them as she slammed into the surface again. "Then we face the gods."

"H-have you met any of the gods before?" Frelina asked, wondering why the mention of the gods filled her with much more dread than that of the sea monsters.

Even just thinking of them made her bones tremble.

Her father didn't know, but she'd found the books he'd kept from her—the ones detailing how the royal families turned on the ones who created them because of how cruel the gods had become, how they had nearly found a way to kill the gods before they finally left the Old World alone.

"I'm not that old," Raine muttered. "So no."

"How old *are* you, actually?" Frelina teased, earning a scowl back.

When silence stretched on for a bit and it became too loaded to listen only to Ydren's soft splashes and the sails shifting with the wind, Frelina spoke again.

"Do you think the wyverns will listen to her?"

Raine looked out over the sea as he responded. "Ydren has taken to her—says she sees herself in Lessia. I'm hoping that's a good sign. But Ydren also didn't grow up with the other wyverns." He let out a breath. "If you think we Fae are ruthless..."

He didn't have to continue for the air around them to turn chilly.

Frelina wrapped the blanket tighter around herself, unable to stop herself from leaning into Raine when another rush of fear danced over her skin.

The Fae didn't say anything as he lifted his arm, allowing her to settle against him.

But it didn't matter. She didn't need to be in his mind to know facing the wyverns, then the gods, and then the rebels and Oakgards' Fae...

It was too much for anyone to survive.

Even without a prophecy hanging over their head.

CHAPTER 16
MERRICK

Merrick set Lessia down on the bed in a cabin that must have been the king's.

He wondered for a second whether he should try to find another room—find somewhere Rioner might not have tainted the air—but when Lessia settled against the wall, stretching out her legs across the bed and expectantly lifting her gaze to his, he only shot her a quick smile as he sat down beside her.

Sitting like this together—her leg pressed against his, her soft breaths the only thing his ears picked up as his eyes traveled across the table and chair standing in the middle of the room and the small tub in the corner—reminded him for a moment of the election.

When stolen moments like this had been the only time he thought he might get with her.

When he'd had to fight with everything in him not to pull her into his arms.

In Ellow his need to hold her—especially when those fucking humans mistreated her—had been so strong he'd often had to force himself to sit on a chair across the room.

It had probably painted his face with a constant scowl, as he hadn't trusted himself not to curl around her. To try to protect her. Hide her from the cruel world they lived in.

Not that she would have let him, back then... He'd sensed how much she'd loathed him, after all—at least in those first few years.

A low sound rumbled in his chest as he remembered the scent of pure hatred that surrounded her every time he entered a room she was in, and he felt Lessia's eyes landing on his face.

Turning toward her, he noticed the slight wince weaving across her face as the bed shifted, and if her eyes hadn't been so soft, so full of love he wasn't certain he deserved, he would have growled in defiance of the fucking king, and of this whole fucking world.

But that's not what she needed right now, so Merrick gently lifted the hands she had in her lap instead, placing them in his own, and blinked against the crimson hue threatening his vision as he studied them.

They'd injured her so damned much.

But he'd fix it. If it was the last fucking thing he did, he would make her whole again.

After a quick glance at the sheets, he decided against using them for fresh bandages.

He didn't want the king's scent touching her skin.

Not for himself.

Well, not *just* for himself.

But for her.

Pulling his tunic over his head, Merrick didn't care that he wouldn't have another to wear.

He'd walk around naked for the rest of his life if that meant Lessia was warm, her wounds were bandaged, and she didn't have to smell the male who'd hurt her so badly.

Who'd turned her into this...

The shell that sat before him.

He could sense she was still in there, though. The soft, gentle, beautiful soul that only wanted the world to be kind to everyone. But she'd hardened, the purpose he'd felt from her before now at the forefront of her mind, all else within her being pushed to the side.

He watched Lessia as he ripped the black tunic into long strips.

Her eyes moved deliberately over his torso, up over his face, then down again across his shoulders, over his stomach, and down to his crossed legs.

She was fucking memorizing what he looked like.

Savoring it.

As if... as if she might not be able to enjoy it much longer.

Again, he felt like growling. Like destroying something—perhaps this entire damned ship. But he forced himself not to—pulled on the last of his patience to keep his hands moving slowly and steadily.

Merrick started talking as he unraveled the already dirty bandages and checked on the deep wound on her wrist. "This will heal in a day or so."

It already looked much better, especially compared to the broken fingers and hand he worked on next.

"This one will take longer." Merrick traced his fingers over her pale skin, sensing the bone beneath it shifting. "You can't use this hand at all for the next few days. It won't heal right if you do."

The wheezing breath falling from her lips told him she was hurting more than she let her body show, and he stilled for a second.

"It will be all right, Lessia. I... I will fix this."

Merrick cursed to himself. He didn't know what the fuck to say. There was so much to fix, and broken fingers were the least of it.

"You... you don't need to fix this," she whispered.

He was glad Frelina and Raine weren't in the room.

He might have killed one of them for how broken her voice sounded.

"You... cannot fix this, Merrick."

Those five words shattered his heart. Hurt worse than anything he'd ever felt before, and made him want to curl into himself, hide within the mounting cloud of souls pressing all around him.

But he wasn't ready to take it in. Wasn't ready to hear that she didn't mean her hands...

So instead he pushed those thoughts away and growled "Watch me" as he continued replacing her bandages.

Lessia remained quiet as he finished, wrapping the strips of fabric higher up her wrist than before to ensure the broken hand would be properly stabilized.

As he did so, flakes of dried blood fell from her skin, whirling in the slight breeze let in by the dark wooden planks of the walls.

Merrick swallowed, telling himself to be fucking nice and not rip her damned clothing to shreds to examine every single injury immediately. Telling himself to be kind like she'd once told him he was.

"May I?" As he gestured to the jacket he'd given her, he felt like slamming his hand into his face when the anger within him still broke through the words he'd meant to be gentle. But he couldn't hold back the fury rising within him like the hot liquid he'd once seen a mountain spit out in a neighboring realm.

When he'd first seen her on the ship, he'd realized she was injured all over—physically as well as mentally. But what he could smell now...

There was so much fucking blood. Some of it might not still paint her skin red, but it was there... It hadn't been washed off, only been replaced by more.

Another vibration in his chest shook the bed.

Lessia only nodded.

His heart could barely hold on when the woman before him raised her arms—the swallow she seemed to have tried to hold back echoing in the second he stared at her.

Merrick bit down on his bottom lip until the skin broke.

She was worried, not for herself but for what he'd think of her. Merrick could sense the flicker of shame within her as he reached for the jacket.

Fuck.

Fuck.

Fuck.

That wouldn't fucking do.

Moving as slowly as he could, Merrick peeled off the jacket he'd helped her into, and he refused to let his eyes drift away when she was finally freed from the fabric.

When Lessia cast her own down, he reached out to lift her chin.

"You're beautiful." Merrick didn't whisper, forcing his voice to remain strong, to be heard clearly.

He wouldn't let that fucking Torkher win by shying away from what he'd done.

Merrick's name was carved on her stomach.

On her sides.

On her arms, even on the one where the black traitor mark appeared starker than ever against her fair skin.

On her chest, right over her heart.

And from the smell of iron and coal dust, he was certain more of Torkher's carvings lined her back.

"You're so fucking beautiful." Merrick made sure his fingers were assured as they whispered over her skin, not cowering from the words now darkening it.

Shifting her, which was easier than he liked since they must have starved her, he confirmed his suspicions.

Like he'd expected, there were even more dark scars of his name branded onto her.

He knew why Torkher had done it.

The fucking bastard.

He'd done it so she'd hate his name—so she'd look at herself and always be reminded of the dark side of Merrick—and so that Merrick would look at her and always know what they'd done to her.

He would not give that fucker the pleasure.

He'd change his damned name if it came to that—maybe go by only the Death Whisperer.

And before that...

Merrick rose from the bed, helping Lessia to the end of it, setting her feet on the floor before he knelt before her.

As he unsheathed the ruby-decorated dagger, he leveled his eyes with her amber ones. "I want you to mark me."

Her eyes flew wide—then quickly narrowed—and he

expected a *No fucking way* was right at the tip of her tongue, but he spoke before she did.

"I can't stand it." Merrick lowered his voice, pressing the dagger into her hands. "I can't stand everyone knowing you're mine"—his eyes dipped to the scars across her body—"if they don't know that I am also yours."

"Merrick," she started.

"Lessia," he interrupted. "As soon as I saw you in that fucking cellar, I was yours. Perhaps even before. Perhaps I've always been yours, and I've just been waiting for you to come into my life."

Merrick slid his hands up her thighs, staring at her.

"I want to wear your name everywhere across my body." Lifting the arm with his own traitor mark, he angled it so the light from the lonely lantern in the room spilled onto it.

"Like this one, I want yours and mine to be the same. You are mine. I am yours. That's just how it is. The good and the bad and the pretty and the ugly. We will fucking share it all. That's how it was meant to be, and it's how it will always be. I want the world to fucking know it. I want everyone I ever meet to see that every part of me—every dark corner of my soul—belongs to you."

"You are insane," she whispered, the hand holding the dagger trembling, and her pale face still moving back and forth.

"Perhaps." His eyes challenged hers. "But if you won't do it, I'll carve your name across my forehead, and I expect it won't look terribly good, as I'll have to do it in a mirror and it might end up backward."

She laughed then.

A cracked, rough, harsh laugh, and it might have been the most beautiful sound he'd ever heard.

"Please." His knees dug into the floorboards, but he didn't care as he moved to lay his chest across her lap, his arms resting gently around her back. "Please, Elessia."

A chill whispered across his bare skin when it was quiet for a moment, but then she whispered, "I promised never to deny you anything."

"You did." His words were muffled as he pressed his face against her legs. "And this is what I want."

"You're insane." She sighed again, and Merrick expected more protest.

But then a cold blade pressed into his skin, and he'd never been so fucking happy to feel pain.

The entire time she worked on him, he whispered the two words he never wanted her to forget.

"You and me."

CHAPTER 17
MERRICK

He stared at the small bundle on the bed that was his mate—at the brown quilt that moved with her chest as she breathed.

She wasn't sleeping. Not yet. But Merrick hoped the breaths that seemed to become more even now as she rested meant her mind would let her drift away soon.

She'd worked on him for the better part of an hour, and Merrick had obeyed her request when she asked him to straighten so she could reach his chest but not look at what she was doing, and had kept his mouth shut after asking her if she needed a break and she'd growled back that she "might cut into something else" if he didn't stop fussing.

He'd watched her face instead. Watched emotions flash across it faster than he was able to pick up. Watched tears, smiles, frowns, and wistfulness pull at her delicate features, trying not to read too much into what had her moving through all those feelings.

Once she was finished, though, he hadn't missed the slight sway of her body, and thankfully, she hadn't protested too much when he wrapped her in the cleanest blanket he could find, ordering her to lie down or he'd make her.

Merrick rolled his eyes at himself.

He wouldn't—it wasn't like he could order her to do anything anymore. As soon as her eyes met his, it was all over.

She held his heart.

His soul.

His everything.

Even his magic seemed to respond to her. The souls moved differently around her now, had done since she accepted him as her mate.

Merrick shook his head as he tore his eyes away from her small body, approaching the full-length mirror that rested against the wall by the tub.

His eyes lingered on the raised basin as he approached.

If she got some sleep, he could get water, maybe even heat it up for her using the small stove already laid out beneath the wooden tub so she could clean up.

His hands clenched the longer he glared at the stupid tub.

A fucking bath.

That's what he could offer her?

Gods, he'd never felt this powerless before.

Not even growing up in that damned camp with the ruthless older soldiers who loved to abuse their power over him and the others whenever they could. That had stopped as soon as he came into his magic. Even the commanders feared him then, giving him a wide berth whenever he decided to stroll around the encampment.

Merrick's eyes were still on the bath as he halted before the mirror.

He could feel the wounds from the markings Lessia had carved into his body begin to heal, the itching already starting, but he refused to touch them. He needed to ensure the coal dust he'd scraped up from the floor around the tub remained inside as the skin closed.

On a deep exhale, Merrick shifted his gaze to the mirror.

He swallowed deeply.

Then swallowed again.

And again.

Again.

But he couldn't stop the warmth building behind his eyes as they swept across his torso—across the words Lessia had marked his skin with.

Meeting dark, glistening eyes in the mirror as his continued to travel upward, the Death Whisperer nearly recoiled, but then he realized they really were his own.

The agony-filled darkness that seemed everlasting, that should have fled the sockets and taken over the world with its depth, was Merrick's, and so was the hot tear that slipped down his cheek.

He couldn't stop staring at it as it made its way down his blood-splattered face, tickling his cheekbone before sliding across his mouth, leaving an unfamiliar salty taste in its wake as it reached his chin and, after lingering for a second, fell to the floor with such a loud drip that he almost worried Lessia would have heard it and woken from what he hoped was now a slumber.

His eyes rose slowly from the shimmering spot of wetness beneath him, back to the mirror.

Lessia hadn't written her name. Or at least not only her name.

There was one spot, just above where his hip bone jutted out, where she'd carved *Elessia*.

Not *Lessia*.

Not *Elessia Rantzier*.

Just *Elessia*.

His heart clenched.

Then his eyes traveled over the other words she'd etched onto his body.

Love.

Freedom.

Peace.

Children.

Unity.

Acceptance.

Friendship.

Family.

Choice.

Future.

A noise left him—one he'd never heard himself utter.

It sounded almost otherworldly, broken and harsh at the same time. Loving and hating and desperate and calm.

Lessia hadn't only marked him as hers.

She'd carved her hopes and dreams onto his skin.

All her wishes were carefully cut, not a single letter bent or deformed.

All but one.

That strange sound wound its way through his throat again.

On the left side of his chest, right over his heart, she'd carved the one thing she longed for the most.

Time.

Her hands must have shaken, or perhaps tears might have obscured her vision when she etched the final word onto him, because it was the only one where the letters weren't perfectly shaped.

Another trail of dampness snaked down his cheek as his eyes trailed the shaky *t*, the stem of the *i* that wasn't aligned with the dot, the *m* that almost looked like an *n*, and the *e* that swept too far out, the line cutting across his skin like the phantom dagger that now pierced his heart.

Two bandaged hands snaked around his body, the fingers on the hand that wasn't broken fluttering over the word—over Merrick's broken heart.

"For only in their ultimate sacrifice can a new world be born—the world they have dreamed of, battled for, and wept over," Lessia whispered as she rested her cheek against his back.

Tears must have stung her own eyes because while her skin was warm against his, wetness soon followed, and Merrick whirled around, pulling her against his chest more firmly than he should have, with all her injuries.

She melted against him, and he pulled her closer yet, wanting nothing more than to fuse them together, wanting something... anything!

Control. Power. Being able to fucking protect this beautiful soul whose heart hammered so hard against his bare chest he could barely take it, especially knowing it might not beat soon.

When she angled her tear-streaked face to his, he slammed his teeth together, telling himself to be strong.

"What was that you just said?" Merrick whispered back, unsure whether he really should ask the question, as he could sense what the answer would be.

Lessia unwound the hands she'd locked around his back, moving them to clasp his face.

He hated the look in her eyes. He hated it with such a vicious rage that his eyes unfocused for the second it took Lessia to speak.

But when she did, he forced himself to calm down—to listen. To be the fucking support she needed even if he hated every word leaving her mouth.

"It's the end of the prophecy." Her full bottom lip shook as she spoke, and he had to bend down and take it between his teeth, gently tugging on it until a soft gasp made its way into her lungs.

The shudder he was rewarded with as he pressed his lips against hers should have heated every inch of skin that aligned with hers, but when he released her and she continued speaking, the ice that had begun to spread across his heart continued until it felt as if it covered everything within him.

"I need to die for this to come true." Lessia's unbound fingers traced over the words, her eyes dropping down to read what she'd etched onto his skin, and when they lingered by the word *future*, he couldn't fucking take it.

Gripping her hand more gently than he wanted, he pulled it around his back, and securing his own hands around her too-cold cheeks, he tilted her face to his again.

"You don't need to die." Merrick tried his best not to

glower, but he could see he wasn't succeeding, based on the defiance that began to shine in Lessia's amber eyes. "You don't. You're choosing to do it!"

"I didn't choose this," she hissed back.

He wanted to scream at her.

She didn't need to sacrifice herself for a world that had done nothing but hurt her.

He wanted to tell her they could get the fuck away from here—hide somewhere in a realm so far away even the gods wouldn't be able to find her.

But then her eyes softened, her lips lifting into the most heartbreaking smile he'd ever seen, and the words floated away like the pressure of his magic, which had been building under his skin.

"I love you so much," she whispered.

He couldn't take it.

The Death Whisperer shut his eyes.

Wanted to cover his ears like a fucking child.

"I do," Lessia continued. "And I would... I would run with you if I thought it would help. But... I saw it in my father's eyes, Merrick. This curse... this prophecy, it'll catch up with us. Besides, what would it say about me if I ran? I've been hiding my entire life, and it's time to step out of the shadows. Even if only for a short while."

Merrick shook his head, his eyes still crushed shut so hard that colors flickered in the darkness before them.

Fabric scratched his cheek as her cold fingers tapped it.

"You and me," she whispered.

Her fingers continued moving across his face.

Too slowly. Too lovingly. Too fucking kindly.

He couldn't take it. It felt as if his heart would burst.

"Please. Look at me."

Fuck.

His eyes flew open. He couldn't say no to her. He couldn't even fucking argue with her.

You love her because of how selfless she is.

How he wished he didn't.

Why couldn't he have been mated to someone fucking selfish?

Someone like himself.

He didn't care about the world. He'd gladly sacrifice every single person he knew if that meant Lessia lived. But...

"I won't be able to change your mind, will I?" Merrick's eyes hungrily roved over her face, wishing to find a single strain of hesitation.

Just one and he'd fucking throw her over his shoulder again and take off.

But there wasn't any in her beautiful, sunny eyes, nor was there any in her soft features as she tried to hike her smile higher.

"I can't have all this, but you can. You all can." Lessia traced her fingers over his mouth, a flicker of her heat tinging the air as she followed the downward curve of his lips. "I'll go to the gods. Maybe... maybe there is something we haven't thought about. But this is my choice, Merrick."

She didn't need to say what she was thinking for Merrick to understand.

You've always respected my choices.

Lessia's fingers moved down from his face, trailing over his bare skin. "I love you," she whispered again. "Please..."

His mind went to the regent.

Maybe he hadn't been such a bastard for taking a choice away from her.

He'd saved her life, after all, and she'd forgiven him...

But as he continued to stare into her warm eyes, the color of honey—of pure goodness—he couldn't do it.

He didn't know what it said about him. He just... he couldn't.

"Please..." she begged softly once more, and Merrick couldn't stop the sweet scent that invaded his senses as she moved closer to him, her hand wandering farther down.

As his hands fell from her cheeks, she shook off the blanket he'd wrapped her in.

She was entirely naked. Naked, but with blood and dirt and dust covering her beautiful skin. Still, she was the most alluring female he'd ever seen.

His hands moved to her shoulders, and a whimper fell from her mouth as he caressed her skin, careful not to press on any of the wounds that might still pain her.

"Merrick," she breathed.

He would never get over hearing her say his name like that.

She was fucking distracting him.

He knew that, but she also wanted this.

She wanted him—needed him. He could smell it. Fucking sense it. And he'd do anything for her.

As his hands drifted across her perfect skin, down her neck, across her collarbone until they grazed her breasts and a wanting sound escaped her, Merrick promised himself he'd give her everything she wished for.

He'd give her all of it. If not in this lifetime, then the next.

And he'd start with time.

If it was the last thing he did in the wretched fucking world, it would be to give this incredible creature all the damned time he could.

Merrick's eyes were burned onto her face as his knuckles brushed her nipples, his body responding immediately when they hardened at his touch.

His cock stretched against the fabric of his breeches, desperate to get out—to feel her warmth wrapping its silky embrace around it. Especially when Lessia pressed her firm breasts against his hands, another whisper of need leaving her.

But he ignored it.

Time. He was taking his time.

"Come here," he rasped, using every ounce of willpower to turn toward the tub.

"That's going to be cold," Lessia protested, her voice still breathy.

Still, he could feel her following him, always aware of her heat, of her soul, just of *her* wherever she was around him.

He didn't respond as he lit the kindling in the stove beneath the tub, making sure it burned bright before he started pouring water into it using the bucket and the strange contraption that allowed water inside through a long tube when Merrick turned a wooden lever.

It took filling the bucket ten times to get the huge tub filled halfway.

He debated whether he should fill it fully, but given how Lessia hovered behind him, the scent that had begun to fill the entire room... he would probably not be able to stop himself from bathing with her, and it'd spill over anyway then.

Rising to his feet, Merrick drew a deep breath, telling himself to be patient, then he turned toward her again.

His eyes widened upon landing on her. Every time he saw her, she was even more gorgeous—a light in the darkness that was his world.

His breath hitched as a shy smile tugged at her features.

Had it been any of his friends reacting like this, he would have made fun of them.

He'd seen her mere seconds ago. But still... it was like seeing her for the first time, whenever his eyes had rested somewhere else but on her.

She was still naked, her skin peppered by goose bumps, but there was no coldness in her eyes as he stalked the few steps to close the distance between them.

"That's going to take forever to warm up." Lessia's eyes bounced to the water behind him before colliding with his again.

"We have time," Merrick responded as he dragged her to him, folding her body into his. "Besides, the plans I have for you..." He leaned down to whisper against her ear, savoring the hair rising on her neck in response. "They include forever."

Lessia inhaled sharply, and he could feel her body tense against his.

Fuck. That had been the wrong thing to say.

Silently cursing himself, Merrick let his lips brush her ear again, his canines grazing her earlobe. "You might want a cold bath when I'm done with you."

A shudder, and not from worry, coursed through her body.

Fucking better. But not good enough.

Merrick ducked his head further, leaving taunting

kisses down her neck, across her sharp collarbone, and up again, lazily kissing and nipping at her skin until her chest began heaving against his.

He dragged his lips higher, kissing her chin, then her cheek, halting right before her mouth.

Her breath was hot as it hit his lips, and she leaned her head back, giving him better access while finding his gaze again.

Gods, he could fucking come at the molten look turning her eyes almost as golden as when she used her magic when she got excited.

He kept his eyes on her as he pressed his lips against hers.

Soft first, but... Merrick groaned as her lips parted for him to reach better.

She even tasted like sunshine.

Like freedom. Like the dreams he'd had when he was younger. The dreams he'd never spoken to anyone about but which included a warm room, a soft voice calling his name, food, and always, always a bed to sleep in.

He couldn't hold back. Angling her head, he deepened their kiss, a growl building in his chest when she responded immediately, winding her arms around his neck to get closer, to kiss him harder.

His little fighter. Injured, tired, dirty, and devastated, and she still responded to him like this.

He was the luckiest fucking male in the realm.

Guiding her backward as their tongues tangled, Merrick nudged her against the short side of the wooden tub, avoiding the heating stove that crackled on the longer side, so her lower back and legs rested against it.

Merrick moved his hands from her shoulders down to her breasts again, fighting a smile when she yelped as his rough skin brushed over her sensitive nipples as he cupped them.

As he weighed the breasts in his hands, his thumbs grazed the nipples once more, flicking them until she squirmed against him.

"So fucking responsive," he said hoarsely.

This was torture. Sweet fucking torture to hold back when all he wanted was to drive his cock into her, filling her as he listened to her cry out her own release.

Moving his hands to slide down her back instead—excruciatingly slowly—he replaced his fingers with his tongue as his hands circled her perfect ass.

Merrick slid his tongue over the hardened nipples as he pressed her against him, letting her feel how hard he was for her and nearly going mad for the harsh pants that left her as she realized just what she was doing to him.

"This is all you," he murmured against her breasts. "You, your perfect fucking body, your soft skin, and your sweet fucking scent drive me insane."

He sucked a nipple into his mouth and gently settled it between his teeth, pulling on it until she cried out.

"I want to make you come until you cry so loud those fucking gods will wonder what is happening." He moved to the other nipple, biting down on it until his name fell from her lips.

"I want to fuck you until my name is the only thing you can remember." His hands moved to her thighs, sliding up to what he was certain was a throbbing warmth between her legs.

When he stopped right beneath it, even as his hands pressed to continue, she actually whined.

"Please," Lessia begged as she arched against him. "Please, Merrick."

He fucking loved it when she begged.

He fucking loved her so much.

But having her like this? All vulnerable and wanton and desperate for him? Calling his fucking name?

It was too much.

His cock ached as he angled his head upward, watching her face pinch as she struggled against his hands, her legs seeking release on their own.

Merrick rid himself of his breeches, and his cock sprang free, bouncing against her leg, and she moaned as it left a drop of his come behind.

Her broken hand twitched. Fucking twitched, as if she contemplated touching him, and he quickly dropped to his knees, ensuring she couldn't reach him.

"Rest your elbows on the tub," Merrick ordered.

It would have been better if she could hold on, but he wasn't risking her damned hands getting more injured because of him.

She didn't argue, and as she shifted down, her elbows rested against the wooden ledge and her scent exploded around him as her beautiful pussy leveled with his face.

Time.

Give it time, he reminded himself.

But he couldn't hold back the sound of approval winding its way up his throat.

She was glistening.

So fucking wet for him.

"Good girl," Merrick grated as his eyes flew over all the hot silkiness before him.

She was so perfect.

His cock twitched remembering how tight she'd been, remembering the warmth folding around him, and he dragged a finger up her thigh, slowly moving it up her stomach, then down again, resting just above her clit.

Another wave of her scent washed over him, and he groaned as heat shot through his limbs. He was grateful she couldn't touch him right now. He might have fucking come if her skin came anywhere near his cock.

Merrick forced himself to move slowly, but as his fingers sank into her warmth, her pussy opening for him as she spread her legs, it proved impossible.

He groaned again as he cupped her, applying the pressure she needed, and as her head lolled back, he began stroking her, letting his fingers travel between her wet folds, his thumb brushing her clit with a featherlight touch until he drew another cry from her.

Gods, she was so wet.

So fucking ready.

He couldn't wait to sink into all that warm wet heat. But not yet.

Sloppy wet sounds filled the room, and Merrick began moving faster, letting his middle finger tease her entrance until she bucked against him, riding his hand.

"You're so fucking good," he praised. "I love it when you take what you want."

She only whimpered in response, and he finally slipped his finger all the way in.

Her moan was as loud as his own.

He'd known it the first time they were together, but this female would be the end of him.

The absolute fucking end.

Adding another finger, Merrick leaned forward, finally tasting her as he increased his speed.

His hand slapped against her pussy as he drove his fingers into her.

Harder.

Faster.

His tongue lapped at her clit, and he nearly fucking came when she screamed his name, then followed with a jumbled mess of words as she pressed herself against his face.

Yes.

Fight for it, he thought as Lessia ground against him.

Always. Fucking. Fight.

Merrick could feel her walls tightening, so he moved faster, thrusting his fingers deeper into her as his teeth skimmed her clit.

She cried out again, and Merrick bit down on the hard bundle, sucking it into his mouth and adding a third finger when her body shot toward him.

Her heart began beating so hard he wondered if he would be able to see it if he looked up, and when her body began convulsing, he continued sucking, mercilessly driving his fingers into her, and when he curved them...

Her body moved like an arrow leaving the bow.

Quivering. Flying. Shooting through the air.

Slowing his movements, Merrick met her there, shifting his speed to gently move his fingers until she came down, and lapping at her pussy until she squirmed, too sensitive for his touch.

He removed his fingers as he rose, trying to ignore his throbbing cock as he took her in.

Her cheeks were flushed and golden eyes glazed.

A smile graced her beautiful lips.

She licked them as her eyes flew down to his

pulsating length, and he couldn't fucking take it when her eyes melted further—like fucking honey dripping into warm tea.

He had to claim her mouth.

The kiss wasn't soft or gentle.

It didn't speak of time or patience. It was urgent and rushed, and he hissed when she bit into his lip, drawing blood.

Her eyes widened, and he could tell she was about to pull back.

Fuck, he couldn't have that.

"No," he growled as he hoisted her legs up around his waist, setting her ass on the ledge before his cock drove into her all the way to the hilt, making her cry out again as he groaned in response to the wet heat.

"Don't hold back on me," he gritted through his teeth as his balls tightened, warning him he wouldn't last long. "Please, never hold back. Not with me."

"Fuck me, then," she ordered, and it was his time to be surprised.

Lessia's brows rose in challenge, but when she opened her mouth, probably to taunt him, he pulled out, then drove into her again so hard the tub shifted beneath them.

Her moan was muffled by his groan. His need for her was fucking all-consuming, and when she started moving against him, her warmth squeezing around him —everywhere—he didn't hold back either.

His hips slammed against her ass as he angled her to get deeper, and Lessia let out a gasp as he thrust up into her, going deeper than ever before, filling her completely.

Merrick pulled almost all the way out before pushing back in, his movements ruthless as the heat within him continued to build. His hand dipped between them, and he cursed when Lessia whimpered his name as he started working her clit again, making his balls ache for release.

Fuck. This fucking female.

"I'm going to fill you soon," he warned as his thrusts became relentless, the force of them making the tub squeak once more. "You're so fucking wet and warm and perfect, and I fucking need you."

He did need her. He didn't say it, but she was the only thing he needed.

That's why she needed to fight. For him.

Because unlike Lessia, Merrick was fucking selfish, and he couldn't live without her.

"I need you too," she whined as her scent became richer, telling him she was close again and causing his fucking mind to go.

"Wrap your arms around my neck," Merrick forced out, the love he had for her at times like this, when she did what he told her without asking, exploding within him.

His thrusts became brutal when her body fused against his and his fingers dug into her ass so hard it would mark her, but when he softened his grip she snarled—actually snarled—at him, so he firmed his grip, his hips working harder as she began shaking and his cock began throbbing.

What was another mark?

That was his last thought before Lessia called his name again, and hers tumbled from his lips as her pussy squeezed his cock, milked it until he spilled within her, curses flying from him as her legs locked around his back, holding him impossibly closer.

Merrick's arms shook as he came down from the high that only she could conjure, and his chest heaved against her as he carefully set her down on the side of the tub again.

Still, the movement made the water within it splash —which it probably had before as well, but they just hadn't noticed—and when the drops landed on Lessia, she grinned at him. A huge, wide, warm smile that sent another rush of heat through Merrick.

"It's actually warm."

CHAPTER 18
LESSIA

An impenetrable mist had formed ahead of their ship, and a chill wove its way down Lessia's back as she stared at it, tried to see anything through the thick white wall, but a sigh rushed out of her as she squinted at the whirling air.

It was useless.

They'd begun to glimpse it a few days ago, and she'd already asked Merrick and Raine several times if they were certain—truly certain—that this was the way they must go.

Unfortunately, it was. This unnamed land between realms that appeared shrouded in mist was where the wyverns supposedly lived, and further in... that's where they'd find the Lakes of Mirrors.

It was believed the wyverns had chosen this location because of its proximity to where Fae could call upon the gods.

Not that anyone did it anymore, not after the war, where the Fae drove the gods from all known realms. No one even ventured out here, as the Fae feared retribution for the bloodshed and violence they'd brought upon the world by turning on their masters.

Lessia wrapped her arms around herself. She wasn't particularly looking forward to meeting the wyverns or the gods.

She could still hear the way the wyverns had whispered her last name—the warning in it.

A warning not to come here?

She wasn't sure, but it hadn't been good.

"You cold?" Frelina sidled up to her, pulling a cloak that Lessia was pretty sure was Raine's around her shoulders.

Dropping her arms, Lessia shook her head. "Just... apprehensive."

Frelina hummed as her eyes also drifted toward the towering wall of clouds before them.

It was so close now. They'd sail into it today.

Lessia fought the urge to fold into herself again.

She needed to be strong, just a little while longer. Just until it was her time, she'd hold it together—be the person the ones she loved could lean on.

She didn't want to see Merrick's eyes fill with that pain she knew he only allowed when he thought she wasn't looking.

But he didn't know she was always looking. She needed to memorize every line of his sharp features, his broad shoulders, his tall and muscular body, before it was too late.

Perhaps it had been rash to tattoo him with her hopes and dreams...

But she'd needed it then—had needed him to know what she wanted.

Because if he knew, maybe… maybe he wouldn't follow her into death but experience all the things she wished she had time to.

But even if she wished for it, she doubted it. Lessia could see his mind working every time his eyes rested on her, how he seemed to explore every possibility of saving her life. Even if it was as useless as trying to see through the damned mist.

"Is she practicing reading your mind again?" Raine called from a level higher up, where he steered the ship right onto the path Lessia wished they could divert from. "Do I need to come save her from perishing from embarrassment?"

"Shut up," Frelina grumbled back. "Besides, I don't need to practice."

Despite her words, flames began licking her sister's cheeks, and Lessia slapped a hand over her mouth, turning away from the two of them when the memory flashed before her eyes of Frelina digging into her mind right after she'd spent two days locked in that room with Merrick showing her his interpretation of love and time.

Lessia knew her sister had only been worried, and she'd felt guilty at the time, leaving Frelina to fend for herself with Raine, but Merrick—and if Lessia was honest, *she*—had needed the time together.

And so, instead of picking up any feelings Lessia might have about their father or perhaps her fate, Frelina had been shown a very detailed memory of Merrick's skills with his fingers.

That's at least what Raine had told them between wheezing bouts of laughter.

Her sister had panicked and sprinted into the room

she'd apparently slept in, and it had taken Lessia hours to get her out again.

Frelina still couldn't meet Merrick's eyes, and Raine teased her sister about it every moment he got, which were many, given there wasn't much else to do on this ship besides talk as they sailed toward the towering wall of white.

Lessia turned to where she knew Merrick was watching her.

His eyes flared when he picked up what feeling coursed through her body, and she could tell he was contemplating dragging her inside the cabin and locking her in the room where they'd spent the majority of the time in the past few days.

But when Raine spoke again, she subtly shook her head, letting her eyes drift toward Ydren, who popped her head over the side of the vessel, curiously watching the four of them, before shifting back to her sister.

Frelina seemed to require some backup right now.

Lessia was certain of her decision to remain by her sister's side when Raine spoke again.

"Little Rantzier, it's been days, and you still light up like fire in winter whenever we mention it." Raine leaned over the gunwale, his hazel eyes glittering even in the gray light enveloping them and the ship. "Where is the sass from our first night together?"

"It's because it was my sister, you bastard." Frelina took a step toward Raine, angling her scowling face to his. "I wish to scrub my entire mind after seeing it, and I'd prefer not to be reminded all the time."

"But it's such fun reminding you." Raine grinned widely before unscrewing the top of his flask and taking a sip. "It's almost as good a distraction as this." He waved the small bottle in the air.

"If you come down here, I'll distract you." Frelina grinned back, although Lessia was unsure whether whatever her sister's lips were doing could be called a smile. It was more of a warning teeth-showing.

Leaning his elbows on the wood, Raine cocked his head. "Such big words for such a small person."

Lessia hid a smile when her sister's leg twitched.

Frelina had definitely been seconds away from stamping her foot.

"Are you one to talk?" Frelina purred, and Lessia had to bite her cheek not to snort when her sister suggestively popped a hip. "I think we both know who would be a coward in the end."

Lessia's eyes almost popped out of their sockets when Frelina went on to toss her hair, then dragged her other hand down her neck as she licked her lips, and she could sense Merrick turn around as well, facing the sea as he fought a deep chuckle.

Raine opened his mouth.

Then closed it again.

"Exactly," Frelina challenged. "Go steer the little ship now, Captain."

The giggle Lessia had suppressed burst out of her when Raine stomped back to the helm, and she could tell Merrick was laughing as well where he stood a few feet away, in the bow, the shaking of his shoulders betraying him.

"What was that?" Lessia asked as Frelina returned to her spot beside her, her words coming out softer than she meant because of the lack of air from her laughter.

"It's just a dumb game we've come up with." Frelina

wouldn't meet her eyes as she rested her hands on the railing, her gaze trailing Ydren swimming beside the ship.

Lessia mirrored the movement, grateful that the past week had healed her hands to the point that she didn't need to wear bandages anymore, even if the broken one still ached at night.

"It doesn't seem too dumb to me," Lessia responded carefully, sensing her sister hadn't been exactly truthful about her feelings, from how her shoulders tensed.

"It is." Frelina's face pinched for a second. "He pretended to flirt with me that first night to distract me from..."

They shared a look, and Lessia didn't have to be a mind reader to know what Frelina was thinking about.

Her father's cold body. The blood beneath him dripping through the wooden planks. The sorrow in Raine's and Merrick's deep voices as they sang the song Fae soldiers sang when one of their own died in battle.

Lessia swallowed hard before she asked, "You don't... like it?"

She'd get Raine to stop if it actually bothered her sister this much. A fierce protectiveness washed over her as she cast her eyes upward toward the red-haired Fae. She'd even use her magic on him, if it came to that.

Especially seeing glassiness fill Frelina's eyes.

"It's... it's not him," Frelina whispered, and pressure laced Lessia's chest. "I... I just will never have the real thing. I know... I know it's horrible what's awaiting you, but... I can't help but be jealous of what you and Merrick have. Even... even what you had with Loche."

Lessia tried everything she could to catch her sister's

eyes, but Frelina refused, the tip of her nose turning pink from holding back tears.

Lessia squeezed the railing, ignoring the soreness in her newly healed hands.

She'd been so wrapped up in her own pain. In Merrick's pain. In her sister's pain over their father's death. But she hadn't thought...

Her sister was right, though. She might not be part of the curse, but with how things were looking now... not many of them would make it out alive, especially the ones of them who weren't vicious centuries-old Fae warriors.

"I'm sorry," Lessia whispered.

"I know." Frelina moved so her shoulder brushed Lessia's. "I'm sorry too."

A thickness filled Lessia's throat as she croaked, "I know."

By birth, the two of them had been doomed. Halflings born to the brother of the king—the king who hated their kind more than anything else.

Her father had tried to give them some kind of life by hiding them away.

But what was life in the shadows?

Yes, Lessia might have wished not to have some of the experiences she'd had to endure...

But she'd lived.

She'd loved.

Frelina, on the other hand...

Tears welled in her eyes as she pressed closer to her younger sister.

Frelina needed time too.

"It's almost upon us," Frelina murmured, and Lessia sensed Merrick had come up behind her, his arms circling her, always protecting her, always there. She leaned into his touch as she met Ydren's large eyes, but as she opened her mouth to respond, the world went white.

And then...

She was alone.

Lessia whirled around, but there was only white around her. Beneath her. Above her.

"Merrick!"

Then:

"Frelina!"

She tried to call their names again, but it was as if the mist around her swallowed her voice, like cotton filled her chest. Stumbling forward on the surprisingly hard floor beneath her, she squinted, throwing her gaze around.

It was all white, but somehow...

The white reminded her of the pressing darkness she'd been forced into in Rioner's cellar, and her pulse began thrumming under her skin, the sound rushing in her ears as she turned her head back and forth, trying to make out something—anything.

Why have you come here, Elessia Rantzier?

Lessia jerked straight at the deep voice, but not from fear. No, for some reason... the voice was familiar.

She waited a beat, trying to get her mind to understand why the voice felt like home.

She doesn't even deign to respond.

Another voice that sounded... Her nails dug into her palms as she blinked at the brightness around her. It was her mother's voice.

Yet... it wasn't.

And the first one... It was Merrick's.

But also not.

"Who are you?" she snarled, fighting the suffocating feeling of the mist filling her lungs.

You came for us, yet you don't know who you seek?

Frelina's voice, but it was also off. Just a tad too high —the tone just a little wrong—and it didn't carry the defiance that laced Frelina's words most of the time.

"You're the wyverns." Lessia tried to keep her voice level as worry for the others formed a ball of unease in her gut and the thick whiteness still fought to suffocate her.

Took you long enough.

They did get Raine's snark perfectly, and she spun toward the voice, almost expecting his red hair to break through the world of white.

But there was nothing.

"What is this?" Lessia asked when it remained quiet, her own heartbeat the only sound pulsating through the mist.

You're asking the wrong questions.

She didn't think it would be possible not to want to hear Merrick's voice.

But this strange one... It was wrong. It was eerie, and the lilt of it raised the hairs on the back of her neck.

"Stop with your mind games," she gritted through her teeth. "Show yourselves."

But we're not the ones with the mind games, are we?

A vision of herself and Loche, with her father and Rioner standing behind them, forced its way into her mind. Agony, pure agony, raced over her skin as she was transported right back to that moment, listening to herself utter, "Forget me. Forget every moment we had alone. Forget you ever felt anything for me. You will only remember me as the spy, the traitor that tried to ruin your election."

Such a dangerous gift.

Lessia watched her own knees buckle before she snapped her eyes shut and snarled, "Enough! I've lived through this enough!"

She really had. Yes, she might feel guilty for the rest of her life for what she'd done to him. Especially now... especially knowing why he'd done it. But she'd decided to live with it.

Like she'd live with every decision she'd made and would make in the future.

Until you won't. We've heard all about your curse, princess of Vastala.

"I am no princess," Lessia hissed, the unease she'd felt hearing this strange version of Merrick's voice shifting into anger, which somehow made it easier to clear her lungs of the strange air. "I claim no allegiance to my uncle. Besides, if you have heard so damned much about me, then you know exactly why I am here. No need for all of these theatrics."

Of course we know. As soon as you tricked that stone into choosing you, we felt you everywhere. Heard and saw and learned everything about you. Who you love. Who you hate. Your fears—and you have many. Your wishes. Yes... the ones you carved into your mate's skin.

"I didn't trick anything. And stop using Merrick's voice," Lessia warned, sensing her magic flicker to life, her eyes reflecting strangely onto the white wall before her.

But you love the Death Whisperer's voice. You fear you'll forget it when you die. And you will.... Trust us.

Lessia refused to let the words sink in.

She would never forget him—it wasn't possible.

She wouldn't let herself.

Whirling, her eyes throwing that ominous glow around her, she thought that the white surrounding her must be some type of magic that let the wyverns see and speak to her.

As soon as you tricked that stone into choosing you, we felt you everywhere. Heard and saw and learned everything about you. They'd betrayed themselves, and... it tasted like magic—the thick white air reminding her of the stickiness of Merrick's souls as they layered around her.

While she couldn't compel magic—the memory of the moment she tried to stop her father's magic drove a sharp pain through her heart—if the wyverns could see her...

The encounter underwater with Ydren surged through her mind, her violet eyes glossing.

I haven't met anyone who could control wyverns before. That's what Raine had told her back on his island.

Something in the air shifted, a tremble—a flicker of uncertainty—and Lessia knew she was right.

Staring straight ahead, watching her own eyes reflect back, she purred, "You will show yourselves, and you will listen to what I have to say."

Told you she was clever.

They did get Frelina's voice right that time, Lessia thought as the world flashed.

Then it went dark for a second before her eyes flew open.

"Lessia! For fuck's sake!" Merrick's eyes were an inch from hers, his gaze flying across her face.

Frelina was a few inches behind him, Raine holding on to her as they stared down at Lessia.

"I'm fine," Lessia said hoarsely, that suffocating feeling lingering.

"You're not fucking fine," Merrick growled, but he appeared to catch himself, his face still hard but lips pressing tightly together when she glared back at him.

Lessia cleared her throat when he remained silent. "I am. I promise."

Merrick's eyes shut for a second as he blew out a breath through his nose, and when they opened, his face softened—at least to her trained eyes.

To Frelina, he probably still looked furious.

Still, when he asked, albeit gruffly, "Do you want to get up?" and she nodded, he was gentle, his arms sliding under hers to help her to stand.

"Your eyes went completely white, and you passed out," Frelina said softly. "You almost scared us to death."

Merrick was terrified is what Frelina's eyes told her, and Lessia stepped closer to the Death Whisperer, leaning into him and wrapping an arm around his waist.

But even though she could hear his heart hammer against his rib cage, when she looked up and met Ydren's eyes, she knew there wasn't time for her to make him feel better.

Lessia bowed her head when Ydren cast hers back, and stated, "The wyverns will be here any moment."

CHAPTER 19
LOCHE

When Zaddock sighed again for the tenth time in minutes, Loche spun around from where he'd stood in the bow, letting the cold wind rush through his hair, and faced his friend.

"I know you're angry, Z, but it was necessary." His eyes bore into Zaddock's blue ones—the ones that appeared to become more and more defiant by the day and that had Loche's gut coil in ways he'd never experienced before.

"I don't understand why I couldn't go with them!" Zaddock shot him a glare back, his entire body twisting with disdain. "You have those Fae bastards. Why do you need me?"

Loche closed his eyes for a moment, trying to find an ounce of patience within him.

Yesterday, he'd sent Amalise, Ardow, and Venko to meet the ship with Geyia and the half-Fae children they'd left behind when they went to find Lessia after that disastrous meeting with King Rioner.

He'd debated for days whether it was worth breaking up the group, especially in enemy waters, but... from what he'd heard from Amalise and the reports from Geyia and Steiner, some of the older Faelings could potentially be quite useful.

They would need them. He didn't want to say it aloud, but while Kerym and Thissian were rumored to be powerful, he'd seen little of their supposedly feared magic the past few days when they'd sailed through Korina's waters, heading toward Ellow and keeping an eye out for the rebels.

And Loche knew Meyah and her people were close. He could feel it in his bones, and his spies had also seen Meyah's ships on the same path they were on.

The final conversation he'd had with Lessia and the others echoed in his mind as his eyes flew across the empty rocky isles flanking his ship.

"Rioner will not risk another failure," Lessia mumbled.

"He won't," Kerym agreed. "He'll come for us. All of us. It's how he works."

Merrick nodded slowly. "You're right. He'll attack when the rebels do. It's what makes most sense. He won't want to waste any more time, and he'll bet on..." The Death Whisperer's face hardened so much with pain that everyone but Lessia and Loche looked away. "He'll bet on Lessia dying in the fight."

Loche couldn't help but let out a shuddering breath when Lessia didn't argue, only stepped closer to the silver-haired Fae, letting him fold both his arms around her.

As if that would protect her. As if any of them could protect her from what was to come.

"So, how can we gain an advantage?" Loche asked when

he couldn't take watching the woman he still loved try to stay strong for another man.

Especially when he knew... Rioner would win the bet. Loche had known the Fae King long enough to know he wouldn't give up, not until Lessia took her final breath.

"We're doing what we can," Kerym responded as his blue eyes landed on one of the copper-haired sisters who appeared to be eyeing him right back, from what Loche could tell. "If we can get the wyverns on our side, we have a chance. And... if we can get the rebels to stand down, we will win."

"Don't forget about Cedar." Lessia's eyes brushed his, but Loche had to look down at the hope that shone in them. "He might convince some of the Fae to, if not fight, at least stand down."

The look Merrick, Kerym, and Thissian shared didn't instill the same hope in Loche.

"We should find a spot to fight that's favorable to us." Kerym's brother's voice was soft, but it wasn't a whisper. "Force Rioner, the Oakgards' Fae, and the rebels to meet us where we are."

Loche's eyes found Zaddock's, and for once, his friend's weren't locked on the blonde woman he followed around.

Nodding as Zaddock's gaze darted north, Loche cleared his throat. "We have such a place. There is an island on the outskirts of Ellow. It mirrors Korina with its high cliffs, but there is a plateau on it as well. It'll allow some of us to be out of the water."

Merrick broke in. "That's good. Rioner will use his water skills in this fight, so if we can strategically place a few of us on land, we can try to counter them. Although those Oakgards' Fae wield earth powers."

"Isn't their magic impacted?" Kerym asked.

"We're not certain how their curse works," Merrick

muttered, the iciness in his voice almost as chilling as the haunted look on his face. "I don't think we can count on it. Besides... they are desperate. And you know as well as I do what happens with desperation in war."

An involuntary chill had Loche raise his shoulders.

So many enemies. So many things that could go wrong, and so few paths to win.

They'd finally decided it was best for everyone if they drew Rioner and the Oakgards' Fae who would fight beside him, as well as the rebels, to the spot outside Ellow. The rebels planned to attack Ellow anyway, and this was the best way to keep his people safe.

"Are you all right, Loche?" Zaddock's voice softened.

Loche definitely didn't prefer it to the grouchiness.

He'd let Zaddock down.

He'd let everyone in Ellow down.

For what? To save the woman he loved.

That had turned out really fucking great. He'd hurt her so badly she'd never look at him the same way again, and who could blame her?

He was so damned stupid.

"I need you here because I don't expect the rebels to *just speak* to us," Loche said, responding to Zaddock's earlier question as he refused to meet his friend's eyes. "I need everyone I can spare, and last I remember, you were quite skilled with the sword."

"Loche..." Zaddock hesitated, and Loche dragged his hands through his hair, wondering how to stop him from asking if he was all right again.

Of course he wasn't.

He'd fucked up so bad. Ellow was in danger. So were his people. His friends.

Lessia.

"We all need to do what we can now." Loche didn't mean for his words to come out so harsh, but guilt was eating him up, and he could hardly stand it.

At least before, he had been able to think about the woman he'd done it for... But now?

It just made it all worse.

"We will." Zaddock placed a hand on his shoulder. "I... I'll be by your side until the end. I made you that vow once, and I will keep it."

Loche fixed his gaze on an especially large rock formation to his left, even as he felt Zaddock's gaze whisper across his face.

Because it would end for them, wouldn't it?

He'd seen it in the Fae warriors' eyes. In Ardow's hesitant nod when Loche asked him to get the Faelings—those who had decided they wanted to fight for Ellow. He'd heard it in Zaddock's shaky voice when he'd spoken to Amalise as she'd climbed into the small rowing boat without a goodbye.

It had only been Lessia who had some ember of hope lighting her amber eyes.

Not for herself... No, he'd seen that same acceptance in her that was mirrored within himself. Neither of them would survive this war, but she had hope for the world...

After everything, she had hope for this realm.

For the people she expected to leave behind.

That's where they differed.

Loche shook his head. He had no idea how she did it.

"Regent." Kerym, the more talkative of the raven-haired twins, approached the two of them, and Zaddock's hand fell from his shoulder as Loche turned to face the Fae.

"What is it?" His brows furrowed as he studied the Siphon Twin, the worry marring his tan forehead.

"I sense something." Kerym met his eyes briefly before his own shot across the water and dark isles around them. "Magic. Someone or something with magic is nearing."

The two sisters—Loche had no idea why they stayed around—approached as well, halting right behind the Fae.

"The rebels are close." Pellie placed a hand on Kerym's shoulder, and Loche didn't miss the slight jerk running through the Fae as he tried to plaster a playful grin across his features as he faced her. "You need to get your brother, handsome."

"How do you know?" Kerym asked, his eyes flitting from the small hand on his shoulder to Pellie's huge green eyes.

"We just do," her sister interrupted. "We need to be ready."

Loche slowly moved his narrowed eyes between the sisters when Zaddock stepped forward. "There. There is a small boat by the formation that looks like a cloud over there."

Loche's eyes shot in the direction his friend waved toward, and sure enough, a small white rowing boat approached them from between the islands.

It was still too far away for him to see clearly, but Kerym, who benefited from a Fae's sharp vision, mumbled, "It's only three people. A woman in the front—she's definitely a shifter—with two half-Fae escorting her."

"How do you know they're escorting her?" Zaddock

asked, and Loche was thankful for it, since the question immediately filled his mind as well.

"They're watching her the way Fae watch their leader." Thissian joined them, throwing a quick look at the small woman still clinging to his brother before shifting his dark blue eyes to Loche's. "They're there for her protection."

"Who is she?" Loche wasn't sure why he asked.

Not when he was certain it must be the elusive rebel leader who always seemed to be a step ahead of him.

For years, his spies had failed to find her. He'd even gone out in search of her himself for a few months, but it had been impossible. It was as if she didn't leave any traces wherever she decided to reside.

"She is who you suspect," Soria responded, stepping closer to him while her sister remained between Kerym and his brother.

Zaddock also stepped forward so they all stood in a row, facing the small boat, which moved so much faster than their own, catching up with them in what felt like seconds, even though they hadn't set anchor.

When the boat sidled up to Loche's ship, a chain was thrown onto their deck, the clanking jarring them all, snapping them out of the thick silence they waited in.

As a ladder followed the chain, landing on the side of the ship with a soft thud, Soria leaned into him and whispered, "You will be all right, regent. Just remember who you are."

His brows snapped together, but he didn't have time to ask what she meant as a dark-haired woman elegantly climbed over the railing, sweeping her long hair over one shoulder when she looked up at the group with a serene smile as the two half-Fae swiftly followed her.

Loche's back shot straight as he took in the familiar face, and when sharp gray eyes landed on his... he couldn't help but gasp, "Mother?"

CHAPTER 20
LESSIA

Lessia still held on to Merrick as the mist parted ahead, the white no longer trailing down Ydren's violet scales as she remained close to their ship, the low hums in her throat echoing around them as she led the way when the fog faded, until it evaporated entirely, revealing a crystal-blue sea filled with large rock formations jutting high above the water.

Despite the warm wind wrapping around them, snow covered the highest peaks towering over the sea, and Lessia frowned as the scent of winter and summer tangling filled her nose.

She could sense Merrick's muscles coiling under the tunic he'd found—the one that was slightly too small but which she'd never complain about seeing him in, as she could watch every ripple playing beneath it—his entire being reacting to the strange sensations around them.

Out of the corner of her eye, she glimpsed Raine approaching them until he stood next to her sister, his massive body so large compared to Frelina's, Lessia took a step closer to her sister, even if she knew Raine wasn't a threat to her.

Merrick stepped with her, and she shot him a quick smile before facing forward again, keeping an eye on Ydren, who appeared nervous, her maw twitching as she whipped her head back and forth.

Then their ship halted so abruptly that they all had to grip the railing not to fall.

"Did we hit something?" Raine hissed.

"No," Merrick said in that low voice that used to terrify her. "Something swam into us."

Ydren let out a squeaking sound before she moved backward, and it was their only warning before the vessel heeled sharply, then slammed back down into the sea.

Merrick dragged her to him, one of his hands locking around her waist as he planted his feet, while the other found his sword.

Lessia shakily unsheathed her ruby-decorated dagger as well—trying not to think about how they hadn't been able to find the one her father had given her, the one with amber stones to mirror her eyes—but when Merrick's grip on her tightened for a second, she knew he'd felt that quick sweep of sadness that washed over her.

She was grateful when Raine pushed Frelina behind him, his curved blades glimmering in the sun, which now hung high above them.

Frelina hadn't wanted to train with weapons when the rest of them had done so on that ship to Ellow a few weeks back, and while the Fae males had tried to convince her, they'd stopped when Lessia had snarled at them.

She'd seen the way Frelina had stared at her daggers, and she suspected that was how Frelina had killed those soldiers who had found their island when her father had been too distraught over their mother's sickness.

A strange sound began thrumming around them, and Lessia pushed aside all other thoughts, apart from staying alive.

Just one more day.

Just a little bit longer.

Vivid colors—as if a rainbow had fallen from the sky and now began spinning around their ship—appeared before her eyes, and even though she blinked, she couldn't make out any shapes, the movements of whatever was swimming in the water around them too fast even for her Fae eyes.

She guessed it was the same for Merrick and Raine, given the vicious rumblings starting in their chests, and when Merrick bent down to press his lips against hers—feverishly, harshly—she knew they were as worried as she was becoming.

Goose bumps peppered her body as she tried to keep her head steady, something inside her warning her not to lose focus, but when Ydren let out a scared sound—one that pierced Lessia's heart like an arrow—she whipped it around.

It was as if she walked into a wall of nausea, and she brought her free hand to her mouth at the same time as Merrick pressed her harder against his quivering body.

"Don't let them get to you," he warned. "They're trying to confuse us."

Lessia started to nod but froze when that voice—the

one that sounded like Merrick's but also didn't—echoed in the air as the colors began spinning even faster.

We're here now, princess of Vastala, but you don't seem to have anything to say.

It switched to her sister's voice.

And you brought one of us. Where did she come from?

"Stop using their voices," Lessia snarled. "And stop whatever it is you're doing."

"Who are you talking to?" Frelina asked, her voice breaking up as Raine dragged her closer to him.

"Maybe she's finally lost it," Raine mumbled when Lessia hesitated, but he quickly snapped his mouth shut when Merrick growled in warning.

"It's the wyverns," Lessia said softly as she tried to listen for those voices again.

It was strange how she heard them. It wasn't like they were in her mind, but... like they were in another's.

She didn't read minds, though...

She's figuring it out. The soul stone...

Hush! The fake Merrick voice filled with anger.

A sharp light shot from Lessia's arm—the one the stone had merged with—and she realized from the gasps leaving Raine and Frelina that even though the rest couldn't hear the voices, they, too, could see the glow.

Merrick only seemed to stiffen further, his grip on her tightening so much she might have complained had they been in another situation.

"The soul stone..." she whispered to herself, feeling that flicker in the air again—the one she'd felt in the white mist.

Fear. Worry. Anger.

"I feel them," Lessia said. "I hear them and I feel them."

We felt you everywhere. Heard and saw and learned everything about you.

"You hear and see and feel me too," she mumbled.

Her mind went to the conversation she'd had with Merrick that first night they had together.

"I feel your emotions." That's what he'd told her when she thought he'd read her mind, but he'd only felt her emotions because of the mate bond.

"We're soul-bonded," Lessia exclaimed.

"What are you talking about?" Frelina's head had begun snapping back and forth despite Raine holding on to her, and her sister's skin color had faded from a soft glow to a green hue.

"You feel them." Merrick leaned down, his stubble brushing her cheek as he stared out across the water, where those colors still revolved like a vibrant rope around the ship, and she realized he was catching on. "You hear them."

They weren't questions.

"You should be able to see them."

Glancing up at him, she realized he didn't mean to *actually* see them, not with her eyes.

She'd been able to compel Raine and Kerym in her mind when they tied their own to it, so if the wyvern's souls were bound to hers and they could hear what she was thinking like the mind-reading Fae... that meant their minds were linked, didn't it?

It was at least worth a try.

"Hold on to me?" She didn't mean for it to come out so soft, but those voices—how they tried to mimic her loved ones—unsettled her.

"Always." Merrick held her gaze until she couldn't

bear it, until she realized there was no way he'd live on and live the dreams she'd hoped might convince him.

Closing her eyes, she focused her gaze inward until the sounds around her muted. Until she didn't feel the wind or the occasional splash of salt water brought by the sea. Until Merrick's arm around her waist was the only thing she could feel.

Her mind was dark, but it wasn't the darkness of Rioner's cellars.

It didn't have the desperation to it.

It was sadness. It was sorrow. It was grief.

It was... her emotions.

But as she looked around, truly made herself look at every dark swirl, she noticed things within the darkness.

A bright light shone ahead, and it looked like the stone Loche had pressed into her hand—the one that now lived within her—and she almost took a step toward it when she realized.

It wasn't the wyvern's light. This one... It belonged to another.

A silver-haired, feared Fae warrior. One who lit fires and lanterns and set her own body and mind alight, driving away even the most unfathomable darkness.

She could taste the love wafting from the sparkling ball.

His and hers combined. Wildness and kindness and loyalty and passion and acceptance. Lessia couldn't help but smile as it sparked brighter when she stayed in that feeling for a moment.

Gods, she loved him so much.

More light poured out of the ball.

I love you too, it seemed to say.

She wished she could stay there—stay in all that

warmth and love and pain-free space—but there wasn't time. Tearing her eyes away, which was much harder than she liked to admit, Lessia scanned the rest of the space.

There was another light. One that was filled with many, almost like a bundle of threads of different colors with a more muted glow. One in particular stood out—a violet thread shining brighter than the others—one that was part of them, but also wasn't. One that was more part of herself.

"Ydren," she whispered, and was rewarded with a slow roll of the thread, almost as if the wyvern heard her.

Another thread also caught her eye. It was golden, thicker than the others, and also appeared to be connected to them all, even Ydren.

After hesitantly walking up to it, Lessia hovered her hand over the bundle.

It purred, almost like a feline, the threads vibrating against each other, and that strange feeling whirled around her—the tangle of emotions so intense she couldn't pick out just one.

"I guess this is it." Lessia aimed for the golden thread, letting her fingers wrap around it.

Her body jerked upright immediately.

Golden eyes set in a large face covered by golden scales—the color reminding her of old honey, a bit darker than her own molten eyes reflected in them—met hers.

She didn't hesitate, and she made sure her instructions were more precise this time.

"I want you to show yourselves, and not like you're doing now. One by one, standing still, please. And I want you to listen to me until I am finished talking."

The threads around the golden ones vibrated for another second before they all stilled, and voices sounded as if from far away.

"Lessia! You did it!" her sister exclaimed.

"Lessia, enough," Merrick urged softly.

But a strange sensation filled her, like she was full of energy, like it was racing across her skin.

And for the first time in a while, she felt...warm.

"Lessia." Merrick's voice became more demanding.

Power.

It was power.

This is what that felt like, she thought as she played with the golden rope, savoring the warmth filling her chest and dancing through every vein and limb.

She was holding so many lives in her hands. Lives that she could tell what to do, that she could control, that she could lead.

"Lessia!"

A surge shot through the darkness, and she blinked, turning her head toward the ball of light she'd eyed before.

It was telling her something.

Open your eyes.

It's enough now.

But was it enough?

She was always weak, always the one beaten down.

The one tortured. The one hurt. The one cast away.

It's enough for now, my little fighter.

She blinked at the light again, and Merrick's love brushed her skin, replacing the powerful heat with his scorching one.

Lessia shook her head as an urge to walk to his light overcame her, but it was the thought that if she could compel the wyverns like this... she could do it to Merrick, too, that finally had her eyes fly open.

Even with the sun above them, it wasn't as bright as Merrick's light had been in her mind, but she still had to bat her eyelids a few times to take in the scene before her.

Wyverns of all colors and sizes floated in the water ahead of them. Behind them. To their sides.

Some of the larger ones had their wings displayed—which she'd learned from Ydren was a sign of warning to an enemy, a sign they could attack at any moment.

Maybe she should have asked the wyverns not to kill them as well.

But as the thought struck her, she realized she could still feel their minds, and when she blinked... she could see it so clearly—she would be able to control them even now.

A large golden wyvern let out a screech that had Merrick pull her against his chest, his sword flying out before them, and from the metallic sound to her right, Raine was also readying himself.

"That's a lot of fucking wyverns," Raine muttered.

"It's fine." Lessia gently shoved at Merrick's arm. "They won't hurt us."

He didn't seem so sure, but as he always did—as he always would do—he released her, and Lessia cast a quick look at their group before she approached the railing.

Frelina's face was white, that greenish hint still present in her cheeks.

Raine seemed focused—his square jaw set as he kept Frelina behind him, his curved blades crossed before them.

Merrick appeared furious, and she almost had to bite back a smile when his black eyes roved over every single wyvern as if he was figuring out where his sword would hurt the most.

Ydren hovered so close to their ship she might have overturned it if she got even an inch closer, and Lessia shot her a wave as she approached the bow, glad that it seemed the wyvern understood, as she swam to stay by Lessia's side.

Squeezing Merrick's hand, Lessia pulled him with her as she stepped up all the way to the railing, focusing her eyes on the large golden one who hadn't stopped glaring at her, and making sure none of the wyverns eyeing Ydren dared inch closer.

"Will you understand me if I speak out loud?"

Lessia's voice cut through the warm air as if it were filled with ice.

The golden wyvern stretched its wings wide, and she fought for her life not to take a step back at the displeasure in its eyes. "Of course we'll understand you, Elessia Rantzier. We're not animals."

From Merrick's harsh exhale, she realized she wasn't the only one who heard them now.

"I didn't mean to offend you." She had no idea how to address the wyverns, but most people and creatures liked to be approached respectfully, so she lowered her chin in a small bow. "May you tell me your name?"

"If you wanted to respect us, you shouldn't have compelled us, princess." The wyvern shook his head wildly. "Your gift is dangerous, and like your ancestors, you wield it too carelessly."

"I..." she started when Merrick snarled, "She wields it with more care than you could ever imagine. She just needed you to fucking listen instead of doing whatever it was you were doing."

Merrick continued under his breath. "Don't you dare apologize. You have not done anything wrong."

Lessia could sense that he truly believed it—that he was proud of her for what she'd done—and she squared her shoulders as she continued.

"Death Whisperer. I didn't think I'd ever see you again." Some of the wyverns around the golden one shifted when the beast spoke Merrick's nickname. "We've heard the stories about you, of course. But some of us also fought beside you and your brethren. You were kind then, kinder to us than most of the Fae."

Merrick didn't respond, and it was quiet for so long that unease crawled across her skin.

"Tell us your name," she demanded when Merrick and the golden wyvern appeared locked in a silent battle of the eyes, the glares radiating from each chilling the air around them.

"I am Auphore, young one. The father of all wyverns alive today."

Her eyes flew across the probably hundreds of wyverns that surrounded them—wyverns of every color she could imagine: blue, green, yellow, a few violets like Ydren, and even some white and black ones.

When her eyes returned to Auphore, something gleamed in his eyes, and she decided not to ask what had been on the tip of her tongue.

It didn't matter anyway.

"You already know who I am, and I am guessing you know why I am here." Lessia held her breath in the thick silence that followed, and she was wondering if she would have to repeat herself when Raine's flask being unscrewed broke the silence, and all heads turned his way.

The red-haired Fae didn't even have the decency to look embarrassed. He only raised his flask to the golden wyvern staring at him and ordered, "Answer her, you old bastard. She is one of the good ones."

"Mind Capturer. Can't say I missed you." Auphore actually rolled his eyes when Raine sipped some of his beloved liquor.

"Enough," Lessia snarled when Raine seemed about to spew something back at the beast. "We don't have time for this back-and-forth. I've come to ask you to join me in one last fight for Havlands. We will go up against Rioner and the Fae on his side, and... we need you."

"*We need you*," Auphore echoed. "You Fae always need *us*, but somehow we never need you."

"I know," Lessia responded, and she could tell Auphore was surprised by how his head cocked, golden eyes widening at the corners. "The Fae have used and abused you—abused what was supposed to be a sacred bond. I will not do that. I only used my magic to get you to listen, and if you say no... I will respect that. But I beg you, please consider helping us one final time."

"You forget we feel you too. We felt that rush of power boil through you, princess of Vastala. It felt good, didn't it? Not to be weak. It's how we know you must have tricked the stone. You can force us to help you, taking away the one thing we always had. Choice."

"I. Am. No. Princess. I seek no power. And I would *never* take away your choice. Never!" She hated how her lip trembled at the end, but Auphore was getting too close to her own frustrations.

She was the one without a choice.

"The stone chose her," Merrick growled. "It was for a fucking reason it chose her—chose anyone!—for the first time in centuries. If Rioner and the others win, they'll come for you. He doesn't like having enemies—albeit enemies in hiding—anywhere in the world. He'll kill every last one of you."

Ydren let out a soft whimper, and on reflex, Lessia stretched out her hand to place it on the wyvern's snout.

Ydren didn't like this, either, and Lessia could tell it unsettled her, being this close to her own species—the sense of not belonging anywhere radiated from the creature right into Lessia's heart.

"Who is that?" Auphore demanded. "Who are you, young wyvern?"

"Her name is Ydren," Lessia answered when Ydren refused to even look his way, the younger wyvern shaking so hard the water around the ship was disturbed.

"I saved her," Raine added. "Her mother and family were captured in the last war, and a group of shifters killed them. I was able to get Ydren out, and she's been staying with me ever since."

Auphore didn't look at Raine as he spoke again. "But you've chosen *her*? Answer me, young one!"

One nod was what Ydren gave him, and Lessia moved closer to her, not fully understanding what *You've chosen her* meant, but feeling some type of way all the same.

"Why? Why her?" Auphore began swimming closer before Lessia ordered "Stop!" as she pulled at the gilded thread she could still feel whispering between her fingers.

"You will not hurt her, or any of the others here."

Lessia didn't recognize her voice as the words left her lips.

It was cold and demanding and… sounded all too similar to her uncle's.

Auphore's eyes went between her and the violet wyvern, his maw opening and closing the same way his leathery wings did.

Merrick made a move to say something, but Lessia placed her other hand on his arm and shook her head. She didn't know why, but she could feel that Auphore needed the time.

Her eyes flicked to Frelina and Raine, and they seemed to understand what she wanted as well, moving their gazes to watch the group of wyverns around them instead.

Lessia counted her heartbeats while she waited.

Thud.

Thud-thud.

Thud.

She'd counted all the way to a thousand when Auphore finally spoke again.

"For the young one, we will come as witnesses."

Her brows furrowed as she lifted her gaze to the wyvern elder. "What does that mean?"

"If you allow Ydren to come back to her family, we will come to the battle. We will stand behind your army, every single one of us. But we will not fight."

"You…" Merrick seethed, but Lessia squeezed his arm again.

"Thank you," she said quickly.

She'd take it. Rioner wouldn't know the wyverns weren't going to fight, and it might scare enough of his people that they could take out the others.

Lessia shot Ydren a quick look when a strangled, sorrow-filled sound vibrated in her long throat. "But Ydren decides for herself if she wants to go. If she wants to stay with us after—that is up to her."

"We would never force her. We just want our family together. You, out of anyone, should understand." Auphore bowed his head for a moment before whipping it back forcefully, and by the way the wyverns dispersed, Lessia guessed it was some kind of order to leave. "I heard you're heading to the Lakes of Mirrors. May I suggest Ydren stays with us for that? It's quite... uncomfortable over there."

Lessia tried to ignore the urge to ask if she could also stay—hide under the protection of these beasts forever.

After a look at the others, she knew it was pointless to try to convince any of them to stay back, so with a soft sigh, she responded. "Yes. We'll return as soon as we can."

Auphore hesitated for a second before doing that head throw again. "If you survive."

CHAPTER 21
LOCHE

The dark-haired woman didn't hesitate as she sauntered up to the group, her movements so familiar Loche had to remind himself he was the regent of Ellow, not the child she'd abused until he couldn't take her or the never-ending stream of men that passed through their small house anymore and he'd finally followed her demand to leave her house at only eight years old.

As she came to a halt before the silent group and he felt the people around him move closer—especially Zaddock, who kept his hand hovering over the sword by his side, and Kerym and Thissian, who stared at the woman and the Fae with strained expressions pulling at their features—Loche also forced himself to remember this woman was a shifter.

He'd seen all the shapes Geyia had shifted into before.

Shifters could become anything—any animal or human they'd come across, they could mimic. The shifters who were especially good could even mirror gestures and body movements, like the swagger his mom used to propel her body forward, making it almost impossible to distinguish them from the real thing.

This could be a mind trick—an illusion to throw him off.

Plastering a smirk onto his face, the one he'd perfected over the years to hide the uncertainty he still felt navigating the rooms of older and more experienced men and women, Loche also took a step forward.

Best not to let her think she had some kind of advantage.

"We can't drain them," Kerym hissed into his ear as he stepped with him. "The curly-haired Fae behind her is blocking our magic. The pale one can blind us, so be ready."

Great, Loche thought as he shot Zaddock a look.

His friend dipped his chin, turning his body toward the Fae with such pale hair and skin that he almost blended into the clouds hovering behind him, and who was focused so hard on the Siphon Twins that he couldn't have noticed Zaddock preparing to take him out at a second's notice.

Loche trusted Zaddock would get to the Fae, even blind. Z hadn't been a great soldier because he was too emotional—he got too distracted in a fight when his friends all fought around him—but he was damned skilled with a sword.

Moving his gaze back to the woman in front, Loche caught her gray eyes.

No time to waste.

"I am guessing you're the rebel leader," Loche

drawled, not bothering to extend a hand. "Seems time we finally met."

"That's not a very warm welcome for your own mother." The shifter he guessed was Meyah clicked her tongue as she slowly dragged her sharp gaze—the one too similar to his own—over the group, stopping at Zaddock when he pulled a deep breath.

"You're not my mother." Loche didn't let himself hesitate a beat as he responded. "I don't know when you met her, but she got around before her death, so I am not too surprised."

Meyah's eyes flashed for a second before she locked down her expression. "Such a strange group of people you surround yourself with. A lowly human—no surprise there, although I did have higher hopes for you. The Siphon Twins. Good to see you again, Kerym." Meyah playfully wrinkled her nose at the Fae, prompting Pellie to move closer to him, and Loche scoffed at the similarity to his mother.

On the island he'd grown up on, in the outskirts of Ellow, she'd been known by everyone for her beauty and her blatant flirting.

There was nothing subtle or sweet about her.

She was the complete opposite of Lessia, and Loche suspected that was also why he'd been drawn to Lessia at first. She didn't see—or care—about her own beauty, and whenever he flirted with her—when he told her the things he'd been thinking about—the blush that crept up her cheeks had warmed him inside out.

He was ripped from his thoughts of Lessia, and despite who the woman before him was, he was grateful for it. Remembering Lessia smile like that with her damned pink cheeks stole all the air from his lungs.

"You two, I don't know." Meyah sniffed the air, and the copper-haired sisters' faces twisted into cold masks so quickly Loche noticed even Kerym's brows flew up for a second. "You smell... I don't know. What are you?"

"We're friends of Lessia, and we heard you weren't very nice to her," Pellie purred, and Loche couldn't help but admire how she managed to fill her voice with such a combination of coldness and disdain.

He'd need to practice replicating it.

"We don't take very well to those who treat our friends unkindly," Soria added, dragging her tongue across her teeth like she was a damned wolf or something, staring at its prey.

While Loche's eyes widened at the sisters, who'd so far mostly been babbling and flirting but now appeared as lethal as the Fae brothers standing beside them, Kerym let out a low laugh.

"Remind me not to get on your bad side," he mumbled.

Thissian rolled his eyes as Pellie responded, "You'd never, handsome."

"You, on the other hand." Pellie's finger shot out so fast Loche thought it might smack Meyah in the face. "You tread very fucking carefully or I'll make your worst nightmares come true."

It was Loche's turn to chuckle, but he made sure to keep it dark as he glared at the rebel leader. "They're right. It's time for us to have a real chat. You must end this rebellion right now, or we're all doomed. I..." Loche ground his teeth before continuing. "I might not have approached our... discussions... in the most amicable way before, but I am here to listen now. I am sure we can find a middle ground before Havlands as we know it is lost and both of our peoples perish."

Meyah's eyes were narrowed to slits as they captured his. "Both of our peoples... You're such a disappointment, Loche. I didn't have particularly high hopes for you... but this... this is what it's come to?"

"Enough with the act," Loche snarled. "Show us your real face."

The woman who looked like his mother threw her head back and cackled. "You keep proving me right, son. After all this time away from you, I thought perhaps my decision to leave you behind had been hasty, but you're as useless and stupid as you always were."

Loche kept his smirk on his face. He'd been called worse growing up and when he fought his way to the regency, and even now he knew what those fuckers in the council whispered behind his back.

"I said enough." Loche took a step forward, and his friends followed, the already strained air growing heavier, whipping salt across their skin as the wind picked up, almost as if it felt the anger rising within him. "We do not have time for your games. And you're doing your people no favors by insulting me."

Meyah laughed again. "You truly don't see it, do you?" Her hand waved lazily toward the tanned Fae behind her, who had an impressive mane of curly black hair falling down his back. "He is blocking all magic."

A hand landed on his forearm, and Loche frowned at Soria when she shot him a small smile, her delicate face moving from side to side ever so slightly.

"So what?" Loche hissed when the rebel leader didn't continue, but Kerym made a sound that made him spin toward the raven-haired Fae, his frown deepening when both he and his brother winced as they met his eyes.

"He's neutralizing magic," Kerym said, his tone almost apologetic. "She can't shift."

She can't shift.

Loche shook his head so violently his hair lashed his cheeks.

No.

Because...

No.

This was not fucking happening.

Loche's hands clenched and unclenched as he tried to lock down the surprise, the unease, the fucking guilt that seemed to have taken a permanent position within his body, and the only question he could get out was "Why?"

Meyah seemed amused as her gaze trailed across his face, reading way too fucking much into it, judging from the way her eyes lit up. "Why am I your mother? Why didn't I tell you who I really was? Why are you such a disappointment? There are so many questions to be answered, don't you think?"

She shook her head, her red lips lifting into a distant smile. "I unfortunately can't answer the last one, but I can tell you that I birthed you. A night with too much to drink, and I wasn't careful enough. And before you ask, I have no idea who your useless human father is. I wasn't happy, of course. It's difficult to get clients when you're with child, although there are a few who seem to prefer it."

She flicked Soria and Pellie a glance. "I wouldn't advise you to go looking for those men, though... they're pretty vile. And it's expensive to take care of children!

You're so needy..." Her top lip curled back in disgust. "The screaming... the sleepless nights. No, you weren't for me."

Meyah tilted her head as Loche only stared back at her.

He'd known she was a terrible mother—that he wasn't wanted. The beatings, the name-calling, the hungry days informed him of as much.

But this?

"I was already part of the rebellion then. It was the only way I could stand letting these humans touch me, knowing that their silver went to the people they hated. Because they hated me, and they hated themselves even more for wanting me." Meyah's eyes lifted to the sky for a moment as she pursed her lips. "Men... idiots, all of them." Her eyes snapped to his again. "Look at you. Falling in love and ruining your life. Was it worth it, son? I saw how she clung to the Death Whisperer when I met her..."

"Enough! It's fucking enough," Kerym snarled when Loche began shaking.

But Loche lifted a hand, silencing him.

He needed to hear this. He needed these answers.

From when he was a child, he'd always known he didn't fit in, that there was something about him that was off—that set him apart from the humans around him. It hadn't just been that he was born to the town whore or that everyone knew and pitied him for how his mother mistreated him.

There had been something else.

An otherness.

It was why he'd recognized it so quickly in Lessia.

He'd seen himself in her.

"She can't hurt me," Loche growled when Kerym continued to argue and Soria's hand on his arm tightened its grip. "I don't care what you call me or how much you hate me. I only want to understand why you are spearheading this damned rebellion and how I can get you to stop."

"Such impatience... I'd heard as much about you. But it all ties together, you see." Meyah tsked. "You were such a disappointment, I had no choice but to set you on this path."

"On. What. Path," Loche gritted between clenched teeth.

He was losing his patience, and despite what he hoped he displayed outwardly, Meyah's words were finding a way through the thick armor he thought he had built around his heart.

Like needles, they weaseled their way through his skin, pricking him where it hurt the most, accompanied by his mother's voice, which loved to echo in his thoughts whenever he doubted himself.

Another woman who doesn't love you.

Because you're worthless.

Loche set his jaw harder at the voice in his mind.

"Remember who you are, regent." Soria's voice was so low that Meyah couldn't hear her.

Moving his eyes to her blue ones, Loche drew a breath.

Then another, until his chest moved rhythmically again and he could focus his eyes on his mother once more.

Meyah opened her mouth as if no time had passed, as if she hadn't noticed how Loche had nearly lost it, and his forehead creased for a moment.

But he didn't have time to ponder it before Meyah spoke again. "You must have wondered by now why you're not a shifter?"

He had, but he remained quiet.

"So useless, even from birth." An exasperated rush of air left the shifter, and the Fae behind her moved for the first time as she began walking back and forth.

Like shadows the half-Fae followed her every step, even as the one with long hair kept his gaze on Kerym and Thissian, who in turn watched Loche with expressions that turned more horrified for every vile word leaving Meyah's mouth.

Zaddock, however, didn't throw Loche any pitying looks—perhaps because he knew him too well, or because he was too preoccupied with tracing every movement of the pale Fae.

"I at least hoped you'd help grow our people when I found out I was having you. But no... you're a halfling without any powers. You're rare, you know? Most half-shifters can at least shift into *one* other form. But not you. No, I tried everything. Throwing you off the roof to see if you'd sprout wings like the birds nesting outside our house. Nothing. Casting you into the water to see if you'd develop gills to breathe. No, I had to get you out, as you only sank and stopped breathing." The expression on the shifter's face was so disgusted that Loche couldn't stop himself from staggering back.

He fucking hated himself for it.

He was used to this, he reminded himself. People despised him, and that was all right. That was how he'd convinced himself he'd be all right when he forced Lessia away; he'd not known warmth before her, and he believed he could just return to that.

But he'd been so wrong.

"When I realized you were no shifter, I had to devise another use for you." Meyah halted so abruptly that the Fae walking a half step behind her nearly stormed into her. "Did you not think it strange that Geyia took you in that first time she saw you? A shifter shunned by everyone? I was the one who convinced her to—although she never truly knew why, of course. She's not strong enough either. Not like me. But she would care for you—she's strange like that—and I knew we needed to get you into the best possible position for our cause, and what better than by ensuring you had some empathy for our kind? And look what we did!" Meyah threw out her hands. "You're the regent! I knew you'd do well in the navy—you at least gained the strength and the build of a shifter—and as soon as we started feeding you all that information? You have a bit of my cunning in you. I didn't think you had enough spine to stand up against us, though. Not after Geyia's weakness and mushiness... But I guess it worked out in the end anyway. Because here you are—begging for me and my people to stand down. Begging for my mercy when you should fight beside us."

Loche only stared at her, unable to meet the gazes of the others, which he felt locked on his face.

His entire life... was a lie.

He hadn't done anything.

Geyia... The information...

"You killed my friends," Loche said in a monotone as the consequences of refusing the rebels' wishes flickered in his mind—the friends they'd attacked and killed because of Loche.

"They were holding you back." Meyah seemed to

study him as well, probably reveling in the fucking pain shooting from every nerve inside him.

Everything was a fucking lie... and the worst part?

There was only one person he wanted to speak to about it. One person who would understand—who would know what he needed. But she wasn't his to need anymore.

His eyes drifted southwest, to where she should be right now, and unfortunately, his mother's gaze followed.

"You miss her?" Meyah asked, her voice mockingly sweet. "Miss the other little halfling who appears as weak as you are. I guess it makes sense why you fell for each other."

Low growls echoed behind him from the Fae twins, and this time even Zaddock halted, his face twisting into the expression that meant he was about to lose control.

"Fuck you," Loche said quietly.

"What did you say?" Meyah's voice remained in that sickly sweet tone.

"I said fuck you," Loche snarled. "Get off my ship before I kill you."

"Oh, but son, I thought we were here to negotiate?" His mother rounded her eyes innocently. "I thought you would give me what I wanted?"

His hand twitched toward his sword.

He wanted nothing more than to tell her to fuck off again, but the fear for his people still whirled within him. He'd already let them down once...

"What do you want, then?" he demanded, his words strained.

Meyah wiggled her brows. "Kneel."

"No!"

Loche first thought he was the one who'd snarled it, but it was Zaddock who took a step forward.

"He will not kneel to you."

Kerym and Thissian made low concurring sounds, and Soria squeezed his arm as if to say *Don't do it.*

After shooting his friends a quick look, confirming what he'd inferred, Loche shook his head sharply. "I will not kneel to you. *Ellow* will not kneel to you."

Meyah shot him another slow, oily smile. "You asked me what I wanted, and all I want is for you to kneel to me and make me the regent of Ellow."

He had always hated his mother. Always. But now?

Hate wasn't a good enough word for the emotions that coursed within him.

Loche only shook his head.

"No?" Meyah laughed again—a laugh that should have been rippling over the wind but that just made his stomach turn—while she shot one of the Fae behind her a look, and when he dropped his gaze...

The air flickered with magic until Lessia stood in his mother's place.

Her golden-brown hair was long and clean, lying in soft waves over her lowered shoulders—the first time in a while he'd seen it like that. Her innocent amber eyes tracked him when he took a stupid, stumbling step toward her.

Then those full lips shot up, her cheeks rounding and pink tinting them...

He had to press his eyes shut.

"Will you not kneel for me?"

Even her voice was spot on.

"Loche," Lessia pleaded. "Look at me, darling."

He could fucking smell her on the wind.

"Loche." Another female voice reached his ears. "Remember who you are."

His eyes flew open.

He was the regent of Ellow.

And this wasn't Lessia. This was his damned mother. The rebel leader. The one who had killed people he loved. Who now planned to kill even more people he cared for.

Loche glared right into the amber eyes before him. "I will *never* bow to you."

The mirror of Lessia flicked her hair, but the irritable expression on her face betrayed Meyah. Lessia would never twist her lips like that, narrow her eyes in disgust, or drag her gaze across his friends with that vicious hint to it.

"Suit yourself."

The world before his eyes went dark.

CHAPTER 22
FRELINA

"Well, that was a waste of time," Raine declared as he lifted his flask to his lips when the final wyvern disappeared into the cerulean sea.

Frelina fought an urge to slap it out of his hand, throw the silver bottle overboard, and let the depths swallow it forever.

"It wasn't," Elessia responded softly, although Frelina could see the twinge of worry flitting across her sister's face when she turned toward the cabins. "They're coming with us."

"But they're not fighting." Raine shook his head. "We have no chance."

Her sister halted with a foot in the air, her back still turned toward them, and it was quiet for a beat, the soft waves lapping the hull the only sound as the ship continued weaving through the island-littered sea, somehow steering itself.

Then Elessia spoke again. "There is always a chance. However small that chance might be."

Frelina winced at the crack snaking its way into her voice, and she took a step forward when Merrick stormed past her, reaching Elessia in a few long strides and swooping her up into his arms, burrowing his face in her neck as he marched them both inside.

"They're in a hurry," Raine muttered as he finally sheathed the swords he'd drawn to protect them. "Guess we have to make the most of it now..."

How he thought those blades would do anything, Frelina didn't know. While they looked terrifying, it didn't seem like they'd do a lick against the hard scales covering the wyverns' massive bodies.

"Can you blame them?" Frelina asked when Raine sighed deeply again, mumbling something about this being "pointless."

Raine rolled his eyes as he made a move to take another damned sip of liquor, and the sight of it ignited a rage within her that burned so hot it seemed her eyes heated as well.

"Do you have no empathy?" Frelina snarled.

"Oh, I have plenty." Raine waved with his flask. "This just cures it."

She ground her teeth so hard her head hurt.

She hated that liquor. She hated how she'd catch Raine's eyes from time to time and see something real only for it to be replaced with muted glossiness as soon as he sipped from his flask.

"Why so angry, little Rantzier?" Raine shook his head, making his hair fly around his face and his reddish stubble sparkle in the sunlight. "I am just saying what everyone is thinking. It is pointless now. We won't win this. We should just run."

What everyone...

She was going to kill this stupid Fae.

Taking a step toward him, Frelina seethed, "Why am I so angry?"

She took another step as her vision colored scarlet.

"Why am I so angry?" she repeated.

"Yes, do tell," Raine responded calmly, only watching her as she closed the distance between them, nearing him where he now leaned on his elbows against the wooden wyvern in the bow.

"Because of you," Frelina spat. "You're so fucking stupid. You're only focusing on forgetting—drinking your damned liquor and floating away in your clouded mind while the rest of us—" She had to clear her throat as her voice broke, and it made her even angrier.

Spit flew from her mouth as she took another step toward him, almost standing chest to chest now.

But she didn't care.

"While the rest of us what?" Raine shot her a lopsided smile that had Frelina lift her hand to smack him.

Unfortunately, he was faster, and he caught the hand as it slashed toward his cheek.

As he held on to her, forcing her body to fully align with his, she could barely see from the anger that overtook her.

"You don't get it!" she screamed. "The rest of us are trying to remember every moment we have left! Can't you see Merrick is nearly breaking? That Elessia is barely holding it together? And still they're both stronger than you are! Elessia is twenty-five years old! Did you know that?"

Frelina was crying now, but it didn't matter; she continued, her words coming out clipped and jumbled. They just needed to get out.

"She is going to die!" she cried. "Do you not understand that? She is walking, talking, going on missions, speaking to fucking wyverns! Instead of hiding away in her misery like you are!"

Raine's smile faded, but he didn't push her off. Instead, he remained quiet, his fingers still wrapped around her wrist as she yelled at him, his chest moving steadily against her wild one.

"You have lived, Raine!" Her voice cracked with every beat of her heart, and she wasn't sure if she imagined it, but it seemed as if Raine pulled her closer yet.

She could at least smell his whiskey-and-wood scent clearly now.

"You... you have loved." Frelina blinked against the tears in her eyes, feeling her cheeks sting from the salt of the ones that had already escaped. "You even found your mate! You have lived while the rest of us... we'll..." A hiccup interrupted her, and she swallowed. "I'll die without any of that. I'll die having lived twenty-four years on an island with only my parents and my sister and..." Another hiccup. "A healer that came once in a while."

An arm wrapped around her. Then another, and her hand fell to his chest when Raine let it go.

As he tried to pull her into the embrace, she slammed the hand against his chest. "Stop it."

It felt good.

It helped.

Frelina lifted her other one and struck it as well against his leather-clad muscles when he tugged at her again. "Stop!"

Smack.

"Stop!"

Smack.

"Stop!"

Smack.

Raine just let her take out her frustrations, his arms loosely lying across her back.

"Fight back!" she screamed when she accidentally met his eyes and there was only kindness in them. Kindness and understanding.

"Fight back!" She hammered both her fists against his body.

Again.

And again.

"F-fight back," she cried.

"Fight..." Her voice drifted away as too much thickness filled her throat.

More tears streamed down her face, and this time when Raine pressed on her lower back, she let him fold her body against his.

Frelina cried like she'd never cried before.

Her entire body shook. Her face scrunched so much she could feel a headache creeping up the back of it. Her skin scraped against Raine's leather tunic as he only held her closer for every hiccup, for every sharp breath, for every whimper and sob.

"It's... it's all a joke to you," Frelina finally got out as the tears came slower. "But... it's not for the rest of us. It's... not a joke."

"I've never said I think it's all a joke." Raine's voice

rumbled through her as it echoed in his chest. "It's no joke to me, little Rantzier."

Frelina sniffed.

She didn't know how to respond. She'd never heard him sound like this.

Glancing up at him, she stiffened.

Tears glistened on the mind-bender's cheeks as well. Tears he didn't bother to hide as he met her eyes, lifting a hand to wipe away her own.

"None of this is a joke to me," Raine continued in a serious voice.

She stared at him as his thumb caressed the warm and wet skin across her cheeks, and the air around them stilled under his slow movements.

She couldn't hear the waves anymore.

Or the wind.

Frelina could only follow the green, brown, and gold swirls in Raine's eyes as he looked back at her.

There was so much more gold than she'd realized. Gold like she knew her own eyes glowed when she used her magic, just like Elessia's. The honey color traced around his irises, almost dancing as the black in his eyes deepened. As it grew...

Frelina hiccuped again.

Raine shook his head, breaking their stare off, and the sounds around them came back.

Soft whistling wind.

Water rippling.

The scent of summer and winter tangling all around.

Her salt-covered cheeks heated before she could stop them, but as she made to take a step back, Raine tightened his hold.

"I..." He blew up his cheeks, releasing a deep breath before continuing. "I want to show you something."

Frelina was about to ask him what he wanted to show her when he caught her eyes again, and somehow, she knew.

Raine nodded, and his mouth twitched as if he tried to lift the corners of it but failed.

Close your eyes.

Frelina did as he asked her in her mind.

As her eyelids fluttered shut, Raine pulled her even closer, but not to comfort her.

No. It was *he* who needed someone to steady him—someone to keep him grounded.

When his memories crashed into her without warning, Frelina understood why.

Ice-filled wind rushed all around him, and an overwhelming tiredness swept through Raine as he pulled open the door to the old tavern.

They'd trained all day, and Merrick had nearly killed him when he lost his temper.

Which might have had something to do with Raine telling all the females flocking around the soldier camp they'd set up outside town that Merrick was looking for a wife.

Despite his cold, stiff limbs, Raine snickered. He'd barely ever seen Merrick take an interest in females. He was too busy brooding and worrying if he was an evil threat to the world to entertain himself with ladies.

Raine, on the other hand...

His snicker turned into a big grin when the warmth of the tavern wrapped around him and Thissian and Kerym waved to him from the back. The warmth seeped through his body, and as it heated his limbs, they hurt even more—but he didn't have time to linger on it as something brushed his nose.

What was that?

Raine whipped his head back and forth until his gaze settled on a tiny little Fae with hair so blonde that it almost seemed white cascading down her back.

His entire being melted.

Then hardened.

Then melted again.

Raine couldn't stop himself from turning fully toward her, and his feet moved of their own accord as they brought him to the female, his gaze locked on her the entire time.

She must have felt him coming because she turned around, and he was rewarded with the darkest eyes he'd ever seen.

She was full of contrasts.

Tiny but with a look in her eyes that would have made males bigger than Raine shrink back.

White hair and black eyes and golden skin.

Full lips in a dainty face.

She was... everything.

He must have stumbled into tables and people because he both felt people push him and heard people curse him.

It didn't matter.

That...

She...

As he halted before her, the barkeep tapped her shoulder, and this little wild creature continued meeting his eyes as she said, "Oh, fuck. I think I might need two drinks because this seems to be my mate."

The memory switched to another, and Frelina could barely breathe from how hard Raine held on to her.

Raine winced at himself in the mirror, pulling at the violet shirt and trousers that clashed horrifically with his red hair while Merrick slapped his hands on his knees and wheezed from laughter.

"You must... must truly love her," his friend got out between fits of laughter.

The memory switched again.

Wearing the same clothes, Raine walked down an alley lined with white flowers, toward the female he loved so much he could barely speak when he was in her presence.

A blur of faces looked up at him from the grass, but he could see only her.

Solana giggled as she reached out a hand and clasped his.

"It's you and me forever now."

More memories flooded Frelina.

Raine and Solana moving into a house with a haunted-looking Merrick helping them.

Sunny days in forests and fields and water.

Holding hands before fires.

Holding hands while cooking.

Love. So much love.

Then another memory.

It was misty outside their house, and Raine tapped his foot while waiting for Solana to come home.

He was hungry, and he'd spent all day preparing a new meal for her.

It definitely shouldn't have taken this long, but he'd burned the first two batches of bread, so he'd had to start over twice.

He'd never admit that to her, though.

When the door burst open, Raine turned around with two glasses of wine and a broad smile on his face.

Finally.

But it was Merrick's terrified and white face that met him.

The glasses fell to the ground, where they shattered in the same way that fear exploded within him.

"He has her," Merrick said, and Raine knew his world was about to change forever.

Frelina started shaking at the next memories that assaulted her mind, and Raine's arms locked around her, his breathing quickening.

War.

Death.

So much fear and terror and so many haunting scenes.

Both within Raine and those around him.

And all the time... Solana in his mind.

Seeing her in Rioner's cellars.

Seeing her beaten and hurt and broken.

When the next memory came, Frelina's knees buckled, and she wondered if Raine hadn't held on to her for support after all, as he pressed her so hard against him that she couldn't move.

Solana was still too thin, but her smile was as bright as ever as she chased Raine through the woods outside their house.

Raine threw a glance to the south as they reached the pebbled path to the small cottage, even if he knew Merrick would never walk down those steps again, not after swearing that oath to Rioner.

The fucking martyr, giving up his own life for Solana and Thissian's and Kerym's mates, making Raine feel equally guilty and so damned grateful.

Solana, always knowing what was going on in his head, wrapped her arms around his waist, looking up at him as she said, "We'll get him out. We'll get strong and then get him away from him."

Raine gave her a smile, albeit a weak one, before his eyes drifted to the woods again.

Something glimmered there, but he didn't have time to react before Solana jerked.

Then jerked again.

Something in him pulled, and as he looked down at his mate, blood bubbled out of the corners of Solana's mouth.

"No!" he screamed as she went limp in his arms.

The thing within him that had pulled snapped.

And his entire world broke.

Frelina panted against the pain that surrounded her, that filled her, that suffocated her.

She knew it was Raine's. This was what he carried each day. But she couldn't shake it.

Her eyes were still closed when Raine's broken whisper brushed her cheek. "Do you see now? Do you see why... why I can't?"

Frelina only nodded, fresh tears falling down her face, mingling with Raine's as he pressed the side of his face against hers.

They gripped each other as if the world would end if they didn't.

And who knew? Perhaps it would.

It wasn't until the air around them truly quieted that they let go of each other, and fear replaced the sorrow within Frelina when mirror images of their ship, of them, of Merrick and Elessia running up the stairs shimmered all around them.

"I guess this is the Lakes of Mirrors," Raine whispered as he wiped his face, releasing her but remaining close as their ship continued traveling on the lake, amid the water that rose around them as if it were walls and met above them to form a ceiling.

CHAPTER 23
LOCHE

Loche gripped his sword as he screamed "Zaddock!"

A groan sounded from one of the Fae twins, and Loche clutched his blade in one hand while grabbing Soria's arm with the other so as not to accidentally stab her in his blindness.

Utter chaos, chaos in damned shadows, ensued.

Loche had no idea who he was fighting, but he pushed his way back to the railing, heart thumping in his chest, keeping Soria between the railing and himself as he slashed with his sword in the darkness.

"Zaddock!" he screamed again, worry for his friend breaking through the adrenaline rushing in his blood.

"I'm alive!" Zaddock responded.

Fucking thankfully.

"So am I, thanks for asking!" Kerym called out. "Not" —metal clangs echoed between the Fae's words—"sure how much longer, though! Thissian?"

The silence that followed was worse than the sword

that ripped into Loche's arm at that second, worse than the fire rushing through the wound, worse than the horrible truths his mother had told him.

Fuck, fighting blind wasn't any fun. Loche groaned as he tried to parry the blows, listening for the rush of wind that should betray them, but it never came.

More slashes did, though, coming from different directions—ones he could never anticipate.

Loche cursed again as he realized whoever he was fighting was playing with him.

"Coward," he hissed as another slice dragged across his side, ripping his skin apart.

It didn't cut deep, only fucking teased him.

"That's no way to speak to your mother," Meyah purred.

"You..." Loche felt Soria press against him, and he pushed back, refusing to let her get into harm's way. "You seem to have many names. Meyah. Mother. Whore. Eliana... wasn't that what you... you told me your name was?" He panted as another of his mother's strikes bit into his skin, this time in his shoulder and deeper than the others.

Maybe she took offense at being called Eliana.

Or perhaps it was *Mother* that was the problem...

Loche laughed when she struck him again.

A hollow, brittle, stupid laugh.

He'd fucking die here.

Blind. Helpless. Useless.

By his mother's hand, like he'd always feared growing up, when she'd been bigger than him.

When she'd been stronger—meaner.

When her punches left him with broken cheekbones and ribs.

When she let him starve until stars flickered before his eyes.

He laughed again as a sword slashed across his chest and hot blood trickled down inside his jacket.

"We... we've truly come full... full circle," Loche got out as he refused to let his hand move to his chest—to press against the wound that must be deeper than the rest, based on how quickly it drained his energy. "I... I just don't get why you didn't kill me back then. Why... why wait until now?"

"This is more fun, isn't it?" his mother chirped, amusement curving every letter.

The arm holding up his sword slackened at the sound.

She was *enjoying* this. Would enjoy killing him. Would surely brag about it after.

How she'd steered his entire life—the regent of fucking Ellow—only to kill him on a ship in the Eiatis Sea.

"No," Soria hissed against his back when it curved. "You do not get to give up, regent. You do not."

He could tell she was out of breath even if her words were sharp, and he wanted to ask her what the fucking point was.

Why couldn't he give up?

The rebels wouldn't back down. His people would suffer. Die.

So would his friends.

Lessia wouldn't survive this.

He knew that now.

Soria pinched him. Fucking pinched him.

When he jerked forward, she snarled "Enough!" in a voice very unlike the one she usually favored. "You are hurting. And rightfully so. But the one you love is also hurting, and she's fighting for her gods-damned life! You need to do the same!"

Lessia's face flashed before his eyes.

Her furious eyes as she stood up to Craven—the defiance in her lifted chin as she stood before an entire audience who despised her. The hope blossoming in her beautiful face as she stared at him from the floor, begging him to love her even when he did everything he could to pretend he didn't.

She never gave up. No matter what this life threw at her.

Fuck. If he died now, if he let Meyah win, Lessia's life would get even harder, and... he owed her more than that.

Loche sucked in a breath, readying himself to pull up any final energy within him—to try to at least get one hit in, perhaps hurt Meyah enough to slow her down when Lessia and the others faced her—when water roared somewhere beneath him.

Wind surged around them, nearly making him stagger with its force.

Wood creaked and screamed, and he might not have the hearing of the Fae, but even Loche could tell it wasn't natural.

His vision came back so abruptly, he had to clamp his eyes shut as the sun pierced them. Keeping his sword before him, Loche squinted until he was used to the cold sunlight and then sliced his gaze around.

Kerym stood above his brother, his eyes bluer than Loche had ever seen them, skin glowing and black hair whipping around his raging face, as the two half-Fae who had shadowed his mother fell to their knees before him.

A broken-off piece of their ship lay beside them, and Loche's eyes flicked for a moment to the mast it had come from before landing on the new ship approaching them, where a group of people stood in the bow, their eyes focused so hard none met his own.

He followed their gazes one by one.

A wind—and not the one nature controlled—directed the sails on his ship and the new one, driven by one or two of the boys.

The mast he'd glimpsed before had been bent at an unnatural angle, and as he snapped his eyes back to the wooden piece on the floor, he realized it must have hit one of the Fae—probably the pale one that had blinded them all.

Water had also wrapped around their ship, holding it in place while drowning the smaller vessel on which his mother had arrived.

His mother.

Loche whirled around, nearly knocking over Soria as she slipped from behind his back, but he didn't apologize when he found his mother running toward the stern, her dark hair flying behind her.

"No!" he screamed as he dropped his heavy sword to follow her. "She's getting away!"

He wasn't sure who he was screaming at, but he could hear someone following him as he sprinted after Meyah, and from the corner of his eye, he glimpsed a rush of wind upsetting the sails before it whirled toward his mother.

But just as it reached her, the air shimmered, and a large eagle took his mother's place, using the damned wind to get up and out so fast none of them had a chance to reach her.

"Fuck!" It might have been wishful thinking, but Loche still pulled the knife he'd once won off Zaddock and threw it with all his might after the bird.

The sun blinded him for a second, but a screech echoed across the seas, and although he couldn't see, he could feel it—feel that the throw that he'd fueled with Lessia's hope, the vow he'd taken to protect his people, and perhaps, just the slightest bit, his hatred for that woman—hit true.

A hand landed on his shoulder when he could finally make out the world again, and when the bird was nowhere to be found in the sky, he turned to find Zaddock's face a few inches from his.

"She'll get what's coming to her," his friend promised in a low voice.

Loche only nodded.

She would.

If not by his hand, by another's, because after what happened here today... there would be war. It was inevitable at this point.

The rebels, Rioner and his Fae, the Oakgards' Fae, and whatever the mixture of Ellow's and Lessia's band of warriors were called would come head-to-head soon.

Probably in the next week, if he'd kept his days straight.

If he didn't kill Meyah, and Lessia didn't... Rioner or any of the other Fae surely would.

She might be a strong shifter, but he'd read about the havoc the Fae could wreak. None of the people on this ship would likely be alive by the end of it, not unless any of them ran, and based on the looks on their faces, he doubted that was a path any of them would start down.

His eyes drifted toward Kerym, who pulled his bloodied brother to his feet.

He'd been wrong to question whether they were as lethal as the rumors stated.

There was nothing kind in Kerym's blue eyes. Nothing soft in his tense body. Nothing human in the snarl as he stared down at the pale Fae, who'd made a low whimper.

Even so, Pellie literally skipped up to Kerym, placing a small hand on his arm when he made a motion to again pull the sword he must have already sheathed. Loche couldn't hear what she said, but it must have been something that broke through the haze of fury that wrapped around the warrior, as he didn't follow through on whatever he'd planned for the Fae kneeling before him.

The other vessel was nearly beside their own now, and he moved his eyes back to Zaddock, noting the blood dripping from the blade still in his hand and realizing his friend must have been more successful in his attempt to fight. He was opening his mouth to tell him thank you when something whistled through the air.

Zaddock jerked, pain filling his eyes.

Loche hadn't been frightened earlier.

Not really—not when everything had been chaos and darkness and violence and pain.

But now? When his friend's eyes widened in agony, that terrifying fear—the one he hated that he still felt—gripped the regent, chilling his blood until it felt like ice flooded him.

The other Fae—the one suppressing magic—limped

up behind them, another sharp weapon ready to fly playing between his fingers.

A fucking throwing star.

Loche didn't think. Hurtling himself forward, he aimed to tackle Zaddock to the ground, praying he wouldn't kill him by forcing the one already stuck to his back deeper.

He realized at the last moment that it wasn't necessary.

A whirlwind of blonde hair flew onto their ship, the small figure throwing what looked like a kitchen knife at the curly-haired Fae, and the knife hit its intended target, right in the eye of the Fae, who had also noticed the movement and turned her way.

He tumbled to the ground the next moment, the throwing star falling with him, clinking as it settled onto the wood.

Loche, who'd managed to stop himself from knocking Zaddock over, let his jaw drop as Amalise didn't even lose speed when she spun in their direction, running up to the equally gaping Zaddock and pulling the star from his back in one swift movement.

His friend, to his credit, only allowed himself a low groan, although Loche could tell he wanted nothing more than to double over at the pain that must consume him, given the dark stain spreading across his light tunic.

Amalise pulled off the scarf she'd had wrapped around her neck, and while she tied it around Zaddock in haste, her fingers seemed gentle, almost probing, as they whispered across his body.

Zaddock just stared.

Stared as she checked on the improvised bandage. Stared as she whirled again, running back to check that the Fae was truly dead. Stared as she called to the others to hurry up as they piled onto their ship.

It wasn't until Amalise tilted her head toward his friend, her lips lifting into a slow smile, that Zaddock appeared to snap out of it.

Loche tore his gaze away.

What brightened his friend's eyes was nothing short of devotion, and while he was happy for him, Loche just... he couldn't. Instead, he approached Geyia and Steiner, who were being helped onto the deck by some of the Faelings, and he noted Kerym and Thissian doing the same, dragging that pale Fae between them.

But his lips curled ever so slightly when he heard Amalise tease, "You appear to be the only one in need of saving, Mr. Brooding Overprotective Soldier Man," with Zaddock's quick response following: "If you're the one doing it, I'll put myself in harm's way every day."

CHAPTER 24

MERRICK

There were so many versions of Lessia.

Merrick might have enjoyed meeting her beautiful eyes everywhere he turned if he hadn't been so vigilant, thanks to the eeriness that layered all around them—that seemed as if it should mist the silver-mirrored water whirling beneath them, beside them, and above them.

Even his souls were quiet. Too quiet. So quiet that he tried to pull on his magic, let that sticky feeling coat his increasingly frosty skin. But there was nothing.

Merrick tried again.

Only emptiness met him.

The feeling was nothing like the Vincere's effects: no pain, no magic fighting beneath the surface to escape the liquid's hold.

But more like... it wasn't there.

He snapped his eyes to Raine, stating what he suspected. "My magic doesn't work here."

Raine nodded, taking a step toward the still teary Frelina.

As Merrick's eyes wandered over her face, the face so similar to Lessia's but which didn't evoke an ounce of the feelings that filled him when he met his mate's warm gaze, he could tell she and Raine had had some kind of moment.

Raine's cheeks looked suspiciously pale, the hands by his side too stiff, and Frelina didn't bother hiding that she must have been crying her eyes out when he'd brought Lessia down into the ship.

Merrick had been worried about Lessia breaking down when he'd carried her inside as well, but she'd only asked to sit on the counter while she allowed him to heat her some soup to try to give some color to her ever-paling cheeks.

Merrick had felt her eyes on him the entire time, but when he finally met them... they hadn't been filled with the sorrow he'd gotten used to in the past days. No, they had been filled with mischief, and when he'd frowned at her, she'd actually giggled before teasing, "I never thought I'd see the Death Whisperer cook for me."

He'd fought the smile tugging at his lips as he stalked up to her, trying hard to keep the scowl that used to feel natural, but that, whenever Lessia was in the room, was impossible to wear for long.

Placing his hands on her thighs, Merrick leaned in close. "I wouldn't call heating up days-old soup cooking."

Lessia leaned right back. "You're feeding me, so I'd say it counts."

He had to fight harder when her breath whispered

over his mouth, her smile widening when his muscles coiled in response.

If she wanted to play...

He'd play.

Positioning his lips right over her own, so close their warmth mingled but they didn't touch, Merrick whispered, "I'd do anything for you. Cook a whole feast if that's what you want."

He'd meant it to come out teasing, had dropped his eyes down to her lips when he spoke, but there must have been a note of vulnerability sneaking into the words. Vulnerability that he would allow only Lessia to see—to hear.

He *would* do anything for her.

Even if it damned killed him, he'd do it.

"I know," she whispered back, pressing her lips softly against his. "That's what kills me."

He hated that the playfulness in her eyes wavered for a second—that those clouds he wasn't used to made the golden flecks within them murky.

He'd promised himself to give her time. He'd promised himself to give her everything she wished for.

Merrick hadn't trusted his words when he noticed her fingers trembling by her sides, so he let his lips and hands respond instead, preparing to make her forget all about any sadness he'd reminded her of when they'd sailed into this damned mirrored land.

Against Lessia's protests, he'd stopped what he'd started, gently tugging her down from the table with a raspy promise that he'd get her up there later. Get her up there and fuck her until her back was raw from sliding against the wood.

She'd blushed at that, but her eyes had flared, that lightheartedness returning.

Something Merrick was grateful for as they ascended the stairs onto the deck again and stared at the mirrored world that was wrapped all around them.

Merrick shook his head as he stepped closer to Lessia when their ship slowed to a stop, the reflection of it—and them—shining everywhere.

He could still smell her arousal—that sweet, beautiful scent that told him she wanted *him* and only him.

She squeezed his arm, an amused tilt to her lips when she glanced up at him before shifting her gaze forward, meeting his eyes in the mirrored wall of water ahead instead.

"What happens now?" Lessia asked, and Merrick was proud of her for not whispering.

He somehow felt like they needed to be careful here, keep their voices low and not awaken whatever slumbered within the mirrored water facing them from all directions, so for her to speak so freely, so unafraid...

"How should we know?" Raine snapped, and Merrick sliced his eyes to his friend, his top lip curling back at his tone.

But he didn't scold him, not when Lessia's little sister had already stomped so hard on his foot that his friend snarled at her.

Merrick respected that she snarled right back, not backing down an inch when the massive red-haired Fae towered over her. The little Rantzier's nostrils flared as she glared at Raine, but when she opened her mouth to tell the Fae warrior off, Lessia raised a hand.

"It's fine," she said softly. "It was a dumb question."

A frown formed across Merrick's forehead, and Lessia must have noticed it because she whispered under her breath, "He's scared."

Merrick's brows lowered further as he moved his gaze from Lessia to Raine.

But she was right. It wasn't just anger in Raine's taut shoulders—in the sharp lines of his usually slack features. There was something in them that Merrick knew his friend had spent decades pushing down.

Something he was fighting for his life trying to keep at bay as he avoided the reflective surfaces with all his might.

Because, unlike the rest of them, Raine wasn't looking around—his gaze remained locked on Frelina, who still glared at him. She must have noticed what Merrick was last to figure out, though, as while her face was painted with defiance, her fingers brushed Raine's when he couldn't hide a shudder running through him, her other small hand lifting to shield his view of the mirrored wall closest to them.

Surprisingly, Raine didn't back away.

He leaned into her instead. Like... she was comforting him.

Merrick dragged his teeth across his bottom lip as he turned to Lessia, who appeared to have been eyeing him while he watched them.

Somehow, he didn't like what he saw in her eyes, especially not when a shaky smile lightened them as she moved her gaze to Frelina and Raine, who'd moved even closer now.

"I know what you're thinking," Merrick hissed. "There is no way."

If he lost her, he'd never move on. There would never be someone who could comfort him. He'd been alone before her, and while he'd make sure there wouldn't be an after her, there was no one else for him.

Lessia didn't respond, but that brightness in her eyes remained.

Merrick opened his mouth to argue with her again—make sure she understood he'd never fucking move on from her, that he wouldn't accept a life without her—when the walls of water around them whirled.

"Fuck," he swore as he flung himself toward Lessia.

But it was too late.

It was as if the world around them liquefied, thick silver waves swallowing everything until they consumed him, wrapped him tight in a bright, cool blanket.

Merrick tried to swear again, but he couldn't speak. He could only watch the strange blanket blur and dance and play before his eyes, holding his limbs hostage, until his head spun.

Blinking, Merrick pushed the fear, not for himself but for Lessia, away as he fought against the nausea and dizziness that seemed to want to pull him under, filling his ears with a buzzing that seemed somehow familiar.

He couldn't allow it. He could feel that if he did, it would be over. How, he didn't know, but a strange feeling raced over his skin, up and down his spine until his insides were as cool as whatever was wrapped around him.

Light exploded before his eyes.

The buzzing quieted.

And then the walls snapped back again, as still as they had been when they sailed in, his reflection's slight distortion the only clue that it wasn't true mirrors he was looking at or standing on.

Merrick was no longer on the ship. His dark boots were planted on the same strange lake that made up the walls ahead of him, behind him, and above him.

Wherever he turned, his own dark eyes stared back at him.

But they weren't really *his* eyes...

No, when he looked closer, he could tell the silver in them was slightly off, his posture not as hostile as he knew it must look like right now, when he sensed the danger lurking all around him, when white-hot rage began burning within him as he realized Lessia was nowhere to be found.

"Where is she?" he snarled when one of the reflections raised an arrogant brow.

That's your first question, Merrick Morshold?

The voice bounced all around him.

Within him.

Thrummed through his blood.

An urge to bow—to submit—washed through him, but he fought it.

He didn't kneel to anyone but her.

He never had and never would.

"Where. Is. She?" he repeated, ignoring the last name he'd never claimed—that he'd never felt worthy of, after hearing the stories of his brave parents—his words so icy he almost expected a white cloud to leave his mouth after each one.

She is here.

His teeth snapped together with a sharp sound.

If the legends were true, the gods couldn't lie.

"Is she safe?" Merrick didn't react as one of the many

reflections of him opened its mouth in a laugh, its eyes twinkling at him when he only stared at it.

She is safe here.

Here.

He didn't like the sound of that.

"How can I *always* make her safe?" Merrick asked as he glanced down at the reflection beneath him.

Its face held pity, and he quickly looked up again.

He preferred the manic laughter to the sadness in those eyes.

You can't.

The voice was matter of fact, void of feeling.

"Why not?" he snarled, the rage that burned hotter with each nonanswer making his fingers twitch, and he wondered for a second what would happen if he plunged his sword into the silver beneath him.

I wouldn't advise trying that.

The laughing reflection threw its head back in a silent cackle, appearing almost frenzied, while another shook its head, waving a finger toward the identical ruby-lined sword on its back.

"Answer my fucking questions, then!" Merrick could feel this was not the way to speak to the gods—his race's creators—but there wasn't time for damned pleasantries.

Besides, he'd never been particularly polite.

The gods could take it or leave it.

A laugh trilled through him—the feeling almost similar to Raine's liquor's first warming licks—and Merrick shook his body, forcing out a sharp breath not to let it affect him.

She must die, Merrick. It's what's been prophesied. It's what must happen.

"No!" He didn't care that he screamed like a damned teenager who hadn't learned to control his temper. He wouldn't accept it.

"How can I save her?" Merrick snarled, his voice reverberating around him, almost mocking him when the echo only picked up the last two words.

Save her.

Save her.

I wouldn't advise trying that, either, Guardian of Death.

Guardian of... Merrick ignored the name when he realized the gods might not have answered his question exactly, but had given him an answer all the same.

"So there is a way?" Merrick began pacing back and forth, his mind racing through different scenarios.

I wouldn't advise it.

His feet moved faster.

Back and forth.

Back and forth.

Back and forth.

"Answer me. Yes or no?"

It was quiet for a while, his harsh breaths mingling with the thuds of his feet hitting the mirrored ground the only things breaking it. But then...

Yes.

But there will be consequences. Severe consequences that you'll most certainly regret. Consequences that will harm both you and her, Guardian of Death.

"I don't care!" Merrick growled. "As long as she is alive, that's all that matters! As long as she's breathing and fucking living, I don't care about anything else."

Really?

Something stilled in the air. Anticipation, maybe, he thought, as his muscles stiffened in response.

Then the wall before him melted, and when Merrick caught a glimpse of Lessia's golden-brown hair, he sprinted toward it.

But there must still have been a barrier between them, as he slammed into something solid—something that had his nose crunching as it forced him to a stop.

Even as hot blood flooded his face, he couldn't tear his eyes away from Lessia.

It wasn't the Lessia he'd sailed here with. This one was clean—her hair longer and sparkling in what seemed like summer sun shining down on her.

Her skin had a shimmering hint to it, and she was clad in a dress, a golden one that reminded him too much of the one Loche had once given her.

It was as if he had conjured the regent.

Merrick could only watch as Lessia noticed the dark-haired man, and when a wide smile spread across her face, a mirroring one softened Loche's features.

A shaky huff left Merrick when Loche opened his arms and Lessia ran right into them, winding her tan arms around his neck, and despite that it shouldn't have been possible for him to hear them, all the loving words Loche whispered into her ear, the promises of a future, of a throne, of a position by his side, ruling Havlands together with kindness instead of fear, pierced Merrick's heart like an arrow.

One of his hands flew to his chest, and he pressed against the quickening beats there as that voice sounded again.

If this is the price... if in the end she chooses him... is it still worth it?

Merrick swallowed against the pain, but he didn't hesitate as he declared, "Without a fucking doubt."

The voice was quiet, but he could feel the flickers of curiosity in the air.

"He is a good man," Merrick forced out. "And if... if she chooses him but that means she's still alive... I will be grateful for it every day of what is left of my wretched life."

The image of Loche and Lessia embracing disappeared.

Just evaporated as if it had never been there at all.

They call you the Death Whisperer here, don't they?

Merrick was about to snap that he didn't give a shit and that wasn't what he was here to talk about, when something—that feeling he couldn't explain—warned him against it.

He remained quiet instead, just watching the empty whiteness ahead.

Such a cruel nickname for someone sensitive enough to connect with all souls. Even the ones who have passed on. You truly are one of my sons.

So he was talking to Preysaih, the god of death, then.

Great. He was apparently the most vindictive of them all.

I see you think us evil, Guardian of Death. But we are merely trying to teach our children the lessons they require in life, giving them the tools they need to survive, like any parent would do. Like you've taught the Rantzier girl how to survive this far.

"What the fuck are we going to learn from Lessia dying?" Merrick growled, whipping his gaze around but only meeting the eyes of his own strange reflections.

You shall see.

But Merrick barely heard him as the real Lessia, the

one with the reddened wrist, with the tangled hair and pale skin, stumbled into his line of vision.

He started banging against whatever was before him —what kept them apart.

But it was useless, and he could only watch as she sat down, crossing her thin legs and somehow appearing to understand more quickly than he had done that the gods wanted them there to listen—wanted to test them.

CHAPTER 25
LESSIA

The reflections around her were wrong.

Lessia had realized it immediately because although she'd tried to avoid mirrors lately—which was how she'd caught Raine's fear when he refused to look around so quickly—every time she accidentally met her eyes in the one hanging in the cabin she and Merrick had claimed on the ship, shadows of desperation had mixed with the light of the small hope that still burned inside her.

The hope that somehow, through everything, refused to be snuffed out.

She wasn't entirely certain what she truly hoped for.

To stay alive?

For her friends to live?

For the world to become a better place?

Lessia shook her head.

The reflections around her didn't have any of that in their golden eyes.

There was anger in one pair. Sorrow in another. Love in a third.

Fear.

Hurt.

Pain.

All the feelings she still carried inside her.

But it was the desperation and hope that kept her going right now. That got her out of bed. That had urgency coursing through her blood at all hours of the day and night.

She felt it now as well, but she'd promised Merrick she'd try to find a way out of her death sentence. And if she was entirely truthful... she wanted that for herself as well.

Hello, child.

The voice rumbling through her was warm, like her mother's embraces whenever she hurt herself growing up, but Lessia still shuddered.

The voice was everywhere. In her mind, in her body, in her blood, filling this entire room, or whatever she was sitting in.

Bracing her hands on her knees, she fought against something wanting to bow her neck, to submit, to... give in.

That small, small ember of hope within her wouldn't allow it.

She was done bowing.

So brave.

Lessia didn't say anything as the melodic voice thrilled through her.

It sounded female—warm and kind and motherly—and it brushed her mind with a familiar swipe, albeit not as forcefully as Raine's or Frelina's mind touch: more elegantly, more... experienced.

This must be Evrene, the god of mind.

"You know why I am here." Lessia didn't phrase it as a question.

If this was a god, she expected they would know every last thing about her.

Her thoughts, wishes, and dreams, and especially her fears.

Of course I do, child. I watched you with the Guardian of Death. I saw the dreams you carved into his flesh.

"Can I have them?" she whispered, already forcing the question out, now, because she knew if she waited, she might lose the nerve.

The air hesitated for a second, but that second was enough for a never-ending hollowness to spread within her.

You may have some of them.

She didn't need to ask which ones.

She could feel it in her brittle bones.

There was no hope of survival, not for her.

"When?" she asked softly, shocked that no tears burned behind her eyes.

She'd been surprised on the ship, too, after the wyverns had declared they weren't fighting, that she hadn't broken apart.

She'd been disappointed, yes, but at least... at least she was fighting. She was doing everything she could now to save Havlands—to save their friends. To make it right with the people she'd wronged.

With Loche.

With Frelina.

Soon.

Thissian had said the gods couldn't lie, and met with these vague answers, Lessia believed him.

She didn't ask for more details, as it was probably best not to know. Instead, she asked the question she'd wondered since she'd found out from Loche who the curse was really about.

"Why me?"

A soft rush of air blew through the room, almost as if someone had expelled a deep sigh.

Lessia waited quietly, the thoughts she'd tried not to allow into her mind when the others were around—since Merrick appeared to be reading her as well as Frelina and Raine, who literally could read minds—breaking free.

In the darkness of the night, when everyone else slept and the waves were the only ones hearing her thoughts, she had wondered why. Why her? Why had she gone through everything she had, just to... die?

All the hurt and the pain and fear, and then the friendship and love and happiness.

Our path for you might not seem simple, Elessia Rantzier. But it is. The prophecy required someone who would be kept hidden from Rioner long enough that he or she would grow up. That's where your father came in. It needed you to experience love, both with your family and your friends, but also with Loche and Merrick, for your soul to crave it. It needed you to feel pain, by Rioner's hand and others, so you would never turn to it, never yield to the darkness your uncle has allowed to fill his soul. We needed someone who wouldn't seek power—who wouldn't want to be queen—ruling the shadows.

Lessia stared at the reflection right before her.

It was the one who looked so in love—who smiled softly as she waved to Lessia.

She recalled the conversation she'd had with Merrick when they were on their way to Raine's island.

He'd been right.

The gods had a hand in everything she'd done—that she'd experienced.

He is clever, the Guardian of Death. It's why he was chosen for you, child. You did forge your own path. And even the gods couldn't have foreseen just how brave you'd become.

Despite everything, a shadow of a smile touched her lips. "He is."

Another clever man's face flickered in her mind. Gray eyes she'd used to let consume her, but which now only spread that dark hollowness she tried to keep at bay.

He will smile again.

She'd only thought the question, but she wasn't surprised the booming voice responded to the fleeting inquiry crossing her mind.

He'll live. And to answer your other question: you needed him at that point in your life. You needed to see that not all those who lead are cruel, with blackened hearts. And he needed you as well.

"But they won't need me any longer," Lessia whispered as the reflection before her smiled again, perhaps in response to the god answering why she'd fallen for Loche first if Merrick was the one she'd always choose in the end.

There is a difference between need and want. Something they both shall learn.

Lessia nodded slowly.

In the silence that followed, she leaned her head back,

looking up at the reflection above her, which seemed to be her own, and listened to her slow heartbeats, savoring each thud of life as it thrummed through the space.

She didn't have any more questions about herself. They'd all been answered now.

She just needed to continue what she was doing—could feel that that was what remained of her fate—and make sure those she loved would be cared for.

"Will I see my parents again?" Lessia asked instead, bringing her eyes down and jerking back when she wasn't met with her own strange amber eyes but instead her father's and the blue ones of her mother.

They looked so real. So loving. So much like they had when she was growing up.

That I may not answer. We do not speak of the afterlife.

The voice sharpened for the first time, and Lessia realized she must have overstepped.

The room chilled as if a phantom breeze rushed through it, and the reflections of her parents cracked, their face contorting, and she didn't know why but she shot to her feet, a cry falling from her lips when her parents also screamed in her mind—their voices so real she tried to cover her ears to drown them out.

But they were inside her.

Lessia's eyes shut as she bent forward, trying to hold herself together as the cries only continued and continued. But she wasn't afraid when arms locked around her, a cheek touching hers as he whispered her name.

Of course Merrick came for her.

She let him hold her until the blood-chilling sounds faded, and when they finally quieted, she spun around in his arms, dry sobs hacking out of her and her chest heaving from pain.

"I know," Merrick whispered. "I know."

He did know. She was sure of that, but even so, she cried into his chest. "I won't see them again. I-I won't—"

Evrene hadn't explicitly said so, but the wind that draped around her had been filled with a touch of despair and fear and loneliness—which hadn't been Lessia's—and she'd understood then.

"I won't..." she echoed.

Merrick was quiet as she continued rambling to herself against his chest, wishing for the tears that, for some reason, refused her—though she knew they might relieve some of the tightness in her broken chest.

It was as if her body wouldn't let her break. Not anymore. As if there wasn't enough space left, with the determination and the fight and the promises she'd made to the living.

But it hurt. It hurt so much, thinking of the loving people she'd had the honor of being a daughter to, the ones she'd never see again, never speak to again.

"They d-didn't know me," she choked out as Merrick pressed her harder into his chest. "T-they died not knowing me. My mother... she didn't even know I existed. And... my father..." A dry sob wrangled from her throat. "He only got to meet this version of me... the broken one... the..."

Lessia's hands balled into fists against Merrick's chest.

It wasn't fair. None of this was fair.

"I know," Merrick echoed, his hands running up and down her back in a slow, rhythmic motion. "I know."

She nodded as he continued whispering the words.

He did know. Perhaps he was the only one who really did know her, and...

Maybe that would have to be enough.

CHAPTER 26
FRELINA

She hated this place.

Frelina knew her face should mirror the emotions within her—the anger and frustration and, if she was honest, the fear at being alone here in this strange world—but the reflections staring back at her carried none of that.

There was sorrow in every face as she spun and whirled to find anywhere without a haunted version of herself looking at her, but in every pair of amber eyes, there was only sadness and despair.

"Stop it," she muttered when the urge to curl up into a ball to hide from the wide eyes tracking her nearly overtook her. "Stop it."

Instead of giving in to the impulse, Frelina closed her eyes, drawing deep breaths to calm herself.

In and out through her nose.

But the air did little to calm her racing heart, and when a deep, melodic voice broke through the strange humming noise—the one she thought she might have heard before but couldn't place—she was ashamed to admit she jumped a foot in the air.

Hello, Frelina Rantzier.

Frelina made herself breathe again. She wasn't interested in speaking to whoever or whatever this was.

That was a lie, child.

Frelina shook her head.

She wasn't going to entertain this. She wasn't here for herself.

They'd come for Lessia. For Merrick. To hopefully find a way to keep her sister alive.

But that's not the only wish you carry in your heart, is it?

A tremor ran down her back. She didn't like this voice. She didn't like it at all.

"Who are you?" Frelina demanded, although her words didn't carry the harshness she'd intended. Her voice had risen at the end, and she winced at herself, finally opening her eyes again.

Those figures around her still glared with that devastating expression, their large eyes filled with tears.

Gods, was that how pathetic she looked?

You do not know me?

How would she...

"You're a god, I presume." She didn't get her voice right that time, either, the fear rippling across her skin making her words shake.

Low laughter traveled through the room, somehow making the mirrored walls contort, their surface swirling with rings like when she threw stones at the water back home.

"How is that funny?" Frelina bit out, eyes tracing the rings as they increased in size and danced around the versions of herself that lived in the mirrors.

You do not need to lie to me, Frelina. I see the fear in your soul. It's taking over. As for your question... my name is Zharra.

The god of life.

She couldn't help but roll her eyes. Wasn't that ironic?

It's no coincidence we speak today, child. We're all called to those who need us the most.

"I don't need you!" Frelina raised her voice, unsure why her gut twisted so hard she nearly bent over. "I am here for Elessia. To save her."

You lie again.

Ice—actual small pieces of ice—blew through the space. The light—Frelina had no idea where it came from—flickered for a second, shifting into dark, then light, then dark, then light again.

I see you. I hear you. I know you. You cannot lie to me. You're scared. Perhaps more than any of your friends here today. And I know why.

"I am not." Her voice wavered so much she needed to take a breath before continuing, the sense of needing to submit to this damned god flooding her and making her bend her neck before she was able to catch herself. "I want to save Elessia!"

I never said you didn't. I said it wasn't your only wish.

Tears began building behind Frelina's eyes, and she blinked frantically to rid herself of them, but it was impossible, especially as the voice spoke again.

You fear you will die alone. That you won't find love or friendship, or experience any of the things you've read about. You fear no one aside from your family will ever care for you. You fear that you'll never feel desire or passion or pain that comes with life.

"Stop it!" Frelina lifted her hands to her ears to shut out the voice, but it only continued booming through her head.

No matter how many walls she slammed up, it broke through every single one as if they were made of feathers that the wind could easily blow away.

You fear that you'll never get that first kiss. That you'll never have a man hold you to whisper sweet words into your ear.

"I said stop it," Frelina cried, tears rushing down her cheeks. "Stop it!"

I've seen how you watch your sister and her mate—

"Stop," Frelina begged. "Please... stop."

Why? You ask yourself these questions each night. Are you too frightened to hear the truth?

An ache spread in Frelina's head from how hard she pressed her hands against the sides of it, and she shut her eyes, the light flickering over her eyelids pulsating red and black.

She didn't want to hear this. She didn't.

Please! Please!

There is no mate for you in Havlands. That much I am allowed to tell you.

Her wails joined the voice now.

"Please," she continued begging. "Please, please, please."

I've seen a future where you die alone. No parents left in this world. A sister sacrificed. Unloved. Living in fear.

"No. No, no, no!" Frelina fell to her knees, surprised at how painful the mirror was as it slammed into her.

The physical pain sliced through her mind, breaking through the panic.

"No," she said again. "No."

She'd always known this. She had never believed she'd get what Elessia had. She didn't deserve it. Not like her sister did.

The sister they were here for.

A shallow breath made its way into her lungs.

This wasn't about Frelina. They weren't here for her. What was happening now... it was a distraction. By the gods who'd cursed her family. By the gods who'd forced her sister to become a pawn in their game.

But they cannot lie, a small voice reminded her.

Frelina's hands dropped to the floor, landing beside her knees.

It didn't matter. So she didn't have a mate?

She had Elessia. She had... friends.

Raine, the stupid, drunk bastard, had somehow become her closest one.

Even Merrick... They understood each other in the way only those who loved someone about to die could understand each other.

You are all alone.

"No!" Her voice didn't shake this time. "No, I am not."

Her eyes opened, and she glared at the tear-streaked faces before her.

"I am *not* alone."

Frelina's hands pressed into the cold floor, and she pushed one of her legs to straighten. Then the other one.

"I am not alone." Frelina repeated the sentence as she got to her feet, as she started walking up to one of the reflections she'd avoided before.

"I am not alone."

Halting right before it, she lifted a hand and pressed it against the glittering wall.

Her reflection—and the eerie, foreign expression on it—melted away, and she nearly fell forward when the entire wall followed, disappearing as if it had never been there in the first place.

Another sound reached her ears, and it stabbed into her heart like a dagger.

Raine was on the ground, head covered with his hands and knees tucked in close as he screamed, "Don't do this to me! Don't do this to me!"

Frelina sprinted up to him, dropping to her knees beside him and grabbing his shoulders. "Raine! It's not real! It's not real!"

The Fae warrior's entire body shook, and something fell from his lap, clinking as it hit the mirrored ground.

That stupid flask.

Frelina hated it so much, but she still picked it up, trying to shove it into Raine's hand.

"Here!" she urged. "This will help."

A scream tore from Raine's throat. One she wished never to hear again.

It wasn't just pain that fueled it. It was agony, torment, and grief. Grief that she'd had a taste of in his memories, but that now was even more raw because... it wasn't muddled.

"Th-they took it!" Raine screamed. "They took it!"

Frelina continued to try to give him the flask, and when he still refused, she unscrewed it herself, her nose immediately wrinkling at the harsh stench.

"Drink!" she tried to demand, but he continued to push it away.

"They took it," he wailed again.

"Took what?" Frelina finally secured the lid, letting

the flask tumble to the floor once more. “What did they take, Raine?”

She didn’t recognize his eyes when he looked up at her.

They were...

Clear. Not bloodshot. Not hazy or glassy but... clear.

Understanding pebbled her skin, and she couldn’t help the slight jerk weaving across her shoulders.

“They took it,” he said again, eyes going wild. “I can’t... I can’t do it. You know I... I can’t.”

“The alcohol? Raine, it’s still in there.” She’d smelled it, after all, and there was no mistaking that smell—not even as it mingled with the strange, otherworldly one of this room.

“No!” Raine shook his head so much his red hair flew around it, nearly whipping her own face. “They took m-my ability.”

“They took your magic?” Frelina could feel the color drain from her face.

Could the gods do that?

“No.” Raine’s eyes went unseeing before they shut, his closed eyelids twitching and features pulling as if he was in great pain. “I can’t... I can’t drink it anymore. They took it from m-me. S-said I was wasting... wasting my life.”

Oh.

Oh, fuck.

“Are... are you sure?”

Frelina didn’t know what to say. She’d finally understood earlier today why he had to drown out the memories, why he relied on that flask like a babe did on its mother.

He couldn’t live without the distraction.

Raine didn't respond.

A low wail, almost a humming sound of pain, echoed around them as he began rocking back and forth.

"Raine!" Frelina shook his shoulders, but he didn't react. "Raine! You're scaring me!"

No response, but that soul-crushing sound continued to build within the space, bouncing off the walls, becoming louder and louder.

The mirrors responded to it, and Frelina watched with wide eyes as their reflections began warping, then cracking, and she realized what was happening.

The Fae before her was breaking.

She'd heard it could happen—had seen up close how near her father had been to losing his mind, how he'd clung to that last bit of sanity only because of Frelina, had seen in Merrick's memories how her sister had turned to rage and guilt to keep herself from being pulled under.

Raine, on the other hand... He'd learned to cope only with alcohol.

If that was gone?

The wailing continued, and her heart, which had already been racing, slammed against her ribs now.

She needed to do something.

Raine rocked into her with every movement forward, and she could feel him slipping.

His mind was wide open when she reached out for it, but she quickly had her own snap back.

It was dark. Empty. Terrifying.

It felt as if her own might fall right down with it, especially now, especially after her devastating interaction with the gods.

You're going to die alone.

It was Raine's voice now, although she knew it wasn't truly his.

It was her mind responding to his anguish, like it always did when other people's memories invaded it.

Raine shook so much under her hands as she held on to his shoulders that she began trembling as well.

You're going to die alone.

You're going to die alone.

Raine's voice continued booming within her despite her attempt to block him, and she realized he was losing control over his magic.

She also realized he had been holding back with her before.

He'd allowed her to push into his mind because this force... whatever was attacking her now... it was all-consuming—so much more powerful than she'd ever experienced.

Frelina gasped when she understood that it wasn't her mind tricking her.

It *was* Raine's voice, but... he wasn't talking to her.

"No," she mumbled. "None of us is dying alone."

Raine didn't respond, his eyes open again but completely unseeing—the beautiful green and gold paling with every moment she tried to look into them.

It fucking terrified her.

"Raine!" she cried. "Raine! You're not dying now! Do you hear me! You can't leave me! You're not alone! You're not alone!"

It was as if she didn't even exist.

She slapped him.

He didn't react.

She slapped him again—harder this time.

He didn't react.

"Raine! You bastard! Wake the fuck up!"

He didn't react.

Frelina's mind spun. What should she do? Her father had never been this bad. Elessia hadn't been this bad, had she?

Merrick had always been there to distract her, keeping her away from the harsh descent into madness that threatened the Fae if they hurt too much, if they lost too many, if the pain managed to consume them.

A whisper of a memory of Merrick carrying Elessia into the ship's cabin floated through her mind.

He always distracted her...

Her thoughts flew to the game she and Raine had been playing.

But it was a *game*, and she'd seen how he jerked back whenever she came too close. He didn't want her, not in the way Elessia wanted Merrick.

You're going to die alone.

Her eyes flicked to the ceiling, meeting those fucking sad ones of her stupid reflection.

You fear that you'll never get that first kiss.

Her eyes dropped to Raine's full lips, the shadow of red stubble around them.

He would kill her. And then probably kill himself.

Frelina moved her arms to wrap around his neck.

No kiss, but she'd try to distract him like she'd done before. Maybe that would be enough.

"Raine," she called softly, trying to morph her voice into the low, seductive one she used when they played with each other. "Raine."

His eyes still seemed to focus and unfocus.

"Raine," she said again as she wrangled herself into his lap.

His arms automatically went around her back to steady her when she lost her balance, and a glimmer of hope awoke in her chest, warming it as she pressed it against Raine's broad one, tightening her grip around his neck and placing her legs on either side of him.

"You're not alone," she whispered when his eyes brushed hers before staring into nothing again.

"I am here. Look at me." Frelina shifted her hands to cup his cheeks.

He did, his hazel eyes wandering over her face before landing on her own.

"I can't." Raine's broken whisper, the pinch of his face that followed, nearly broke her resolve.

"You can." Frelina smiled, ignoring how tight her cheeks were from all the salt from her tears. "You're not alone."

Raine just stared at her.

Drawing a steadying breath, Frelina wiggled her brows.

"We're here together." She slowly trailed her eyes over his face as she moved closer, trying to keep a sly smile on her face. "You and me."

Raine didn't back away as she stilled an inch from him, but some of the color on his cheeks returned, his eyes deepening.

"You know they told me I would die alone." Frelina licked her lips, and she didn't miss Raine's eyes following. "Do you know what I think?"

He shook his head.

"I don't think so, since the most feared Fae warrior in the world keeps flirting with me."

Something sounded in Raine's chest.

It wasn't a laugh or even a chuckle, but she'd take it,

especially as more color returned to his eyes. Frelina began to pull away, pushing her feet into the ground when Raine's face contorted again, and the sound she'd heard before began echoing between her ears.

"I... I can't," Raine whispered. "Not without..."

Settling into his lap again, she brushed her thumbs over his cheeks. "What can I do?"

Raine's eyes were dry as they held hers, but it didn't matter. They were still the saddest ones she'd ever seen.

"What can I do, Raine?" she whispered back as he let out a sorrow-filled rush of air. "How can I help you?"

"I don't... I need..."

He looked so young. A lost boy with sad eyes and wild hair who held on to her as if she were the only toy he had left in the world.

Her heart ached for him.

For the male who'd loved so much only to have it ripped away from him. For the loneliness she could sense in him—the one she shared.

Pursing her lips, she made a decision.

"Use me," Frelina said quietly.

Raine's arms tightened around her. "What?"

"Use me." She said it louder. "Use me as a distraction."

Raine's brows snapped together, and he began shaking his head.

"I won't live long. The gods basically confirmed it. Neither will you, the way this war is going. You don't love me. I... I don't love you. She'll forgive you."

Frelina's cheeks heated when Raine shook his head again.

"Why not? You've been with others, haven't you?"

His silence was enough.

"So why not me? Use me, Raine. Use me until we've either won this war or moved on to the afterlife—whatever comes first. I need it too. I don't... I don't want to be alone anymore."

It was true. She didn't want to be alone in a cold bed, fear trickling through her veins until she finally fell into fitful sleep. If she was to die soon, and there wasn't someone special out there waiting for her anyway, what did it matter?

Raine still didn't say anything, and embarrassment washed over her.

What had she been thinking? Was she that desperate to make sure he didn't lose it?

Or... that desperate for company herself?

She laughed weakly as she began rising, releasing his face, but Raine's grip tightened, and he dragged her down again, boring his eyes into hers.

"Little Rantzier," he whispered, his voice gravelly. "You sure?"

Something warm—and not from the shame still tinting her cheeks—ignited in her core.

She nodded.

Raine watched her for a moment, and the air crackled in the room. "You're really sure? You want this? You want... me?"

She nodded again, allowing him to see her mind—to know that she meant every word. See that she didn't want to be alone. See the things she wanted to feel—to know—before she died.

Raine blinked.

Then one of his hands moved to her chin and slid down her throat until he'd tilted her head back.

"I won't be gentle," Raine warned. "That's not who I

am. That's not what I can offer you. This isn't love, little Rantzier. This is—"

"Good," Frelina interrupted, that heat within her spreading. "That's what I was counting on."

His lips were on hers in the next moment.

He hadn't lied.

It wasn't gentle. It was desperate. It was salty.

It was need, it was fear, it was shared loneliness.

It was teeth clashing, lips crashing together so harshly that iron filled her mouth.

It was a tightening hand around her neck, restricting her air, as he shifted her head even farther back, devouring her mouth.

It was a hard nip that had her gasp, and a tongue finding its way into her mouth to play.

Frelina loved every moment of it.

She was alive.

She felt... wild. Free.

She had no idea if her response was good, but she savored each groan that shook his body as he roughly shifted her so she was pressed fully against him, and when he left her mouth to nip at her chin, then moved down to suck and bite at her throat...

A sound she'd never made before echoed around the room, filling the air with want and need and desire.

"Good to know," Raine rasped as he continued down, biting into her collarbone as she began rocking back and forth in his lap. "Good. To. Know."

She moaned again as he returned to her mouth, but as she began pulling at his tunic, Raine stopped her, his eyes finally fully focused again.

Panting, she stared at him, glad when she realized his chest was moving up and down as wildly as her own.

"Not yet." Raine kissed her again, so hard she sucked his bottom lip into her mouth and sank her teeth into it.

It only made him laugh, and another piece of hope settled within Frelina's chest.

"I think we'll have some fun distracting each other." His words dripped with promise, and despite everything that had happened, liquid heat pooled in her entire body as Raine got them both to their feet. "But we need to get out of this damned place."

CHAPTER 27
MERRICK

He didn't know four little words would just about kill him.

But hearing Lessia ask "Can I have them?" was as excruciating as when he'd once been captured and tortured for weeks by enemy Fae.

Having to watch the rest of her conversation with Evrene play out... no, it was a pain he wouldn't wish even on Rioner.

Lessia's warm body clung to his, and he held her closer, trying to push down the rage at the gods for what they'd done to her. For what they continued to do to her.

The violent trembles running through her had calmed a while ago, but she'd still gripped his jacket so tightly he hadn't dared move, not even to try to study her face, try to see if this was what would finally break her.

His pulse thrummed over his skin, and he knew Lessia could sense it as she glanced up at him, a wrinkle of worry forming over her brows.

Leaning down, Merrick kissed that wrinkle, then moved to press his lips against hers.

Only once, but he couldn't stand not touching her.

Not after today. Not after everything.

As he pulled back, Lessia began whispering, "I am s—"

He didn't stop the rage this time as he placed a finger over her lips. "No."

Her beautiful eyes widened at his command.

"You do not apologize." Merrick wished he could say he was calm, but he was anything but as he continued. "It's them who should apologize. It's them who should fucking crawl at your feet, begging for your forgiveness."

Merrick lifted his chin, fixing his eyes on the reflection of the two of them in the ceiling.

"Do you hear me?" he screamed, his vision going in and out from fury. "You should fucking apologize, and when the time comes... I am going to fucking make you! I am going to make each and every one of you kneel before her like the queen she is!"

He knew that if he'd had magic right now, the souls would race unchecked through the room—searching for the gods he knew they also hated, for reasons he hadn't understood before but that were becoming clearer to him by the second.

"Merrick," Lessia urged. "Merrick, be careful."

"Why?" He flung his gaze down to Lessia again. "What else can they do to us now? What else can they threaten us with?"

She stared back at him, her eyes darkening and some of that defiance he fucking loved shifting her features into the Lessia he knew would fight until her last breath.

His little fighter.

A loud silence enveloped them as they watched each other, and Merrick could barely believe his eyes as his mate seemed to sharpen with every second, not an ounce of the sorrow flickering in her hard gaze.

"You're right," she said simply, her eyes burning into his. "You're right."

He was. And he was going to fucking save her. Now that he knew there was a chance, he would make sure he stayed beside her every damned step of the way, even if it would drive her crazy.

He'd fucking kill the gods if that's what it took. Make each of them pay in blood for the pain they'd caused her.

"I know I'm right," Merrick rasped as he bent down to claim her lips again, continuing to speak against them when he came up for air. "Fuck them, Lessia. Fuck fate. Fuck this place. Let's get those wyverns, go to war, kill the king, and fucking win."

She kissed him. Kissed him with a feverish urgency that told him she would fight to the end, even if what he'd just said was unlikely to happen, and he couldn't help but groan when his body responded to it, his cock already awakening when she dragged her nails down the back of his neck.

"Here?" Merrick mumbled as she began undressing, her fingers not hesitating as they unbuttoned the jacket he'd given her a few days ago.

"Let them watch." Lessia lifted her chin, her eyes sparkling as she dragged a finger along his neckline. "Let them see they can't break me. Let them see I am not scared anymore. Let them see I won't bow to them and their fucking curse."

Fuck. He'd never loved her as much as he did now.

She was a damned goddess.

A goddess who began undressing slowly, seductively, in a way that had his jaw slacken and only allowed him to remain still and watch.

Her tunic dropped first, her perfect breasts reflecting all around him, the nipples drawing in and hardening as he dragged his gaze over them.

After undoing her boots, one at a time, she slowly slid her breeches down until she stood before him only in her silky undergarments, soft skin on full display and head still lifted high, her beautiful golden-brown hair tumbling down her straight back.

The carvings of his name on her body and the traitor mark sweeping across her arm only made her more magnificent.

She was real. She was real and she was here and she was his.

Merrick nearly lost it when he caught the damp spot on the white fabric between her legs.

She was already wet, and he could fucking smell it.

His cock twitched again, more painfully now, but he ignored it, unwilling to speed this up a second more than he had to.

"Is that for me?" he asked roughly.

Lessia smiled as she dragged a hand down her front, squeezing a breast before sliding it down to her stomach and hovering right above the waistline of the delicate piece of clothing.

"Of course it's for you," she whispered. "I'm yours, Merrick. I'm always yours."

He closed his eyes for a moment, committing that sentence to memory.

I'm yours, Merrick.

He fucking loved it when she said his name.

She never did it in fear, like most others, but emphasized each letter, taking care to pronounce it with all the love he could feel rolling off her. Even during the election, she'd pronounced it differently, at least when she'd stopped calling him *death boy*. It hadn't been with love then, but some kind of mutual respect—one he hadn't heard in connection with this name since he was young.

"You are mine," he echoed, his voice rough. "You will always be mine as I will always be yours. As I always have been."

She smiled wider. "What do you want me to do?"

He must have frowned because she continued. "I told you I'd do anything for you. What would you want me to do?"

Merrick groaned.

He was so fucking lucky. So undeserving of this beautiful, selfless, loving creature.

He promised himself again to give her all the wishes she carved onto his skin. He was going to take care of her —love her—if it was the last fucking thing he did in this realm.

"Come here." Merrick reached out a hand. "Let me make you feel good."

He would have died to watch her touch herself, see what she did to make herself utter the noises he dreamed of every night, but he couldn't ask it.

Not now, not when every bone and nerve and part of his soul craved to protect her—care for her.

She did enough fighting alone. This was his responsibility.

And he'd enjoy every damned second of it.

Lessia slowly approached him, and if his eyes could have, they would have eaten her up. He let them slide over her long legs, over her undergarments where the wet spot had grown, over her hip bones and stomach, savoring her full breasts and then moving to her beautiful face.

"You are fucking perfect." Merrick reached out a hand and touched her cheek when she stilled before him. "Every inch of you is perfect. You're the goddess, Lessia. Not them. No one else but you."

He believed it. This golden-dipped female was not of this world. She couldn't be, not when all this world was pain and cruelty and she was kindness and light and perfection.

She didn't shy away from his roving eyes.

Her chin only lifted higher, her lips curling a little bit more, and Merrick didn't bite down on the grin spreading across his face.

"Good girl," he rasped, so damned proud of her, and just a bit proud of himself to see her believe his words.

Lessia's eyes heated as she stared back at him, and he smiled wider as he dropped to his knees before her.

The shiver jerking her body was everything he wanted to see.

"You like this?" He tilted his head upward, watching as her cheeks colored.

Merrick's low laugh rumbled through the room. "Of course you do. My little fighter likes her man on his knees before her. Likes to see him serve her like the goddess she is."

She actually moaned, and he hadn't even touched her.

"Yes," Merrick continued, feeling his balls tighten when he could smell her responding to his words. "Do you want to hear that I'd do anything for you? Do you want to hear that I'm going to fuck you in this place, making the gods of our world watch as I please you, as I submit to your every command?"

Lessia squirmed before him, and he had to clench his hands not to touch her.

Not yet.

"I am going to fuck you until you're screaming my name so loudly these fucking mirrors threaten to break. But first..." Merrick fixed his eyes on her beautiful pussy hidden by the white silk. "First, I am going to taste you. I am going to commit every swirl of your pussy to memory."

"Please, Merrick," she whimpered, and it was all he needed to hear.

"You don't need to beg. Never for me." Merrick didn't let her respond as he pressed her thighs wide, making sure she stood steady before he trailed a finger down her stomach, hovering right above the white silk.

"I want to rip these apart," Merrick growled. "They're in my way."

He hooked his finger under her panty line, pulling it out and letting it snap back, eliciting another cry from Lessia.

Those fucking sounds made him nearly spill right into his trousers.

"Maybe I should," Merrick mused when Lessia squirmed again, trying to press her legs together for some release, although she didn't fight him too much when he refused her. "I like the idea of you walking around without them. Knowing that I can slip my hand down at any moment and touch the pussy that's always wet for me."

"Merrick," she whined.

"But I won't. At least not today."

He really did struggle not to rip the innocent fabric apart. Because while Lessia was kind and sweet and light, she wasn't innocent, and he loved how she responded to his dirty words. How she gave him as much back.

"Fuck," he swore when his cock pulsated and he used a hand to adjust it.

Not that it helped when Lessia followed the hand with fucking hunger in her eyes.

He couldn't wait anymore. Merrick didn't give her a warning as he roughly yanked her underwear aside, sinking his mouth into her pink pussy, one hand sliding around to grab her ass and the other shoving her thighs even wider.

He groaned as her flavors flooded his mouth.

"You taste so fucking good," he growled against her shaking pussy, using his tongue to lap at her folds, then switching to move in circles over her clit.

His little fighter responded exactly as he'd known she would.

She wrapped her hands in his hair and pulled at it, crying out with each steady swipe of his tongue.

Merrick sucked and licked, making sure not an inch was missed as he devoured her, alternating between lazy strokes of his tongue and the sharp nips at her bud that seemed to drive her crazy.

As he glanced up from her glistening pussy, he watched her head fall back, her eyes closing as she moaned his name, again and again, and he continued, teasing her hole with his tongue until she cried out, her teeth sinking into her bottom lip as her body began trembling.

"Yes," Merrick mumbled against her skin. "Fight for it. Fight for what's yours."

Her nails dug into his scalp as he sucked on her clit again, and Merrick slid the hand keeping her legs apart up her thigh, using his thumb to circle her entrance while he continued to eat her.

Her breaths came quicker now, her chest heaving above him, making her stomach clench and unclench, and he shifted, using his thumb to press hard against her bud as his tongue speared into her, drawing out another scream.

"My name," Merrick purred. "You scream my name when you come."

She didn't disappoint as his name began spilling from her lips.

Merrick began lapping at her faster, in rhythm with her panting, his tongue darting in and out of her while his thumb moved faster and faster over her clit.

Allowing himself another glance up, he drank in her pink cheeks, her wild golden eyes as they opened to stare down at him, and he stopped his merciless nibbling and sucking to whisper in awe, "Look at you. You're so beautiful."

"Merrick." She sucked in a breath as he continued working her with his thumb, her eyes never leaving his. "Merrick. Merrick. Merrick."

His gaze lifted to the ceiling, and he demanded, "Look at us."

His fucking good girl did exactly what he asked, and as soon as her eyes met his in the mirror above and she could see him on his knees, face shining from her juices, he moved his hand to drive a finger into her at the same time as his mouth attacked her clit again, all the while watching her.

She screamed his name, her breaths becoming shallow, causing her entire body to quiver, and he started moving his finger faster, sucking harder on her bud.

"Look at us," he mumbled before he added a second finger, dipping them in and out until she thrust against them, her body straining so hard he knew she was close.

"Take it. Take what you deserve, my queen."

She did. Lessia started riding his hand, speeding up his movements until her moans and the wet sound of her pussy sliding along his fingers were the only things to be heard in the room.

His cock bulged in his trousers, and he knew he needed to fuck her soon, especially when her perfect pussy tightened around his fingers, lighting his body on fire.

With his eyes on hers in the mirror, he bit down on her clit while ruthlessly shoving his fingers inside her.

"Merrick." His name was like a prayer on her lips, and then her breath stuttered, her face pinching but eyes never closing as her pussy strangled his fingers, wetness and near unbearable heat flooding his hand.

Merrick growled as he stared back at her, and when she also continued meeting his eyes, that heat that made them molten not fading away but deepening, he dragged her drenched undergarment down, before ordering "Lie down."

Helping her shaking legs to fold, Merrick settled her onto her back, allowing himself a quick look in the mirrors around them—seeing so many magnificent versions of his perfect mate—before freeing his cock from the restraining breeches and pulling his tunic over his head.

Fisting his cock in one hand, squeezing it up and down to pace himself, he lay down atop her, using his other arm to keep most of his weight off her.

She protested at that, her hands moving to his back, nails digging into his muscles before piercing his skin, dragging down from his shoulder blades to his ass.

"So eager," Merrick purred.

Lessia narrowed her eyes at him, shoving at the hand holding his shaft and wrapping her own smaller one around the tip.

He could barely fucking believe it when she used her thumb to sweep off the wetness already forming there and then brought it to her lips to taste.

Merrick had to close his eyes for a moment, take a deep breath so as not to just drive into her and spill everything he had.

Fuck, she was so fucking perfect.

His cock heated, swelling even more under her touch when she dipped her hand back down, and he smiled when her eyes widened.

Leaning his forehead on hers, he whispered, "I love you. I love you so fucking much."

She kissed him softly, in complete contrast with the eager hand beginning to milk his cock, moving up and down with a fervent speed.

"I love you too," she said against his lips. "I love you with all the broken pieces I have."

Merrick's muscles coiled, but not in pleasure.

Gently removing her hand from his hard length, he brought it to her chest, and still keeping his body from crushing hers with the other one, he responded, "You're not broken, Lessia."

He slid his cock against her wetness, forcing down the groan spilling into his throat at how her jaw slackened, her eyes melting into his.

"You're not broken," he repeated as he lifted further, wanting—no, needing—to watch as he slid into her. As they became one, as they were meant to be.

He ground against her pussy again, coating his cock in her glistening wetness, before nudging her legs farther apart and thrusting his hips until his pulsating cock pushed inside her.

They exhaled at the same time, their eyes holding each other's hostage.

Merrick started moving, forcing his eyes to remain open as they threatened to close at the pleasure.

She was so wet. So fucking warm.

Lessia started shaking again, but as her eyelids fluttered, he ordered, "Eyes on me."

She obliged immediately, and he had to bend to kiss her, claim her full lips until they swelled from the force—from the passion—of their clashing.

Merrick slid almost the entire way out, even as his cock screamed at him for leaving the warmth, and then he thrust.

Hard.

Sinking all the way inside her until his hips slammed against hers.

Her eyes rolled back into her head as her back arched off the mirror.

"Eyes on me when I fuck you," Merrick rasped again, and Lessia's golden ones flew open, colliding with his in the way that always had his stomach heat.

Fuck, it should have been illegal to love someone like he loved her.

It was as if his heart wanted to burst out of his body, take over the entire world, drive everything and everyone else away.

He needed only her. But... he needed her so fucking much.

Lessia seemed to catch on to what he was thinking because her fingers began moving over his back again, nails scratching against his skin, impatient and wanting.

He wouldn't disappoint her.

Merrick moved, thrusting deep inside her as her legs spread even farther. Pushing himself up on the arm by her side, he watched her beautiful body shake beneath him, how her breasts bounced with each shove of his cock, and how she reached up to meet him—to allow him to go even deeper.

Fuck. When her hips rolled to meet his, he couldn't hold back anymore.

"Arms around my neck," Merrick growled, and when Lessia locked her hands, holding on tight, he started pumping into her, thrills of heat racing down his back with each thrust as he drove into her harder and harder and harder.

"Merrick," she cried, her body tensing and arms gripping him tighter.

"Lessia," he groaned back, the sheen of sweat that covered them both making their bodies slick as he slammed his cock into her, and he couldn't resist the urge to mark her—even if his name was now permanently etched into her skin.

"Fuck," he swore as her pussy contracted around him, and he nestled his face into her neck, biting down on her sensitive skin until she cried out again, her heat nearly choking his cock as she came, his name streaming from her mouth in a rambling mess.

Heat filled Merrick, and his balls throbbed as he swirled his tongue over the mating mark, and when her blood touched his lips... it was over.

Blood rushed within him, and he came harder than he ever had before, spilling deep into her as she held on to him, whispering how much she loved him.

Over and over.

CHAPTER 28
LOCHE

Geyia stood by the stove in the cramped cabin, and while they had brought little food with them in their haste to leave to find Lessia, his friend must have managed to whip something up, from the mouthwatering smells filling the small room.

Loche apparently wasn't the only one starving, as almost every inch of the room was filled with people. Around the same table he sat at, Zaddock and Amalise were seated beside each other, the former still staring at her while she ignored him.

The copper-haired sisters had taken the seats beside Loche, while Kerym had slipped onto the chair beside Pellie, his blue eyes—which were still eerily strong in color, apparently from siphoning almost all the pale Fae's energy—wandering over the small woman, something like curiosity on his face.

Thissian, who'd been stabbed in the gut, suffering a wound so deep no human would have survived, sat against a wall, his face still blanched but eyes sharp as they took in the room the same way Loche did.

Ardow and Venko sat beside him, the former offering to get Thissian something but being rewarded only with a dismissive wave of the Fae's hand.

Around them, the Faelings had spread out, making themselves at home on Loche's ship after abandoning the smaller one they'd come on, although they kept huddled together, throwing somewhat suspicious looks at the Siphon Twins.

He'd decided with Geyia and Steiner that it would be best if they remained together, not just because they might need that magic he'd only caught a glimpse of when the Faelings saved them from Meyah, but because they were running out of time.

Geyia and the others had told him they'd raced away from several strange ships when they left Ellow's water, and that the whispers in Ellow confirmed they only had days until the rebels attacked.

Thankfully, they'd also seen his soldiers follow the orders he'd borrowed Raine's eagle to deliver.

His men—following the orders he'd sent—were rounding up all the men and women in Ellow who were willing to fight, putting them on the ships they had left from the last war, and sending all those too old or young or sick to the caves for safety.

Some of them might be rebels, as Loche had refused to cause mistrust and chaos already before the fight began, but he harbored a small hope that if they saw their friends and neighbors fall at the rebels' swords, they might reconsider.

It was a fragile hope, of course, but if Lessia of all

people could keep a small flame burning after everything... so could he.

Loche's eyes stayed on some of the younger Faelings. There was a boy there who looked only twelve or thirteen, his body lanky in the way Loche's had been when he finally grew at eleven, and his raven hair messy in a way that told him the child didn't care what it looked like.

It was almost too much when gray eyes met his. Even if they were darker than his own, they carried the same suspicion Loche hadn't been able to erase after his own years on the streets.

From what Lessia had told him, these Faelings hadn't had it easy.

Still, they were here. They were fighting. For this fucking wretched world. For Ellow—a nation that hadn't been kind to them either.

Those gray eyes continued to bore into his own, and Loche found himself struggling to look away, something stirring in him when more eyes turned his way, sizing him up.

A white-haired woman, one who seemed to be the leader of the Faelings, found his eyes briefly before she winced—actually winced at him—and turned away, backing up a few steps.

One by one, the half-Fae focused on Geyia again, their eyes lighting up when she threw quips their way, exactly like she'd done with Loche when they got to know each other to make him comfortable with her—every pair but the gray ones that had captured Loche's eyes first.

They narrowed as they swept over Loche's dark clothing—the simple but expensive cut of his trousers and shirt—and a feeling of unease crept up on the regent when he realized what ill-fitting clothing they were all clad in.

Loche cleared his throat, and before he realized what he was doing, he addressed the Faelings, silencing the soft smattering of plates and hushed conversations in the room.

"I promise you, if we win the war, things will be different. Ellow will be different." He nodded once as he sought the young boy's eyes before meeting each pair around him. "You will not need to hide anymore. Not from anyone."

It was quiet for a second, and the mistrust tensing in the air was palpable as the gray-eyed young boy spoke up.

"That's not why we're here." One of his arms shot out, sweeping across the group. "Lessia fought for us when no one else would. We will fight for her until our last breath if that's what it takes."

His eyes held a wisdom that was too old for his age as he continued. "You might be regent, but you didn't do *anything* for us. Even if you must have known what it was like. And from what I've now heard, you're a *halfling* yourself." He spat out the vile word as if it was hard for him to even let his lips touch it.

"Ledger!" Geyia's wide eyes flew to Loche before she stepped toward the boy. "That's no—"

Loche lifted a hand, rising from his chair. "It's fine, Geyia."

Pushing his chair in, he looked around the room. At his friends. At the Fae warriors. At the Faelings, shying away from Ledger, who still kept his chin raised, although Loche could tell his small hands shook even if he tried to hide them behind his back.

"He's right." Loche forced himself not to swallow in the silence. "Ledger here is right. I didn't do anything for you. It wasn't until Lessia opened my eyes that I understood what was happening right under my nose." He rested his hands on the back of the chair. "I've made many, many mistakes in the past years. With my people... with my friends. With those I love."

Loche paused for a second, making sure he was certain of what he was planning to say next.

There wasn't an ounce of hesitation within him.

"That's why I will step down as regent after this war. Ellow needs to heal. Our people need to heal. And we need a fresh start for that. I claimed this seat unjustly, and... I risked everything... I..."

"Loche," Zaddock pleaded. "This isn't necessary. We need you. Ellow needs you."

"But it is." Loche couldn't not swallow then, his throat itching for some reason. "I love Ellow. So much. But that's why I need to do this."

"No," Pellie broke in, a serene smile softening her features. "But the fact that you're willing to do it proves that you're what Ellow needs."

Loche began shaking his head, but Pellie continued, her long hair swishing over her shoulder as she turned more toward him. "We all make mistakes, regent. It's what we do after that counts."

Pellie shot a quick look at her sister before finding Loche's eyes once more. "We've seen you hurt for Lessia, but you still stand behind her, broken heart and all. We've seen you being lied to, deceived, and tricked, but you still believe in a different world. We've seen you care

—care more than we think the cold, lethal Loche ever wanted anyone to know he could—for your people, your friends, even the Fae. That's why your people will need you more than ever when this is over." Her smile grew wider. "That's why we believe in you."

Loche just stared at her; then a rough voice broke in.

"Who are you, woman?" Kerym seemed almost mesmerized, his blues shining when Pellie turned back toward him.

"You'll find out soon enough," Pellie teased, her hand touching his cheek briefly. "When it's time."

The Fae warrior blushed. Crimson bloomed across his sharp cheekbones, his eyes widening as they followed the hand Pellie placed back in her lap, and Loche realized he wasn't the only one who was openly gawking when a raspy laugh rang behind him.

"I don't care who or what you are, but the fact that you made my crude brother blush..." Thissian had to gasp for air. "That... I'll always love you for."

Thissian's laughter broke the suffocating tension, and conversations began around the room again, plates being handed out by Geyia and Steiner, and even those gray eyes that had been locked on him left to focus on the bowls of soup being pressed into the Faelings' hands.

Loche accidentally met Thissian's eyes as he waved Geyia away, wanting her to give the others food first, and he couldn't help but notice how the blue eyes were so similar to his brother's but darker, harder, as if they carried so much more pain.

He almost missed it when the Fae inclined his head.

"She's right, you know." Thissian's legs shook when he used the wall to get up from his seated position and started toward the door.

Loche found himself following him, and in a comfortable silence, they ascended the stairs to the deck, where a cool breeze had Loche grateful for the jacket he wore. They crossed the deck until Thissian folded his legs over the railing and sat on it, letting his feet dangle over the frothing sea beneath.

Mirroring his position, Loche swung his own legs over, letting the sense of his gut churning wash across the lingering sorrow he hadn't been able to shake after the meeting with his mother.

"She *is* right," Thissian said again. "You are a good man, regent."

Loche scoffed, his eyes on the darkening horizon where only a few orange flames licked the sea.

"You might not believe it, but everyone else does." Thissian sighed, the rush of air sounding similar to the wind ripping into Loche's jacket.

"I feel your pain, you know. I might not be an empath like the white-haired Faeling girl, but even I can taste it. Kerym can too."

Loche sneaked a look at the Fae, but his eyes were forward, almost unseeingly staring out into the evening light.

"I'm fine," Loche muttered when Thissian said nothing else.

"I'm sure you are. But it's also all right not to be," the warrior responded. "You're lucky humans don't have mates. It would be worse. Much worse."

Loche filled his lungs with salty air. "Was it... was it hard for him?" he asked.

Thissian turned his way, and Loche met his eyes as a sad smile curved the Fae's mouth.

"It nearly killed him. But he would have let her go. If she'd chosen you, he would have let her go."

Loche shook his head. Merrick was a better man than he would ever be.

"You're letting her go too."

Thissian frowned when Loche scoffed again. "But you are. I saw you comfort her before we left. Merrick saw it too. You took some of her pain away. Some of her guilt."

"That was nothing." Loche waved dismissively.

He still hated himself, knowing that if she showed one sign—just one—that she might still want him, he'd fight for his life to win her back.

"It's never nothing to carry pain because you're relieving another."

Loche chewed his lip as he observed Thissian.

He seemed strangely confident of that.

His mind went to Kerym's bright blue eyes, then to Thissian's sorrow-muddled ones, and understanding knitted in his stomach.

"You're taking his pain, aren't you?" Loche asked.

Thissian was silent for a moment.

"You can never tell him," the Fae finally offered. "He was... He loves so hard, my brother. Lessia reminds me of him sometimes. He loves unconditionally, doesn't care if it's right or wrong, and doesn't care if he loves people more than they love him. When she... when our mates died... he nearly did too. I had to do something."

Loche took a steadying breath. "Is it worth it?"

Thissian didn't hesitate. "To see him blush like today? To see him smile and laugh and maybe even feel something again? It's worth all the damned pain in the world."

CHAPTER 29
LESSIA

Lessia looked out over the snow-covered rock formations, the question of how the snow remained even in this warm weather vaguely crossing her mind before she turned to her sister, who stood beside her on the ship sailing toward where they'd last encountered the wyverns.

Frelina's cheeks were still red for some reason—exactly like they had been when they'd found each other amongst the mirrored waters and quickly escaped the gods-damned lands.

As soon as she and Merrick had dressed again back in that horrid mirrored place, Lessia had somehow known how to get out.

Walking up to one of the reflections, which appeared to be her normal one based on the rosy cheeks and the small satisfied smile Merrick couldn't seem to get enough of, as he'd made sure she came apart twice more—once with his fingers and then again with his skilled mouth—before he allowed her to get up, she'd pressed a hand against the surface.

As soon as she touched it, it melted away, revealing a disturbed Raine and a flustered Frelina staring right back at them.

Lessia's heart had skipped a beat when she met their eyes—worry that they had somehow been forced to watch her and Merrick coursing through her veins—but she'd realized they'd been occupied with their own experiences when Raine hadn't immediately cracked one of his jokes, as he surely would have if they'd seen what Lessia and Merrick had been up to.

It was as if the thought of Raine made him materialize, and she frowned as she watched him and Merrick take up the spot beside her, both males resting their hands on the railing, even if Merrick managed to stand as close to her as possible, aligning every inch of skin he could with hers.

She wasn't too bothered by it, not just because she obviously enjoyed having him close but because she'd noticed what he tried to do lately.

He didn't rush her in the mornings anymore.

He kissed her whenever he got a chance.

Whispered words into her ear that he'd usually saved for when they were alone, ignoring Raine's quips about them being mushy.

Touched her everywhere he could.

Made jokes that weren't particularly funny but that made her laugh all the same because of his studious expression.

He was giving her what she'd wished for: time, love, friendship, acceptance. And he was clearly trying to give her the one thing she knew he couldn't... a future.

Her brows snapped together when Merrick remained quiet. His eyes drifted her way like they usually did, but they also... kept returning to his friend, and when they did so, there was something, a twinge of worry, disturbing the silver swirls within his eyes.

Lessia's eyes followed, trailing over the burly Fae. There was something about Raine that irked her as well.

"What happened to you?" Lessia asked softly when Raine, who must have felt her eyes on him, threw a look her way.

Frelina stiffened on her other side, and Lessia sliced her gaze her sister's way.

Why did she look... guilty?

"And what happened to you, Lina?" she continued when no one spoke up.

Silence. It was just... silence.

All right then.

"Did they... speak to you?" Lessia tried.

Nothing.

Raine still looked so unnatural, and why was there guilt in his green-and-gold eyes too? The green-and-gold eyes that were... clear?

"You're sober," Lessia gasped. "Aren't you?"

Raine's jaw tightened, still no sound leaving him, but she didn't need to hear it from him.

He'd looked so strange to her because he was walking entirely straight, because his features weren't the mixture of hardness and softness she'd gotten used to, because his hands shook in the way they did whenever he hadn't had a drink in a while.

She hadn't seen his flask either. Not on the mirrored, arched path leading them to the ship. Not as they got on the ship and it began moving. Not the entire time they'd collected themselves, got ready to get the wyverns and sail to Ellow.

"Was it... did the gods do something to you?" Lessia searched Raine's eyes, noting the wince weaving across his face as he swallowed.

He swallowed three more times before he finally spoke.

"They believe I was wasting the life they'd given me," he said quietly. "They took it... the liquor... Zharra... she said that I can't use it to get through life anymore. That like any of the children she gives life to, I need to experience it or..." Raine swallowed again. "Move on."

"She spoke to me as well," Frelina interrupted. "For being the god of life, she isn't the most cheerful, is she? She casually informed me I'd die alone."

Lessia slipped her hand into Frelina's when she heard the fear breaking through what Frelina probably had meant to sound indifferent. Squeezing, Lessia declared, "You won't."

But the words sounded as empty as she felt. The gods couldn't lie. They could evade and elude and distract... but not lie.

The whole group jerked when Merrick's whispers boomed around them, and Lessia dropped Frelina's hand to grab her dagger, her eyes wide as she cast them around.

Raine had gripped his blades, too, and Frelina bared her teeth as she stepped closer to Lessia.

Merrick was the only one who looked... relaxed?

"What the fuck?" Raine spat when Merrick actually started laughing.

Nostrils flaring, Lessia thought Raine's question was

pretty accurate, especially as that sticky feeling layered over her.

She might not hate it as much as she used to—for some reason, his whispers more caressed than threatened her nowadays—but still... she could do without.

"Those bastards..." Merrick's laugh rumbled around her, and she would have smiled at the expression on his face if she had a clue what was going on.

It was Frelina who finally kicked Merrick's shin, causing the Death Whisperer to rein his magic in when she hissed, "What are you doing?"

It took a few moments for Merrick to catch his breath, but when he did, a thrill—and not the good kind—raced down Lessia's spine. Merrick must have noticed because his arm wrapped around her shoulders, pressing her against him as he spoke.

"Those fucking gods... they tried to take our hope." His dark eyes bore into Lessia's when a frown pulled at her forehead.

"I heard what they told you. They tried to make sure you'd follow that fucking prophecy by making you believe there was no other way. Frelina..." The hand not caressing her skin waved toward her sister. "They knew her inner wish was to experience more than the island you grew up on. Of course they'd tell her she'd die alone. But we all die alone! It doesn't matter how loved we are... in that final moment, our souls are alone. Trust me... I know."

Merrick's voice softened when he turned his head in Raine's direction. "And for you, my friend. It must have been the easiest of all... taking the one fucking thing that makes this life bearable for you. They took my magic in there, Raine! There was nothing of it under my skin, just... silence. But they did it for a reason! They do everything for a reason. And as you all noticed, it's definitely back. I'm sure you'll be able to drink again if that's what you wish. They... the gods are scared of what we can do. I can feel it."

Lessia just stared at him.

She'd never seen Merrick like this. Rage and love and hope and vengefulness all tangled across his sharp features—almost as if he wasn't sure whether to scowl or smile.

But his eyes sparkled. His hair glittered in the setting sun. And finally, it appeared that determination won over all of them, his jaw setting, brows drawing down, and mouth settling on a cold smile that Lessia knew was directed toward the gods.

"Hope," she mumbled. "You truly believe that?"

Merrick bent down to kiss her. "I do. They wanted us to stop fighting this fucking prophecy, so they tried to take away the one thing we care about most. But they couldn't lie to me, not when I asked for what I needed in a way they couldn't escape."

She didn't need to ask what Merrick had demanded to know from the gods. There was only one reason they'd gone there, after all.

Hope... She fought a chill raking down her back. Such a delicate thing.

Lessia caught Raine's eyes, and she could tell he wasn't convinced. Like her, doubt appeared to creep all over his skin.

She'd felt it back there—how the small ember of hope within her had finally been quenched.

But if it made Merrick happy?

If he smiled like this a little bit more?

Who was she to tell him he was wrong?

So when he kissed her again, she let him.

But when he finally pulled back as water splashed beneath them and the wyverns circled the vessel, Ydren leading the way, she could tell Merrick was the only one interested in the beasts' company.

Frelina and Raine stood silently beside each other, each seemingly carrying heavy weights on their shoulders, barely reacting when water splashed onto the ship from the wyverns' thick tails.

And when Raine met her eyes again... No, there was no hope in them.

Lessia had to look away, especially when a tear fell down Raine's cheek as he shook his head at Merrick, who'd lifted a hand to welcome Ydren back.

Don't, she thought, lowering the mental walls she'd gotten used to keeping up whenever Raine was around, since there was no telling when he'd decide to peek into her mind. *Don't take this away from him.*

I won't. Raine's voice was sad even in her mind. *But he's mistaken, Lessia. I was the same in the beginning with Solana. I thought... there was no way it could end like this. But...*

Maybe he is. She gave Raine a sad smile behind Merrick's back. *But even so, let him. Let him have hope for all of us.*

Like guilt, hope kept a person moving.

Those two feelings had been the strongest for her at different times in her life.

Guilt had kept her alive in Rioner's cellars. Guilt had guided her in Ellow and through the election.

And hope? It was hope Merrick had instilled in her

when she fought her way back to strength. When he'd kept her steady. When he'd fought for her. And now?

She wasn't certain which one had her step up beside her mate, grip his hand firmly, and smile widely before moving her gaze to the wyverns beginning to swim beside them as they headed north.

To Ellow.

To her friends.

To war.

CHAPTER 30
FRELINA

The wind had gotten colder, and Frelina was almost beginning to rethink her wish to visit Ellow when little flakes of snow filled the air.

It was supposed to be spring here.

In Vastala, it would get cooler in the winter, but not like this.

Not with snow and ice and whatever the wind that actually hurt her cheeks was called.

Frelina shuddered as she caught Elessia approaching her from the corner of her eye.

As her sister offered Frelina a blanket—one that must have been their dear uncle's, based on the thick lining and beautiful gold stitching weaving through the black fabric—Elessia gave her a soft smile.

One Frelina had come to hate over the past few days as they'd raced toward Ellow.

It wasn't her sister's real smile. It was... *fake* was the wrong word, but it was just... wrong. Like the reflections back in the Lakes of Mirrors, it wasn't her sister's usual grin—it wasn't her real face.

Frelina could tell Merrick hated it, too, based on his brooding scowl every time Elessia threw it his way.

Her sister didn't appear to care, though. Elessia didn't go silent like the rest of them had after what they'd been through, didn't draw back into her room like Frelina had come to do, especially as Raine didn't even deign to meet her eyes anymore, clearly regretting what had happened between them in the heat of the moment back in the gods' land.

It was as if Elessia was trying to fit as much conversation and company into their days as she could.

She kept asking Frelina about mundane things like what she and their father liked to eat when they'd been living back at their home isle.

What had come of the horses they'd kept in the stable behind the modest cottage?

Did the isle still smell like salt and forest, and did the sun warm the white cliffs where they had to watch out for the Vastala snakes that King Rioner kept breeding and letting out into the wild? The ones that swam, too, which Frelina hated more than anything else.

Elessia did the same to Merrick, and while he entertained her, his answers usually became shorter and shorter with each question until he'd pull Elessia down into his lap, kissing her so passionately that Frelina had to leave the room.

Raine was the only one who refused to speak to her. Elessia had tried for a day or two, but realized quickly that the Fae either didn't want to talk or didn't even listen.

"Are you all right?" Elessia asked carefully as she

made sure the blanket was wrapped tightly around Frelina's shoulders.

Frelina nodded. "I'm fine. I am just sick of being on a ship. Feels like it's been forever since I had solid ground beneath my feet."

Elessia laughed. A quick, breathy laugh, but one that still warmed Frelina's heart. "I know what you mean. The mirror place definitely wasn't solid or steady."

Ydren popped out of the water, probably at the sound of Elessia's voice, like she had done every day they'd traveled, just watching and waiting until Elessia crawled over the railing and got onto the beast's back, riding there beside the ship until Merrick couldn't stand being away from her and got her to return.

"She's calling you," Frelina mumbled when the wyvern made a purring sound—one that didn't really sound feline but that she guessed was supposed to be soothing, based on how rounded Ydren's eyes were.

Elessia shot her another one of those strange smiles. "She doesn't feel comfortable with the other wyverns yet. She... she and I... we understand each other."

Frelina made a concurring noise.

Elessia had told her the other wyverns swam deep beneath them, their leader apparently not trusting the group not to lead them into an ambush, and while she hadn't spent much more time with them apart from that first meeting, she could understand why Ydren was hesitant.

None of them seemed particularly friendly.

"You should go." Frelina tried to soften her voice, not let any sadness seep into it.

She knew Elessia would do anything for her. She could feel it in every touch, in every smile, in every time her sister checked on her. But it... it just wasn't enough.

Frelina missed the banter and friendship with Raine.

She didn't care about the kiss or whether there would be any more, although she wouldn't say no if he wanted to continue to pursue whatever they had started back in the lands of gods.

It had felt good to find someone who wasn't her family and who actually cared for her. Who thought she was funny. Who didn't treat her like something they needed to be careful with.

But now he barely looked her in the eyes, even when she'd noticed he hadn't touched the flask, which had begun collecting dust on a shelf in the kitchen.

"Are you sure?" Elessia's eyes narrowed, and Frelina quickly dragged her downward lips into a forced smile.

Not that it would fool her sister, but if Elessia was allowed to walk around with a grin that should have been the definition of somberness, Frelina should as well.

"I'm sure." Restlessness settled in Frelina's bones. "I am going to find Raine."

She'd been too scared to talk to him the past few days, but what was the point?

They might all be dead in a week... and she didn't want a stupid kiss to ruin what could be her final days.

Elessia already had one leg over the railing when she stilled, her face tilting to study Frelina. "Did something happen between you two? I know he's been strange the past few days, but I just chalked it up to him not drinking anymore..."

The smile on her face shook, but Frelina kept her sister's gaze. "Nothing that can't be solved."

She hoped, at least.

Elessia bowed her head, but her eyes were still unsure, so Frelina hurried to begin backing away. "Go on. Your pet needs you."

Her smile did firm the slightest bit when Ydren screeched at her, trying to splash a wave of water onto the deck, but thankfully, it wasn't far to the door to the stairs leading down to the cabins where they all slept, and where Raine appeared to spend most of his time.

As she opened the creaking door, which took quite some effort since the wood had swelled from the water either the sea or Rioner must have cast against it for years, she heard Elessia assure the wyvern that "she was just trying to be funny, I promise," and Frelina shook her head as she offered Merrick a quick wave where he sat against one of the masts, watching her sister with those dark eyes that never rested.

She kept her feet moving swiftly down the stairs, unwilling to lose her nerve now that she'd worked it up, and within moments she stood outside Raine's door.

Frelina lifted and lowered her hand a few times, reminding herself of what she wanted to say to him, when the door flew open, revealing a Raine with messier hair than usual and more stubble than she'd ever seen shadowing his strong chin.

Her eyes flew to his heaving chest for a second before she also sucked in a breath, the words she'd memorized pouring out of her. "I know you regret the kiss... and what we said. While I don't, it's totally fine. I just... I want us—"

Raine gripped her arm so forcefully she stumbled into the room, and even before she'd regained her balance, he'd slammed the door behind her and thrust her against it.

"I—"

Raine didn't let her finish that sentence, either, before he covered her mouth with his own, groaning "Finally" into it.

The kiss was as urgent as the one before, and he groaned so loudly when she responded that heat exploded between her legs at the sound.

"I thought..." Raine kissed her again. "I thought you'd never fucking come."

Frelina opened her mouth for his demanding tongue, and he didn't hesitate as he angled her head, his fingers wrapping around her chin to position her as he seemed to like her.

Head tilted, Frelina kissed him back, alternating between crashing her lips against his and sucking on his bottom lip when she needed a break.

"Fuck," Raine swore when a whimper escaped her as the hand not holding on to her chin began exploring her body, finding her ass and pressing her against his hardness.

"Fuck," Raine echoed when she arched into his touch, grinding against what must be his cock, using it to find some relief from the burning need between her legs. "Is... is this okay?"

Is this...

Frelina wrangled her hands into his hair, which definitely needed a wash, not that she cared too much right now, when the only thing she wanted was to have him closer—have something—and despite the waves of desire washing through her gut, she dragged his head back so she could meet his eyes.

"Don't you dare ask me if this is okay," she hissed. "You said you wouldn't be gentle. This... this is an exchange of needs. Like we agreed. I use you, and you use me."

Raine's hand dropped from her chin, and an involuntary sound left her when it found her other ass cheek and he used it to roughly lift her off the ground, forcing her to wrap her legs around him as he pressed her back against the wooden door.

His stubble scraped against her chin as he kissed her again, harder, making her lips swell and ache with each rough press of his own.

When he pulled back, the green and gold in his eyes swirled, and there was a wild edge to them—one that had her move her throbbing pussy over his clothed cock so hard he growled.

"So eager, little Rantzier," he mumbled as one of his hands found her hair, fingers tangling in it as he pulled her head back until pain from her scalp mingled with pleasure.

She couldn't help but moan at the sensation, and it felt as if she needed to escape her clothes, maybe even her skin, and crawl under Raine's when he rasped, "Good to know."

Still, after Raine had attacked her throat, licking and sucking and nibbling until she was panting, he stilled with his lips hovering over hers, hand still fisting her hair, keeping her from moving a single inch.

"Have you... have you been fucked before?" Raine asked hoarsely, and she didn't miss how his cock twitched against her.

"No," she snarled, trying not to meet his eyes,

although it proved hard when his grip tightened even further in her hair. "Is that a problem?"

Please don't be a problem.

She wasn't sure who she begged.

But she wanted this. Fucking needed this.

I need this, too, little Rantzier.

Oh.

Raine's laugh rumbled against her, and despite the heat shooting across her face, her eyes closed at the sensation of his length pressing into her, even through their clothes, and how his cock seemed to grow even harder at her response.

And it's not a fucking problem. But... we're taking it slow.

Something like a growl left her throat, and Raine laughed harder.

I said slow. Not gentle.

When his lips still waited above hers a few moments later—as if he was giving her a silent choice whether she wanted to stop—she used the last strength in her trembling legs to slide over his hardness. *What are you waiting for?*

Raine didn't respond to her question as he turned them both around, taking long steps to the table standing in the middle of the room and setting her down on it.

Empty.

That's what she felt when Raine released her, wrangling her own hands out of his hair and stepping back.

"Undress," he ordered.

A thrill of heat crept down her spine at his words, but she didn't move right away, a feeling of... not unease but hesitation cutting through her muddled thoughts.

My motto is usually "women first," but I'll make an exception.

There was amusement lacing Raine's words in her mind, but somehow it felt easier not to speak out loud—like when she'd spoken to him that day after her father's death.

Thank you, she thought back.

Oh, you should be thanking me. Raine's brows rose playfully as he undid his boots and kicked them across the room.

His tunic went next, revealing a broad chest with dark red hair covering the top of it.

She was certain her eyes were as wide as they'd ever been following the coiling muscles, how they played beneath his skin, leading down into a sharp V between his hips, a trail of the same crimson hair that wove across his chest pointing the way to—

There went his trousers.

Frelina swallowed.

She obviously didn't have anything to compare it to, but that... his cock was huge.

I assure you, it stands well against other males.

A nervous giggle bubbled out of her, and she could tell Raine had a hard time hiding his smile as well, as he gave her a gesture that it was her turn.

Frelina moved before she could overthink it, shuffling off her own boots, which she hadn't bothered tying since all she did was walk across this stupid ship, then dragging her shirt over her head and starting work on her trousers.

It proved quite difficult while sitting, but as she was about to get down from the table, Raine approached her.

Halting with her hands wrapped around the side of

the table, she watched him as he firmly placed a hand between her breasts, pushing her until she had to let go of the edge to fall onto her back.

Allow me.

His touch wasn't gentle, but it wasn't rushed, either, as he trailed his hands over her chest and down her stomach until it flipped, then started pulling her trousers off one inch at a time.

The air in the room seemed to cool as more of her naked body was revealed, but her skin didn't react to it. On the contrary, for each sharp breath leaving Raine as he exposed more and more of her, it was as if she was lit on fire.

Flames licked not only within her gut but down her legs and up her arms and neck.

Frelina realized she was panting as well when the fabric fell to the floor, and wetness pooled between her thighs as she felt Raine's heated gaze fly across her body.

So beautiful.

She was about to scold him for the softness in his thought when he shoved her legs apart, leaned over her, and cupped her pussy.

Oh.

Frelina cried out as his fingers squeezed, applying exactly the relief she'd been looking for, but the sound was swallowed when Raine claimed her mouth again, biting down onto her lip until she moaned into his own.

Today is about you. I want you to be ready when I fuck you. Because I will definitely not be gentle.

An image of her pressed up against the door, her nipples rubbing almost painfully against the wood while Raine held on to her hair, pulling it so the back of her head rested on his shoulder while he thrust that huge cock into her from behind formed in her mind.

She almost came right then, especially as Raine began moving his fingers on top of her cotton undergarments.

That's what I'm planning for you.

Frelina couldn't respond, neither in words nor thoughts, as Raine continued to kiss her while moving his fingers until the friction of the fabric and the pressure from them had her on the edge.

So responsive.

The words in her mind were almost guttural grunts at this point, and she could tell Raine was as affected as she was from the way he fisted his cock, squeezing it until wetness formed over the tip.

I'm going to touch you now.

It wasn't a question, and thank the fucking gods for that, because she wasn't sure if she could have even gotten out a nod.

Her body jerked as Raine slipped his hand into her underwear, sliding down easily because of how wet she was. She could hear his fingers gliding over her pussy, the wet sound having her eyes roll back into her head.

Raine wasn't even kissing her anymore, more like panting into her mouth as his thumb found her clit and the other fingers parted her slick folds, and her back flew off the table when the tip of his middle finger teased her entrance.

More... I... Don't stop.

Frelina began shamelessly rubbing against him when his thumb didn't press hard enough, when that finger teased too much...

P-please.

She didn't care that she was begging when heat swelled in the lower parts of her stomach, but Raine seemed to love it, from the loud growl shaking not only her but the table he now leaned his other hand on while the one working her began moving faster.

Fuck, you're already so ready for me.

Stars danced before her eyes when his finger slid in deeper, and before she knew what she was doing, Frelina rolled her hips, driving it all the way in until his knuckle slammed against her pussy.

She and Raine moaned in sync.

Please, she begged again.

Yes. With that single word, Raine began thrusting his finger in and out, speeding up until her hips started rolling again, needing more, needing him to go harder.

"So ready," he groaned into her mouth as he added a second finger. "Next time... it'll be my cock feeling all this wet softness."

At the same time as Raine started driving into her hard, he dragged his nail over her clit.

That did it.

Frelina squeezed her eyes shut so hard crimson light danced before them, and she bit down on something—Raine's lip, she thought—as her body convulsed, something even wetter, hotter rushing through her pussy until every muscle within her stopped working.

Fuck.

Fuck. Fuck. Fuck.

That wasn't a fuck, little Rantzier. Raine gently shifted her to the side of the table, and she watched in fascination as he lay down beside her and began stroking his cock as he watched her come down from her orgasm. *I... I can't wait to actually fuck you... to fuck your wet pussy.*

With that, streams of white shot across Raine's stomach, and his groans echoed around the wooden-walled room as he slowed his movements until he finally stilled completely.

Frelina didn't know what came over her, but as he continued watching her, she dragged a finger through the thick fluid painting his muscles and brought it to her mouth, tasting it.

It was salty and strange, but it didn't taste that bad, she thought as she glanced over to Raine.

He met her eyes for a moment before throwing his head back and growling into her mind, *Fuck. Now I need to come again.*

Despite his words, though, he only dragged her to him so her back rested against his sticky stomach, and in what seemed like seconds, the Fae warrior fell into a deep sleep.

Hard table and all.

CHAPTER 31
LESSIA

Salt stung her eyes, and she tried to shield her face behind Ydren's thick neck when another tall wave threatened to rush over them as the wyvern swam through the water.

Ydren didn't always seem to realize that unlike her, Lessia wasn't built for water, and while she didn't mind it—wasn't afraid of its depths like she'd learned Frelina was—she couldn't keep being slapped around by the strong waves that had started rolling in as soon as they closed in on Ellow's borders.

Lessia stared at the familiar landscape taking shape over the islands dotting the dark ocean around them.

Ellow... She didn't know what to feel anymore for the nation she'd called home for the past five years.

There had been a time when she'd have argued with anyone—even Merrick—that this was where she was meant to be. But now?

Even if there was a chance for her to survive this war,

she wasn't sure she'd choose to stay here anymore. The ship, while being Rioner's, had felt more like home for the past few days than the house on Asker she no longer missed.

She knew it was because of Merrick and Frelina, and perhaps because she allowed herself to feel every happy emotion they evoked in her, that she reveled in her feelings. Even Raine, who seemed to have perked up today and came armed with his usual crude comments, made her smile.

Merrick was certain something had happened between Raine and Frelina, had apparently seen her sister sneak out of Raine's room in the middle of the night, but Frelina and the Fae warrior seemed equally happy, so Lessia let it be. If they could find even an ounce of happiness with what was to come...

Her heart swelled as she cast a glance back to the ship, where Merrick watched her as he always did, while Frelina and Raine seemed to be occupied with their endless teasing on the deck above him.

They'd be all right. She had to believe that.

Merrick had been happy when he realized there was still some hope within her, forcing her to continue their journey, keeping her spirits up even when it seemed like he expected her to break apart each night she snuggled into his arms.

He just didn't realize it wasn't for herself.

Ydren made a sharp sound, jerking her neck so hard that Lessia almost fell off.

"What did you do that for?" she snapped at the wyvern when the latter turned her lethal head to glare at Lessia.

The soft glow from Lessia's arm shone bright even in the cold wintery light that had yet to break into full spring in Ellow, and like she had ever since that stone merged with her, she somehow understood what the wyvern was thinking.

"I'm not pitying myself." Lessia glared back at her. "I am not. I am merely enjoying whatever time I have left."

The wyvern scoffed, sending streams of water through her nostrils.

"What do you want me to do!" Lessia snarled, unable to keep from showing the beast her teeth, although they had little on Ydren's razor-sharp, feet-long ones. "I'm fighting as much as I can. I will fight for them, but I'll also fight for myself. I am not planning on rolling over and dying, if that's what you think!"

The wyvern hissed at her, the rush of the air splashing more water onto Lessia's face, and Ydren's violet eyes flashed as they stared into her own.

"I know you're strong, Ydren."

It wasn't a struggle for Lessia to lower her voice. They'd had this fight every day since they started the journey back to Ellow.

It had started with Lessia refusing to allow Ydren to join the war, telling her that the other wyverns were all staying back.

But the wyvern wasn't having it. She'd pouted and cried and pleaded with Lessia every day for her to change her position. Had told her repeatedly that if Lessia allowed her to fight, Ydren could protect her, make sure the king didn't come near her.

But Lessia didn't want to. Ydren might be older than she was—somewhere around seventy years in the way humans counted—but Auphore had told Lessia enough for her to realize Ydren was barely more than a child still.

Like the Fae, wyverns could live almost forever unless injured, but they didn't mature as quickly as the Fae did.

Ydren was technically an adolescent. A clever and stubborn one, Lessia thought as Ydren began the soft whimpers that she knew damn well broke Lessia's heart.

Her heart, but not her resolve, because if she wanted to somehow get all the wyverns to fight willingly, sacrificing one of their own—a near child, at that—was probably not advisable.

A large tear snaked its way down Ydren's snout, lingering on one of her scales before it fell into the sea beneath them, and the beast's sad eyes held on to Lessia's.

"I would miss you too," Lessia croaked, holding on for her life not to let her shaking hands lose their grip on the spikes lining Ydren's neck as the wyvern's sorrow struck her chest like a fist.

"I'd miss all of you," she continued, throwing another look at the ship and trying to keep the warmth in her chest from being overtaken by the fear of leaving them all behind. "I'd miss you so much."

Ydren blinked at her, and Lessia could tell the wyvern was holding back more tears.

"I can't say it's all going to be fine." Lessia smiled through the words she knew were harsh, but she'd appreciated how Merrick never lied to her—never tried to gloss over the truth—and wanted to do the same for her new friend. "But this is life, Ydren. The life the gods created and we try to navigate. It may not be fair, it may not be fun, but this right here... it's living. It's fighting. It's loving. It's... all I can do."

Ydren opened her maw in a silent cry, one that Lessia knew could have echoed across the ocean but that the wyvern quelled for the fear of rebels getting to them before they could get to their friends, and Lessia stroked her soft scales, trying to share some of the calm that had settled within her at the Lakes of Mirrors.

The gods *had* given her time.

She'd realized that when she'd spoken to Evrene.

They'd given her a loving family.

They'd given her friends she couldn't even dream up.

They'd given her not one but two loves.

One that she hoped would turn into another great friendship before her life was over, and another... another that she pinched herself every day to make sure it was real.

Merrick was...

She couldn't help the smile breaking out across her face as she thought of the Death Whisperer, the Fae everyone feared, who was grumpy and broody and sharp but who stared at her like she was his sun, his only reason for waking up every day.

The Fae who drove her mad with desire every time his fingers found a bit of her naked skin.

The Fae who whispered his own dreams to her when he thought she was sleeping.

She'd almost thought she'd dreamed it the first time. But the night after, when her breathing had slowed after Merrick had exhausted her with every perfect thrust of his hips and lap of his tongue, he'd held her against his chest and told her their story.

The one where they hosted everyone they knew at a mating ceremony.

The one where he asked for her father's hand like humans did and dropped to a knee before her, begging her to also marry him when she laughed at him, since it had only been days since their formal mating.

The one where she carried his children while he built them all a home on the island she'd grown up on, making sure they all knew of Alarin, their brave grandfather, who'd died to ensure they could be born.

She'd dreamed of it every night after that. Of silver-haired children running through the tall grass of her childhood home, exactly like she had done. Of a sweaty, smiling Merrick coming into a stone cabin for dinner, lifting her and settling her on the table before kissing the life out of her. Of late nights before a sparkling fire and summer days on the cliffs and winter rides through the forest.

It was what made her keep smiling throughout the day when other thoughts—the ones far more threatening—claimed her mind.

Even if that smile wasn't exactly her regular one.

It was strange, the happiness of what could have been—a future she could nearly taste but would never realize.

She knew they all saw through her new smile, but the fact that they didn't call her out on it made her love them even more.

Ydren jerked beneath her, and Lessia snapped her head forward when a low rumble racked the wyvern's strong body.

Her eyes rounded as she beheld the scene ahead.

Thirty or so of Ellow's warships stood side by side

before an impossibly steep, dark cliff—one that reminded her of those skirting Korina. There were several inlets in the cliff, making this side of the island look almost like a comb, with tall ebony teeth shooting up from the water.

In front, twenty feet or so ahead of the others, Loche's ship proudly floated, the sail that bore his own symbol, the one he'd apparently only raised the day he was elected six years ago, stark against the dark island.

The mark was fitting, Lessia thought as she nudged Ydren to bring her back to the ship.

Almost the shape of a heart, it had what looked like a bolt of lightning splitting it, tearing the two sides apart. Only a small piece at the bottom sealed them together, fighting to keep each side from tumbling away from the other.

"Stay with the other wyverns when I am not around," she ordered Ydren as Merrick reached out his arms to help her onto what had once been Rioner's vessel, which she now claimed as her own. "I doubt the humans will know what to make of you."

With a hiss that Lessia hoped was agreement, Ydren dove into the dark water just as Lessia jumped, right into Merrick's arms.

His lips tickled her ear as he held on to her far longer than needed, and she blushed when he whispered, "If you continue to tire yourself from riding her all day, I might begin to get jealous. I'd much prefer to be the one you have those beautiful legs wrapped around."

She went to peck him, but Merrick captured her lips in a more passionate, deeper kiss than she'd expected, and she was slightly lightheaded when he finally set her down.

Swatting at him when she noted the smirk on his face, she finally turned back to the group of people who had begun gathering in the bows of every ship.

Lessia knew exactly why Merrick kept his hand sliding up and down her back as rows and rows of humans glared at them as they sailed up to the ship where Loche stood in the front, his hand shielding his eyes from the sun setting behind them.

CHAPTER 32
LOCHE

The damned wyvern.

Of course she'd come riding in on it.

He'd watched Merrick, Raine, and Ardow riding off on it last time, but seeing Lessia do the same...

He shook his head. It seemed insane.

And dangerous.

Loche squinted against the setting sun, which made the four figures in the bow of Rioner's ship look like dark shadows staring back at him. Dark shadows who stood shoulder to shoulder, ready to protect each other at any hint of a threat.

The regent didn't need to cast his gaze around to realize why Lessia and the rest seemed so tense. He could feel the eyes of his people tracking not only the ship approaching them but also him, their regent, always monitoring, shadowing, and evaluating his every movement.

Loche let out a weary breath.

These people weren't even the worst of them.

His men had struggled to get the noble families to agree to come to this place—to leave the safety of their castles and mansions. In the end, only five had shown up, with the others sending the people in their employ while they stayed back like the cowards they were.

As if anyone would be safe...

Loche scoffed so loudly that Zaddock and some of his other closest men turned toward him.

Their masks shone like polished leather as the sun reflected on them when Loche jerked his head dismissively, and they turned to face straight ahead again.

He'd told them the masks weren't needed anymore, but his men had opted for them anyway. And why not? They were terrifying. It was why he had chosen them, after all.

Maybe they'd give their enemies a second's pause, and a second was all that his men needed to stay alive.

They were long, silent moments before Lessia's ship finally dropped its sails and Raine steered it around so it sidled up beside his own, facing south—the direction from which they expected both the rebels and Rioner and his Fae to come.

Loche's men reacted instantly when he raised his hand, and without Loche having to call out orders, they caught the ropes Merrick threw out, tying their ships together with knots that would be easy to undo should the ships need to flee or separate in the fighting to come.

They'd practiced these knots in the navy, but somehow Loche had never expected the need for them to appear.

Yet here they were.

Lessia was the first to step onto their ship, using her hands, which Loche was happy to see seemed healed, to swing herself onto the deck. He watched her eye his men for a moment, something he couldn't quite read crossing her features, before she turned toward him, a hesitant smile spreading across her face.

Knowing what was expected of him, knowing every soul on the ships around him would scrutinize any and all interactions with her, Loche didn't smile back, although he did try to soften his eyes as he met her halfway.

Lessia chewed her lip for a moment, but her eyes darted sideways, noting the thousands of people facing their way, climbing up masts and onto railings to see the regent meet the one who betrayed him—the one who was sent into their elections to spy—and her chin dipped. Only for half a second, but that was enough for Loche to know she understood.

"You came back," he greeted her, noting his men standing straighter at the cold tone—the one that made them confident Loche had moved past the emotions that had made him bring Lessia to their home, to their haven.

"Of course we did." Lessia wrung her hands, eyes fighting not to move sideways, and shoulders trying to remain lowered under the heaviness of the gazes on them.

Loche could tell it wasn't an act. She'd always hated standing before crowds like this, and while some people had had her back during the election, they all knew what she'd done now—knew of her affiliation with the Fae king.

After helping Lessia's sister—the girl he'd only seen

once, on that horrible day when they said goodbye to their father—onto the deck, Merrick and Raine approached as well, and Loche could tell Merrick struggled not to pull Lessia to his side when she continued to shift her weight from foot to foot, as if she was preparing to flee.

But it appeared as if the Fae warrior also knew what was at stake, as he reached out a hand to shake Loche's, with Raine following as soon as the silver-haired Fae released his firm grip.

"Regent," Merrick greeted. "It seems you've chosen a good spot."

His dark eyes flickered over the cliffs behind them—the ones where Loche planned to place most of his archers, including the ones with the best aim.

Loche only offered a sharp nod to acknowledge the Fae's words. "Did you get the wyverns to come?"

Cold danced down his back when Lessia winced, and the Fae kept their features locked in the strange way only Fae could.

That they'd get the wyverns to help was how Loche had convinced most of his people to trust Lessia again. He'd spun a tale of her bravery, of her wish for forgiveness, and how she'd do anything to save Ellow, not to cause more mistrust than already filled the wind caressing the warships.

He certainly didn't want anyone to know about the prophecy, especially once the king appeared. While he hadn't fought in a war before, he knew what fear and desperation did to people. They would sacrifice Lessia without a second thought about what could happen after.

"They did come," Lessia finally responded. "But they will not fight. Not yet."

Loche momentarily shut his eyes, blowing out a deep breath.

"We'll place them on either side of this island, regent. Just having them there will be enough to scare most Fae."

He opened his eyes when Raine spoke, and something in his gut sparked at the Fae's appearance.

Raine looked... different.

But he didn't have time to linger on it. Not right now. So, Loche inclined his head an inch. "Understood. Make sure they keep away from our ships. I'd prefer my people not be eaten before the fight."

"They don't eat—" Lessia shut her mouth when Loche glared at her.

"We'll keep them away," she promised, neck bending to his will.

He hated how they had to play this game, but he *was* regent, and he needed his people to believe in his strength and power right now. They couldn't afford any doubt. Not when there was no time to reclaim it.

"Good." Loche threw out an arm behind him. "My men believe the rebels are coming in two days, so there is little time left. We were just about to finalize the strategic positions and plans, so I'd suggest you join us."

Lessia nodded, gravitating toward Merrick, who stood almost shoulder to shoulder with her, and Loche noted how their fingers brushed. Just for a moment, but it appeared to calm her.

He waited for a pang of jealousy to hit his chest, but when Lessia's eyes found his, it didn't come. As with

Raine, there was something about Lessia that was different.

An innocence had been taken from her—one that used to whirl in her beautiful, gilded eyes even when pain had painted them darker. Once again, he found himself grateful to the Fae who whispered something in her ear that had her cheeks flush in the way he used to love.

Even if things had been different—if it had been Loche standing in Merrick's place—he couldn't have offered her that comfort.

His duty was to Ellow—to his people.

Like it should be. Like it always would be.

Placing a hand over his mouth as if he needed to cough, turning his back to most of his men—all but Zaddock—Loche offered quietly, "There are some people who are very eager to see you, Lessia. I'd suggest you go into the cabins first, and then you can join us. I'd like to get Merrick's and Raine's thoughts, anyway."

The smile Lessia gave him almost had him stumble back, and Loche could tell he wasn't the only one affected when Lessia's little sister wiped at her eyes, and even Raine cleared his throat as he steadied his feet.

Merrick was the only one who wasn't watching Lessia. His dark eyes bore into Loche's instead, and the air became loaded as the Fae bowed to him, a deep bow filled with respect, before the Fae offered, "We're at your service, regent."

Loche didn't know how to respond, so when a chirpy voice broke through the tension surrounding the group, he was eternally grateful.

"I'll make sure she finds her way on this gigantic ship," Amalise said as she skipped across the deck, tapping Zaddock playfully on the back before walking up and grabbing Lessia's and Frelina's hands, wholly ignoring the two Fae warriors.

Loche caught Lessia's sister's eyes as she was dragged past them, and he hadn't realized just how alike they were until the younger Rantzier trailed her gaze over his face and mumbled "You're not so bad" before Amalise rushed her away.

"Don't take too long," Zaddock called as Amalise opened the door leading down to the kitchen and sleeping cabins.

"We won't," Amalise called back. "I know you need our expertise, what with the war and all."

"I just need you." Zaddock grinned, his brows rising in challenge when Amalise stumbled.

As Lessia began laughing and even her sister's mouth twitched, Loche and the others heard Amalise mutter "Save a man's life once and somehow he thinks you're in love with him" before the door shut behind them.

"She *is* in love with me," Zaddock said with a broader grin. "She just doesn't want to admit it yet."

Loche was pretty sure his friend was right, and while it wasn't what they needed to discuss, Zaddock and Amalise's exchange had cleared the air, made it a little easier to breathe, and when he turned to the Fae warriors and waved for them to join him, it somehow felt like a small part of the responsibility he carried lightened.

"We have around thirty ships here, each with five hundred or so people and soldiers on them. Not all are trained, but we asked whoever was willing to defend Ellow to come," Loche explained as they walked toward the stern, where the shadows were deeper from the towering cliffs. "We are a bit low on weapons, especially since the shipments from Vastala stopped during the election, but we'll make do. I was planning on placing my archers on the plateau up there."

"How many men will fit?" Merrick gestured to the large piece of rock jutting out above their ships, casting most of those behind this one in shade.

"A couple hundred, we believe," Zaddock said as he took the spot by Loche's side when they stopped a few feet from the railing. "Kerym and Thissian have already agreed that one of them will join the troops up there, while the other will fight from the water."

"Makes sense." Raine nodded as his eyes flew over the island, back to the water, and across the ships that Loche had felt were plenty but under the Fae warrior's scrutinizing gaze appeared to become fewer and fewer by the second. "Merrick, you should remain on the ship, take out as many of the soldiers in the bows of the attacking ships as you can until your magic runs out. I will have a better overview from the cliff. I'll go after the captains to start—to save my energy—make sure they break formation."

A muscle ticked in Merrick's jaw, and he eyed his friend before shifting his examination to Loche. "Rioner always puts those that can do the most damage—the water wielders, the fire wielders, the wind wielders—at the front of his line. I don't know Meyah's strategy, but I can only assume she'll do the same. I can take out many, but not all, not when I need to ensure I don't kill any of our own."

Loche was about to snarl that Merrick definitely couldn't fucking risk his people, remembering too well that night on the cliff in Ellow when he'd figured out who Lessia and Merrick truly were and discovered how terrifying Merrick could be in his element, but Merrick continued speaking before he had the chance.

"I won't." Understanding glimmered in the Fae's dark eyes. "I'll work with the Faelings on the ship to figure out where best to place them. They're young, so they'll run out of magic quickly, and since I don't expect many of them to know how to fight any other way, we'll need to ensure they can get away fast. I don't stand for young ones being harmed."

"Fair," Loche declared. "We have some younger ones on our side, too, but I am placing them all in the archer lineup, keeping the front line to my experienced soldiers. Will this strategy also work for the rebels? We haven't had any sightings of Rioner or the Oakgards' ships, not that that is saying much, but we expect the rebels to come first."

"It's how Rioner likes it," Merrick said in a voice that should have chilled the water beneath to ice. "Where do you think the shifter ruler got the idea to get the Fae and humans to take out each other in the previous war? It's been a tactic of the Rantziers for millennia."

"But it should still work for the rebels," Raine added, stepping toward Merrick, whose face was shifting with rage. "Even if they have some magic wielders amongst the half-Fae, they'll be untrained."

"They have quite a few," Loche responded, continuing when the Fae males stared at him. "We have a prisoner on this ship who has given us some useful information. Not that we could get much more out of him than what his friends could do, as Meyah"—Loche forced himself not to let any emotion fill his face as he spoke of his mother—"seems to keep everything she can under wraps."

Merrick nodded once, and irritation flitted across Loche's skin at the slight narrowing of the Fae's eyes—the way he seemed to see through his regent mask.

But then a screech had them all jerk their heads up, and all but Raine went for their weapons when a huge shadow blocked their view of the sky.

An arrow shot into the air from another ship, but the eagle swerved swiftly, letting out another ear-splitting cry before its wings whipped salty air in their faces as it landed on Raine's outstretched arm.

"About time," he mumbled as he unclasped a piece of parchment from the creature's leg.

"Who?" Merrick demanded.

A slow smile spread across Raine's face. "Everyone."

Zaddock looked as confused as Loche felt, and thankfully Raine expanded. "I sent for my friends. The only ones I trust—the ones I've been living with for the past decades. They took their fucking time, but they've decided to help us. They hate Rioner as much as we do, so I offered a fine price for whoever killed him... It seems they responded well to it."

"A price?" Zaddock still appeared perplexed as he shot Loche a glance.

"I offered my house to whoever manages to kill the bastard." Raine shared a look with Merrick, and the warmth passing between the males flickered in the air for a moment before Merrick placed a hand on the crimson-haired Fae's shoulder, something dangerously close to glossiness shading his already dark eyes.

"When?" Merrick asked quietly.

"A while ago," Raine responded, his voice also lowering. "You're not the only one who wants to keep her alive, you know."

Another silence stretched across the ship, but it wasn't an uncomfortable one.

It was an agreement.

Understanding.

Hope for the half-Fae girl who had affected each of the four men in some way.

Hope... for them all.

CHAPTER 33

MERRICK

"They're at least... passionate." Kerym bumped his elbow into Merrick's side as they watched the Faelings practice what Merrick had asked of them.

Merrick hummed, his eyes fixed on the three who would be helpful during this fight.

Two of the Faelings were water wielders, and they seemed used to working with each other, one favoring steering the ocean as it was, while the other would freeze his friend's waves whenever it pleased him.

The skill would come in handy, especially for the ships taking the lead, whether rebel or Fae.

If these two could stop one or two of them—perhaps even have them collide with some of the others—it would give the others time to prepare their weapons, would give himself, Kerym, Raine, and Thissian time to take out as many as they could before the inevitable physical battle would begin.

The third Faeling, a dark-haired, gray-eyed male who

hovered around Lessia whenever she was around, was a wind wielder, and they'd all watched in awe as he managed to move entire ships in the direction he wanted, or blew through a group of Loche's men so hard they all tumbled to the wood beneath them.

The rest of the Faelings had gifts that either were too unpolished or just wouldn't be helpful in war—like the white-haired girl Merrick had spotted before but stayed far away from those years he'd followed Lessia around in Ellow.

He believed her name was Kalia, and while she had a strong gift—one that reminded him of Kerym's and Thissian's—it wasn't offensive.

Sure, she could sense all the emotions around her, perhaps even see who was frightened enough that he or she would be a sure kill, but she was getting overwhelmed already.

Merrick had sent her down to Geyia, the shifter Loche was apparently friends with, to help with the food when he'd realized the half-Fae was sensing the fear, worry, tension, and other emotions filling those around them.

"Three is more than we could ask for," Thissian said softly. "With Raine's friends coming, too, we'll be able to stand strong against the rebels."

Merrick's eyes traveled to Lessia, who was patting the dark-haired Faeling on the back, smiling at him as she said something.

They would be able to stand against the rebels, but not the Fae. Not when they'd all have used up their magic to keep the rebels at bay, and especially if the Oakgards' Fae had magic.

He'd heard they could wield all the elements as long

as they were connected to that specific element—that they drew power from the world around them—allowing them to continue fueling their energy without food or sleep, like the Fae in Vastala.

"We'll do what we can, Merrick," Thissian continued, his eyes following Merrick's own. "I'll keep an eye on her."

"So will I," Raine said. "I'll keep her sister with me, and she will prioritize tracking Lessia, since she's not fighting."

As if Merrick would let Lessia leave his side. There was a way to save her, and it was up to him to fucking find it—to ensure he made that promise of future a reality.

"They will try to take you out first," Kerym broke in. "You know this, Merrick. It's how it always is. You'll need to keep moving around, use that speed of yours to your advantage."

Merrick bared his teeth at his friend. "Her life comes first. I am not leaving her."

"What can you do for her if you die?" Kerym shot back. "Thissian will stay by her. They always underestimate us. Why, I don't know, since our powers are clearly superior."

Raine rolled his eyes while Merrick took a step toward Kerym. "I. Will. Not. Leave. Her. There is nothing, fucking nothing, that can stop me from being right by her side."

Thissian slammed an arm across his brother's chest when Kerym seemed to ready himself to argue. "Kerym, enough. You wouldn't have left Mishah if she were here. Elessia is his mate, and he gets to decide what he wants to do."

Kerym's chest puffed out under Thissian's arm, and his voice shook as he snarled, "I know that! But what's the point if he dies instead? Shall we welcome her with open arms to our sad little group? Hey, Lessia. Life without your mate is fucking miserable, apart from the small moments when you get distracted. But do you know what? It hurts even more after those moments because then you feel so fucking guilty you wish to die as well! Do you think she wants that, Merrick? Do you think anyone wants that?"

Merrick stared at his friend, at how a shaking began in his shoulders, then moved to his entire body, and he didn't miss Thissian's agony-filled face whitening, his arm falling to his side as if it took too much to keep it up.

Even Raine made a choked sound, his eyes flying to Lessia's sister, who stormed toward them, eyes wide with fear.

Fear that resounded within Merrick when he found another pair of golden eyes—ones that were far too close and that made his entire being ache with how much worry weighed them down as they swept across his face.

He only glared back at her.

Fuck this. Fuck all this pain and worry and fear.

Merrick snarled so loudly that Frelina backed up, and even his friends took a step back when his magic roiled in the air, the power from it shifting across the ship, quieting those who had watched the Faelings practice.

Only Lessia remained planted in place, her face morphing into a mask of defiance that he knew meant she was about to tell him to fucking listen to his friends.

Which he was definitely not planning on doing.

"Come." Merrick gripped her hand, forcing down a

smile when she squeezed his back in a way that made him believe she wanted it to hurt.

As if she could ever hurt him by touching him. And this... this grip meant that she was angry.

Good. It was good to be angry in war. Better than being afraid. Better than worrying.

"Where are we going?" Lessia hissed when Merrick began dragging her across the deck.

"You and I need to talk." Merrick's eyes remained on the steep cliff, the steps leading up to it, and he continued pulling on her hand to make her move faster as he fought against the souls pressing all around him, even under his skin, making his pulse thrum wildly—and not in a fun way.

"Why can't we just talk here?"

Merrick threw a look over his shoulder and found Lessia frowning at him while his friends, some of Loche's soldiers, and the Faelings gaped as they watched them get off the ship.

"Because," Merrick forced out, trying to keep his tone level while his whispers whipped the air around them. "If I stay, I might kill someone, and I don't think that'd be great for morale, do you?"

Lessia pursed her lips, but she must have realized he meant it because she remained quiet as Merrick lifted her onto the ship behind them and dragged her across that one as well while the soldiers parted, giving them a wide berth, until they reached the gangway leading them to the island.

The isle was rocky and barren and suited Merrick's fury perfectly.

They stayed quiet as they climbed the steps leading

up to the plateau, and it wasn't until Merrick dragged her to the end of it and sat down with his legs dangling off, making sure Lessia followed, that he began speaking again.

"I know what you're going to say." Merrick didn't look her way even when he felt her eyes move across his face.

He didn't trust himself not to take her and run if he did.

"But I am doing the fucking best I can," Merrick continued, hating how angry he sounded and hoping Lessia knew his anger wasn't directed at her, despite the way it might come across. "I have said it before. I don't give *one shit* about this damned world. Or about the people down there. Fuck, I don't give a shit about any of it. The only thing I care about is sitting right next to me."

Lessia's hand, which he'd let go of as they sat down, found its way into his again as he shuddered.

"I'm not living without you!" Merrick glared so hard at the horizon that it blurred. "I don't care that the others can do it, that they might be stronger than I ever will be. That they might even find some light once in a while. My purpose in this life was to find you, and I believe also to keep you alive, so that's the one damned thing I am going to do. This is *my* fucking choice."

"Okay."

"So I am going to fucking—" Merrick's words drifted off with the wind when he realized she'd spoken.

Okay?

"What did you say?" He had to face her now; he couldn't not do it, couldn't not allow himself to savor every moment, every second with her.

"I said okay," Lessia responded, her eyes falling into his, no defiance, no fight, no fake smile touching them.

"Why?" Merrick stared at her as she shuffled closer on the cliff, sliding one of her legs between his own until she half sat in his lap.

Pressing her nose into his cheek, Lessia whispered, "Because I don't want to live without you either."

Well... Fuck.

Merrick's heart pounded so hard in his chest that he was sure Lessia could hear it.

He'd prepared a whole speech when he stomped up those stairs, as he'd been certain she'd fucking fight for her life for him to change his mind.

"So you'll stay by me?"

Lessia wove a hand into his hair, dragging her nails down his scalp. "I'll try."

"Lessia," he warned quietly.

"I am also doing the best I can." Her whisper was sharper now. "I will try. I will fight. I do promise you that. But I cannot see the future, Merrick. I do not know what will happen once we're in the midst of it all. You'll have to take it or leave it."

He ground his teeth, everything in him wanting to demand more of her—order her to promise him everything he wished.

But that wasn't what he did.

That wasn't what she wanted.

That wasn't who they were.

Merrick and Lessia... They were respect, they were fight, they were hope, they were... love.

So, instead, he folded an arm around her back and said, "Okay."

Lessia nodded, her soft skin rubbing against his

rough cheek, and they were quiet for a while, listening to the bustle that had picked up on the ships, where soldiers were putting out weapons, where his friends probably shared the final decisions they'd agreed upon today with Loche, where everyone prepared for one last evening before the rebels were expected to show tomorrow.

It wasn't until Lessia began fidgeting with her dagger, the ruby one his mother had once owned—or at least so he'd been told growing up—that Merrick cleared his throat.

"We'll get the other one back."

He'd seen how she often grasped for it—the amber-decorated twin to the dagger now in her hand—the one her father had gifted her when she came of age.

They'd searched the entire ship for it, gone through each drawer and dusty box, but Rioner must have seen it for what it was—a royal weapon—and taken it when he fled the ship.

"Yes," Lessia said simply as she tucked the other into its sheath again.

"Tell me something," she asked as Merrick couldn't help but move her fully onto his lap, securing her legs sideways across his own so he could continue looking at her.

"What do you want me to tell you?" Merrick smiled at her.

The smile was weak. But it was a real one.

They'd started this game on the ship on the way here, when Lessia hadn't been able to stop herself from asking questions all day, every day. But she'd been too tired at night to come up with new ones—so she'd started asking him to tell her things he thought of—and he loved how it reminded him of when he'd told her how everything had changed between them back in Ellow.

"What's your family name?"

He shook his head, teasing, "Of all the questions..."

But Lessia only popped a brow back at him, so Merrick shrugged. "Morshold."

"It fits you." Lessia tilted her head as if examining him, humming to herself. "It really does."

Poking a finger into her side until she let out a slight squeal, Merrick laughed softly. "I've never really gone by it. Since I never met my parents, it didn't feel right somehow—carrying a family name when I didn't have a family. It's what Raine and the others did, so... I kind of just did the same."

"I know what you mean." Lessia leaned her head on his shoulder, holding his eyes whenever her eyelashes didn't sweep across her fair cheeks. "I know I've used the Rantzier name, but after that day... after what he did to my father... I don't want it anymore."

Merrick wanted to ask her then.

Ask her the question he carried around like a precious gemstone.

Ask her to marry him—or to allow him to organize a mating ceremony—whatever she preferred, but to do something that would tie her to him, make her his official family.

Ask her to do the honor of taking his name.

Or he'd take hers.

He didn't give a shit that it was Rantzier.

He'd wear it proudly if it meant his and hers were the same.

But something in her eyes told him it wasn't the time.

They'd go to war tomorrow, and she... she didn't want to be reminded they might never get to do it. That's what the emotions drifting from her told him, so Merrick only held her closer and whispered, "I love you, Elessia. Whatever name you might choose to carry."

CHAPTER 34
FRELINA

The anticipation in the air was so palpable that Frelina felt like she could reach out, rip a piece from the starry sky, and pop it into her mouth.

All day, the humans on the ships had prepared for the war they expected to descend upon them tomorrow, finding their weapons and their positions and saying what needed to be said to their friends and families.

But it wasn't just war nerves that made the atmosphere electric. Loche had declared that there would be a feast tonight, and amidst all the sharp and shiny weapons, some of the humans had dragged up instruments, gathering them on the four ships right behind Loche's own.

Others had huddled together over small ship stoves and open fires, cooking whatever they could come up with, creating what, at least to Frelina, looked like a lavish feast, with bread, soup, fish, and even meat being plated and sent across the ships, ensuring all would be able to fill their stomachs.

Barrels of wine had also been carried out, and when she'd walked past a group of Loche's horrifying soldiers —she honestly didn't understand how Lessia hadn't fled the nation as soon as she'd laid eyes on those birdlike masks—they'd pressed a wooden cup into her hands with a curt "Keep track of it, or you'll have to drink directly from the tap."

Frelina had mostly stayed in the background, apart from when Kerym lost his shit at Merrick, and she'd spent fifteen minutes scolding all three Fae warriors, telling them it wasn't the time to tell Merrick what to do.

Besides, she wanted him near her sister at all times. She firmly believed he, out of anyone, could keep her alive.

Elessia listened to him, even when he didn't believe it, and Frelina had seen how he'd directed the Faelings and even some of the humans earlier in the day. They all had a lot of respect for the Fae, and not because they were frightened of him.

Frelina snorted to herself as she leaned her arms on the railing of Rioner's ship, watching as the humans started gathering, the first hesitant ones beginning to fill their plates.

At least they didn't respect him *only* because they feared him. Merrick knew what he was talking about; it was clear to anyone who deigned to listen a second to his grumpy voice. So if he believed he could save Elessia, so did Frelina.

She moved to look at the deck behind her.

Speaking of grumpy Fae...

She had watched Raine today, too—how he'd steered clear of the barrels of wine; how he'd refused to meet her eyes when she'd yelled at him, Kerym, and Thissian; how much guilt coiled Raine's shoulders when he'd finally retreated into his chambers when someone had offered him a bow and arrow and he'd jerked back as if they would burn him.

Too much of a reminder of Solana, Frelina guessed.

Her thoughts went to the beautiful blonde Fae Raine had shown her in her memories, and she wondered what she'd think of Frelina.

"I'm just trying to keep him alive," Frelina whispered to herself, wondering if the words would ever reach Raine's mate. "He's still yours. He'll always be yours. I hope it's okay that I just... borrow him for a little?"

She wanted to think that the feisty female she'd watched die would approve—that hopefully she loved Raine enough to see he was only using Frelina as a distraction.

Just for this war.

Just for today, Frelina promised herself as she made her way down into the depths of the ship, trying to ignore the butterflies awakening in her stomach at the prospect of seeing Raine's heated eyes again.

She didn't bother knocking before she opened his door, and she wasn't surprised to find him on his bed, staring up at the ceiling, his blades—which he'd apparently been attempting to polish, based on the rags spread out everywhere—left on the floor.

"Can I come in?" she asked as she closed the door and made her way over.

"Haven't you already done so?" Raine didn't look her way as she halted before the bed.

Nerves kicked in, and Frelina wiped her hands on her trousers, deciding it was better to sit down on the end of the bed rather than stand above him.

"The others are beginning to eat up there," she said after Raine had only sighed twice.

"So?"

She rolled her eyes at the Fae, who wore an expression fit for a child. "So? I am guessing you're hungry. That's why I came down here to get you."

Raine laughed, but not in his usual teasing way.

It was raspy and brutal and mean.

"I doubt that's why you came down here."

She couldn't stop the blood rushing to her face, especially when Raine glanced at her down his nose.

"You came here so I'd fuck you." There was no warmth in Raine's voice.

No lilt of friendship or even respect.

"Little Rantzier can't get enough of the mind-bender's fingers, is that it? You came here to use me again. To settle your battle nerves with an orgasm, perhaps?"

"No." She began shaking her head when Raine continued.

"Don't lie, it's unbecoming. Remember that I've seen how lonely you are." He laughed that awful laugh again. "You're so damn afraid of dying alone that you'll take any scrap I'll give you."

"Stop it," Frelina snarled. "You're just feeling guilty and taking it out on me."

"Don't pretend like you wouldn't suck my cock if I whipped it out right now. Anything for a little company, is that it?" Raine began sitting up, and she couldn't stop herself from meeting his cold eyes. "So fucking sad. I thought your sister was broken... but it's you who are the broken one, isn't it?"

"Stop it, Raine," she repeated. "I know what you're

doing, and it won't work on me."

"Don't say my name like that," he growled before he began ripping his shirt off.

"I said stop," Frelina said again, her hands gripping the blanket when Raine's eyes went crazed.

Gods, he was such an idiot.

She held back a scoff. As if *she* was the broken one.

"Isn't this what you came for?" Raine was in her face now. "For a quick fuck before we all die tomorrow?"

The harsh lines of his face twisted and blurred as rage sprang into her eyes, and Frelina shot up from the bed when the urge to slap him became almost unbearable.

"Fuck you," she hissed as she started toward the door, that bottomless depth of loneliness fighting to wrap its sharp claws around her heart even though she knew why Raine was doing this. "You're pushing me away because it's easier to deal with the guilt than maybe feeling happy for a change. You're such an idiot."

She fumbled with the handle. "Fuck," she swore again, and despite the rage burning hot within her, tears clouded her vision as another rush of cold loneliness feathered across her skin.

As more stupid tears made their way down her cheeks, she kept messing up when she tried to open the door, and angry sobs shook her until she hiccuped loudly, the sound muted only by her fist slamming against the damned door so she could get out.

A hand snaked around her waist as she struggled, and she hiccuped again. "L-leave me alone. I might know why you're doing this, but that doesn't mean I need to take it."

"Frelina. Fuck, Frelina, wait." Another curse brushed her ear, and she struggled against Raine's hold.

"Get off me!" she screamed, praying that Lessia and Merrick had returned from wherever they'd sneaked off to and would hear her. "Get the fuck off me!"

But no one came to the door, and Raine didn't release her.

"Fuck," he snapped again. "I'm sorry, little Rantzier. I didn't... I didn't mean it. I was just... I don't know. Fuck! Please stop crying. I can't take it."

"F-fuck you," she stuttered, fighting against his grip around her waist, kicking her legs and scratching at his arms. "I am not crying over you! And I said, let me go!"

She didn't need to ask again.

Frelina almost fell when Raine removed his arm, but she quickly moved away from his steadying hand on her shoulder when she regained her balance.

Raine was panting as much as she was, and she fucking hated him for the tears that streamed down his cheeks as he stared back at her.

"I'm sorry, Frelina." Raine reached out a hand, which she slapped away. "I... I fucked up."

"Fuck you." She hiccuped again, but she'd gotten control over the tears, angrily wiping her sleeves across her face to dry them. "You're such a bastard, Raine."

"I know." His head hung between his shoulders. "I really am."

"You're an asshole." Her panting slowed as she stared at him, watching her words land but not hurt.

Almost... almost as if he wanted them, as if he welcomed them.

Gods, of course he fucking did.

And he said Merrick was a martyr...

"I know." Raine lifted his eyes to hers. "I know I am all those things, and I'm sorry you had to be the one to deal with it."

Frelina slammed her hand against the door again. "Stop it!"

Raine didn't move as she stepped up to him, tapping a finger hard into his chest.

"I get that you're feeling guilty. I get that it hurts!" She refused to let him look away when he tried, her gaze holding his hostage. "I get it. But I thought we were friends, Raine! You could fucking talk to me instead of trying to drive me away."

"I know." His eyes flitted between hers as he mumbled the only words he seemed to be able to express.

Frelina continued poking his chest, emphasizing each word she hissed at him. "You are a fucking adult, Raine. Use your words."

"I..." Raine hesitated but finally seemed to get it together when she widened her eyes at him. "I just don't know what the right thing to do is. With everything going on... war... emotions are high, Frelina, and I just don't want you to take whatever this is the wrong way. For you to think I have anything to offer you."

She threw her head back and groaned before responding. "I am not asking you for love. I am not asking you for *anything*. You needed someone, and so did I. It was a mutually beneficial agreement, you dumb bastard! I don't pine for you at night. I don't dream of weddings and children and eternal love. I just wanted to fucking experience *something*, anything, before I potentially die tomorrow!"

"It's just..." Raine gripped the hand she kept driving into his chest. "I need you to know... I promised her forever."

Despite her previous words, something twisted deep in Frelina's gut, into that space she hadn't dared look too hard into, but she made herself ignore it as she stared up at the stupid Fae warrior.

"I don't want her place, Raine. I am your friend. Or at least I thought we were friends before today. I... I just didn't want to be alone tonight," she added quietly, wondering why she did this to herself, why she was vulnerable with him after the vile things he'd said to her.

Frelina sniffed, realizing she'd lost her grasp on her tears once more, and she began turning when Raine pulled her to him.

"Don't cry because of me," he whispered as he cupped her cheeks. "Please don't cry, little Rantzier."

"I'm n-not," she forced out. "I don't... I don't care about you. I don't care about anything."

After swiping his thumb over one cheek, Raine bent down, and she froze when he pressed his lips beneath her eye, capturing with his tongue the tears still falling there.

Don't start lying to me now, please. I'm sorry I was a bastard asshole.

His mouth left her skin, but he didn't move back, and she glanced at him from under wet lashes.

What are you doing? Frelina frowned when Raine seemed to hold a silent fight within himself, the fingers on the hand still cupping the cheek he hadn't kissed caressing her skin in slow, rhythmic movements.

You do care. Raine's eyes burned into hers. *You care so much, and you have so few to do it for.*

Frelina shook her head, but Raine stopped the movement. *I care too. I care too fucking much, and it's eating me alive. I might be centuries old, but I don't fucking know how to deal with this! I don't know what to do with you!*

Her eyes rolled upward to the dusty planks lining the ceiling. *Who's the liar now?*

The air stilled for a moment.

Then Raine's lips were on hers.

This time, though, it wasn't harsh and desperate and almost painful. It was soft, probing: a question whether she would allow him in.

What are you doing? She remained still as his mouth tentatively explored hers.

I do care, Frelina. His words were as slow, as cautious, as his kiss. *I do care about you, and I am so fucking sorry for what I said.*

She tried to hold back. She really did. But when Raine retreated, his lips leaving hers, she couldn't.

Melting into him, she wound her arms around his neck, and he groaned as he found her mouth again, fusing them together as if that was the one thing in the world that could save them.

I don't want to hurt you.

She could tell he was being sincere: the worry was as clear as the yearning brimming under his skin, building within him, which made the hands running up and down her back twitch as he restrained them from exploring every bit of skin they could find.

Then don't hurt me, Raine. I don't ask for promises or commitments. I only... I only ask that you don't push me away when you're hurting—that you treat me like you would a friend.

His tongue sought access, and when she opened for

him, pressing her body harder against his own, he growled into her mouth.

It won't happen again. Raine's thoughts came choppier now, a fiery hint to them that told her he was on the edge of giving in entirely to his desires. *I'm so sorry.*

I know. Frelina unwound one of her arms around his neck, slid it down his broad chest, and tentatively sought out what she'd been so curious to touch.

Raine stood entirely still as she cupped his hard length, letting her fingers squeeze and explore until something deep rumbled in his chest and his forehead fell to her shoulder, leaving her mouth as he drew deep breaths.

Fuck, little Rantzier, if you continue, I am going to come in my trousers, and I haven't done that since I was an adolescent.

She giggled at that, even as his words made heat shoot between her legs, that wetness Raine had coaxed out of her last time flooding her.

Raine sniffed the air, and his cock became impossibly harder under her fingers as he groaned, "You smell so damned good."

Lifting his head, even as Frelina began moving her hand faster, realizing that the friction of her hand on the fabric was driving him insane, Raine found her gaze, and her pulse thrummed at the look in his eyes.

Raine chuckled quietly as he pressed a thumb against her neck, feeling her racing pulse. "Are you sure? Even with everything I've told you? With everything I've done?"

She nodded, suddenly breathless as she responded, "It's only battle nerves, right?"

Raine swallowed, his eyes moving across her face as if to find any sign of hesitation or uncertainty.

I'm sure. She let him in fully again, allowed him to see that she didn't want anything more from him than company, than for him to settle the fire he'd started deep inside her. *Just battle nerves, Raine.*

"Right," he mumbled, the corners of his eyes creasing and something she couldn't quite read flashing across his features.

Frelina shook her head before she stood up on her toes and crashed her mouth against his.

I want this, you dumb bastard. I want you.

She bit his lip until one of those guttural growls rumbled against her.

I want you, too, little Rantzier.

She smiled at him as his hands became more assured, and when he noticed it, he closed his eyes for a second before swooping her up in his arms.

It was as if they'd come to a mutual agreement because when Raine carried her over to the bed, clumsily shedding their clothes on the way, they left their minds open, letting the other see precisely what they wanted—what they were feeling.

He really did want her.

Frelina didn't think it was possible to be more desperate than she'd been last time, but seeing the images forming in Raine's mind, feeling how his mouth dried as his eyes roved over her naked body, from her breasts down to her pussy, which he'd noticed was already wet, made her wild.

Her nails dug into his scalp as he settled her on the bed, and she knew he allowed it, but she pulled him with her, forcing his hard body to press down on her own until his cock slid between her folds.

She moaned as he began rubbing it against her, moving over her clit and down again, coating it in her wetness.

The sounds alone were almost enough for her to come, and she tugged at his hair to make him move faster, push down harder… anything.

If this was battle nerves, perhaps war wasn't so bad after all, she thought as Raine slipped a hand between them, his weight coming off her, making her let out a disapproving sound, but then his thumb found her clit as his cock continued sliding over her pussy, and she cried out at the pleasure.

I'm going to get you ready. Raine's hot breath danced over her mouth as he teased her lips, his thumb brushing over her clit, again and again, while he refused her his kiss.

She whimpered when he rolled off her, but he swallowed the sound with his mouth, finally crashing it against hers while he dipped the tip of his middle finger into her pussy.

Her back shot off the bed, but Raine gently pressed her body down again, kissing her until she moaned into his mouth.

Then he began moving, and she had no idea what noises left her, and she honestly didn't care as Raine's finger drove in and out while his thumb worked her clit until she started thrusting her body to meet his movements.

You are so fucking wet.

Raine groaned as he added another finger, and when

Frelina cried out his name, he swore loudly, driving his fingers deeper as he pressed down on her sensitive nub until her breathing stuttered.

And when he added a final finger... Her legs fell fully open as her eyes slammed shut, and she bit down on her bottom lip as the heat exploded through her stomach, sparking through every nerve and vein as she came undone.

Raine kissed her, using his teeth to get her to release her lip, and the gentle kisses somehow made the orgasm more powerful—more real.

When her limbs stopped trembling, Raine rose on his elbows, shaking his head with a small smile as he looked down at her. She met his eyes for a second, but Frelina quickly closed her own when something almost... tender brightened the gold in them.

She could feel him continue to watch her, so she conjured the image he'd shown her last, when he'd fucked her against the door, trying to break up the strange tension that flickered through the room.

If you ask me if I am sure, I am going to kill you. She grinned, relieved, when she opened her eyes again and his own flared at her words and at the images of his cock driving into her that she continued sending into his mind.

"Fuck." Raine shook his head again, and she moaned even though he hadn't even touched her yet when he wrapped his hand around his long, hard shaft and shifted so he hovered over her.

You're going to feel so fucking good.

Frelina closed her eyes as Raine released his cock, settling his hands beside her as he crowned her entrance.

Look at me.

She wasn't sure if he'd meant for her to hear the softness in his voice, but her eyes flew open anyway, and there was no teasing smile—no cocky hardness in Raine's eyes as he stared back at her.

She held her breath as Raine thrust his hips and gently pushed inside her.

It didn't hurt.

She had somehow expected it to, but it was as if her stomach was set on fire, everything heating and swelling when Raine stared at her like that.

As if she were something extraordinary.

"Frelina," he moaned, and she could sense his pleasure as he pulled out, almost the entire way, before sinking into her, merging them entirely.

She cried out at the slight burning sensation, but Raine claimed her mouth, murmuring over her lips, "Frelina, Frelina, Frelina."

When she responded to it, her hips lifting an inch off the table, Raine started moving faster, thrusting deeper into her while her hands tangled in his hair and she held on to him, letting him lead.

He filled her so perfectly—his thick cock sliding in deep before he almost pulled it out fully and drove into her again.

Raine's lips moved to her neck, and she cried out again when he began sucking on her sensitive skin while one of his hands found her breast and he twisted her hard nipple. The pain mingling with the pleasure was...

Incredible, Raine murmured into her mind. *Like you.*

He continued pumping her, and her skin lit on fire as he moved his lips farther down, sucking a nipple into his mouth and biting it.

Don't stop. Don't stop, she begged, and he bit down

harder until she lifted her hips more for him to glide deeper.

His cock hit something deep within her, and Raine used a hand to press her knee up, somehow finding a way to thrust himself all the way in to the hilt, and Frelina couldn't take it...

I'm... I'm... She didn't know what she was trying to say, but Raine growled against her breast, his sharp teeth rasping against it as he thought, *I'm right there with you.*

His cock twitched in response, and that was that. Frelina's blood raced, her pulse beating so wildly she thought she might pass out as her eyes shut, stars and moons and suns dancing in the darkness.

Raine groaned as he drove into her—harder and harder—until her pussy closed around his cock, squeezing it, and they cried out as one as warm, hot wetness spilled within her.

Raine's head fell to the mattress beside her, and they were both silent as they caught their breaths, the bed squeaking from their untamedness.

"I think I'm ready to die now," Frelina mumbled as she played with a strand of his long hair.

Raine's laugh exploded through the room, and when he rolled off her, he pulled her body to his own, nestling his face into her neck as he whispered, "I plan on keeping you alive for a long, long time."

Frelina swatted at him, closing her mind as she caught a glimpse of just how much Raine meant what he said.

She would not read anything into it.

Just like he wanted.

Like she wanted.

He seemed to fall deep into thought, his hand tracing

over her stomach in slow, deliberate circles, and a sense of unrest swept through the room so swiftly that Frelina wiggled out and got to her feet.

She struggled to look at him as she mumbled, "Let's get to the party. I'm sure Elessia is desperate to be saved from talking to too many people."

CHAPTER 35
LESSIA

Lessia sat with her friends, warmth that shouldn't have found its way into her chest the night before war still clawing through as she let her eyes rest on each of them.

Kalia was seated beside her, her white hair fastened into a tight braid that hung over her shoulder as she kept one eye on the makeshift dance floor ahead and one on the Faelings moving about the ships.

While the humans, under Loche's orders, hadn't said a bad word to any of them, a sense of apprehension filled the air whenever one came too close, especially when it was Lessia—although given what she'd done to them, that made complete sense.

Right now, most of the Faelings sat on some of the empty wine barrels lining the stern of Loche's ship, watching as humans swung each other around to the soft tunes. Exactly like she, Amalise, and Ardow had done the past few hours, catching up on seemingly mundane things, but the things Lessia wanted to remember, should everything go as she expected tomorrow.

Lessia waved to Ledger as he ran past them, watching as he approached a group of humans to refill his cup, and she couldn't help but smile when the gray-eyed boy threw around quips that made even the most uneasy man in the group laugh.

"What are you thinking about?" Ardow leaned over Amalise's lap to look at her, and she was glad the guilt that had painted his gaze darker ever since she'd helped him escape Ellow was nearly erased.

They'd set those grievances aside, especially once Ardow had understood just how far Meyah had led him astray, and she'd heard from both Amalise and Zaddock how Ardow had apologized not only to Loche but to every human he came across, and how he and Venko had done everything they could to prepare for tomorrow.

Venko was the one who'd provided the abundance of food that lay on the serving trays around them, and he'd also funded several of the ships, donating weapons and other resources to ensure they were all fully stocked.

And Ardow... She knew that guilt still lingered somewhere inside him, because he'd fought to be on Loche's ship, to be placed with the group that would be positioned in the bow, meeting the rebels first, to maybe, just maybe, make some of the ones he knew pause before they blindly threw themselves into the fight.

She smiled at Ardow when he raised his brows.

What had he asked, again?

What she was thinking about?

Lessia met Amalise's eyes before she spoke. "If there is some way I can convince you not to be on that ship tomorrow."

Amalise hummed in agreement before she bore her eyes into Lessia's. "I don't understand why I have to be on the stupid cliff while you both stand in the front lines."

This was why Lessia had lost every fight with Ardow today about his decision. Merrick would be in the bow of Rioner's ship, and since she'd promised to try to be right next to him the entire time...

"You know why," Lessia said softly, praying that Amalise wouldn't start crying, like she had twice today. "He needs to know I'm safe."

"He's a good man." Zaddock strolled up to them, and Lessia and Ardow shared a glance when Amalise tried her best not to look his way, her legs dangling lazily over the edge of the barrel. "I wish I could do the same, but you'll be safer on the cliff, Amalise."

"Who is going to save you when you get another knife in your back, then?" Amalise snapped, her eyes slitting as she glared at Loche's right-hand man.

"Are you worried about me?" Zaddock shot back as he stepped closer, blue eyes twinkling as they flickered over her friend.

"No," Amalise muttered, her arms crossing over her chest. "I just think my talents will be wasted on that stupid cliff."

"She is worried about me," Zaddock mouthed to Lessia when she snickered, and she realized he must have had a cup or two of the wine because his face didn't have the sharp lines it usually did when Amalise was around. The ones that made Lessia believe he was on high alert at all times, looking for any danger that might pose a threat to her friend.

"I. Am. Not." Amalise went red when Ardow also began laughing. "Stop that!"

Amalise went to slap Ardow when Zaddock swept in and grabbed her hand, swiftly bending his back in a bow. Looking up at her while keeping his body bent, Zaddock asked, "Will you do me the honor of a dance?"

Amalise pulled at her hand, but even Lessia could see it was half-heartedly, especially as Zaddock's gaze filled with innocent hope.

"Just one," he continued softly, and Lessia had the urge to look away—the moment seeming too private. "If I die from one of those daggers to the back tomorrow, you'll still have made me the luckiest man alive if you just give me one."

When Amalise hesitated, Ardow shoved her off the barrel with a "For fuck's sake, you two are going to make me cry," and Zaddock sent her friend a drunken salute before he led a bloodred Amalise onto the dance floor.

Ardow did have tears in his eyes as they caught Lessia's again, and he cleared his throat. "She is really giving him a hard time."

"You know why," Lessia responded as she watched Amalise's blonde hair sway over the arms Zaddock had wrapped around her. "She is scared of getting hurt again."

Ardow enveloped one of the hands in her lap with his own. "I know. But if the past months have taught me anything, it's that time is not on our side." He turned to her, and the air between them became heavy with seriousness. "I haven't apologized enough for what I did to you—to all of you."

Lessia began waving her other hand, but when Ardow whispered "Please," she dropped it again.

"I fucked up, Lessia." His eyes searched hers. "So, so bad. But I am doing what I can to make up for it."

"I know, Ard." She did know. She could see it in his eyes, in his shoulders, in his back, and in his gait. "It's all right."

"It's not..." Emotions raced over his face. "I can't help but think I set everything in motion with my actions, and"—his voice broke—"your father."

Lessia took a shaky breath. "Was not your fault. His death wasn't anyone's fault but Rioner's." She squeezed Ardow's trembling hand. "I understand why you did what you did. Even here, even now, when we're all fighting on the same side, there is a divide. We all see it. And it needs to change."

Her eyes reflected in his, not in the way they did when her magic captured someone's mind but in understanding, and Ardow's pinched face finally softened.

"Do you think we'll be alive to see it happen? See humans and Fae and half-Fae and shifters unite as one?" Ardow asked, his voice barely a whisper as Venko approached them.

Her grip on his hand tightened further.

"I don't know," she admitted. "But I have to believe it *will* happen."

"Believe what will happen?" Venko asked as he rested a hand on Ardow's leg, the other lifting a goblet of wine to his lips.

"That our men will finally ask us to dance," Lessia said, blinking away any wetness that might have formed in her eyes.

"That's why I came over here." Venko grinned. "But I think your man is still on the other ship waiting for Raine's friends, so I can wait."

"No, no." Lessia shook her head. "I'll be fine."

"Don't be silly," Ardow responded. "We'll wait until Merrick is back."

"No, you go ahead." Lessia pressed Ardow's hand back into his lap. "I could do with a few minutes alone."

She actually could use some time by herself. All day she'd been catching up with the Faelings, with Ardow and Amalise and Soria and Pellie—she honestly had no idea why the sisters still were here, deciding to fight, when she'd never seen them do much more than drink wine and bed men—and while she'd found that short time with Merrick on the cliff, her pulse was still heightened from all the socialization.

Ardow seemed to read as much into her expression because he bowed his head before jumping off the barrel, and with a squeeze of her knee, he led Venko onto the dance floor, taking up a spot beside Amalise and Zaddock, who were still moving in a circle even though Lessia was quite certain this would count as a second dance.

The two men pressed their cheeks against each other's, Ardow's auburn hair mixing with Venko's blond mane as they held on to each other, moving elegantly but slowly from side to side as they appeared to be having a whispered conversation, judging from how their lips moved.

More warmth welled within her as she watched her two best friends.

"We've come quite far from those drunken nights," Lessia whispered to herself when first Ardow, then Amalise, shot her a soft smile.

"What did you say?"

She jerked back at Loche's voice, making the barrel

shake, and Loche had to grip it so her sudden movement wouldn't make it fall over, taking her with it.

"Sorry," he mumbled when it finally stilled. "I heard you wanted to be alone, but I just wanted to say hi."

Lessia gripped the edge of the barrel as she stared back at him. He seemed... not calmer but focused, no pain brimming in his eyes as they met hers, and she heard herself order, "Sit."

"Are you sure? I don't need to." Loche threw a look at the dance floor, but no one was paying them any attention, not with the drinks flowing and music building.

"I'm sure." She smiled at him, patting the barrel beside her. "Sit."

As he did what she said, hoisting himself on top of it much more effortlessly than she'd crawled onto her own, he shot her a smile back. "You're not dancing?"

She shook her head, eyes darting to her own ship for a second.

Loche nodded once. "Raine's party just arrived. I was heading over there myself to greet them, but I heard they couldn't find Raine, so I thought I'd come here to check first."

Lessia had a suspicion about exactly where Raine was, since her sister hadn't been sighted, either, and she'd heard some strange noises when she'd finally returned to the ship to drop the daggers she'd been given in preparation for tomorrow, but if they wanted some time alone, she would not be the one to out them.

So she only mumbled something incoherent as her eyes drifted toward her friends again.

A silence settled between them, but it wasn't a loaded one, and she turned back toward Loche when she sensed him watching her.

"I'm sorry for what I put you through," he blurted when their eyes met again, and she didn't have time to do more than gape when he continued. "I... just wanted to have it said."

Lessia knew very well why these apologies were streaming out of people. She'd heard enough of them as she walked through different groups of people on the ships today. People were worried, scared that by the end of tomorrow, it would be too late.

"I'm sorry too," she said, offering him a weak smile. "We really messed this up, didn't we?"

Loche's lips lifted into an equally forced smile. "Maybe we did. Maybe we didn't. Maybe this was exactly what we were meant to do."

She eyed him for a moment, making sure he was sincere. "Maybe," she responded.

Because maybe they'd been exactly what each other needed in those moments—a beacon of hope, a mutual understanding, a bond between misunderstood people.

Loche's mouth twitched like he was reading her thoughts. "Make sure you bring the same rage tomorrow as when Craven dared open his mouth."

Lessia huffed a laugh, even knowing the older man's fate. "I'll do my best. And... you do the same, all right?"

She'd heard from the others about Meyah—that she was Loche's mother—and while she'd been shocked, there was something in her that had known that he was different. That he wasn't entirely human, that like herself, he was... something else.

Loche dipped his chin, and he began to make his way off the barrel when one of his men signaled him, and they both noted Raine and Frelina walking over the brow between their ship and Loche's. But as he was about to walk away, he turned to her again, placing a hand over her own.

"I'm happy you have him," he said in a voice that should have been too soft to be the regent's. "I truly am. He's... he's a good man, Lessia."

She smiled at him, not a forced one this time. "I know."

Loche nodded again before heading over to the man who'd waved him down, saying something to her sister that had her turn around and head Lessia's way while Raine quickly disappeared to the other ship.

That warmth sneaking through her body took a permanent spot in Lessia's chest.

She and Loche would be all right. She believed that now.

CHAPTER 36
LESSIA

"And where have you been?" Lessia teased as Frelina leaned her elbows on Lessia's knees, resting her chin in her hands as she looked up at her.

"I'm sure you already know," Frelina mumbled, pink creeping over her cheeks. "Raine asked us to come say hi to his friends, unless you plan on sitting here all night."

Lessia grinned at her sister as she let Frelina drag her off the barrel she'd been planted on for far too long, and they rushed their steps to catch up with Loche and the soldier walking straight-backed beside him.

When they had a few steps left, Lessia leaned into Frelina. "Is he good to you?"

Frelina raised a brow, and Lessia had to laugh at the look in her eyes.

"I guess I know better than to ask that." Lessia laughed again as they fell into step with Loche, and more happiness warmed her gut when her sister elbowed her, a smile brightening her features.

Like Merrick, Raine wasn't sunshine and rainbows but dark clouds and storms, although he must be doing something right if he could lighten Frelina's steps almost to skips.

Their giggles quieted when voices drifted toward them, amplified over the water, and Lessia couldn't help the prickle of irritation that crawled over her scalp when she recognized the voice of Iviry, the flirtatious Fae she'd met in the tavern on Midhrok, over the rest.

Her upper lip had curled even before they circled the bend of the ship, and Iviry's flame-like hair shone like burnt gold in the moonlight ahead.

"A Rantzier, Raine. Out of all people?" Iviry and Raine stood with their backs to where Lessia and the rest approached, with Merrick ahead of them and a group of Fae unloading weapons from a smaller ship behind him.

Lessia felt Frelina stiffen beside her, and she disliked Iviry even more as her sister slowed her strides.

"It's not like that," Raine muttered. "She's... a distraction."

A hiss shot through Lessia's teeth, and she was about to storm up to smack Raine's and Iviry's thick heads together when Frelina grabbed her hand.

"Don't." Frelina's eyes were hard as they held on to Lessia's. "Just leave it."

Lessia shook her head, locking eyes with Loche over Frelina, and she noted that even his jaw flexed as he moved his glare to the Fae ahead.

That damned...

"Who is she?" Frelina demanded under her breath.

Merrick had just noticed them approaching, and Lessia hurried to whisper, "Iviry. We don't like her." It was childish and probably unfair, but she couldn't help it.

As she uttered the name, the fiery-haired Fae spun around, and her eyes went wide as she took in the group, licks of crimson that mirrored Raine's hair weaving up her neck.

Yes, you should be fucking ashamed, Lessia thought as she moved closer to her sister while Merrick overtook Iviry and Raine to meet them.

Raine's eyes were also wide when he turned around, and she noted them fixing on her sister, something passing between them every step as they reached the group. But while his eyes softened at the same time as her sister relaxed, Iviry's gaze seemed to get wider and wider, her hand flying to her chest as if she needed to calm her heart.

Lessia gave Merrick a meaningful look when he slung an arm over her shoulders, and when he followed it, he stilled, pulling both Lessia and Frelina to halt about three or four feet away from Raine and the annoying female.

Loche also stopped, his confused gaze meeting hers before he asked, "What's going on?"

Merrick laughed, actually laughed, in the strained silence.

Then Raine followed, his deep chuckle making Loche's dark brows pull down as low as Lessia expected her own were.

Her sister also looked bewildered as Raine closed the distance between them, offering Frelina his arm as he got out between snickers, "Come on, let's get some water and I'll tell you."

Frelina shrugged at her as she let Raine lead her

away, and Lessia turned to Merrick, her hands flying out in a questioning gesture. Merrick didn't respond to her silent question; he only tilted his head to Iviry, who remained still as a statue as she stared at them.

No...

As she stared at... Loche.

Lessia slowly moved her gaze between them.

She stared at him like... Merrick did her.

"Oh, shit," Lessia mumbled. "No way."

She waited for a jolt of jealousy to hit her and send her spiraling like it had back on Raine's island, when Iviry tried to make Merrick dance with her. But it never came. Not even a nudge of pain could be found within her. There was only surprise, an element of amusement, and maybe... if she was truthful, a little bit of relief.

"What is happening?" Loche demanded again when Lessia realized she was also staring at him.

Merrick pulled her closer, and she could sense him getting ready to steer her away when Iviry's strangled response came.

"Y-you're my mate."

"I... What?" Loche tried to keep Lessia's eyes, but Merrick had already begun turning them back to Loche's ship, and she only had time to shoot him an apologetic grimace before his eyes were ripped from hers.

Bursts of laughter still shook Merrick's shoulders a couple of times as they left Iviry and Loche on their own, since the soldier who had come with his regent must have read the situation and hurried after them, and Lessia let out a shocked giggle herself as she met Merrick's eyes.

"That was..."

"Strange." Merrick finished her sentence. "But knowing Iviry... it kind of makes sense."

She was about to respond with something even more childish than what she'd told Frelina about Iviry when she caught herself.

Lessia didn't know her.

Maybe she was a wonderful person.

Merrick laughed again, clearly sensing the wrangling emotions within her.

"No, you didn't read her wrong." He steered her toward the dance floor she'd been watching all night as he spoke. "Iviry can be mean and shallow and rude, and she enjoys being the center of attention. But she is also loyal and brave and fiercely protective of those she cares about. She rose very quickly in the ranks amongst the Rantzier troops because of it, becoming the first female commander when she was merely a century old."

Lessia threw a glance over her shoulder.

Neither Iviry nor Loche appeared to have moved a muscle.

"Why did she end up on Raine's island, then?" she asked as she turned forward again.

"Because she believes everyone has a right to life." Merrick's eyes moved between hers. "She caught some of her soldiers forcing a group of half-Fae children to beat each other to death for sport, and... well, it didn't end well for them. Rioner found out what she did, so she fled."

So... she was a kind person.

Lessia was about to scold herself for the thoughts she'd had about the Fae when Merrick brushed his lips over hers. "No need for you to feel guilty. I kind of enjoyed seeing you jealous," he murmured against her mouth. "Come. I want to dance."

Lessia scoffed playfully even while allowing him to shift her into his arms as he backed her toward the music. "Why? You hate dancing."

"Because we can." Merrick's eyes went serious for a second before he blinked and pressed her against his chest, where his heart beat a steady rhythm that heated her blood as she listened to it.

They weren't even really near the dance floor. Their slow movements, the ones she'd fallen for so hard on Raine's island, shifted them closer to the side of the ship, keeping them within earshot of the music but away from the crowd.

Resting her cheek against his chest, she let him steer her in a small circle, let his hands and heart be the only things she focused on while her eyes swept over the group ahead, where firelight, from the small lanterns placed across the ship and railing, brightened smiling faces.

Her friends still danced there, and she was glad to see almost all the Faelings joining in, Kalia even dancing with a human man who didn't seem to know whether he should be enthralled or terrified by the white-haired beauty in his arms.

When Lessia finally looked away and lifted her face to his, Merrick bent down and kissed her.

His lips were soft, warm, moving lazily with hers.

As if they had all the time in the world.

As if this wasn't the night before battle and many of the people on this ship probably wouldn't see another sunset.

A sigh escaped Lessia, and he pulled back to look at her, mouth slightly red from their kissing and eyes filled with silver swirls that moved with the music.

"Is it bad that I am happy right now?" Lessia whispered when Merrick only continued to drink her in.

Because despite everything, she was. She was surrounded by everyone she loved. She'd seen each of them smile for a different reason.

"No." Merrick rested his forehead against hers. "No, it's not."

They stood like that, silent and still, until she whispered, "There is only one thing that could make me happier."

He must have sensed where her mind went because Merrick responded with a low groan, hands on her back moving down to her ass, pressing her against his hardening cock. "I thought you'd never ask."

After whipping his head around, he gestured for her to follow him up a staircase she believed led up to the upper deck where Loche's soldiers usually stood guard.

It was now dark apart from a single lantern shining its light on the wooden wheel and the small stools standing around it. A few bottles littered the floor, probably from the soldiers' precelebrations before they were allowed to leave their posts.

Merrick took a lap around the deck—to make sure no one else had gotten the same idea they had, she presumed—and as she waited for him, Lessia picked at some of the items left on the shelf beside the captain's chair.

There were a few coins, a sticky deck of cards, and some glasses, but it was the silver-encased mirror that drew Lessia's attention, and she smiled as she picked it up, remembering her mother having a similar one that she would let Lessia and Frelina borrow sometimes when they wanted to play dress-up.

Catching a glimpse of herself in the mirror, she froze.

The woman looking back at her looked... happy. Content. Excited. With rosy cheeks and bright eyes and hair that she'd finally combed.

For the first time in a long time, Lessia could see the girl she'd once been.

The one who'd been carefree, unafraid, excited for what life could potentially bring.

The one who'd read books about romance and adventure and who'd wished for all that for herself.

The one who'd argued with her parents over bedtimes and food and rules she was expected to follow, and who'd believed not being allowed to ride alone in the forest was the greatest punishment of all.

Her parents' faces formed in her mind. Her mother's kind smile when Lessia helped her with dinner. Her father's proud claps when she learned how to ride.

Then her father's face morphed into one of pain—the desperation for forgiveness that darkened his amber eyes nearly making her double over when it was replaced with emptiness, his soul finally joining her mother's in the afterlife.

The memory refused her air, but as she fought for it, the hand that still held the mirror trembling, her reflection only smiled wider, a strange laughter echoing around her, sounding both as if it were right there and as if it were far away.

Frelina's eyes, void of life, took her father's place.

Then Amalise's.

Ardow's.

Loche's.

Ledger's.

Kerym's.

Raine's.

Her reflection mocked her, the deranged smile growing wider and wider with every breath Lessia's body denied her.

"No," she breathed when an image of Merrick's bloodied and lifeless body—the one Rioner's guard had loved to conjure—took over her thoughts.

Whirling around, Lessia smashed the mirror so hard against the railing that its pieces rained down on the floor beneath, and she was glad this part of the ship was empty as she dropped the rest to the ground, winding her fingers around the wooden handrail and forcing air down into her lungs.

Steps rang behind her, and Merrick's voice was a mixture of fear and anger when he asked, "What happened?"

She only shook her head, struggling for breath to keep herself upright, and Merrick seemed to understand as he picked up a piece of the broken mirror off the floor.

Wrapping his arms around her, his chest began guiding her own breathing, his voice in her ear, whispering "I'm here. I'm here," calming her erratic pulse.

Still, pain nearly had her double over.

Pain because days like today were numbered, if not over.

Pain because tomorrow there would be so much hurt and death and fear.

Pain because she might never again see the smiles she had today, the ones that had given her hope that maybe... in some faraway future, it would all be all right.

A sob cracked through her chest when she had enough air for it, and Merrick held on to her as she began shaking.

He didn't ask again if she was all right or what had happened; he only kept her upright, kept her together, made sure the pieces he'd tried to build up didn't shatter like the mirror beneath them.

Lessia shut her eyes, trying to find a place for all that hurt within her.

But it didn't want to be locked down.

It needed to be seen, to be heard, to be felt.

A low wail built within her, starting in her chest, then whistling through her throat, and when it finally wouldn't be held back from leaving her lips, she spun into Merrick's chest, muffling the sound by letting it seep into his leather tunic so the people still dancing on the deck below wouldn't hear.

"Give it to me," Merrick said hoarsely. "Give it all to me."

She continued, her fingers digging into his clothing, holding on as she let the fear and pain and worry and distress leave her with that horrible sound while Merrick continued whispering, "Give it to me, Lessia. I can take it."

She didn't know how much time had passed when her throat began aching, when her fingers went stiff, when her eyes dried, but when she began to come to, the people beneath them were still drinking and dancing as she threw a peek their way.

Swallowing the last of the cry, she looked up at the

Death Whisperer, wishing that the sense of falling she got every time she looked into his eyes was real—that she could fall right into him and never come back out.

Her eyes drowned in Merrick's dark ones as she whispered, "I don't want to do this, Merrick."

He was the only one she could tell. Because she knew he *could* take it, that his whispered words weren't empty ones. Still, there was no hiding the brokenness in his voice as he responded, "I know. I know, my little fighter."

She didn't have tears left, but her vision was still muddled as she looked up at him, letting her eyes tell him everything she couldn't.

That she didn't want to do this. That she didn't want to die. That she wished for all the futures and dreams she had carved into Merrick's skin, and those he'd dared speak only into the night.

She didn't even blink as she let his night-sky gaze envelop her, and she tried to stay in the consuming sensation, allowing it to respond to everything she didn't say with its own wishes and dreams.

The longer she stared into his eyes, the more frantic a frenzy welled within her veins, and it was as if Merrick read her mind because he reached for her at the same time as she jumped up on him.

The kiss wasn't tender, nor did it feel like they had time.

It was agony and despair, and she needed more of it.

Merrick wrapped her hair in his fist, tugging at it so he could kiss her harder, and she didn't care about anything other than having his skilled tongue play with hers.

When he sat her down on the railing, she didn't give one shit whether anyone could see or hear them, and she tugged on his trousers until they slipped down his legs and his hard cock sprang free.

As she whimpered "Please," Merrick growled softly, and he relieved her of her own trousers, forcing them over her boots to gain access faster.

Pulling her undergarments aside, his fingers whispered over her already drenched pussy before he roughly pulled her toward him and thrust into her so hard he sank in to the hilt with one drive.

Merrick swallowed Lessia's cry with his lips, crashing them against her own as he began moving, pushing into her with one deliberate thrust at a time.

Shifting her arms so they were locked around his neck, Merrick began sliding in deeper, harder, and his mouth left hers to move to her ear, whispering "Give. It. To. Me" in rhythm with his movements.

As he trailed his lips lower, never losing the speed of his thrusts, her pussy contracted around his thick hardness. Then his teeth sank into her skin, and Merrick's hand flew to cover the cry leaving her as the orgasm shot up from the pit of her gut through her stomach and out into her entire body.

He continued to push his cock up into her until his body jerked, his cock twitching, and he spilled within her with one final thrust.

They came down together, and even when their breathing became normal and the heat in her veins chilled, Merrick held on to her, refusing their bodies any space as he rested his forehead against her shoulder.

It wasn't until Lessia finally straightened, and Merrick gave her a quick peck before helping her down and into her clothes again, that she realized her shirt was wet where he'd leaned his face.

But neither of them said anything as they made their way back to their cabin—not to sleep, not when the sun had just started peeking over the horizon, but to at least change and get their weapons to prepare for what the new day would bring.

CHAPTER 37
LOCHE

The mood across the ships couldn't be more different from the one of last night.

Gone was the passion and bristling energy and laughter, and in their places a suffocating silence stretched out across the sea, allowing even the faintest murmur that might occur across the thirty or so ships now floating in what he hoped would be an impenetrable row to be heard by everyone.

Loche glanced around the ship where he stood. They'd ended up deciding to keep Rioner's ship in the middle, with him and Lessia and the Fae who would not be atop the cliff standing in the center of it, while Zaddock and Ardow led his best troop of soldiers in the bow.

Around them, each ship was filled with armed soldiers, all bearing the Ellow crest on their chests or arms, and behind them, atop the dark cliff jutting out over the vessels, Kerym and Raine led the best archers, with the Faelings who would fight dispersed between them.

The bluest eyes he'd ever seen collided with his own, and he quickly looked away when Iviry's gaze swept across his face from where she stood beside Merrick, Lessia, and Thissian.

Y-you're my mate.

Loche couldn't even begin to consider the implications of this, even if he somehow sensed her around him now, like a shadow that wasn't his own but followed him all the same.

They'd stared at each other for what felt like an eternity before Loche had excused himself and retreated to his room, where he'd spent the night looking out the window at the stars and moon that reflected in the too-calm sea.

He'd felt her eyes on him all morning, when they'd eaten a quick breakfast and then made all the final preparations, but she hadn't approached him, and for that he was thankful.

What would he even say?

What could he offer her but disappointment?

Loche shook his head as one of the two copper-haired sisters strolled up to the group of Fae, her hair not as fiery as Iviry's but still so similar that he looked away, instead tracking Lessia, who cast him a quick smile as she passed him on her way to the stern, where that terrifying sea wyvern rose from the water, large droplets rushing down her long neck and glistening atop the thick dark spikes lining her violet-scaled body.

The scene before his eyes seemed too tender, too sweet, for a beast and half-Fae, but he couldn't tear his eyes away when the wyvern settled her head against Lessia's body while she wrapped her arms around it, whispering something Loche couldn't pick up into the creature's ear.

"Their bond is a fierce and fragile one." Merrick placed a hand on Loche's shoulder, a gesture the regent would have felt the urge to shake off only a few days ago but that now filled him with a strange sense of gratitude for the Fae. "They are made of the same cloth, those two. History has seen it before, like it shall see it again. In war—"

"Unlikely allies find that the threads of their souls are woven from the same loom, that they were bound together even before the birth of their realm and their gods. That their past is linked as their future always shall be." Soria smiled as she approached them, not the Fae, as Loche believed she'd first intended.

Merrick frowned at her, his hand dropping from Loche's shoulder. "You know our old sayings?"

"They're not *your* sayings. You Fae always think you come up with everything, don't you?" Soria tsked before continuing. "Their truth comes from the magic of our worlds, from those who see it and guard it and mold it."

"So they come from the gods, then?" Loche asked when he felt Iviry's eyes on him again, turning more toward Soria as she sidled up beside Merrick.

Not that he'd ever heard of the saying Soria and Merrick were referring to, but everyone believed the gods had created these realms, even if neither humans nor Fae worshipped them anymore.

Soria threw her head back and laughed. "The gods have as much to do with it as this ship, my dear regent."

He kept his eyes on her when he caught Iviry and

Thissian walking up to them, the former throwing her long hair over her shoulder as she stared at Soria.

"You're a guardian," Iviry exclaimed. "As soon as I saw you, I felt it, but I couldn't believe... Not here... But the magic in your veins screams for you to free it."

"A guardian," Merrick mused. "I didn't know we had those in this realm."

"We don't." Thissian shook his head, his dark ocean eyes sharp as he stopped before Soria. "Do you know what you are?"

She glared up at the raven-haired Fae, and once again, Loche felt something strange from her. As if this small woman truly was more than met the eye.

"Of course I do." Soria dragged a hand through her short hair, her eyes challenging as they swept across each person in the group. "My sister and I have always known."

"Have known what?" Lessia joined them, and Loche was secretly glad he wasn't the only one who appeared utterly confused as he stared between the Fae and whatever Soria was. "What's going on?"

"You have a guardian in your midst," Iviry responded, and if Loche hadn't known better, he might have thought something had happened between the two of them because Iviry's tone had a slight frost to it, and there was a mirroring hint lining Lessia's usually warm eyes.

"And what's a guardian?" A crease twisted the skin between her brows as Lessia looked from Soria to the others.

"You might know us better as witches." Soria's smile took an apologetic form. "We call ourselves guardians, as we're meant to keep the balance of magic in worlds where that balance is needed not to give one kind of creature too much power."

"Witches..." Lessia seemed to taste the word, each letter rolling slowly off her tongue. "But we don't have witches in Havlands? I read all about your kind when I was younger. My... my father used to tease me that I'd become obsessed... but being able to cast spells... I found it so fascinating."

"Well, you've had me and Pellie here for a few years." Soria winced when Lessia's frown deepened. "I'm sorry I never told you."

"Why didn't you?" Lessia met Loche's eyes as she chewed on her lip, and he could tell she wasn't sure whether she should be worried about the sisters' secret.

Merrick couldn't, either, apparently, as he stepped closer to her, making sure she wasn't standing alone as she stared out across the group.

"I..." For a moment Soria's eyes rose to the cliff where her sister should be standing, then came back to Lessia's. "We were sold to someone in Havlands when we were very young—as a secret weapon this person could wield should they need to. But then you noticed us that day... noticed the sadness and fear the person pretending to be our mother instilled in us, and you didn't just walk away. You *saw* us, Lessia. And then you did something about it."

Soria shook her head, her smile returning. "We knew you were special then, and we could see you needed help, so we stayed... perhaps too long, but when we began to find out other things about you, we were in too deep, and we knew we needed to see this through."

Lessia appeared lost for words, her hand slipping into Merrick's as a million thoughts raced across her face.

"Can you help us with protection today?" Iviry broke in. "I... I traveled to a realm far away from here once, and the witches there could cast protection spells that would ward off enemies. They had me walk in circles for an entire month before they deemed me a nonthreat."

A whisper of hope brushed Loche's skin—hope that he'd thought he'd quelled—until Soria shook her head. "Our magic doesn't work here. You already sensed it."

"Iviry can read others' magic," Merrick whispered to Lessia, but Loche realized he did it loudly enough so he also could hear the information. "She'll be able to tell Thissian who to drain first."

Loche couldn't stop himself from looking at Iviry then, and when she found his eyes, something in his gut turned, but not in a bad way, and he didn't immediately look away this time.

That was when the drums started.

The group fell silent as the loud rumbling rushed across the sea, followed by the harsh sounds of trumpets and war cries—many human but some entirely animal.

Loche stood frozen as ship after ship appeared on the horizon, the sun's orange light illuminating them from behind, making them seem larger than he knew they really were.

Lessia moved swiftly beside him, and the entire group looked on as she waved the wyvern away, telling her to join the hundreds who'd begun popping up out of the sea, their colorful scales shining against the dark water and forming a rainbow barrier to his nation lying behind them.

When the beast followed Lessia's orders, which in the end were more like begging, the group faced forward, and moving nearly as one, they approached his soldiers in the bow, backs straight and chins raised high as they waited for the ships sailing straight for them.

Voices from his people joined the eerie drums and noises, and he couldn't let himself look directly but he knew people were embracing, saying goodbye and good luck, and he could barely stand it when Lessia tilted her blanched face to Merrick, who'd taken the spot beside Loche, and whispered, "I'm scared."

Loche's hands formed tight fists, his eyes going unseeing as Merrick pressed his forehead against that of the girl with the golden hair and eyes and whispered back, "So am I."

The Fae's words made fear drive its harsh claws into Loche's chest, and for the first time, he let himself feel it.

He was scared too.

So fucking scared.

Not for himself but for Ellow, for his people, for his friends who stood all around and above him.

A hand touched his, and while he didn't look to the side, he somehow knew it was Iviry, could feel her fear mixed with determination and focus.

"For Ellow," she said quietly, but with so many Fae around her, they all heard it, and despite fear keeping a strangled grip on his throat, something else thickened it as well when the two words began echoing all around him.

"For Ellow."

CHAPTER 38
FRELINA

Her pulse beat in rhythm with the drums that struck across the calm sea, and she didn't know what to do with her hands when the ships came into view, one terrifying sail at a time.

Frelina had asked for a few daggers, not that she was exceptionally skilled with them, but she didn't want to go entirely without weapons even if she wasn't in the midst of the fighting. They all hung by her waist for now, the blades bumping against her thighs whenever she moved, which was a lot, since she couldn't seem to stop shifting from foot to foot.

She caught the eyes of the white-haired half-Fae she'd heard was called Kalia before she turned them forward again, but she didn't miss the apprehension simmering in the woman's light eyes as she did so.

She, Kalia, and the other Faelings without offensive skills were huddled together by the cliff's edge—the one farthest away from the stairs leading down to the bay with the ships.

To her side, she knew Raine stood beside Kerym, the two of them instructing the human archers, the Faelings, and Raine's friends, who'd use their magic to fight from up here.

Thud.

Thud.

Thud.

Her heart hammered against her ribs as the drumming grew louder, and Frelina pressed both hands against her chest as the ships began sailing toward them. Sailing way too fast toward their own ships, which just seemed to become smaller and smaller below.

There were so many of them ahead. She'd counted that there were thirty-two ships of their own keeping steady on the sea in the cove, but crossing the sea were at least as many.

Ripped flags trailed from every mast—a mixture of Ellow's and Vastala's—some of them sparking from embers as the rebels on the ships set them aflame.

She had to seek out the hazel eyes she, for some reason, found soothing when her pulse continued to pound in her ears, and Frelina was grateful when Raine turned away from his sharp-eyed brother to face her fully.

He didn't say or mouth anything, but he didn't need to.

She could tell he wanted her to focus on what he and Merrick had asked of her: keep track of Lessia at all costs.

She hadn't protested. Frelina wasn't a fighter, not like the Fae and humans around her, who stood tall, their faces growing more and more focused as those ships neared. Not even like Lessia and Amalise, who didn't want but had learned to survive—to kill—because they had to. She'd gotten lucky that one time she'd killed the soldiers who had found their home—they'd been careless, and she'd been close enough that driving a dagger into each of their backs hadn't proved too difficult. So if she could keep her sister safe somehow by ensuring Rioner or anyone else couldn't sneak up on her, she would.

Frelina nodded, and Raine broke their stare.

Taking a step forward, Frelina made sure Lessia was in full view. She wouldn't be able to hear her from up here, but down below, her sister's golden-brown hair reflected the sun, and Merrick's distinctive silver hair was even easier to find amid the crowd of brown and black and blond scalps.

Staring from Lessia to the ships, Frelina shuddered.

If she thought their own ships looked small compared to those ahead, her sister seemed... tiny. Tiny and fragile.

"She'll be all right."

Frelina looked to the side when Amalise spoke, and she tried to give the blonde a smile when she settled beside her, her small hands waving toward her sister.

"She's a fighter," Amalise continued. "I think she's always been. You should have seen her when she arrived in Ellow... she was hardly more than a whisper of a person, but she clawed herself back to life. Fought every day to stay alive and every night not to succumb to the darkness that seems to follow her around."

Frelina nodded, the knot in her throat preventing her from replying.

Thankfully, a deeper voice broke in as Kerym approached them, the girl with the long copper hair trailing in his wake. "She really is."

Kerym leaned over the edge of the cliff, much farther out than Frelina ever would dare. "And she has Thissian and Merrick. Neither will allow anything to happen to her."

Frelina nodded again, as if it were the only thing she could do, when Amalise's face whitened, her eyes flying to the south.

Snapping her head the same way, Frelina had to hold on to Kerym's arm when Vastala's ships—the ones she'd seen drawings of in her father's study growing up—sailed toward them, keeping far away from where the wyverns formed a barrier against Ellow but still straight for the ships beneath them.

A sound of terror, one she might have been embarrassed about in another setting, betrayed her, and there wasn't much more than sheer willpower keeping her standing by the edge as the ships flew toward them.

"It's not Rioner." Raine's warm presence came up behind her, and she didn't care that they were surrounded by people as she spun around, releasing Kerym to take his outstretched hand.

"How do you know?" Amalise demanded, her voice shaking in the way Frelina would have expected her own to.

"The sails," Kerym murmured as he pulled the small woman behind him to his side, something stirring between them before his gaze sliced back to Raine. "It's the Reinsdors. And behind them... that's the Hjelmsons and the Driksters."

"Who are they?" Pellie asked softly.

"Some of the most prominent noble families in Vastala," Kerym said as he placed a hand over his brow to see better. "Seems they might have brought some friends too."

"They came for her," Raine breathed. "They really came for her."

Pride swelled in Frelina's chest, and she could tell even the mighty Fae warriors were touched by how Raine held on to her hand and Kerym blinked rapidly.

More of that pride worked its way into her limbs when Amalise took her other hand, and Kerym and Pellie shifted so they all stood in a row, with curious humans and other Fae shuffling forward behind them.

While they were fighting for Ellow, for a world where those who tried to rule with fear would not succeed, where Rioner and the rebels couldn't force their way to power, her sister had had a hand in how these groups came together—made people believe in something.

Frelina laughed as hesitant calls began rising behind and beneath her when more humans noticed the ships coming to their aid.

But that laugh faded as the ships slowed, then halted completely, a safe distance away from their cove and the wyverns waiting an equal distance from them, but to the north.

"Why are they stopping?" Venko, Ardow's man, stepped up to the ledge, his light eyes near slits as they stared into the sun.

Worried whispers rushed through the crowd behind her, and Frelina couldn't do anything but stare at the group surrounding her sister—watch how their hands fell to their sides and their faces dropped to the ship's deck.

"They're not fighting." Kerym tensed beside her,

before he jerked his head backward, eyes flying up to the blue sky. "The fucking cowards."

Frelina gave him a quick glance but then focused on Lessia, who, unlike the others, hadn't backed away from leaning over the railing, her arm still outstretched in greeting.

Frelina's thumping heart slowed with the pain lacing her chest, and she didn't know why she made herself continue looking at the painful scene beneath her, the small hand reaching for help that wouldn't come.

Raine, who'd also been watching their friends below, slowly lifted his gaze. "She's thanking them."

"Why the fuck is she thanking them!" Amalise's eyes could have killed someone when they swept past Frelina. "They're just... standing there."

"It's a warning," Raine said quietly. "They came to warn her."

"That Rioner is coming, right?" Frelina added when Amalise continued her choppy breathing, holding back an anger she was justified in letting free. "They're warning her he's coming today as well."

Raine didn't say anything, nor did anyone else, as they all looked out over the vast sea and the armada of rebel ships spreading out threateningly across it.

They'd known Rioner was coming. But... like herself, she guessed the others had held out hope that maybe, just maybe, they'd be able to quell one threat at a time. But the ships now moving with the slow waves had eradicated what was left of that fragile hope.

"So we fight," Kerym said in that voice she knew he wanted to sound playful—to drum up some bravery in the men and women around him—but that sounded mostly hollow to her ears.

"You all know what you need to be doing," Raine declared as he slapped his friend on the back.

Releasing Frelina's hand, he raised his to touch her cheek. "So do you. Don't let her out of your sight, little Rantzier. And I won't let you out of mine. Whatever happens... I'll look out for you."

She leaned into his warm hand for a second, allowing herself a moment of stupid wishful thinking.

That they could win this.

That they'd all get out alive.

That she and Raine... that there might be some kind of future for them.

He seemed to read too much into her eyes, even with her mind carefully closed, because he leaned down to kiss her, and the entire time, his eyes swam with emotions.

The kiss was brief, barely more than his lips pressing against the corner of her mouth, but it still made the ball of apprehension in her gut grow.

When Raine opened his mouth, that tension still filling his eyes, she placed a finger on it. "Don't. Don't make me a promise you won't be able to keep."

Raine stared at her, and it felt like it always did, like he truly *saw* her, for a second. Then he nodded, and with another quick touch of her face, he moved back to his position, starting to scream out orders to the archers, telling them where to aim and where not to bother.

She didn't look behind her as she approached the edge again, forcing her mind only to focus on the sister that had tilted her head Frelina's way, and she tried with everything in her to get her lips to curl upward as she raised a hand toward Elessia.

The sun lit only half her sister's face, but Frelina

thought it looked like she mouthed something, perhaps even called it out, but the words were taken by the wind.

Frelina squinted as she moved closer to the edge, cupping her lips and mouthing, “What?”

Elessia’s eyes looked... Frelina sliced her eyes farther when Elessia’s lips formed two words, and it wasn’t blood anymore that ran through her veins when she realized what they were.

“Behind you!”

Whirling around, Frelina noted the dark cloud rushing for them, and she wasn’t the only one, based on the screams and taste of terror that the wind whipped all around them.

She blinked at the cloud, the darkness so impenetrable it looked like the night itself was making its way toward them, but then Amalise screamed, “It’s birds!”

With shaking hands, Frelina reached for her small blades as people began shuffling in panic around her.

Amalise was right. Massive birds flew in a huge formation, their black feathers blocking any bit of light that tried to shine through them, and she was about to step back when she realized at the last second that she stood on a cliff.

“It’s a trap,” she said to herself.

“It’s a trap!” she screamed when people around her ignored Raine and Kerym’s orders and began running down the stairs, down to the vessels that would soon be surrounded by those ships.

But her words were drowned in the stomping of feet and clinking of weapons, and few followed Raine’s bellow to “Shoot them! Shoot them down!” when blades and rocks and other things Frelina couldn’t see but that cut into their skin when they hit began raining down from the sky, dropped from the birds' lethal claws.

Something smacked into her forehead, and she pressed the back of her hand against it when her skin split open, using her other one to throw a blade upward, praying it wouldn't come tumbling down and kill one of their own.

In the next second the birds were upon them, and wherever she spun, the cliff was in complete turmoil, birds and humans and Fae alike fighting for their lives, blood splattering onto stones with bodies falling off the cliff to her side, while others received daggers in their backs, dead bodies slamming into those trying to run, taking them with them into the depths of the seas.

"Frelina!"

She heard Raine's cry somewhere in the chaos, but she didn't dare search for him.

Not when one of those lethal birds, the ones that looked like live versions of the masks Loche's men wore—surely not a coincidence, Frelina thought as her heart began pounding in her ears—stalked toward her, crowding her against the edge while it snapped its sharp beak at her.

Opening her mind, she sent a fast goodbye, hoping that Raine would live to convey it to Elessia. Then she gripped the daggers in her hand, knowing they'd do little, being about half the size of that damned razor-sharp beak.

CHAPTER 39
MERRICK

The ships were upon them faster than should have been possible—propelled forward by something other than mere wind—and when Merrick looked out over the groups, finding the sharp eyes of the enemy half-Fae and shifters in the bow, he knew neither Raine nor Kerym nor any of those on the cliff would be of help.

Merrick and the others on the ships had been able only to watch as the shadowy formation of birds appeared in the sky, flying straight for their friends, and while he'd felt the same urge as Lessia, who'd thrown herself toward the back of the ship, trying to head for the cliff—for her sister—when the screaming began, he'd forced them both to stay back.

Even now, he kept a firm grip on Lessia's wrist, ignoring the hiss she sent his way as she struggled against his hold.

"Listen to me," he hissed back at her. "Raine has her. He won't let anything happen to her!"

Lessia's eyes still burned, that defiance he loved making them almost glow in the early daylight, so he continued, ushering out the words and turning her fully toward him so she wouldn't have to watch the bodies falling from the cliffs—although he could do little about the cries that cut off when they broke against the harsh water.

"We can't abandon this ship, Lessia." He shot a look around, grateful when her eyes followed. "The hope driving these people is already fragile. If we leave, it'll be lost."

Her mouth twisted a few times, eyes darting to either side as if she struggled to keep them ahead, but finally she nodded. "You're... you're right."

"Stay with me." Merrick wanted nothing more than to kiss her again, but there wasn't time, not with the ships closing in on them and the losing battle he knew was being fought on the cliff above.

He'd seen and heard it all before, and knew what the screams of horror meant, the ones that made everyone standing across the ships wince as they cast glances upward.

He could only hope his friends would find a way out of it.

Lessia seemed to understand because she drew a deep breath before forcing her body forward, unsheathing a few daggers hanging by her waist and holding on tightly to their hilts.

Even if her hands were steady, Merrick struggled to do the same, struggled to follow his own damned orders, because seeing her here, in the midst of this...

He wanted her far fucking away. But there was nowhere to flee, and she'd never forgive him if he gave in to the urge. So instead the Death Whisperer turned forward, allowing the souls to take a step closer to their world, readying them for the right moment.

The one coming too soon.

"We need to keep the line," Merrick screamed when the humans before him began backing up, nervous features twisting into fearful ones as they noticed the forms some of the shifters had taken as the ships sailed into the cove.

Snakes and massive felines seemed to be the preferred choice, long, thick bodies weaving around tall masts and roars joining the drums and war cries from those opting not to shift—or from the humans and Fae who couldn't.

"They are human underneath!" Merrick continued bellowing when a particularly ferocious cry drifted toward them from a pure-black feline twice his size. "They bleed and die like the rest of us!"

Still, a few of the men turned and ran, and the air that was already filled with screams and the smell of iron —both from weapons and from the blood of the fighting above them—shifted into the despair and terror Merrick was entirely too familiar with.

Men always thought war was about glory and bravery... but it wasn't. It was dirt and blood and fear and doing whatever it fucking took to stay alive. There was no chivalry, no elegant swipes of swords or perfect footwork. Only desperation to stay alive, and sometimes a bit of luck.

"Get ready," he said through his teeth when Lessia followed him as he stepped forward.

She didn't look at him, but she nodded, her eyes

already sweeping across the animals and people, seeing who'd come onto their ship first.

It wouldn't be any of the ones in the bow, though, not if Merrick had anything to say about it.

Ardow, of all people, began echoing his message when more people backed up, screaming, "Hold the line! Hold the line!" as the ships grew bigger and bigger, soon casting theirs in shade.

"Here we go," Thissian muttered on his other side as the screech of wood tore through the air, letting them know the ships were prepared to cast out brows to lock their ships together, not allowing anyone to sail away. Or perhaps they were readying to sail their ships into their own vessels.

Merrick had seen both happen before.

From just staring at the chaos above, Loche appeared to have awoken to the threat before them, and Merrick was glad Iviry shadowed the regent when he stormed forward, encouraging some of his more hesitant men to do the same.

When the ships were about forty feet away, Merrick turned to his dark-haired friend. "Ready?"

Thissian shot him a grin, one Merrick knew was a feeble attempt to mirror his brother's but that he still appreciated.

"Already ahead of you." Thissian jerked his head so his raven mane whipped the air, and Merrick realized his dark eyes were glittering, his skin glowing—even the color of his hair seemed to deepen.

They'd used to joke about that growing up, that Thissian and Kerym always looked their best after battle, while the rest would be bloodied and dirty and pale from tiredness.

But after Thissian had admitted to him it nearly killed him to look in a mirror, knowing the energy bristling under his skin, making him feel like he could take over the world, came from the dead bodies strewn across the battlefield, Merrick had shut it down every time Raine brought it up.

Giving his friend a quick tap on the shoulder, Merrick also faced forward, hoping the forewarning Loche had given his men about his magic would be enough not to send more people running, as he couldn't stop the wind from filling with stickiness, the magic layering over the others even when he tried to keep it contained to a certain area.

Lessia moved closer to him when the air roiled, and for a second, everything around him quieted as the whispers from those who'd already passed—many in situations like this—exploded between his ears.

Then it all came back—louder and wilder and more vicious.

A huff left Merrick as he released his grip on his magic, shoving the souls out wide, ensuring he took out at least a few people on each ship from the enemy fleet that spread out on either side of him.

He didn't look at Lessia as screams began and cut off, animals shifting into their human forms as they fell from wherever they'd been standing when their lives were ripped away, and already-cold bodies slammed into wood before tumbling into the water that had begun to whirl with red from the many lives yet lost.

Merrick's breathing became labored as he steered his magic, keeping it away from the people on either side of him in the lineup of their own ships, who just stared as the rebels bled and died, and he closed his eyes when a young man—someone who couldn't have been much older than Lessia—crashed into their ship, eyes unseeing and body twisted at a strange angle.

The air in his lungs thickened as a veil of crimson colored the darkness before his eyes, and he struggled for a moment to remember where he was, only hearing someone call "Enough, Merrick. It's enough" as if from far away.

It wasn't enough. Merrick allowed his magic to stretch out farther, let the fury of the souls and the terror of those they took with them to the afterlife flow through him until they were all he could feel. Until the whispers were the only thing pressing around him, within him—the only thing filling his ears.

"Enough! Merrick, stop!" someone called again, but it was easy to ignore them.

There were too many living souls before him.

He needed to do this.

For her.

Merrick almost didn't notice when Lessia's hand slipped into his, but as he panted, giving more of himself than he'd ever done to thin out the line of enemies that just kept refilling ahead—to give the people here, his friends, his brothers, his... Lessia... a chance—her voice muted the whispers, broke through the haze of rage that always overtook him when he let them free, and he glanced down at her as she continued speaking to him.

"I love you." She smiled as she said it, and continued smiling as she pressed his hand. "I love you so much."

Merrick blinked at her, sensing another's hand on his back.

"Enough, Merrick. I can feel that you're on the edge."

Thissian's voice.

Lessia's smile didn't dim as she whipped her head to the side, the hand not holding on to his flying out to send something silver through the air. Something that lodged in flesh, with a groan following.

"You and me," she whispered, and the world around him came to as he pulled on his magic, reined in the souls wanting, pushing, shoving to be free.

"They're on the ship!" Thissian screamed, slapping the last of Merrick's muddled thoughts out of him.

Whirling around, he drew his sword in one motion, and he couldn't help but relish the feel of Lessia's warm body lining up with his own—the sensation so different from the cold wrath that had been wrapped around him only seconds ago.

Even here—even in war, she was... everything.

"Remember," Merrick whispered hurriedly as metal hitting metal rang ahead, the rebels who'd survived his attack not hesitating as they stormed their ship and those around them, animals and humans and Fae crying out as they collided. "Stay behind your weapons. Don't let them corner you—"

"I know," Lessia interjected, a soft edge to her tone. "You've taught me well."

He glanced at her, and she offered him a crooked smile as she let another dagger fly, one that lodged in the back of a shifter that had sprinted for Ardow's unprotected back.

"Thanks, Lia!" he called out, the smile he shot them contrasting with the fear in his eyes.

Lessia seemed to have noticed it as well, given the sense of worry rolling through her, but they didn't have time to discuss it as a group of half-Fae descended upon them.

Fuck, they were so young.

Twenty- or thirtysomethings, barely past their Faeling age.

He cursed the rebel leader as his sword sliced open the guts of one of them, the male falling to the ground, clutching the wound Merrick knew wouldn't heal before he died.

The fucking leaders somehow never found their way into the front lines, allowing their people to die for them and their stupid fucking causes, and he was so sick of it.

Lessia danced beside him, ducking under swords and flying weapons so fast that her unbound hair flew around them, but Merrick snarled at her when he realized what she was doing. "Do. Not. Hesitate!"

She winced as she caught his eyes, the grimace deepening as she finally dug a dagger into a half-Fae's chest, her eyes narrowing, not with anger but with chest-cracking pain.

"I know..." Merrick parried a blow from a particularly large half-Fae, the male's eyes crazed with fright, probably as he realized who'd just disarmed him.

"Pass safely," Merrick whispered as he sliced with his sword, swiftly severing the head of the young male, unwilling to let him suffer more pain or fear than necessary.

Lessia let out a choking sound beside him as she kicked off a shifter, one that transformed back into her human form as blood spurted from her neck, splattering all over his beautiful mate before the body slammed into the floor.

Touching the back of her hand to her bloodied face, Lessia blinked, and Merrick knew she was about to realize exactly what the costs of war were.

The shame and guilt that came with surviving.

Fuck! He sliced open a wolf's neck before throwing its body into another group of rebels sprinting for them, then caught Lessia's hand and dragged her to him.

"Don't think!" He didn't have time to be soothing, his sharp voice making her snap her eyes to his. "After... we'll deal with it after."

He glared at her until she nodded. Only once, but it was enough for Merrick.

He spun around again, his heart sinking as he took in the scene before him.

Ardow and Zaddock had been backed into a corner, exactly like Merrick always instructed his soldiers to do with their enemies because they would not get a single moment's break and the tiredness would make them sloppy.

Loche still fought bravely, even with the onslaught of shifters and half-Fae going after him, and while Iviry kept her distance from him, she fought to take down anyone who tried to sneak up on the regent.

However, his soldiers were dying all around him, and Merrick could tell the regent was struggling not to give in to the fear that always crept up when watching your friends die—his gray eyes darkened with each body crumpling to the ground.

Thissian had streaks already forming down his bloodied face from the many bodies strewn around him —from the tears Merrick knew would continue falling until the battle was over.

As Merrick's eyes landed on the Siphon Twin, he was glad that even after a century away from each other, the latter instinctively followed his movements.

Thissian's gaze followed his own as he snapped it to

where Loche was about to be surrounded, satisfied grins on the faces of the rebels stalking toward him.

The eight men slowed their pace as if they wanted to take their time, and Loche must have understood what everyone else did as he started backing up, the regent truly looking his young age as what was about to happen sank in.

"No!" Lessia sprinted forward at the same time as Iviry tried to get to the human leader, but the latter was blocked by that giant black feline, the shifter seemingly more skilled than her dead companions: she snapped her jaw at the fiery-haired Fae, forcing her back again.

Merrick also started running when Lessia jumped over dead bodies to reach her friend, only stopping to slam a fist into a half-Fae's face before continuing the stumbling run.

"Lessia!" he screamed when she didn't notice the snake coiling up the side of the ship, its vicious tongue flicking the air as it headed right for her. "Lessia, no!"

More fucking rebels got in his way, and he didn't bother sparing their pain as he struck them wherever he could reach, pushing and shoving as much as slicing with his sword to get to her.

"Lessia!" His voice shook as more and more rebels piled in between them, and he could only catch glimpses of her terrified face as the snake—a mirror of the damned one Rioner loved so much—rose above her, opening its lethal jaws and showing off long, sharp fangs.

"Please!" Merrick didn't care that he begged as he killed more rebels. "Please!"

He needed to get to her!

Merrick groaned as someone's strike hit true, slicing

open his jacket in the back, but he didn't even spin around as Lessia lifted her thin arms, looking so fucking small in the snake's shadow and holding the fucking dagger he'd given her, its rubies mocking him with their shine.

He fought blindly now, refusing to take his eyes off her as the snake dove.

People died around him, beneath him, and Merrick had no fucking clue how while his breath caught in his throat when Lessia managed to roll away.

But the snake didn't let up.

It just went for her. Again and again.

Even Loche screamed her name, and the rebels surrounding him threw glances at the reptile fighting the young woman, catching Ardow, who'd sneaked up on them to help, and nearly disarming him with their first retaliatory strikes.

That's when Lessia made her mistake.

"No!" Merrick's scream echoed across the ship as her amber eyes moved to the regent and the snake saw its opportunity.

Whipping its tail, it slammed his mate to the deck, and the sickening crack of her head hitting wood seemed to quiet the entire ship.

Then the snake plunged again, maw open to show off already glistening teeth.

It was all Merrick could do to stay upright as he stumbled forward, running right over dead and injured rebels and soldiers as he tried to get to her.

Realization that he wouldn't make it drove into his chest like the sword he struck another rebel with, and the scream leaving him wasn't of this world as the long fangs readied themselves to close around Lessia's limp body.

Then a mess of darkness jumped in between Lessia and the snake, and Merrick didn't know what was worse.

Hearing the sickening crunch of bones and teeth sinking into soft flesh.

Or Thissian's dark blue eyes latching onto his as they drained of color.

Merrick screamed again.

A scream of rage. Of pain. Of the fucking unfairness.

He threw his sword.

It drove right through the snake's eye, so hard it pierced its entire skull.

He didn't know if it was real, but it was as if the world parted for him, and he reached his mate and friend in mere seconds.

Lessia was already on her knees, Thissian's face in her lap as her hands moved over his body, unsure which gaping wound to press on, which one could stop the blood pumping the life out of him.

It didn't matter. Merrick could see it even before he fell to his knees.

"Thissian," he whispered, taking one of the Fae warrior's hands in his own. "Fuck, Thissian..."

The Siphon Twin smiled at him, blood bubbling out of the corners of his mouth. "D-don't... thank me."

"You..." Merrick couldn't get the words out.

He knew why Thissian had done it.

He could see it in his friend's eyes.

It was for him. For Lessia. For the two of them not to have to feel the pain he carried with him each day.

Something warm and damp fell down Merrick's

cheeks, and the damned Fae dying in his mate's lap laughed. A choked, coughing laugh.

"Now—" Thissian coughed again. "Now I've seen everything."

The most horrible sound left Lessia. "I'm s-sorry. It's..."

"Stop." Thissian moved his other hand excruciatingly slowly to take Lessia's in his own. "It-it's been... it's my time."

More warmth touched Merrick's face, and there were so many things he wanted to say. So fucking many things, and still no words made it past the lump in his throat.

"I... I know," Thissian forced out, more blood streaming down his chin at the effort. "Tell... tell him."

Merrick couldn't speak. Nothing would fucking come out. Only more of that warm wetness. But Lessia's voice was surprisingly strong as she answered, "We'll tell him. He'll know how and why. Thank... thank you."

Another low sound rumbled in Thissian's throat, but no words left the warrior's lips.

His eyes stayed on Merrick's, though, until they glossed, then went unseeing, then never moved again.

CHAPTER 40
FRELINA

Frelina had always loved animals, but she'd have to reconsider her stance on birds as the vicious one before her snapped its beak at her again, and Frelina crushed herself against the stone to get away from the sharp bite.

It had already managed to rip into her, and her daggers had lain useless on the ground since the bird's last strike. Blood trickled down both her arms and her side where it had taken a chunk out of her flesh.

Frelina whimpered as rocks bit into the wound on her side as she whirled to get away from another attack, sweat forming on her forehead and stinging her eyes.

When she'd thought of her death, she never imagined being eaten alive by a fucking bird. Weren't they supposed to just eat plants and worms anyway?

"Fuck you!" Frelina screamed as the bird nipped at her shoulder when she wasn't fast enough to avoid the next strike.

The bird screeched, almost as if in laughter, and it pissed her off even more.

As it came down on her again, Frelina jabbed out with her hand, and even though it wasn't a hard blow, she managed to get a slap in, driving the bird's face away from her own.

"Seems quite inefficient. Allow me, little one."

She shot her eyes up at Kerym's voice, and they widened at how his skin began glowing, how his hair started to shine and reflect the sun, and how the bloodshot lines in his eyes faded.

"Makes me look quite handsome, no?" Kerym grinned at her stunned expression, and her eyes swept over him, then moved to Pellie, who stood behind him, her eyes also wide, in not surprise but rather... vigilance.

They were as blue as Kerym's as they moved from Frelina to the bird, and as Frelina followed them, she sucked in a breath.

In the bird's place, there was now a woman. One who might be only a few years older than herself. One who appeared barely able to stand, letting out a sound of... sleepiness? Yes, it was a damned yawn that made the woman's mouth form an O.

"What are you waiting for?" Kerym nodded toward the woman. "She won't fight back."

Frelina's eyes went even wider. Did he mean...

Kerym rolled his eyes, and before even a muscle moved in Frelina's body, he shot forward and slammed a fist into the shifter's face, making her tumble to the ground, although her chest still rose and fell, almost as if she...

"She'll be taking a nice, long nap." Kerym reached out

a hand when Frelina only stared at him. "You didn't think I was going to kill her, did you?"

Frelina still only stared at him.

"You did." Kerym's eyes flew upward again. "It's no fun when they can't fight back."

Fight...

Right. There was fighting.

If she strained her ears, she could hear it.

The screams coming from both the cliff and the ships beneath them.

She could smell the blood too. It must paint the water red now, judging from how much it tinged the air, from how the biting wind whirled the metallic scent all around them.

Frelina shook her head, trying to get her thoughts to gather.

But it proved to be a struggle, and she wavered as she finally stepped toward the Fae as he dragged a hand through his inky-black hair.

"You've lost a lot of blood." Pellie was suddenly by her side, and then someone blonde...

"Come, you need to sit down." Amalise snaked an arm around Frelina's waist when her eyes snagged on Kerym again. "There is a spot here you can hide."

For some reason, Frelina held back, even as she glimpsed shadows and metal reflections moving somewhere out of the corner of her eyes, even as she heard the sounds come closer, voices screaming to get them and birds snapping their beaks.

Kerym stood so still.

Like a statue, only his black hair danced around his face. Even his eyes...

"Wait," she mumbled as she freed herself from the

women's hold and took the three steps needed to reach the Fae.

Placing a hand on his arm, she jerked.

Then Frelina doubled over.

There was so much pain. It was all around her. In her blood. In her thoughts. In her body.

She released him as if she'd burned herself, and Pellie was instantly by her side, but her blue eyes were on Kerym, her fingers tracing his face.

"Something is wrong," he mumbled. "It's... It hurts so much. I—"

Pellie hushed him, her eyes filling with tears as she swallowed loudly.

"Kerym—" she started, but loud steps drowned her words, and Frelina realized their moment of reprieve was over.

Rebels stormed their small corner, and Amalise turned a white face in their direction before trying to get around them—to get help or get away, Frelina didn't know, but it was useless.

They were surrounded in seconds.

Six men—two half-Fae, their pointed ears and tall frames betraying them, and the rest shifters, Frelina guessed, based on their strange smells—stalked toward them, low chuckles reverberating against the dark stone on either side of Frelina.

"We knew you'd lose," one of the half-Fae taunted as his eyes roved over Frelina's body, his tongue wetting his lips as he followed the blood that still flowed from her wounds. "But we did think you'd put up a better fight."

"You just wait," Amalise tried to sneer, but the words hollowed when one of the shifters howled with laughter. "We—"

"For what? The wyverns who haven't moved a muscle since the bloodshed began? For the three Fae ships just floating out there, watching you die? No one else is coming." The shifter transformed his hand into a claw with which he swiped at Amalise, thankfully catching only air as the blonde jumped back.

Frelina pulled her to her left side, while Kerym and Pellie stood on her right.

She allowed herself one glance at the Fae, but he was still staring out over the chaos beneath them, his face twisting with so much pain that Frelina struggled to continue watching him.

"Kerym," she hissed under her breath. "Kerym!"

Pellie leaned forward to meet her eyes, and Frelina didn't like the bottomless sorrow deepening her blue ones as she shook her head.

So Kerym would be of no help. Frelina's mind whirled, her hand moving to press on the deeper wound in her shoulder, trying not to fall into the muddled mess she'd been before.

Thankfully, it seemed more adrenaline began pumping through her body, and when the group neared, more of the shifters following their friend's example and opting for those claws instead of weapons, she decided to do whatever she could.

"Someone is coming," Frelina forced out.

The asshole Fae who hadn't stopped staring at her laughed again, but she raised a bloodied hand.

"Kill us if you wish, but you won't live much longer either."

That had them at least halting, shooting glances around.

This was her only chance.

"I'm sure you've heard the rumors that your leader is trying to squash, but Rioner is on his way here. Those ships you mocked? They were a warning. A courtesy to *our leader*, who is trying to stop all of us dying, including you damned rebels!"

"Do you—" one of the younger shifters started, but the Fae snarled so loudly at him he closed his mouth again.

"Lies," he spat. "Meyah told us they'd try to mess with our heads."

"It's not—" Amalise tried to break in, but another swipe of those claws, closer this time, had her gasp as Frelina pulled on her hand to get her out of the way.

"We've heard all about your mind-control powers," the Fae continued, spit flying from his thick lips as he moved again, crowding them against the wall.

Everyone but Kerym, who Pellie couldn't even get to move an inch now, even as she slapped him, cried at him, and pulled at his hand.

He just... stood there.

"That's one of the Siphon Twins." The Fae waved a hand toward Kerym. "Did he take his own energy? He looks dead."

Frelina's heart had never beat so hard as when the Fae drove a fist right into Kerym's face, making Pellie cry even harder, clinging to him and begging him to move. But he still didn't.

"Kerym!" Frelina screamed as blood formed a trail from his nose over his mouth and down his neck. "Wake up!"

"Shut up!"

Frelina didn't have time to react as the half-Fae's hand struck her instead, sending her face slamming into the stone with a crack she prayed wasn't her skull breaking open.

She tried to blink, but it was pointless as the Fae punched her again, on the other side of her face this time, making her hurtle into Amalise, whose arms flew around her.

Frelina's head lolled forward, and the blonde's arms were the only thing holding her up as strange suns began flickering before her eyes.

"Frelina!" Amalise shook her, but it only made it worse, those suns spinning faster until she vomited—apparently to someone's disgust, as she heard them exclaim "Just fucking kill her!"

"Frelina!" Amalise cried into her ear now. "Look at me!"

She couldn't open her eyes. It was...

Too heavy...

Too much.

"Do you know who she is?" That half-Fae's harsh voice was like nails being hammered into her head. "That's Frelina Rantzier! Didn't you see her eyes and hair? I shall want to have fun with her before we kill her and nail her to my ship."

"F-fuck you," Amalise spat as Frelina felt arms drag her away from her friend. "Leave her a—"

Something hard hit flesh and bones, and Frelina squinted to see Amalise's knees colliding with the ground as that claw swiped across her chest, making blood spurt all over the already dark ground.

"Pl... please," Frelina whimpered as the Fae continued pulling her away from her friends. "K-Kerym," she cried, but her words were only whispers, too low even for a Fae's hearing.

Her head was turned away from the group when hands wrapped around her neck, and she didn't have time to draw another breath before her air supply was cut off.

Red-lined eyes burned into hers, and she would have winced if she could at the vile breath fanning across her face as the half-Fae spat at her, "Do you know what your dear uncle did to us? He had us killed for sport in the streets. He'd chain some of us up until we died in our own filth, on fucking display! Do you know what for? Stealing food from damned trash cans!"

"I..." she tried, but her eyes bulged as the male tightened his grip.

"You carry his fucking name! You and your sister and your uncle and anyone else left with the Rantzier blood are going to die. We're going to display you like Rioner did us. A fucking example for others, hanging down the gates to his castle."

She could feel her life draining.

A sense of tiredness, of warmth, wrapped around her as she started choking, and Frelina struggled to keep her eyes open when she realized the male was continuing to speak, but the words were lost on her, his moving mouth only occupying her gaze.

He wasn't evil, she thought as she began drifting away, her body convulsing under his hard grip.

He was in pain.

Like all the rest of them.

And he thought she was to blame for it.

Somewhere around her, the screaming intensified, and Frelina found herself smiling when she pictured her mother and father running toward her, perhaps even in a field like the one outside their home.

Then something pressed against her mouth, and she pushed half-heartedly at a hard presence before her as the thing touching her lips pried them open, forcing warm air down her throat.

There was no strength left inside her, and she let whoever it was tilt her head back, continuing to make her chest rise and fall by blowing their breath into her.

It took a long time for her body to react, and when it did, the first thing that left her was a whine. Then a cough. Then something warm pressed against the side of her face, and the words "Breathe. Just breathe, please" brushed her ear.

She did as they told her, too tired to fight, even as the image of her parents faded and muddled.

"Breathe, little Rantzier. Breathe for me."

Wetness pressed against her cheek, her nose, her forehead, and she wrinkled it when she started coming to, feeling hard ground and rocks digging into her lower half while her upper body rested on something soft.

"Look at me," the person coaxed, and again she just followed the orders.

Eyes opening, she looked right into green-and-gold ones.

Her body relaxed as they swept over her face, and when Raine bent down to kiss her cheek, kiss her forehead, hugging her closer, she started crying.

Not the soft tears she found trickling down the red-haired Fae's face, but full-on sobbing, with snot rushing out of her nose and panicked convulsions.

Raine just held her. He didn't hush her, he didn't say it was all going to be all right, he didn't speak into her mind. He just let her cry.

"Th-they were... h-he was..." Frelina sobbed, and she

didn't know if it was from the relief of having been saved or from guilt as she found the male's head severed from his body beside them, his eyes still raging, even in death.

"I know," Raine finally whispered. "This... is what war does. It's horrible and painful and fucking devastating."

Frelina crushed her eyelids shut as she cried into his jacket, her hands fisting the leather as Raine strengthened his hold almost until it hurt.

Finally, finally, the sobs softened, and she pulled a breath into her hurting throat. Then another one, and another, until she could look up at Raine, finding his eyes already there for her.

For a long moment, he just stared at her.

"I thought I lost you," he eventually said, something like surprise sneaking into his low tone. "I thought... I..." His eyes closed for a second before they bore into hers again. "I can't lose you. I... don't want to."

Frelina didn't think as she pulled at his jacket again so he fell right into her lips, the urgency making their teeth clatter together.

She didn't care. She didn't care that it was wet and salty.

She needed it.

"I don't want to lose you," she whispered when he pulled back.

Then she opened her mind and let him see that she wanted him.

In every way she could have him.

What was the point in lying now? To him or herself?

She could hear the fighting, which didn't take a single break around them. Could smell the death and despair.

"I..." Raine's features sagged. "I don't... I can't..."

"I know," she responded quickly. "Just... for now... Let's... just pretend."

Pretend until she died, and then he could pretend that this... whatever was between them wasn't bigger than he realized.

She could see it in his eyes. Raine searched her face, and she could tell there was more he wanted to say, but instead he pressed his forehead against her own and sighed.

When she nodded, Raine got them both to her feet, and his hand didn't release its grip on her own as they faced the fighting again, the swords and daggers clinking as they met each other and the humans screaming as the birds ripped chunks of their bodies or lifted them off the ground and threw them off the cliffs with their strong claws.

The scene before them was devastating, and it was clear... they were losing.

Quickly.

"We need to get out of here." Zaddock's face appeared to her left, and she didn't have time to wonder where he'd come from when he pointed behind Venko, who stood beside him. "There is a hidden path over there. It'll bring us to the ships."

Frelina only now noticed the woman in his arms, and she pressed a hand to her chest in relief, her neck bending back, when Amalise's blue eyes opened to her own.

The blonde looked from Frelina up to Zaddock's chiseled features, and she had the gall to grimace. "You're the one who saved me? I will never hear the end of this."

Loche's right-hand man only smiled at her. "Come on. They're not doing so fine down there either."

Frelina caught the look Zaddock cast Kerym's way, and something within her froze as the former took a shuddering breath before waving for them all to follow Venko as he started down a narrow, rocky path.

While she was glad Kerym seemed able to move again, when Raine squeezed her hand, she knew, somehow she knew, it would only get worse from here.

CHAPTER 41

LESSIA

Lessia could still hear the horrible sound of the snake ripping into Thissian's body, how its fangs had cracked through his rib cage, punctured his lungs, and burrowed deep into his flesh before Merrick killed it.

She had never wished for something as much as she wished she could have given Merrick more time with Thissian, because the devastation across his face was like nothing she'd seen before.

But the fighting didn't let up.

The world around them continued, even if one of the good ones, perhaps even one of the great ones, who'd spent centuries in it, no longer did.

After throwing two of her last three daggers to keep more rebels away—she refused to part with the one Merrick had gifted her—she had to drag the Death Whisperer to his feet and order him to help her move Thissian's body to the side.

Lessia tried to cover his broken limbs with a piece of

black tarp whispering in the wind, and all the while she prayed his body wouldn't get injured further, mostly for Kerym, but also for herself and Merrick and anyone else Thissian's gentle soul had touched.

Like her father, he deserved a hero's journey into the afterlife.

When she finished, Merrick had snapped out of his static state, but he remained a step before her as they started toward the others, no longer allowing any space between his body and hers as his sword slashed through the rebels daring to come close and his other hand held on to her with a grip that nearly restricted her blood flow.

Perhaps the one good thing Thissian's wasteful death had brought was that it seemed like their side had found some renewed energy.

It was as if they all fought for the Fae warrior—for his sacrifice—pouring everything they had into what Thissian had died for.

For the people on these ships to live on.

But even so, Loche's eyes shone with tiredness when she found them, and Ardow wasn't holding back his cries of devastation as another half-Fae fell at his hands.

Even Soria, who had been staying away from the worst of it, was bloodied and dusty now, hollow-faced, having had to defend herself against two shifters who'd separated her from the others.

It was all so damned useless.

Lessia clenched her jaw as she followed Merrick, seemingly set on helping Iviry as she struggled against that terrifying cat.

Everywhere around them lay dead bodies, and the floor was thick with blood. Loche's soldiers, some with their masks still on, were strewn across the deck—only a few of those brave men who'd decided to remain in the bow still fighting beside their leader.

Rebels were mixed amongst them, their faces in death no longer twisted with anger but soft, lonely, young...

A group of Faelings who looked too similar to those she'd grown up with lay together, eyes shut, almost as if they'd decided to live and die as one, and Lessia briefly wondered if she'd recognize any of the faces if she looked closer.

Not that she would. She knew now what Merrick had once spoken of. War... it wasn't anything other than waste. Pure useless fucking waste.

She tore her eyes away from the bodies as Merrick's almost unnatural movements—the ones that made her realize he was as impacted as she was—added more to the piles on the floor.

They finally made it to Iviry, and with Merrick's help, the Fae female cornered the shifter. It appeared they'd both gotten a few strikes and bites in, as Iviry panted, holding a hand clutched to a deep injury in her arm, while the feline jerked, limping backward as it hissed at Merrick, who continued driving it into a corner, his snarls as animalistic as the ones from the cat before him.

When Merrick lifted his sword, the air flickered, and he hesitated when a woman, perhaps in her mid-fifties, with black hair and gray eyes, tumbled to the ground, eyes sharp but unable to hide her fear as they fixed on the Fae's blade.

Iviry did not. Storming forward, she bared her sharp teeth, pushing Merrick out of the way when he didn't strike, and lifted her sword.

"Don't!"

It was as if that one word from Loche broke through any and all spells of fury Iviry had been under, and while she frowned, her hand fell to her side, the tip of the blade scratching across the wood as it met it.

Loche's breathing was as heavy as his mate's when he stormed forward, ducking under a dagger that whistled over his head—a dagger belonging to someone Ardow took down in the next second, as he tried to follow—before he slid to a stop beside Iviry.

Lessia was torn between watching and running for Ardow, who now fought the last three rebels on their ship, but when Merrick growled and stomped toward them, taking out two before they even had the chance to turn around, she kept her gaze on Loche and the two women staring at him—the gray-eyed one from the floor and Iviry from the other side of the sitting woman, the Fae female looking as if she would rather continue to fight the shifter than talk to the regent.

"She is to be taken prisoner," Loche said quietly, but not without firmness.

The shifter started cackling—a wild, manic cackle—before she responded, "So my son cares for me after all."

Lessia didn't have it in her to react to the shifter's words, and neither did anyone else, which seemed to anger the woman, from the sneer marring her face.

Iviry looked from the shifter who Lessia now knew was Meyah, the rebel leader, to the regent, and while confusion danced over her beautiful features, she didn't ask, something Lessia knew Loche would appreciate.

And even though Iviry didn't look her way, Lessia saw a moment of understanding, a dip of Soria's chin as she approached the Fae, which Iviry returned a moment later.

"I do not care for you." Loche sounded almost bored.

But Lessia knew better. He was exhausted. Utterly, devastatingly exhausted. She could tell the Fae with the fiery hair also understood it from how she stepped around Soria, moving discreetly to his side, although she made no move to touch him.

When he continued speaking, his voice went in and out, his face looking as run down as Lessia felt.

Glancing around, seeing all his men dead on the ground...

Even Zaddock was nowhere to be seen.

She also stepped toward the human ruler, and Loche threw her a look—one of gratitude—as he ordered, "I need you to call off your people."

Loche's arm swept to their right, and as Lessia followed it, she realized most ships had fared far worse than their own, more rebels piling onto them from the second and third row, with screams and panic and fear trailing off them like smoke from a fire.

To their left was the same thing, and when Lessia's eyes moved upward...

She couldn't. It was complete devastation up there, with bodies lying on almost every other step of the winding staircase, and on the plateau, those shifters had gathered, not a single one of their own people in sight.

"I'm here." Merrick's hand pressed against her lower back, and all she could do was nod as she leaned into him, not allowing her thoughts to drift off from what was happening before her eyes.

"I said call them off!" Loche's voice rose an octave when his mother threw her head back and laughed that awful laugh again—the one Lessia now recognized, even if the shifter bore her real form.

"I will... not," Meyah got out in between cackles. "You will have to kill me, son. If you have the guts. But alas... they won't stop then either."

The muscles in Loche's jaw worked as Ardow limped up to Lessia's other side, and she touched his hand as he placed it on her shoulder.

A harsh breath rushed through the regent's teeth as he picked up one of the daggers Lessia had thrown that hadn't lodged in someone's gut or chest, and Lessia couldn't look as he brought it to his mother's throat.

The pain exploding in his eyes wasn't for Meyah.

Merrick seemed to understand it as well, as he shuddered beside her, pressing the side of his body to her own as she stared out across the ocean.

The pain in Loche's eyes was for himself. For the person he'd become once he killed his mother.

For the person he'd leave behind.

After today... Lessia understood it completely.

She'd counted her kills. Sixteen rebels, many her own age, had fallen at her blades. Sixteen souls she'd have to remember the rest of her life, and perhaps even in the next one.

"Do it. Don't be a fucking coward for once in your life, and do it," his mom hissed, and Lessia's gaze drifted farther out across the sea, toward where the wyverns still floated and then to where...

Where were the Reinsdor ships?

Lessia spun around as Loche said something to his mother, the words fading into the wind as her heart began beating harder.

"No," she breathed as her eyes snapped to the southwest, where the tallest part of the rocky island behind them towered, a straight, dark wall driving its way deep into the sea, the waves crashing harshly against it.

Almost half their ships had been forced over there, forced between the curved edges that jutted out on either side.

Nearly as many rebel ships blocked their exit, the thick chains falling from them into the sea betraying how they'd anchored themselves there, making sure Loche's ships could not escape while the fighting continued.

The struggle was still as loud and frantic as theirs had been in the beginning—the humans and rebels over there were more evenly skilled—but that wasn't what made the last of Lessia's verve leave her and crawl through the gaps in the wooden planks beneath her.

It was the hundred-foot wave chasing the Reinsdor ships toward that same inlet, how the wave curved around them, allowing them only to sail forward.

It was the armada of Fae ships behind it, a gilded one in the middle—the one that she knew Rioner must be standing in, in the bow, directing the wave.

It was the ships docking on the other side of the island, somehow coming from the north, with flags she didn't recognize and with Fae who were now mounting the isle, molding the rock before her eyes so it built stairways leading directly above the trap.

"Merrick!" There was no other word in her mind, and he must have heard the pure terror in her voice because he spun, his dark eyes taking in the scene quicker than she had.

"Fuck! Chain her or kill her, Loche! We need to go!" Merrick screamed so loudly that everyone on their ship and several on the ones beside them looked over, then moved to what was about to unfold around them.

Rebel and nonrebel froze as one before they ceased all fighting, weapons clanging to the floor as they were abandoned. People were running back to the ships, trying to get away from the Fae soldiers who would follow the wave, aiming to crush those who now had nowhere to go in the cove.

Loche looked exactly how Lessia felt, his face so ashen she worried he might pass out. "What do we do?"

She knew that had it been a different situation, Merrick might have teased the regent for turning fully to him, but Merrick didn't even blink as he responded, "We run."

"No—" Lessia started, but Merrick dragged her to him, his face so hard that it reminded her of how it had looked when they first got to know each other.

"If we leave now, we *might* survive. I say *might*, Lessia!" Merrick's dark eyes whirled with such emotion that she whimpered at the sight. "I know! I know how much it hurts! Trust me! But they are already dead! They're not getting out of there—not with that wave and the fucking anchors of the rebel ships."

Another hand folded around her arm as she shook her head.

Loche.

"He's right, Lessia." The regent jerked his head toward where Iviry had already begun strapping weapons onto her tall body, her eyes flying to the cove and the ships trapped within as she did it. "We need to go!"

"There is a boat back here! It's small, but we'll fit on it."

Lessia's blood ran cold at the new voice before she realized it belonged to Zaddock, and she knew warmth should have filled her at the sight of him, of Amalise in his arms, injured but alive, of her sister walking hand in hand with a bloodied Raine, of Pellie and Kerym trailing behind them, of Venko running right into Ardow's arms.

They were alive.

But it was as if ice had permanently taken the place of her usually warm blood, and when Kerym searched the group, his blue eyes more muddled than she'd ever seen them, she actually shivered beneath the sheen of sweat covering her skin.

His eyes captured hers, and she shook her head at his silent question.

Kerym didn't scream.

He didn't even cry.

It was as if he knew.

He let Pellie take his hand as he asked, "Where?"

Lessia slapped a hand over her mouth, violent sobs beginning to shake her body, and not even Merrick's hand on her back helped anymore as her eyes darted to where they'd left Thissian, and Kerym walked right over, sinking to his knees and lying down across his brother's chest.

Pellie sat right beside him, her hand whitening under the pressure of Kerym's grip, but the woman didn't complain once as Kerym seemed to hold on to her with everything left within him.

"We need to go," Zaddock urged, and although his face did not betray his fear, his arms did.

They shook as they held on to her friend, and Lessia knew Amalise must be truly injured because she didn't make a joke about it—she only turned her face in to

Zaddock's neck when Kerym's low wailing began folding all around them.

Lessia couldn't stand the sound.

Nor could she stand her sister clinging to Raine while he looked down at her, seemingly as devastated as Kerym as he pressed his forehead against Frelina's.

Not even watching Soria help Loche chain his mother to the ship, her screams of betrayal layering across the crimson-stained water, was bearable.

Actual tears flooded the regent's eyes as they traveled to his people—the ones now caged between the tall, curved cliffs and the equally tall wave.

Lessia's gaze flew to the scene where both the people of Ellow and the rebels had started to realize the trap they'd been driven into.

Blood-curdling screams bounced against the water, and panicking rebels and humans alike jumped into the sea when rocks began falling upon them, lifted into the air by invisible hands, steered by the Fae on the cliffs above them, while the merciless wave neared faster than should have been possible even with magic.

It must have been the Oakgards' Fae who stood upon that dark cliff, Lessia realized with a sinking heart, given their tan skin and darker features, the more rounded ears they sported, and... their magic definitely worked.

Her eyes snagged on the wyverns who hadn't moved backward, but not forward, either, their colorful scales seemingly too gaudy for the abominable sight ahead of them.

Rage, moving as fast through her body as the damned wave ahead, surged within her, and Lessia didn't care that Merrick said something, his hand tugging at her own.

Shutting him out, she turned inward, screaming at the wyvern leader. *Are you just going to let us die? Is that what you stand for?*

It was easy to find the bond within her, the one forever tying her to the cowardly creatures, and she tugged on it when Auphore didn't respond quickly enough.

We won't make it in time, Elessia.

Try! she screamed back at him. *Just! Fucking! Try!*

She would have compelled him, and in turn all the other wyverns, as that's how the bond must have worked.

She would have forcefully pulled on all those strings.

But Auphore sounded truly crushed as he responded, *It's too late.*

"No!" Lessia realized she screamed it out loud when the truth of Auphore's words sank in.

The wyverns were too far behind the wave.

Lessia shook off Merrick's hand as she ran to the railing, and her voice cracked and trembled as she turned her scream to the Fae above them—the only ones who might hear her plea.

"Please!" she cried. "Please don't do this! Please stop!"

Lessia could feel eyes on her, their warmth shifting over her face.

But the rocks kept falling.

And the wave Rioner was conjuring kept rushing.

Merrick sprinted to her side when she collapsed against the railing, her hands barely holding her body up.

Fear, desperation, and despair filled the air.

From her friends behind her.

From Kerym's wails.

From Meyah's pleading.

From the cries of the people ahead.

Both the ones trying to flee and the ones realizing this was it—that this was the end.

She couldn't take it. She couldn't... just fucking stand here... couldn't just run.

Please! There must be something—

Another sound joined the ones pounding in Lessia's ears.

A softer one.

A low cry and a hum and a demand all at once.

Peeking over the railing once more, Lessia met Ydren's violet gaze—the wyvern hadn't listened to her after all—and as soon as she did...

She knew what she must do.

She could see the same determination in the young wyvern's eyes as she inclined her head to Lessia, and without looking behind her, Lessia started crawling over the thick wooden rail, when a hand—a gentle, begging touch—stopped her movement.

Her body didn't give her a choice, and she turned to meet Merrick's eyes.

"Please." His whisper shattered every piece of her heart, and as she opened her mouth, his hand locked around her wrist. "*Please.*"

Ydren screeched behind them again.

And there wasn't time.

She didn't have the time to tell him everything she felt for him, why she had to do this, why he had made her strong enough to do this.

So instead, she let the magic brimming under her skin set her eyes on fire, and she'd never hated herself as much as she did in the moment she purred "Let me go" to her mate.

His fingers released her immediately.

Lessia didn't look back as she threw herself onto Ydren's back, nearly falling from her when the wyvern took off as fast as the wave that raced toward them.

CHAPTER 42
LOCHE

Something had happened.

Loche couldn't describe it, but it was as if the world around him stilled, and he looked up from his mother's scowling face to find Merrick by himself at the stern of the ship.

The Fae didn't seem injured, but something was off...

Lessia wasn't beside him.

Loche's head snapped from side to side, finding the witch sisters watching over Kerym as he screamed out his sorrow over his brother, finding Zaddock gently setting Amalise on her feet, seeing Raine and Frelina holding on to each other as if they were the only ones left in the world, but...

No Lessia.

Even before he lifted his blurred vision to the scene that didn't just break his heart but snapped his entire soul in two, he knew.

Somehow, he could feel it in his bones.

Sure enough, a violet reflection with a smaller

golden one atop it—stark against the light blue horizon—raced toward the wave and the ship behind it.

As if in a trance, Loche stumbled across the deck, his eyes never leaving the wyvern and the woman riding on it, watching as they swam closer and closer to the armada—led by the gilded ship, where they could now make out Rioner standing in the bow, his dark green cape flowing behind him and hands raised above his head.

Loche didn't know what to say as he took the spot beside Merrick.

The Fae whose skin usually glowed subtly golden looked like a wraith, those dark eyes that intimidated even Loche at his worst moments so empty and full at the same time, as if he didn't know what to feel.

"She told me to let her go," Merrick said in a monotone.

Loche's stomach turned at the torment darkening the Death Whisperer's face.

"Where is she?" It appeared as if the rest of them noticed the world was no longer the same, because the silence that followed Frelina's scream... it had Loche swerve, and he pretended that he placed a hand on Merrick's shoulder to comfort him, but really, he needed it as much himself.

"Where?" Lessia's sister cried. "Where is she?"

No one responded, but Loche heard the group behind them approach, and he'd never felt anything like it when they silently took the places around them: Zaddock, Amalise, and Iviry by Loche's side. Kerym and the sisters by Merrick. Ardow and Venko holding on to each other as they sidled up by Zaddock.

And finally, Frelina sprinted up to the railing, her scream echoing across the bay. "No! Elessia! No!"

The redheaded Fae came up behind her, and he didn't react as Frelina fought the arms he placed around her waist, holding her back from diving into the sea.

As if she'd be able to catch up with her sister, who was now mere moments from reaching the ship.

"No, no, no," Frelina cried, her fists slamming against the railing. "Please! We have to do something!"

"Little..." Raine winced as he caught Loche's eyes after watching Merrick, who appeared to lose all hope beside him. "Frelina... there is nothing we can do to stop her."

"What is she doing?" Zaddock breathed when they saw something red glint in the air by Lessia's hand as she used the wyvern's spikes to climb higher, almost settling herself by the creature's head.

"She is killing the king." Merrick had begun rocking back and forth, and the movement shifted Loche as well as he kept his hold on the Fae's shoulder. "She is killing him. And she is killing herself."

Kerym had stopped his wailing, but a low cry began building again in the Fae warrior's chest—one that didn't belong there—one that Loche knew he'd have nightmares about for the rest of his life.

The sisters joined in, hums of sorrow whirring in their bodies.

Then Amalise started sobbing, her tears running freely.

Then Ardow broke apart, falling to the deck as Venko tried to hold him together.

Iviry was quiet beside him, but Loche felt the fear

rolling off the Fae, and he didn't recoil when her hand brushed his.

Still, Loche didn't know what terrified him the most.

Merrick's face—the rage and fury and sorrow and love and pride that didn't seem to be able to decide which emotion was strongest—or how small Lessia looked as she repositioned herself on that wyvern.

The world around them quieted, almost as if the entire realm held its breath.

And... perhaps it did.

The strange Fae above them stopped throwing their rocks, only watching the lone half-Fae and her wyvern rushing toward one hundred Fae ships.

The people on the vessels around them stopped their fleeing—the humans and rebels unable to tear their eyes away from the golden-brown-haired woman with the most beautiful amber eyes who carried all their fates as she rushed toward an entire army.

While the Reinsdor ships still sailed to get away from the towering water, Loche could see how the Fae on them turned backward, not to watch the water but to follow Lessia's wild ride.

Even in the bay, even with the wave still coming for them, people were watching.

Waiting.

Wondering what that one woman could do.

His damned mother had quieted as well.

If he didn't know better, Loche would have thought he saw Rioner's own men wince, their faces tinged with shame, as they watched Lessia ready herself atop the violet wyvern.

Because she was readying herself.

A glacial chill wove its way down Loche's back, raising every hair on his body.

The ruby-decorated dagger in her hand was clearly visible now, and Lessia's bared teeth glinted in the sunlight as Ydren ducked and swerved and dove to escape the waves Rioner tried to send their way. Rioner, who stood straight-backed, smirking in the bow, surrounded by hundreds of his soldiers.

There was no fear in the king's eyes, and yet... that coldness spread through Loche. He didn't know how the world around them could be so silent.

But as Lessia and Ydren managed to get within thirty feet of the gilded ship, everything else slowed down.

No one breathed.

No one moved.

Even the wind died down.

The entire sea could hear Lessia's scream as Ydren flew out of the water, the sun shining through her leathery wings, and the crimson dagger went flying.

"This is for us!"

It was such a simple statement, but somehow it seemed to rush through every person who watched the scene unfolding, and Loche wasn't the only one who staggered at the sincerity of Lessia's words.

The *us* wasn't just the ones standing on this ship and the ones Loche had funded around them.

The *us* was the rebels.

The *us* was the half-Fae and shifters.

The *us* was humans and Fae who stood with them and against them.

The *us* was even the Oakgards' Fae above them.

Loche's eyes fixed on Lessia's shining blade whistling through the air. Something else met the dagger halfway, and Loche thought he saw a cross of gold and red, before his wide eyes watched Lessia's dagger hit true.

It lodged itself right in Rioner's chest, his surprised expression shifting to one of pain before the king fell backward and the soaring wave splashed into the sea.

It was entirely silent for a second, the only sound the wall of water being swallowed again by the sea.

Then someone cheered.

The cheer was lonely at first, before more of them erupted.

In the bay.

Around them.

Clapping joined the voices.

Rioner's ships sailed more slowly, and the Fae on the cliffs began mumbling amongst themselves.

The wyverns, who'd until now remained still, approached hesitantly, their colorful scales painting the water in every color Loche could imagine.

It was relief, happiness, confusion, and hope all at once that mounted around them.

The fighting didn't recommence.

Rebels held on to humans as they watched Rioner's ship come to a complete halt.

"She saved us."

"The half-Fae saved us."

The whispered words filled the air until every rebel and human ship called Lessia's name.

"Lessia!"

"Lessia!"

"Lessia!"

They yelled her name like a chant, and Loche couldn't help but let a smile tug at his lips.

Lessia probably hated every second of it.

His eyes went to search for her, for the wyvern who hadn't yet returned to the sea, when the worst sound he'd ever heard shook the realm.

Merrick's scream made the chill he'd felt before feel like a warm breeze.

Every muscle in Loche's body coiled, and he could barely move enough to watch Ydren screech as she whipped her wings, flying straight for their ship.

Something dark dripped into the water beneath them, painting Ydren's scales on its way down, and Loche didn't have to smell the air for iron to understand what it was.

The moments it took the beast to reach them were the worst in Loche's life.

The worst until Ydren's wings nearly tripped them all as she landed on the deck, breaking apart the railing in her haste.

The sounds leaving Merrick were mirrored in the wyvern, but the Fae didn't hesitate as he sprinted up to Ydren, pulling something into his arms.

Someone...

Someone who was too still. Too peaceful. Too... injured.

A dagger with beautiful amber stones covering the hilt was embedded deep in Lessia's chest. But that chest... it moved, and as Loche sank to his knees beside the sitting Merrick and Lessia, who lay halfway across his lap, her eyes were open.

The others came running after him, and falling to the deck, they surrounded the woman he'd loved more than anything, each one, even Iviry, placing a hand on her damp body.

No one said anything, but Loche wasn't surprised,

since the tears that had started watering his cheeks now wetted the faces of everyone around him.

Large tears rushed down the Death Whisperer's face as he whispered, "I hate... I fucking hate how much I love you. And I hate you for doing that... but... I am so fucking proud of you. Do you hear that?"

Everyone watched as Lessia reached up a hand to cup Merrick's cheek, and even if the moment should be too vulnerable—too personal—they couldn't look away as she whispered back, "I know. I know."

Then she coughed, a bloodied, wet cough that made Frelina's sobs turn into a shriek.

Loche's throat constricted further when Lessia tried to smile at her sister, moving her hand to clasp at Frelina's after Raine released his grip on it, although he shifted to fold his arms around the younger Rantzier.

"Look at you two," Lessia said hoarsely. "I love you."

Loche wanted to tell her to stop—that those words sounded too much like a goodbye.

He wasn't the only one, as Merrick let out one of those bone-crushing sounds and Kerym folded into himself, whispering "Golden Eyes" almost as if in prayer.

Ardow and Amalise looked on the verge of fainting as they gripped each other, staring down into Lessia's quickly paling face.

Still, Lessia kept her smile as she forced out, "Carefree, r-remember?"

Amalise screamed at that, but Zaddock quickly got hold of her, and the blonde collapsed against his chest, her cries muted by the fabric of his dark jacket.

Ardow managed to smile back. "You know it, Lia."

But somehow his words were worse than Amalise's

screams, and Venko leaned his head on Ardow's shoulder when he sat back on his heels.

It was quiet for a beat before Iviry reached out, placing two fingers beside the dagger that must have just missed Lessia's heart.

The women didn't say anything as they stared at each other, but for some reason, the fiery-haired one nodded before she also sat back.

Soria and Pellie blinked at Lessia, their hands moving as one to touch hers as something silent also passed between the three of them.

Loche didn't know where to look when Lessia turned to him, but he shook his head, eyes dimming with tears as she smiled wider, everything they'd ever said and everything they'd never had shining in those damned golden eyes.

She seemed to realize he couldn't do it because she only touched his knee before looking up at Merrick again, eyes trailing over every sharp angle of his features, across the hands that he kept around her face, across his heaving chest—so alive, so vigorous compared to her own crackling one.

The tension was so thick, the sorrow so deep, Loche could hardly breathe.

"I..." Lessia swallowed another bloody cough before continuing. "I-I heard I won your house, Raine. Best... believe I will take it."

Zaddock burst out with a shocked laugh, and while the rest hesitated, when Lessia lifted a shaky brow, they all started giggling, breaking up the tense moment.

Loche's laugh mixed with strange sobs, and his vision blurred completely as he tried to gain control of his body and mind.

"You... you'll have it all. But I'm keeping the liquor. Gods know I need it after today," Raine responded as the group calmed down, and Loche waited for Lessia to snap something back.

But it remained quiet.

Against his will, his eyes focused again.

There was no more movement in her chest. There was no more life in her eyes, which were still turned upward, looking into Merrick's. There was no strength in the hand she'd used to touch each of their souls.

Loche couldn't breathe, and his body began shaking as he watched the Death Whisperer break apart before his eyes, limbs falling limp to his sides, body folding over Lessia's as he mumbled, "No. Just... just fight a little more. Please... Lessia!"

More screams filled the air.

Frelina was lifted away by Raine as she collapsed.

Amalise was impossible to move from the floor, so Zaddock just lay down with her, holding together whatever pieces he could.

Ardow stared into the air while Venko mumbled a soft goodbye.

The sisters hugged each other, their faces so pale it almost seemed as if they'd join their friend.

He couldn't... No. Loche shook his head as he got to his feet, stumbling backward, right into waiting arms.

Somehow, he knew they were Iviry's, and he didn't know how his body could respond so quickly, but it did, spinning around and pulling the Fae so hard to his chest that air rushed out of her lungs.

She didn't say anything, but she let Loche hold on to her, keep something steady in the fucked-up world that was now their own.

The one where... Lessia no longer lived.

They stood like that until Merrick's mumbles became harder, louder, more focused.

"No," the Fae snarled. "I won't accept this."

"Merrick," Kerym tried, his tear-stricken face the mirror of his friend's.

"No!" Merrick was screaming now. "This can't be happening! I refuse! Do you hear that! I fucking refuse! I... I am getting her back. I have... have to do something!"

"There is nothing you can do," Soria said softly as she tried to approach the Death Whisperer. "It was prophesied by the gods, Merrick. And so it shall be."

"Fuck the gods!" Merrick screamed back at her. "Fuck them and fuck fate and fuck everything! Lessia hated all of that!"

The air started whirling, oily layers wrapping all around them.

"Merrick, no!" Kerym sharpened his tone. "You'll kill all of us."

Merrick's eyes were wild as they flew across the group, the darkness in them deep enough to swallow them all. "Do you think I give one shit?"

The world exploded.

Loche wasn't sure whether Iviry was still in his arms as whispers flooded the air, the floor, his mind, his body.

They were everywhere.

If he thought he couldn't breathe before, it was nothing compared to now.

The air shifted, and Loche could hear them so clearly now—their voices brushing against every inch of his skin. They were everything and nothing, and he couldn't move as they pressed against him, pushed everywhere, until the entire world went dark.

CHAPTER 43
LESSIA

Her hands flew to her chest, and Lessia gasped when she couldn't find the dagger that had hurt so badly.

Glancing down at herself, she frowned.

She wasn't wearing the damp fighting leathers anymore.

Instead...

Was this one of the dresses her mother had made her growing up?

It was, she decided as she placed her hands in the soft grass and pushed herself to a seated position. She recognized her mother's stitching, the beautiful golden patterns she liked to sew into their dresses to accentuate her and Frelina's hair and eyes.

Lessia splayed her fingers over the cotton, straightening the blue skirt before getting to her feet and looking around.

Home.

She was... home.

Ahead lay the forest she'd been riding in growing up. Behind her were the cliffs and the water that remained warm year-round. And to her left... that was their house, the door invitingly open as if it just waited for her to enter.

She wondered momentarily if this was another trick, if she'd perhaps never escaped Rioner's capture and this was one of Torkher's visions.

But it didn't feel like it.

It felt real.

She could smell the grass and the salt in the wind.

She could feel the sun warming her skin.

And... there was no undertone of fear.

She felt truly... home.

Lessia started walking to the house when it appeared to call for her.

She must be dead.

She remembered riding on Ydren, the determination within her as they swam to avoid Rioner's waves, the certainty that she was in the right place at the right time.

Somehow, she'd known she'd succeed. Even when she first met Rioner's eyes and he'd grinned at her—too sure of his abilities—she'd known he was about to die.

She'd felt a moment of pure relief when her dagger found its way into his heart. Relief that shattered when the dagger he'd thrown—the one her father had once gifted her—settled in her flesh.

Lessia had fought with every nerve and cell within her to stay alive until Ydren did what Lessia silently begged her to do: bring her back to Merrick.

To see his eyes one final time.

Tears threatened Lessia again as she walked the familiar path, but they weren't of sorrow.

She couldn't have asked for a better goodbye.

Every person she loved had been there, and while she knew they would be hurting now, she'd done whatever she could to protect them—to let them *live*.

A smile broke through the tears as she stepped over the threshold and the scent of her favorite vegetable soup washed over her, but Lessia's brows narrowed when she realized it wasn't her mother standing by the stove but another woman.

A very short Fae with long white hair and eyes as dark as Merrick's but without the silver swirls, which lit up as she turned to face Lessia.

"I've been waiting for you," she chirped as she skipped to Lessia and pressed a goblet of rich red wine into her hands. "I've waited for you forever! Come, sit down!"

Still confused, Lessia did as she asked, her hands moving the cup to her lips before she knew what she was doing, and she groaned as the flavors exploded within her mouth.

"Good, right?" The Fae grinned at her before taking a swig from her own glass.

Lessia only nodded, her fingers moving across the cup as she eyed the female before her.

"You're probably wondering who I am." The smile brightening her features only seemed to grow as the woman tilted her head to study Lessia.

"I am." Somehow, Lessia wasn't worried, though. Not just because this woman was maybe a head shorter than her, so she'd hopefully be able to take her in a fight, but because she felt... familiar.

"Oh!" The woman wiggled her brows. "I think I'd

take you. After all, I trained with Raine and Merrick far longer than a few weeks."

Lessia slitted her eyes again. "And so you are?"

"Solana." The female showed off all her white teeth. "I know Raine has spoken of me."

Even with the smile, something glossy glinted in her dark eyes, and Lessia couldn't help but jerk at the sharp tug in her chest as she stared into them.

This was Raine's mate.

"He misses you," Lessia said softly when the Fae remained quiet, watching as Lessia took in what she'd told her.

"Oh, I know." Solana's eyes moved to the window for a moment. "Even if this place is lovely, it's been torment watching him slowly kill himself. I... Some days I would just do what he did and drink myself into a stupor to make the time pass."

Lessia played with the rim of the cup, swirling her finger across it. "I don't blame you."

Solana shrugged. "Time holds the power to both mend and wound. We were lucky. We had years together."

Years...

Years Lessia and Merrick wouldn't have.

Solana must have caught the sadness ripping into Lessia's heart, because she hurried to smile again. "I don't think it's over for you two. Not yet."

"What do you mean?" Despite the summer warmth drifting through the room, Lessia shivered. She already missed Merrick so much she could hardly pull air into her lungs, but she didn't want him to come here.

To join her. To die.

"This place." Solana swept her thin arm across the

room, to the windows with the forest beyond and the glittering sea peeking over the cliffs. "It took me a while to figure out what it was, but once I did... I've been waiting ever since."

"So what is it?" Lessia took another pull of wine.

"It's the afterlife but also not." Solana refilled their cups before continuing. "For those of us whose soul is ripped in two when we're separated from our mate... we can't rest until both souls do so."

Lessia swallowed. "Until you both die?"

"No. Until we move on." Her white hair sparkled as she tossed it back, away from her face. "I've come to understand we might not always be reunited in death, not immediately at least. For some of us... there are bigger plans, but we need to wait until the one who lives on finds something or someone to fill the aching wound, so that the one who passed can finally go peacefully."

Lessia shook her head. "He won't do that."

She'd seen it in Merrick's eyes. He'd never move on from this.

He'd rather die.

"I'm not talking about Merrick." Solana leaned back in her chair, her smile spreading widely. "Raine is fighting it right now, but I feel it. A few weeks ago, the world around me started flickering, a calm peace layering over me for a few moments until it was ripped away again. But it's been happening more frequently since..."

"He met my sister." Lessia watched the Fae for any anger, perhaps even jealousy, but there was none in the deep darkness.

"Yes," Solana responded. "Frelina is good for him. She challenges him. She understands him. She trusts him, and he trusts her. Raine and I were complete opposites... and that's what he needed back then. But now? He needs someone like him. Someone who will understand him when he is at his worst. Someone like your sister."

Lessia smiled as she thought back to how Raine had held on to Frelina. She'd known in that moment that he'd take care of her, and it had allowed her to let in some of that darkness pressing at the corners of her eyes.

"Will you tell him?" Solana reached over the table for Lessia's hand, and her grip was surprisingly firm for such a small female. "Will you tell him to be happy? To love again? He deserves it. And... so does she."

Tears, but not like those of her friends in her final moments, made Solana's eyes glitter. "Tell him... we'll find each other again when it's time, and when we do... someone is waiting for Frelina as well."

"Who?" Lessia's eyes widened and then rounded further as the world before her eyes distorted.

"That, I may not say." Solana's voice drifted in and out, and she glanced behind her when everything continued to flicker, like a sputtering candle about to burn out. "Now, it seems your mate is about to break every rule the gods ever put in place." Solana squeezed her hand. "Good luck."

Lessia blinked, and in the next moment, she stood before a bridge, the halfway point veiled in dark shadows, but not ones that scared her. She could feel Merrick's presence all around her, his voice breaking through the whispers—the near shouts—filling her ears.

There was a small light shining in that darkness—a familiar one, like a lantern leading her home—and he was calling to her from it. As she took a step onto the bridge, Merrick's voice, his command to find him, grew louder.

"You and me," she said. "You and me."

She repeated the words as she neared the thick shadows where the whispers appeared to grow louder, and as she was about to take the first step into it, a hand folded around her own.

Merrick pulled her right into the darkness, but his silver being was all she could see—it was all that mattered—and he didn't even let her speak before he kissed her with such passion she was surprised the shadows didn't evaporate into steam.

"I'm here," he mumbled against her lips when she wound her arms around his neck, her body desperate to know this was real. "I'm always here."

"I know," she whispered back when his lips released hers. "I know."

There was no fear within her as Merrick pulled them deeper into the heavy darkness, because she knew...

He would always, always be there to light the way for her.

CHAPTER 44

MERRICK

He had no fucking clue what he was doing.

Still, Merrick followed the feeling roiling within him, all the while making sure his grip on Lessia never loosened, because he knew if he lost her in… whatever this damned darkness that enveloped them was… there was no finding her again.

The sensation within him was so strange. There was happiness, yes, near euphoria at feeling Lessia's hand in his own. But something else also whirred through his veins. A strange emptiness that also made him feel complete.

An awareness that began as soon as he gave up all grip on his magic and let those souls break down the barrier between their worlds entirely.

He'd cut a deal. If they let him over to the dead's side, he'd let them roam free.

Merrick had no idea what they would come back to, but his words to Kerym had been true.

He didn't care as long as Lessia was with him.

If they were all dead... if she'd hate him for it...

Then so be it.

A small light shone ahead, one that got bigger and bigger the more Merrick let that feeling that pulled deep within his gut reign.

Lessia moved closer to him, and he switched his grip on her, keeping one arm over her shoulders and the other hand holding on to her small one, somehow knowing that a force would try to rip them apart, keep her from the land of the living, as the gods had meant it to be.

Fuck the gods, Merrick thought again as he began fighting his way through the thickening darkness, nearly dragging Lessia with him until the light flickered teasingly before them.

Who'd decided that they could set the rules? They fucked them all over, again and again, and he wasn't about to let them get away with it.

With a growl that made the shadows shake around him, he forced a foot through the light, pushing Lessia ahead as he grasped the edges, and even as he felt blood begin rushing from his nose, he pressed on. Fought and shoved and tore at the bright hole until it snapped open and they tumbled right into blinding brightness.

It took a few moments for Merrick to get his bearings, but when he did, he realized he was still on the floor, Lessia in his lap, and the others in the mourning positions they'd been in before, albeit their faces more terrified and shocked than grief stricken.

Merrick's heart pounded as he looked down at his mate, but there wasn't even a question as her eyes flew open and she reached up to kiss him, her lips so demanding he groaned right into them before kissing her in return.

Merrick shook his head as he pulled back, but he couldn't look away from Lessia, needing to see her take a breath as the dagger fell to the floor as if it had never cracked through her rib cage, needing to see her smile back at him, needing to see her look around in wonder at their friends.

It wasn't until all color drained from her face that he tore his eyes away, fear clutching around his heart like the shadows had pressed on them before, and for the first time in his life Merrick was stunned into silence when he followed Lessia's gaze, hearing her trembling question, "Who... who are they?"

All around them, people knelt.

But they didn't look like their friends, who stood dispersed amongst the thousands upon thousands of kneeling bodies—the ones that floated over the sea, in the air, all around them.

They were shadows—ghosts, wraiths... Souls.

Not a word passed the Death Whisperer's lips, not even when Soria and Pellie each dropped to a knee as well, their eyes as wide as his own, and the witch sisters whispered as one, "And so a soulbinder shall help her rise to take her throne—her right as a veiled queen."

Acknowledgments

I have to start by thanking you, the reader.

Since I began publishing this series, I have gained thousands of readers, and you all are making my dreams come true. Thank you for loving my characters and stories as much as I do. Thank you for spreading the word about my books. Thank you for being the most amazing, kind people I've ever had the pleasure of meeting. Thank you for the messages, emails, and DMs. YOU are the reason I stayed up those late nights and got up those early mornings to finish this book in time, and you're the reason why I smile every time I dive back into the world of Havlands. I promise you I will never take it for granted.

To Michael, my husband.

Thank you for celebrating every moment of my journey with me, and for always proudly telling people that "my wife is an author" and what my books are about. This book wouldn't have been possible without you cheering me on.

To Amanda, my friend, PA, Alpha Reader, and just the best sounding board.

Thank you for believing so much in me, especially when I don't do it myself. Thank you for reading those messy first drafts and for rooting for me every step of the way. Thank you for always being willing to bounce ideas, listen as I rant, and for never judging me when I change my mind (even if it's for the twentieth time, haha!).

To Cecilia, my Beta Reader and fellow Swede-writing-romantasy-in-English.

Thank you so much for always catching the small things, and for always being up for chats about our characters, stories or journeys.

To my Street Team.

I am so lucky to have you. Our chat is my highlight, and I am so grateful that you help me spread the word, send encouragement, come up with amazing ideas and beautiful content, and that you are also my friends that I get to celebrate both the big and the small moments with.

To Elyse, my fantastic editor.

What would I do without you? Thank you for making my stories the absolute best they can be, and for always being someone I can bounce ideas with and get advice from. And thank you so much for always teaching me the niche things that I forget to research, it makes my day every time I learn a new term or word.

Also by Sophia St. Germain

Series

Echo of Wings

Echo of Deceit

Echo of Wrath (coming 2026)

A new series within the same universe as Compelling Fates Saga will also be announced fall 2025. Books one and two are planned to be released in 2026.

ISBN: PB: 978-91-990040-9-9, HB: 978-91-989689-5-8, eBook: 978-91-990041-4-3

Made in the USA
Coppell, TX
11 February 2026

71779003R00298